No More
Wasted Time

BEVERLY PRESTON

Congrats Jeanne,
always be
sin fully sexy!

Beverly Preston

Cover designed by Yevinn Graphic at www.yevinn.com.

Visit Beverly at **www.beverlypreston.com**.

ISBN: 1469905833

ISBN-13: 978-1469905839

To Don

You are the love of my life and the man of my dreams

Thanks for loving me

—just right—

ACKNOWLEDGMENTS

A book never writes itself, and finding the courage to put my blip of a dream to paper took some coaxing. I would like to thank my family and friends who supported me in my endeavors, listened when I cried, and gave me words of encouragement. Your support and friendship are priceless. Sandy Mohn and Sherrie Lee, you are the best mother and sister anyone could hope for. Karen Collins, you motivated me to keep going and be true to myself. Jewel Peck, you thought my sex scenes were a little too sweet in the beginning; hope you enjoy the rewrites! Lynette Owens, you taught me how to manifest and make my dreams come true. Lynn Bieker, thank you for being my faithful friend for over twenty-three years.

I would also like to thank Natascha Jaffa, my friend and editor.

Yevinn Graphics, thanks for making my cover art smoking HOT.

Geoff Schumacher, you gave me some invaluable advice in the very beginning. Without it, I wouldn't have gotten this far.

Morgan Kearns, you inspire me.

Ellen, I hope you read this someday; thanks for making me laugh. Without watching your program, there would be no dream. Finally, I would like to give a big thank you to my kids, Stephen, Cody, Caylee and Jordyn. I couldn't ask for better children. You inspire me every day to be a better person. Jordyn, thanks for making the best walnut chicken dinner.

And a very special thanks to Caylee for agonizing over every line with me, laughing with me, and giving the best words of encouragement exactly when I needed them the most. Love you.

CHAPTER ONE

Tess Matthews nearly ran face first into the biggest pair of boobs she'd ever seen.

"Holy shit! Whew. That was close."

The Las Vegas airport bustled with tourists hoping to win millions, party like a rock star or pretend to be someone else for a weekend. The sweltering July heat always brought the craziest of crazies to town and today was no exception.

"That might've hurt." Tess' oldest daughter Tracy giggled. "You would've had two black eyes."

"Two *huge* black eyes." Her youngest daughter JC clarified, elbowing Tess in the ribs, encouraging her to peek at the elderly couple dressed-to-impress Vegas style. As if she hadn't just collided with another woman's vast amount of cleavage because of them. Her daughters pointed at the woman in her late seventies sporting bleach blond hair, red six-inch heels, black spandex pants and a form fitting purple shirt. Her spray-tanned, saggy arm clung to the shoulder of a frail man dressed in black leather pants and vest.

"Wow, Mom, was that a smile?" JC asked sarcastically.

Tess ignored the comment. "Did you put copies of your passports in each of your suitcases in case it gets lost or stolen? Be sure to keep your phone in your…"

"Front pocket, we've got it. You've gone over this ten times already." JC rolled her eyes.

"You know we'll be responsible." Tracy reminded her. "Look Mom, it took me two months of bribing JC with Starbucks to get her to come with me and I planned this entire trip by myself. I've been dreaming of going to France, Venice and Rome for-"

"Don't forget about Greece." JC interrupted. "That's where all the *really* hot guys are going to be. According to the movies I've seen, Mr. tall, dark, and handsome is going to be waiting for us when we step off the plane."

"Mom, are you sure you don't want to come with us to Europe? It'd be so much more fun." Tracy asked as they passed through airport security.

"Yeah, come with us. There might even be cute old men your age." JC hunched her lean body forward, imitating an old man using a cane as she peered through her long caramel hair.

"Thanks, JC. Thanks a lot. Maybe you could even drum me up a guy without a wheelchair or a walker or a cane, since they'd be my age." Tess joked back, completely conscious of her forty-four years.

"Maybe you'll find a hunky Polynesian fire dancer in Bora Bora," JC's jade eyes sparkled mischievously.

"All right, that's enough out of you, missy. I have no interest in hunky fire dancers."

"Maybe it's about time you get interested," JC mumbled under her breath.

"Seriously, Mom, are you positive you don't want to come with us instead?" Tracy reiterated. "You're going to be by yourself in the honeymoon capital of the world."

Detecting worry in Tracy's brilliant blue eyes, she slipped her arm over her daughters shoulder. "I know you're concerned, but I've made up my mind. I need to do this."

When Tess had informed her three kids ten days ago that she booked a trip for herself, they'd thought she was joking. The fact that her destination was Bora Bora only made it worse. They thought she'd finally gone off the deep end. Merely taking off, escaping on an unplanned and unpredicted spur of the moment trip seemed completely out of character for Tess. Usually, every trip she took needed to be neurotically organized and planned to perfection. This trip would be difficult. Bora Bora wasn't exactly a place where people went to feel sad or recover.

It was a lover's paradise.

Her twenty-three year old son John thought she acted so

irrational, he offered to go with her.

Tess explained to her children that this trip would help bring her closure. Her perfectly planned future vanished a year ago. She hated not knowing where her life was heading, only existing from day to day. It needed to change. She needed to say goodbye.

For the last ten days, Tess had rehearsed saying goodbye to her girls, convincing herself they'd be fine. *Just let them go. Say goodbye and let them get on their plane. They'll be safe.* Approaching their gate, she pulled her girls in for an airtight squeeze. "Have a great time. Take pictures for me. Stay with your tour group."

"Yes, Mom." Tracy smirked.

"Remember, don't put all your money in the same place in case you get pick-pocketed."

"Got it." JC shook her head with an impish attitude. "Try to have some fun, Mom. It'll be good for you. Love you."

Tracy tossed her long dark coppery hair to the side as she adjusted her backpack. She kissed Tess' cheek and whispered in her ear. "I hope you find what you're searching for. I love you, Momma. Be safe."

Tracy and JC sauntered away, turning back to flash their beautiful smiles. Tess exhaled deeply as she waved goodbye, "Try to keep your little sister out of trouble!"

Standing alone, Tess realized exactly how much she'd come to depend on the love and closeness of her kids over the last year. It seemed as though they were taking care of her, instead of the other way around.

She knew Tracy would watch over her little sister. She'd always been the mature levelheaded child. It was JC she worried about. Her youngest daughter was boy crazy.

Tess rushed toward her gate to make her flight on time. Happy couples, young and old, filled the gate area, leaving her with an uncomfortable pit in her stomach. Tess couldn't help but wonder if she'd made the right choice traveling to Bora Bora by herself. Richard was gone and he wasn't coming back.

Waiting for her flight to be called, she settled back into her seat, and closed her eyes. *Damn I miss you. It just doesn't make sense. Hell, nothing makes sense anymore.*

It'd been over a year since his death and she still couldn't believe he was gone. Richard had always been active, healthy and in perfect shape. How could he die of a heart attack? It seemed like only yesterday she received the worst news of her life. The horrific memory of running down the hospital hallway, door after door passing by in a slow motion still brought tears to her eyes even now. The agony on her son's tear soaked face as he stood in the sterile hallway was etched into the fabric of her memories forever. She was too late.

Tess and Richard were married twenty-five years, sharing a love most people only dreamed of. She couldn't get past the fact she hadn't made it to the hospital in time to tell him how much she loved him. Nightmares still haunted her. She would never be able to hear him laugh, hold his hand, kiss his lips, or tell him how much she loved him again.

Tess' phone rang jolting her back to reality. "Hi, John."

"Hey, Mom, I'm glad I caught you before your plane leaves. Did the girls' plane get off okay? I tried to call them, but it went to voicemail."

"They should be in the air already."

"They're going to have so much fun." A hint of envy hung in John's husky voice.

"Hey, you could've gone with them."

"Yeah, umm, no, thanks. Between Tracy and her museums and architecture, and JC chasing her hot guys... I think I'd rather stay home and work. Maybe get a little riding in, too. Anyway I wanted to tell you…"

"I know. You think it's a bad idea to go to Bora Bora by myself. I'm going to be sad and lonely…your sisters already discussed this with me."

"Actually, I wanted to tell you I understand why you're going, and I support your decision. We just want you to be happy. You need to start smiling again. It's not good for you to be sad all the time Mom. If this is what it takes then I'm behind you one hundred percent."

"Oh." Tess' throat tightened. "Thanks for being my rock the past year."

"I love you, Mom. Be safe and I'll see you in two weeks. Come home with a smile on your face. Okay?"

"I'll try. Don't forget to bring in the mail and be sure to-"

"I know. I'll take care of everything."

Tess could always count on her son to be dependable, just like his dad. In fact, other than his dark brown hair, John was a spitting image of Richard. He sported his father's jade green eyes, and muscular physique. Even their mannerisms were identical. His smile, laugh, and hand gestures mimicked his fathers.

Tess jumped at the woman's voice announcing, "Ladies and gentlemen, we are now boarding Pacific Air flight 227 to Bora Bora."

After three flights and a boat ride, Tess watched painfully as two blissful couples sat beside her on the boat gazing in awe at the breathtaking tropical surroundings. Glancing down at her luggage that contained Richard's ashes, she almost uttered out loud, God I miss you. Turning her thoughts and gaze away from the lovers, she stared out over the indescribable turquoise lagoon emulating a painter's pallet of blues and greens.

Tess glimpsed the thatch roofing of the over-water bungalows in the distance. Lush tropical valleys lay between black jagged mountains and swaying palm trees lined the soft white sand beach.

Soft Tahitian music serenaded the boat passengers as they approached the dock. Resort staff greeted them with warm smiles. A lovely, older, dark-skinned woman handed each passenger a lei and a cool wet cloth infused with the fragrance of Tiare flower.

Tess dabbed her neck with the refreshing cloth. She ambled down the dock following the pathway bordered with pink hibiscus flowers. Swept away by the tranquil setting, her heart began to soften as she strolled by the exotic landscape and beachfront villas.

"Paradise," she whispered, taking in the sultry air and sweet scent of the exquisite lei draped around her neck. For the first time in over a year, she felt at peace. Bora Bora had become her home away from home. Coming here felt as comfortable as slipping into her favorite jeans.

The resort was everything she'd expected and more, filled with traditional Polynesian architecture and exquisite furnishings hand crafted by local artisans. Tess admired the craftsmanship of the open-air lobby while waiting for her turn at check-in.

"*Ia Orana*, Mrs. Mathews." The clerk greeted and offered a Mai Tai. "Thank you for staying with us again. It appears you will be staying in one of our beach bungalows with a private plunge pool. Would you be interested in upgrading your stay to an over-water bungalow? There are several available."

"No, thank you. The beach bungalow is my favorite." As soon as the words left her lips, she remembered the lure of the plunge pool. She and Richard used to walk through the gate of their private bungalow, undress, and slip into the warm water. Never even bothering to unpack.

"Of course. Mrs. Mathews you're in bungalow-"

"Actually, do you have an over-water bungalow available near the coral gardens?" Tess asked, realizing the plunge pool wouldn't have quite the same ambiance as it on previous trips.

"We have bungalow 35 available. It's at the very end of the North Pier facing the lagoon. It's ideal for snorkeling and you have a view of Mount Otemanu."

"That sounds perfect."

"If you'd like to finish your drink, your luggage will be taken to your bungalow momentarily. Enjoy your stay."

Tess sipped her Mai Tai and munched on fresh pineapple.

The pier leading to her bungalow perched on stilts above the turquoise lagoon. She stopped to watch an eel swim beneath it and spotted a gray figure with ghost-like movements just under the sand. Tess exhaled heavily, pleased with her decision to switch rooms. The over-water bungalows came equipped with a glass panel in the floor giving her complete access to watch the fish swimming below.

Stepping into her bungalow, she relaxed taking in the tranquil décor of rich mahogany furnishings and vibrant Tahitian art. Tess opened the glass doors leading to the deck where two chaise lounges sat and a private outdoor shower beckoned.

Standing at the edge of the luxurious bed, she stared down at pink flower petals fanned out perfectly into the shape of a heart.

"I sure as hell won't being needing those." She tossed her bag onto the crisp white linens, scattering the petals to the floor.

A ladder at the edge of the deck gave access to the lagoon merely yards away from the coral gardens. Unable to wait for the pleasure the warm waters gave her, she changed into her bikini, grabbed her snorkel gear and slipped into the turquoise lagoon. Drifting above the coral, she swam side-by-side with vibrant canary-yellow, electric-blue, and tangerine-orange schools of fish.

After snorkeling, Tess retreated from the late afternoon sun. She wasn't in the mood to see the famous Tahitian Fire Dancers, so she ordered room service, dinner and a bottle of wine. The romantic sight of lovers holding hands, gazing into each other's eyes, and knowing where the night would lead them wasn't something she wanted to think about.

Tomorrow Tess would book a private excursion with Mr. Rene on his boat, just as they'd always done in the past. Swimming with black-tip reef sharks and stingrays had always been their favorite excursion. Plunging into the clear water, observing sharks as they swam within two feet of them seemed almost dream-like. All their friends back home thought they were crazy, even by Las Vegas standards. Nevertheless, for Tess and Richard, it was always first on their to-do list. *Well close to the first thing*, she thought with a smile.

The night grew darker as she finished a second glass of wine, gazing up at the stars as they began to put on a brilliant show. The memories filling her mind now were as vivid as the fish swimming in the coral beneath her bungalow. Tess knew this beautiful blue lagoon is where Richard would want to be. She'd brought his ashes with her, so he could swim in his favorite underwater playground forever and Tess would swim with him one last time.

CHAPTER TWO

The next morning, Tess awoke to the sound of Tahitian music playing softly in the distance. Sunlight filled the room, and a balmy breeze blew through the open glass doors. Gazing beyond the end of her bed, Mount Otemanu crested over the top of her toes, giving the illusion that they were holding up the towering volcanic peak. She giggled, *If this place is heaven on earth, it must be Mother Nature's bedroom.*

Dangling her feet over the side of her bed, she extended her arms, stretching out the best night's sleep she'd had in a year. Tess ambled to the bathroom inspecting a basket on the counter filled with soaps and oils infused with the scent of vanilla and coconut. She rubbed on the oil leaving her skin silky smooth and then ran her fingers through her long, wavy, rich brown hair, giving it the perfect amount of luster and control. No brush needed. This is paradise.

Tess threw on a little blue dress and strolled down to breakfast poolside, enjoying delicious fruit and a cup of strong coffee. She wandered over to the activities desk, lounging on a luxurious white chaise, and waited for the woman behind the counter to finish checking in new guests. She inhaled deeply again, catching a whiff of the orchid leis the couple wore around their necks.

Tess could only see the back of the couple from where she sat. The man had a fit athletic build and dark, brown hair peppered with gray. The woman dressed in heels and a red, backless dress, accentuating her pale skin. Though sunglasses covered much of her face, she was very attractive with long, blonde hair falling to her waist.

He spoke to the Tahitian woman in a deep friendly voice that sounded familiar. Tess studied the man, listening harder to see if she knew him. He casually stood at the counter in flip-flops, dark jeans and a white dress shirt. *If he'd turn to the side a little, I can get a better look.* He turned away and Tess shrugged. *No, I don't think I know him.*

The woman draped her arm around him, tilting her head to the side so the large woven black hat she wore wouldn't brush against his face. Tess listened as she asked, "Can you tell me where the nearest shopping district is? I didn't see any big buildings as we flew over."

"Shopping district?"

"You know. A mall or shops, places like Gucci, Bebe…"

"We have a lovely boutique here at the resort and there are several shops and local craftsmen at the outdoor market on the main island."

"Are you serious?" the blonde whined. "Tommy, you said you'd take me shopping. Now what am I going to do while we're here? I didn't bring anything nice to wear because I was going to buy a new dress."

If Tess hadn't seen the woman's arms around the man, she'd sworn the girl was his daughter. A very spoiled daughter.

"Mariah, I told you I'm coming here to relax, not to go shopping. I need some down time. There's a beautiful pool you can sunbathe next to. I want to try some snorkeling and go hiking, too. I'm sure you have something to wear in the suitcases you brought." Irritation sat heavily in his voice.

"Hiking! I thought you were teasing when you said that. I can't sunbathe too much. I have a shoot in two weeks. Besides, how many days can you look at fish underwater?" She pouted, running her fingers through his hair.

He subtlety shrugged her off.

The clerk offered them a Mai Tai, stating their luggage would be taken to their room momentarily.

Tess' mouth gaped open with the look of "unbelievable" written all over her face when the man turned from the counter. She recognized him immediately.

Tom Clemmins, famous actor and Hollywood hottie was

staying in her resort.

His lips pulled to one side, grinning at Tess. She timidly smiled back. Her face turning redder by the second, Tess was embarrassed for eavesdropping on their conversation. She stood, moving toward the counter. As he passed by, their shoulders almost brushed and his dark eyes locked on hers, making it impossible for Tess to look away.

"What can I do for you, Mrs. Mathews?" the desk clerk asked.

"What? Hmm? Holy crap it's hot." Tess muttered, wiping the trickle of sweat from the nape of her neck.

"Would you like a wet cloth or a cold drink?"

"No. No, thank you. I need to book a private shark tour with Mr. Rene."

"He has an opening tomorrow morning if you'd like a half day tour. If you'd prefer a full day, it will be several days before he has anything available."

"Tomorrow morning is perfect."

Tess smiled to herself, listening to the couple on the chaise behind her. *That poor girl isn't going to win this argument. There aren't many shops on the island. Especially not the names she's dropping.* Tahitian people were very humble and the most elaborate things here besides the resorts, were their pearls. Tess almost laughed aloud at the thought of the young woman meandering through a pearl farm in the outfit she had on.

"How many people will be joining you tomorrow, Mrs. Mathews?"

Tess' smile faded from her lips, "Just me." She shuddered, sensing someone was staring at her from behind.

"You're all set. Private tour for one. Mr. Rene will be waiting for you on the dock at 7:45am. You should eat breakfast prior to leaving and Mr. Rene will prepare lunch on a beautiful private *motu*. Can I be of any further assistance?"

"No, *Maruruu*." She smiled appreciatively.

As she turned to leave, Tom Clemmins and his girlfriend were finishing their drinks. Tess knew she wasn't his wife because it was well publicized he dated a lot and had never married. She wondered if they were staying on the same pier as she was, or if maybe they had a villa. He flashed a grin at Tess as she passed by and his girlfriend still pouted her beautiful lips.

Holy crap he's good looking. Tess placed her clammy fingers to her neck, feeling the blood pulse through her veins. "What the heck is wrong with me?" she muttered under her breath. Running into movie stars and professional athletes wasn't uncommon in Bora Bora or even in Las Vegas. Tess had never been awestruck by movie stars or famous people. She never understood people's fascination with fame and fortune. After all, neither made them a nice person. *I must be tense about tomorrow.*

Returning to her bungalow, she put on her bikini bottoms, grabbed a book her daughters had packed in her suitcase and strolled out onto her deck to sunbathe.

Her mind kept wandering to magical moments with Richard, so she tossed the book to the side. Yearning for the lost comfort of his arms, Tess slipped into the lagoon, immersing herself into the warmth of his favorite underwater paradise.

As the sun dipped lower in the sky, she lugged herself up the steps and into the shower. The hot water caressed her skin, washing away the saltwater. The exotic sensual atmosphere made her body ache for the tender touch of his strong hands against her skin. She wrapped her arms across her chest, holding herself for comfort as she cried.

Mentally exhausted, she ordered dinner in again. As Tess lay on a chaise star gazing, she found herself thinking of another star, Tom Clemmins. *How could anyone come to a place like this and want the main attraction to be shopping? How could that woman not just want to take him to bed?* Her thoughts stirred with curiosity as she drifted off to sleep.

Tess hadn't slept well. Her thoughts weighed heavy with the difficult task lying in front of her. She'd wallowed in grief for over a year, but today she needed to pick up the pieces of her shattered life. Today was the day she would say goodbye to Richard.

It sounded silly, but sometimes Tess felt Richard watching over her, and today she wanted to look good for him. She wore a black bikini, her favorite cut-off jean shorts, white tank top, waterproof mascara and lip-gloss.

Richards's ashes rested in a wooden box with a hand-carved manta ray on the lid. She took a deep breath, and picked up the box, tracing her fingertips over the carving. Holding back the tears that pricked her eyes, Tess packed the box into her snorkel gear bag and walked out the door.

After grabbing breakfast, she headed for the dock. Tess arrived early, so she relaxed on a bench waiting for the boat. At 7:40, she could hear Mr. Rene coming as he sang a Tahitian song while strumming a little guitar. Palm fronds and beautiful pink flowers wrapped around the poles holding up the shade tarp. He serenaded her as he pulled up to the dock.

"*Ia Orana*," he said joyfully. "It's a beautiful day."

She stepped onto his boat with a huge grin. Tess couldn't help but love Mr. Rene with his immense white smile, jet-black hair and dark russet skin covered with tribal tattoos. "*Ia Orana* Mr. Rene, it's wonderful to see you again."

"Yes, yes, welcome," he said reaching for her gear. As Tess lifted her sunglasses he said, "Mrs. Blue Eyes…is that you? It is you! You look beautiful this morning. I have not seen you in such a long time." Mr. Rene wrapped his brawny arms around her, giving her a big Tahitian welcome.

"It has been too long." Tess agreed, smiling at the nickname he'd given her years ago. Mr. Rene had always been infatuated with her striking azure blue eyes, teasing that if he were not a married man he would steal her away from Richard and make her his woman.

"Mrs. Blue Eyes, are you catching the other ferry to the main island?" He asked in confusion, glancing at the gear she loaded on his boat.

"No I'm on tour with you this morning. Sharks!"

"I don't think so, Mrs. Blue Eyes. I have a tour with someone else today. Let me check my papers," he muttered, reaching behind the steering wheel. "I have a different name on my ticket. You're not here under a different name, are you? Where is the Mr. Blue Eyes?"

"No, my name is the same." She knew he was politely asking if she'd gotten a divorce. "I'm by myself this trip."

Completely baffled, he cocked his head to the side with a frown.

"I lost my husband last year."

Mr. Rene gasped. "Oh no! I'm sorry for you. Oh! I am so sorry." Compassion filled his voice as he pulled her into his chest, patting her on the back.

Her voice climbed an octane higher, hoping there wasn't a problem. "Whose name is on the ticket?"

Releasing her from his brawny arms, he thumbed through his paperwork. "Let me see... a Mr. Clemmins."

"What? You've got to be kidding me! That woman didn't even want to get in the water," she sneered. "Mr. Rene, there must be a mistake. I booked this tour before Mr. Clemmins checked into the resort."

This cannot be happening.

"I'm sorry, Mrs. Blue Eyes. I didn't realize it was you who had booked the tour this morning."

Her hands trembled. "What do you mean, you didn't realize it was me?"

"You know, I don't make much money for my family. My oldest son goes to college now in France. The man offered more than double my normal rate. How could I refuse?"

Tess growled. "You gave him my tour? He out-bid me!" Starting to pace, she whipped around to see Tom Clemmins moseying down the dock wearing a haughty smile.

"Mr. Rene, this is important to me. I'm trying to say goodbye to my husband. You don't understand."

"Good morning." Tom said cheerfully, stepping onto the boat.

"Maybe for you." Tess shot back.

Tom flinched, exhaling out a small laugh over her reaction, bringing Tess' irritation from a simmer to a full-blown boil.

Mr. Rene gripped Tom Clemmins hand. "*Ia Orana.* Welcome. I am Mr. Rene. You must be Mr. Clemmins? Do you have any gear? Or if not Mr. Rene has all of the gear you will need. Mask, flippers, I have every size."

"Perfect. The woman at the front desk said you'd have everything. I have my trunks and sun screen, so yep, I'm ready."

"Mr. Rene!" Tess threw her hands in the air, clearly gesturing, *What the hell?*

Tom Clemmins stared at Tess in disbelief. "Is something wrong? Is there a problem with the boat?" he asked.

"No, no problem with my boat, it runs-" Mr. Rene insisted.

"Yes, something is wrong. I booked this boat yesterday for a private tour. Do you remember seeing me at check-in?" She attempted to make an effort to sound civil, but in reality, snarled at him.

Tom Clemmins lowered his sunglasses, exposing his dark brown eyes. "The blue dress, right?"

Tess' mouth dropped open at his admission. "You booked this tour after me. Or more like you stole it out from underneath me!" She fumed with a blistering glare.

His lips curled back into a grin. "Well, I can guarantee you that I didn't steal your tour. They must have double booked our reservation."

"Double booking? You mean double payment?" Growing more annoyed by the second, Tess' eyes narrowed, uninterested in his smooth talk and brilliant white smile. Standing her ground, she placed her hands on her hips and lifted her chin. "Look, I'm sure you're used to getting your way, but not today. I am not getting off this boat. I *need* this tour."

"I didn't ask you to get off the boat. I'm sure we can work something out. It's only the two of us and there seems to be plenty of room. I don't mind if we go together. And for the record, I don't always get my way."

"There's plenty of room, of course, of course," Mr. Rene agreed.

"I *really* need a private tour, Mr. Rene. If I don't go today then it'll be another week. I can't wait!" She pleaded with her eyes.

Mr. Rene would never hurt her feelings intentionally and had no previous knowledge of her plans. How could she blame him? He could probably use the extra money, but she needed to say goodbye right now. Tess didn't want to wait another moment, fearing she might change her mind about letting Richard go. Tess had planned this moment perfectly and Mr. Fucking Hollywood was ruining it for her.

Realizing she wasn't going to get her way, Tess shuddered, fighting back tears of anger and disappointment. "You said the two of us. Are you coming alone?" No way in hell could she be stuck on a boat for five hours with his girlfriend. The whining would push her over the edge.

"Yes, I'm by myself," Tom replied.

She glared at him with as much bitterness as she could muster. "What did you have to do? Send her to the main island so she could go shopping?"

Mr. Rene stepped in, placing his hand on her rigid shoulder. "Look, Mrs. Blue Eyes, it's just the two of you. You're almost by yourself. You love this tour. It's your favorite. I'll take you to a lovely *motu* for lunch."

"Fine." Tess conceded. She'd never been so disappointed in her life.

Mr. Rene sighed in relief. "See, I knew this would work. Is everyone ready? Okay then, let's go."

As they pulled away from the dock, the serenade began again. Tess sulked in her own thoughts, incensed with Tom Clemmins for intruding on her snorkeling tour. Her dreams of a 'perfect goodbye' were wrecked.

I can't believe he out bid me. Unbelievable! At least he didn't make me get off the boat.

CHAPTER THREE

Tess watched as Tom Clemmins sat blissfully at the back of the boat, soaking up the sunshine, taking in the amazing colors of the lagoon, while she was unraveling at the seams. She fidgeted in her seat. If she had any chance of getting through the day, she couldn't be angry when saying goodbye to Richard. And she sure as hell didn't want to sound like Tom Clemmins' whiny date back at check-in.

Grasping a hold of her frayed emotions, Tess glanced toward the young man steering the boat. "Who's your new skipper?"

"This is my youngest son, Riatia," Mr. Rene said ruefully.

She acknowledged with a nod.

God. I think I just had a meltdown. The man probably paid double so he could have the day to himself. Embarrassed about their confrontation, Tess closed her eyes, took a deep breath and headed to the back of the boat.

As she approached, he spoke first in a low comforting tone, holding his hand out hesitantly. "I'm sorry about the....mix up. Maybe we should start over. I don't want you to be mad at me all day, I'm Tom."

Schmoozer! Tess reached for his hand. "Tom Clemmins, right?" she stated matter-of-factly, unimpressed by his celebrity. "I'm Tess, Tess Mathews. I recognized you at check-in yesterday. I'm sorry for being rude back at the dock. I'm just frustrated. I needed some time alone, no offense."

"I know how you feel. I've been working too much. I needed to get away, far away. This place is beautiful. The color of the water is so many shades of blue. I've never seen anything like it."

"Have you ever been to Bora Bora before?"

"Nope, first time. First time snorkeling, too."

"Well, you picked the perfect place. The snorkeling here is superb. The coral gardens are filled with the most exotic fish." She rambled on. "The reef sharks are my favorite. They'll be amazing today. They get so close you can almost touch them."

"From the boat?" he asked with a puzzled look.

Tess chuckled, apparently someone at check-in failed to tell Mr. Clemmins everything about the tour. "No...you can almost touch them...in the water."

"You actually get in the water with sharks?" he asked apprehensively, color quickly fading from his cheeks. "I thought we watched them feed the sharks from the boat."

"No. You truly do get in the water with them." Tess grinned mischievously, unsure if she wanted to tell him that the black-tip reef sharks were harmless. She wanted to watch him sweat a bit longer. "The sharks are fairly tame. They hardly ever attack people." She figured he deserved this for taking her tour.

His eyebrows creased. "I'm not sure if I want to get in the water with sharks. You're kidding me, right? Do you seriously get in the water with sharks?"

"Most of them are only five or six feet long. There's nothing to worry about. You won't be the one feeding them. That's Riatia's job." She enjoyed the nice shade of avocado coloring his cheeks.

"Oh, I don't think so. I'll just wait on the boat. I think I'll pass."

She couldn't take it any longer, fearing if he turned any greener, he'd puke. "I'm only teasing you. There's never been a shark attack here. The black tip reef sharks are actually very docile." Tess tried not to laugh aloud.

"What? That's not even funny. You're just kidding me about the sharks?" Color returned to his cheeks. "So...you really don't get in the water with them?"

"Oh yes it was funny. And yes, *we* are really going to get in the water with the sharks. They don't attack." She found herself slightly charmed by the playfulness between them. He still looked fearful, and she didn't want him to be afraid. "Seriously, you're going to love it."

"How many times have you done this?" he asked as if she

were crazy.

"Maybe a dozen, it's one of my favorite things to do here."

The boat slowed and Riatia tied a rope onto a metal poll sticking out of the coral with a florescent orange flag waving from its top. Peering over the side of the boat into the crystal clear lagoon, they could see vibrant coral, schools of fish and even the ripples in the sand. Mr. Rene gave Tom proper instructions; stay next to him, keep your arms at your side, no flippers on with the sharks in the water and enjoy the show.

Speedo? Tess snickered noticing Tom didn't have his swim trunks on. "You brought trunks didn't you?"

"I did, but I figured there'd be a place to change." He smirked.

"I'll turn around or if you'd prefer to wait until I get off the boat…"

"No, no, you can just turn around." His lips curled up on one side into a gorgeous heart-stopping smile.

Tess slid out of her tank top and cutoffs, waiting curiously to see what he'd look like in his trunks.

"Ready!" he said. Tom nervously peering over the edge of the boat, observing several black tips slicing through the water's surface.

Riatia swam twenty yards out, calling in the sharks with dead fish.

Tess checked Tom out nonchalantly while pulling her hair back into a ponytail. He had great arms with the perfect amount of muscle. His black trunks hung low on his waist, exposing a chiseled six-pack. *Well at least I'll have a nice view for the day. Tess Mathews that was a little shallow.* Her heartbeat drummed loudly in her ears. Jesus, get it together. *It's not as if you haven't seen attractive men before.* She merely hadn't taken notice of one in twenty-five years.

Mr. Rene handed "Mr. Tom" a mask and snorkel.

Tess fine-tuned her mask, resting it on her forehead. She watched him wipe the sweat from his hands to adjust his mask. She placed her hand on his forearm. "I promise. You'll love it."

He huffed out an uncomfortable chuckle. Following her lead, they turned their backs to the lagoon and plunged backward into the warm lagoon.

A camera hung from Tess' wrist on a rubber band. "Did you bring an underwater camera?"

"No, I didn't even think about it," he shrugged with disappointment.

"Do you want me to take some pictures of you with the sharks?"

He glanced at her oddly as they bobbed in the water. "I don't really want pictures. Thanks anyway."

"How come? You may never get to do this again. Believe me. Your friends are going to want to see these pictures." She didn't understand. Surely, Tom Clemmins loved getting his picture taken; he fronted dozens of magazine covers.

"I don't think so." Tom raised one eyebrow skeptically, glancing at the camera.

"Seriously? I promise, I'll email them to you." Tess realized by the suspicious look on his face, it wasn't that he didn't think she wouldn't send them; Tom didn't want the world to see them. "Are you afraid I'm going to sell them or something?" Tess asked with her mouth wide open, insulted that Tom didn't trust her.

He gazed through the water under his chin observing a dozen sharks starting to come in. Riatia floated in front of them feeding the sharks right out of his hand. "My vacations are private to me. It's happened a dozen times before. I'm sure you've seen some of the photos in the rag magazines."

"Come on, I would never do anything like that, I promise! Look, I'll even give you the camera when we're done. You can send me the pictures. You have to have memories of this."

He hesitated for a few more seconds.

"You can trust me."

"Deal. But if I get eaten by a shark, you can sell the pictures," he joked, lowering his mask into the water and began watching the show.

"Deal."

They drifted in the crystal clear lagoon alongside twenty to thirty sharks feeding merely feet in front of them. As sharks approached Tom, he instinctually stretched his hand out to touch the magnificent gray creatures. Tess reached out, gently tugging on his arm, pulling it back so he'd return to the boat with all ten fingers. They smiled through their masks, watching in amazement as sharks opened their jaws to snag fish right out of Riatia's hand. Tess took great pictures of Tom with six-foot sharks in the background, swimming effortlessly with only a swish of their tail.

When they ran out of fish, and the sharks disbursed, everyone retreated back to the boat. Tom talked nonstop for twenty minutes while Mr. Rene took them to their next destination. Tess laughed at Tom describing the sharks in animation. His arms stretched out fully while imitating the sharks thrashing about, ripping the fish heads off.

"It's a good thing I took pictures for you. All your friends will think you're full of shit if that's how you're going to tell the story." Tess giggled mimicking him with her arms extended as far as they would reach.

"Next stop, sting rays," said Mr. Rene.

They stood in chest deep water with their feet spread apart, allowing the rays to glide between their legs. At least twenty stingrays swam gracefully around them with ghost-like movements, almost as if they danced to ballet in slow motion. The stingrays loved Mr. Rene, encircling him and fluttering their wings to swim up on his chest, so he could pet and kiss them. Their dark gray skin felt like rubber as their wings fluttered against Tess and Tom's chest, so they could give the stingrays kisses, too.

Mesmerized in the moment, Tom rambled on enthusiastically as they headed for their next location. He rested his warm hand on her shoulder, stealing the air from her lungs as a tingling sensation swept over her skin. "You were right, that was incredible. I'll admit, I was chicken at first, but once the sharks started to come in, I completely forgot about being nervous. I think I liked the sharks more than the sting rays."

Guilt crept into her heart for enjoying herself. Tess didn't come here for fun. It almost felt like she was cheating on Richard to notice another man. She hardly ever noticed other men before, and never cheated, not once in all the years they were together.

Tess still hadn't done what she came there for. She considered asking Mr. Rene to drop her off at a separate *motu* while they ate lunch, but doubted he would leave her by herself.

"Here, just like I promised," she handed him the camera.

"I'm sorry. It's not that I don't trust you. It's just…"

"Really, it's okay. I understand. It must be hard not knowing who you can trust. I don't know how you do it. I'll give you my address, just make sure you send me copies of photos you want me to have, okay."

Mr. Rene interrupted. "Don't put your camera away, Mrs. Blue Eyes. We are going to snorkel a large coral reef after lunch."

"I thought we were doing a half day tour."

Tom smirked. "You were, but I booked the full day. Is that all right or do you need to get back?"

"No, that's great." She paused for a moment before laughing aloud. "Did you steal some other unlucky couple's afternoon appointment?"

His dark brown eyes flirted mischievously. "No! I did not. Not that I know of. Maybe."

They laughed together now. Tess relaxed, knowing she had more time to figure out how to be alone with Richard.

Tom lay on his back stretched out on a bench with his sunglasses on, one hand propped behind his head and the other rested casually on his hip with two fingers tucked into the band of his trunks. She needed to plan a course of action to get away by herself, but Tess could barely even think straight peering at his lean sculpted physique from behind her sunglasses. *I wonder how old he is? I bet he runs. Maybe he swims. He has to be in his late forties. He definitely takes care of himself. Is he flexing? He's doing that on purpose to torture me. Holy crap!* Tempted to reach out and touch the muscular chords running down his arm, she finally forced herself to look the other direction.

At last, the *motu* appeared in the distance. Tess couldn't wait to jump into the water to cool off. Her mind raced in all different directions. Pushing the image of Tom lying on the bench out of her head, she moved on to the task that lay before her. This was it. Tess would be able to do what she came here for.

"What's going on?" Tom asked lifting his head.

"Lunch, it's time to eat." She smiled.

Mr. Rene handed each of them a coconut with a straw and a

lovely purple flower sticking out the top. "I will get lunch ready. You can swim or relax on this beautiful *motu*. I will set up a table in a moment."

Tom held his mask and flippers in his hands. "I'm going to go snorkel, do you want to come with me?"

"No, thanks. I'm going to chill out for a bit."

He headed for the water. Tess waited until she saw his snorkel sticking out of the water before she grabbed her snorkel gear and proceeded off the boat.

Mr. Rene stopped her, "You are going to go snorkel with Mr. Tom?"

"Actually, do you remember what I told you I came here to do?"

"To say goodbye," he whispered sadly.

"Can you please keep Mr. Tom busy, so I can have some privacy on the other side of the *motu*?"

"By yourself?" he asked hesitantly.

"I promise I'll be back in an hour."

He nodded reluctantly.

Tess intended on spending the morning reminiscing of their time spent together in Bora Bora, but the day turned out very different than she planned. She wasn't going to be disappointed though. Maybe it was better this way. Richard wouldn't want her to be heartbroken in a place this beautiful.

On the other side of the *motu*, Tess found a magnificent white sand beach. Tall palm trees swayed in the sultry breeze and a coconut lay in the sand split open with a palm tree growing out of it.

Tess plopped down on the soft sand with her box in her hand, gazing around at the dreamlike surroundings. *Richard would've loved this beach.* She always believed everything happened for a reason, and she thought of that now, staring out over the lagoon. If she would've done the half-day tour by herself, she'd be on a different *motu* now and this spot was perfect. She wouldn't want Richard to be anywhere else.

Looking down at the hand carved box, she reflected to the time Richard bought it. They'd tried on several occasions to snorkel with the giant manta rays. Every time, the manta rays were a no-show. On their last trip to Bora Bora, Richard found the carved box while shopping at the market. He'd said, "Well if I can't snorkel with them, I'm going to take one home with me." Tess had even taken a picture of him holding up the box, pointing to the manta ray lid and pouting his lip out because they eluded him once again. Tears spilled down her face as she chuckled remembering the moment.

Memories replayed through her mind like a movie. The passion they shared still filled her heart. She missed him, his touch, his kisses, his smell, the feel of his hand in hers and his arms around her. She wanted to hear his deep voice and feel the warmth of his body next to hers.

Relieved to finally be there in the moment, but overwhelmed with sadness, Tess wanted closure yet didn't want to let him go. Allowing him to slip out of her hands would feel so final, as if she were letting him slip away from her forever. Richard wouldn't be at home with her anymore. *I can do this. I need to do this. I have to do this.*

Tess waded into the lagoon with Richard for the last time, talking to him aloud. "I miss you so much, baby. You were the best husband, lover and friend I could've ever asked for in life. I know everything happens for a reason, but I don't understand why you had to leave me." She opened the manta ray box, scattering his ashes into the gentle surf.

She sat in the warm sand, sobbing while the waves washed over her.

Gazing out over the ocean, serenity and peacefulness fell over Tess, certain Richard would be happy here. She stood up, forcing herself to leave. She blew a kiss toward the lagoon. "I love you and I miss you, Richard. Have fun here, baby."

Mr. Rene's face showed relief to see her trudging down the beach. "Come eat. Please, Mrs. Blue Eyes, lunch is delicious. I have a fresh drink for you, too. Come, come, sit," he said with a tender smile.

She tried to eat, but wasn't hungry, so she laid a towel down on the sand and nodded off. The sound of Mr. Rene's guitar woke Tess. She sat up wondering how long she dozed off for. It wasn't Mr. Rene playing the guitar; it was Tom. Mr. Rene touched her shoulder. "Are you ready to go, Mrs.?"

"Umm hum."

Tom handed the guitar to Mr. Rene and followed behind Tess as she climbed back on the boat.

Tess sat dazed and numb, watching the scenery pass by. Tom joined her on the bench, tears immediately rolled down the tip of her nose as she tried to hold back sniffles. She couldn't bear to look at him, so she bowed her head clasping her hands between her knees.

He rubbed his hand across her back. "I'm sorry Tess. Mr. Rene told me about your husband."

"Thanks." Without thinking, without hesitation, and without explanation, she leaned back resting her head against his shoulder and the tears came again. Tom didn't move. He kept his arm around her, softly stroking her shoulder, holding her fingers with his other hand.

They stayed that way, not saying a word, until they reached the coral reef. "We don't have to snorkel here. I'll understand if you want to go back to your bungalow. You probably need some sleep."

"I'm fine, really. Go ahead."

She appreciated his kindness, but didn't want to ruin his adventure. Tess lay numb on the bench, attempting to pull herself together while Tom and Riatia snorkeled. She wondered what amazing creatures Richard would see on his journey. *Have you found the manta rays all ready? Are you swimming alongside the boat right now?* Sitting upright, she leaned over the edge of the boat, peering into the lagoon. *Are you right here with me now?*

Mr. Rene blew his conch shell. It was time to go.

Silence filled the boat ride back to the resort. Not an awkward silence, but an exhausted silence. The lagoon reflected a mirror image of blue glass, as *motus* passed them by. Tom lightly stroked her shoulder. The feelings that had stirred within her earlier subsided and it was nice to have his arm around her for comfort. It wasn't the day she planned, but it was a beautiful day.

As they approached the dock, Tess didn't quite know what to say. In a strange way, it seemed as if they'd been on a bizarre blind date. "I hope I didn't ruin your day. I'm sure this wasn't what you bargained for on your first snorkeling trip. A complete stranger breaking down crying all over your shoulder." She smiled apologetically.

"Oddly enough, I feel like I've known you for years. Women don't usually yell at me until they've known me a few days." He joked, making her burst out laughing.

"Seriously, Tess, I really need to apologize. I hope I didn't ruin your moment. I feel horrible. If I'd known, I would've stepped aside and let you take the tour by yourself. I'm truly sorry."

"If you wouldn't have *stolen* my tour, you mean." She poked him in the side. "I'm just kidding. Actually, I'm glad you were here. It helped me in an odd way."

His long tapered finger brushed her hair out of her face, tucking behind her ear.

"I owe you an apology, too," she admitted.

"Apologize to me, why?"

"You're not what I thought you'd be," Tess confessed.

"Am I supposed to take that as a compliment?" His lip curled into a gorgeous grin.

"Yes. Yes, you are. You were fun today and very charming. I enjoyed your company. I didn't expect you to be so laid back, and you did let me cry on your shoulder."

"Honestly Tess, I would've never gotten into the water with sharks if you weren't here. I'd be left with only a very boring story of how I observed sharks from the safety of a boat. If you leave me your address at the front desk I promise to send you copies of the pictures." He chuckled reaching down to hug her.

Tess' heart began to thump erratically as she wrapped her arms around his waist, not wanting to let go of him.

"Don't stay gone for so long, Mrs. Blue eyes." Mr. Rene patted her back.

Tess went to her bungalow, lay across the bed, and cried herself to sleep.

31

CHAPTER FOUR

Tess' cheeks were red from sunburn, eyes puffy from crying, and hair untamed and wild from salt water. Her stomach growled with hunger, but she couldn't go to breakfast like this. She dragged herself into the shower outside on the deck, letting the cool water sooth her warm skin.

Tess heard someone knocking on her door. She didn't want to be caught naked in the shower by housekeeping, so she grabbed a towel and tiptoed over to answer the door.

She cracked open the door expecting to see housekeeping.

"Good morning." Tom's irresistible grin broadened, taking in her towel-clad body. "Did I catch you in the shower?"

Heat immediately rippled through her core. "No, I always look like this when I answer the door in the morning," she replied with a sarcastic smile. "What's up?"

"Can I come in? It'll only take a minute, or...I could come back."

"Come on in. Have a seat. Just give me a couple of minutes to rinse the conditioner out of my hair." She tiptoed back to the shower.

Tom followed her to the deck, taking a seat on the chaise. The open-air shower consisted of no more than three teakwood walls. Tess could barely see over the top without standing on her toes. She felt exhilarated standing naked with only a small wooden wall between them. She peeked over the wall to see him grinning at her, looking hotter than ever in flip-flops, khaki shorts, a black T-shirt and dark sunglasses.

"How are you this morning?" he asked sincerely.

"I feel...peaceful actually. Thanks. What brings you to my

door this morning?"

"I have a proposition for you, Tess."

She liked the way he said her name, kind of slowly and drawn out. "I don't have to steal anything do I?"

"Ha, ha very funny. I booked another tour today with Mr. Rene to see the manta rays. I wondered if you'd be interested in joining me. I'd like to make up for interfering with your tour yesterday. And for the record, I didn't steal a tour from some unlucky couple today. Mr. Rene assured me his brother-in-law would do their tour for him."

"I don't have to pay for it, do I? Because I'm sure it's going to cost double the normal tour fee." She laughed aloud.

"Nope, it's on me."

Tess stepped out of the shower with her towel wrapped around her. "Can I eat first?"

"Sure. Mr. Rene should be here in thirty minutes, but if you need more time we'll wait. Take your time."

Tom stood to leave. Tess sensed his eyes on her. She automatically straightened her back, pushing her ass out. Tom smiled from ear to ear.

"What?" she asked shyly.

"Nothing. I'll see you in a few minutes. I'm glad you said yes, I wasn't sure if you'd be up for it."

"Of course I'll go with you. Thanks for thinking of me. I've never gotten to see the manta rays. Hopefully they won't be a no-show." She wanted to ask about his girlfriend. "Just the two of us, right?"

"Yep, just the two of us."

"See you in thirty minutes." She peeked her head out the door to watch him mosey down the pier. *Holy crap!*

Tess slipped a sheer white bathing suit cover over an electric blue bikini. She hit the buffet and made it to the dock in thirty minutes.

Mr. Rene sang to her as she strolled down the dock. "*Ia Orana*, it's a beautiful day, Mrs. Blue Eyes."

"*Ia Orana*. It is a gorgeous day. Hopefully the mantas will show themselves. Mr. Tom isn't here yet?"

"He forgot something. He will be right back."

Sure enough, Tom strode down the dock. As he stepped onto the boat, Tess fought back the urge to throw her arms around his neck and hug him hello. *What the hell is wrong with me?*

"That was fast. I thought for sure I'd be waiting at least thirty minutes for you." He sounded exceptionally cheerful.

She exhaled heavily to release the breath she'd been holding. "It doesn't take me very long to get ready. I'm easy."

"Really? I would've never guessed."

"That's not what I meant." Heat rose to her cheeks as she poked him in the ribs.

"I'm only teasing. I ran down to the front desk and got another underwater camera." Tom reached for her hand and slipped the camera around her wrist. "With any luck, we'll get to use it today. I brought my regular camera, too. It won't bother you if I take pictures, will it? I'll make sure you get copies and…I asked the nice lady at the front desk to leave me your address."

"She's going to leave you my address?" Tess' mouth hung open in shock. "Did you have to pay her for it or did you use that voice you use on her?"

"I'm not sure what you are referring to, but no, I simply asked nicely."

"I'll bet."

The bright blue sky made for a magnificent day. The motion of the boat on the water relaxed Tess as they chatted about their excursion from the day before.

"So Tess, where are you from?"

"I live in Las Vegas."

"Really?" he said in surprise.

"Yeah, why? Does that shock you?"

"Well, kind of. I've been to Vegas, and you don't look like the typical Vegas-type girl."

"I'm not a *Vegas-type* girl. Vegas isn't just about gambling, nightlife and clubbing. Regular people live there, too," she explained, unsure how to take his comment. "Where did you think I lived?"

"Oh, I don't know, you look like a California girl, very natural." Beneath his sunglasses, Tom's eyes wandered from her head to her toes.

Knowing Tom fully enjoyed toying with her, Tess stared him straight in the eye. "I'll take that as a compliment. I am all natural." She liked her shape and didn't feel the need to surgically enhance her body or face. Everything was still where it was supposed to be.

He grinned in a way that made her blush. "Oh, believe me, I meant it as a compliment." Tom snapped a picture of her fiery cheeks.

"Where do you live?"

"I have a couple of houses, but I don't really have a permanent residence. I work a lot, so I'm not home too often. I'm trying to slow down so I can have more time off," he paused for a minute. "Do you have kids?"

"Three kids. JC is eighteen and starting her first year in college. Tracy's twenty-one, in her third year of college. And John's twenty-three. I'm lucky. They're good kids. We're close."

"Where does your daughter go to college?"

"UNLV, but both my girls are going to Colorado College this fall. Tracy did her first year there and loved it. She decided to go back and JC wanted to go with her. They love to snowboard."

"I have a cabin about an hour from there. If your girls like to do anything outdoors, they'll love it." Tom hesitated. "How long were you married? I don't mean to pry. I'm just curious."

"It's all right, I promise I won't break down and cry today." She smirked self-consciously. "We were married twenty-five years."

"Wow. You must've gotten married awfully young. Twenty-five years is a long time, how did you do it? Don't get me wrong. I take my hat off to you. I think it's great, but I can't even get past twenty-five days with a woman."

"I was 19 when we married." She wasn't embarrassed of her age, but in truth didn't want to tell him. "I was genuinely lucky. For us, it was incredible."

"I haven't had the best of luck with dates and marriage always sounds like too much work. Most of my friends are married, some several times, but the jury is still out on whether or not they're happy together," he remarked sarcastically.

"That's actually sad. It's kind of a waste of your life not to be happy. Why bother getting married if you're going to be miserable together? Life's too short. Don't you think?"

"Hey, I can't even get to girlfriend, let alone to 'I do'. So I definitely agree."

"I'm not going to lie. It's a lot of work, but we truly liked each other and loved being together."

Mr. Rene broke into their conversation. "We are here. This is the best spot for the manta rays."

Both grinned in anticipation. She took off her sunglasses and turned to slip out of her cover-up. The thought of Tom changing into his trunks right behind her sent an unexpected surge of heat through her core. He rested his warm hand on her shoulder. Goose bumps covered her body. She clutched onto the metal shade poll for support, fearing her legs might give out from under her. *Holy crap.*

"Ready? Let's do this." Tom cocked his head to the side and stared at her in astonishment. "You have the most beautiful blue eyes I think I've ever seen."

"Thanks," she squeaked. Tess swallowed the sudden overwhelming desire to kiss him.

They peered over the edge of the boat, staring down into the dark abyss. Tess turned her back to the dark water and adjusted her mask. Tom huffed out a chuckle as he stepped directly in front of her and poked her in the tummy with his pointer finger, sending her reeling over the edge into the water.

"Oh, that's it!" She splashed him with water as he stood on the boat. "So this is how it's gonna be?"

"Yep. This is definitely how it's gonna be." He confirmed with a grin, tossing his flippers into the lagoon before diving in himself.

She splashed water in his face again when he surfaced. Straightening the mask over her eyes, she teased, "You're falling behind." With a kick of her flippers, she swam to catch up with Mr. Rene.

When Tom finally joined them, Mr. Rene smiled, "Are you two ready now?"

Tess squirted a fountain of water from her mouth in Tom's direction. They both answered, "Yep."

The deep cavern changed the shade of the lagoon to midnight blue and the underwater trench acted like an underwater freeway for marine life. They spotted stingrays, turtles, eels, and schools of fish, but it looked as if the morning was going to be a bust.

Tom swam up from behind and lightly touched the back of her thigh, reaching to squeeze her fingers. She smiled through her mask, and he pointed downward into the deep dark water. Five huge black and white manta rays gracefully danced their way toward them. They were enormous, their wingspan at least twenty feet across. The dark figures swam in sync doing back rolls and side twists and turns. He slipped the camera from her wrist and snapped pictures of her with the magnificent rays. Tess reached for the camera, pointing downward. Tom dove down twelve feet and Tess took amazing shots of him diving alongside the manta rays.

The majestic manta rays disappeared back into the darkness as swiftly as they appeared before them. Both were elated as they ripped their masks off, lifting their heads out of the water.

"That was amazing! I can't believe how enormous they are." Tom was beside himself.

Overcome with excitement, Tess threw her arms around his neck. "That was awesome! They swim so gracefully, like they're dancing. Finally, they showed up for me." Her arms still clung to his neck, and her legs automatically floated up to wrap around his waist.

"I was afraid you didn't see them at first. I swam over as fast as I could, so you wouldn't miss them." His strong hands slid beneath her bottom and slightly adjusted her position for a more comfortable fit. Tom's fingers rested on her hips as they treaded water together.

At that moment, Tess realized she'd wrapped herself around him. She froze. The desire to kiss him was almost unbearable. Her heart hammered in her chest as they bobbed up and down in the lagoon. The touch of his skin uncoiled an ache deep within.

Her gaze followed her fingers as they coasted across his shoulders and draped behind his nape. Their eyes locked upon each other.

Mr. Rene blew his conch shell, breaking the spell. A smile touched his lips. She untangled herself from his lap and they swam for the boat.

"I have a perfect place for lunch today. We will celebrate the show the great mantas put on for us."

Tess sat beside Tom unable to stop her feelings of confusion. Her attraction for Tom had grown during their excursions, but so did the feelings of guilt and cheating. Richard always wanted to see the manta rays, he tried so many times, and today with Tom, they finally emerged from the depths. The carved box from the day before consumed her thoughts, certain Richard had already found his way to the majestic rays.

"Are you okay, Tess?" Tom softly brushed his hand across her shoulders.

"I was just thinking. Do you ever think things happen for a reason? Like they're supposed to happen that way in life, good or bad?"

"Actually, I do believe that."

"Me too."

He eyed her curiously, but she simply gazed out over the water.

They stopped for lunch on a beautiful unspoiled *motu*. Tess and Tom strolled around the island talking about "the great manta adventure". Mr. Rene prepared coconut cocktails with an incredible lunch. After, Tom explored the *motu* taking pictures while Tess relaxed on the beach with her toes in the warm water. Calmness settled over her.

"Would you like to stay here in paradise, or would you like to snorkel some coral reefs?" asked Mr. Rene.

Tom sat beside her in the sand.

"I'd love to relax for a while, wouldn't you?" She asked.

"Sure," Tom agreed. "Your back is getting red. Would you like me to put some sunscreen on it? I bought this great oil in the lobby this morning. It's made with coconut oil and vanilla."

She chuckled when he held up a bottle of her favorite monoi oil. "You could use some on your back, too." Tess buried her guilt and shrugged off the fact that a gorgeous woman waited back at the resort for him. She wanted his hands on her. Tess missed being touched by a man, even if only a casual contact of his hand on her shoulder.

They laid out beach towels and Tom handed her the oil as he turned his back toward her. His body felt fit under her hands. Her fingers wrapped around his sides, feeling every muscle in his back and shoulders. Her heartbeat pounded in her ears and her hands trembled from nervousness.

He faced her, taking the bottle from her fingers. "Lay down, I'll do your back."

She did as he asked, giggling nervously as he drizzled oil down her back. His hands were amazing, as he massaged her back with the perfect amount of pressure, rubbing the sides of her waist. He slipped the tips of his fingers under the edges of her bottoms. "Your cheeks are a little red."

Extremely aroused, Tess held her breath, using all of her concentration not to moan aloud. "It's from s…snorkeling. You know, face down," she said, practically panting.

"There you go. How's that?" he asked playfully.

"Oh yeah, that's great, thanks." She could barely talk.

"Are you okay?"

"Yep." She nodded, taking in a gulp of air.

"I can put some more oil on you, if you think I missed a spot."

Tom lay on his side next to her with his head propped up on his elbow.

"That's really not fair," she groaned.

"Why, whatever do you mean?" he asked, his voice thick with amusement.

"I haven't had anyone's hands on me, including my own, in over a year." She shoved her face into the beach towel. "I can't believe I said that out loud. You are totally messing with me on purpose."

"Tess, it sounds like you're complaining," he pointed out sweetly.

"Oh no, I'm not complaining." It came out muffled, her face still buried in the towel. *What the hell was I thinking coming here like this? I should've taken care of myself a long time ago.*

Mr. Rene blew his conch shell. "Lunch is ready."

"Go ahead. I'll be there in a minute," she stammered, hiding her face in the towel.

"I'm sorry, really I am. Let me help you up."

Tess waved her hand at him to go away, so she could collect herself.

"I know you're hungry. Seriously, I'll play nice."

She smiled to herself and lifted her hand for him to help her up. After lunch, Tess swam in the shallow turquoise water while Tom received a crash course in Tahitian culture from Mr. Rene. The conch shell blew again. The boat was loaded and it was time to go.

They sat beside each other on the bench, their shoulders gently brushing every time the boat hit a swell. The motion of the waves and heat from his skin relaxed her.

"Tom, can I ask you a personal question?"

"Sure."

"How does a man who seems so…wonderful and kind and gorgeous, have a girlfriend like the one I saw in the lobby? I mean, she's beautiful, I understand the physical attraction but how do you put up with her?"

"First off, did you just refer to me as wonderful, kind and gorgeous?" He grinned.

Tess flushed and wrinkled her nose. "Shit."

He chuckled, smiling immensely. "Second, she's not my girlfriend. It's more like an out of town date. I didn't want to come here by myself so…she seemed nicer three days ago. Sometimes it's more for show, you know, aspiring actress or model. It gives them publicity, and it keeps me in the magazines, too. Honestly, I just haven't found someone I'd like enough to keep around." He shrugged nonchalantly.

"Ever?" Tess asked with surprise.

"Not really, maybe a few times when I was younger, but it didn't work out."

"Oh."

"I travel a lot and my work has always come first. My date didn't want to come out and have fun with me, so I'm sure as hell not going to sit by the pool all day," he said matter-of-factly. "Besides, I'm having a great time with you."

"It's probably just as well she didn't come with you today." Tess bit her lip with a naughty grin.

Tom smiled, too. "What do you mean?"

"Well, if she would've been here, I'm sure I might've felt bad. When I knocked her overboard and took you back to my bungalow!"

"Is that so?" Hidden under his gorgeous grin lay a candid question.

"Yes, that is so," she flirted brazenly.

Unsure if it was Tom, Bora Bora, or the fact she'd been alone for so long, Tess wanted to take him to bed. She wanted to feel his warm lips and hands on her body. Even more so, she yearned to touch him, everywhere. The mere thought of tasting him sent her pulse rocketing.

He stroked her shoulder with his fingertips. Every inch of her body craved his touch. She sighed several times, trying to calm herself down. It took every ounce of self-control to keep her hands and lips to herself.

As they approached the resort, the boat slowed. Tess would never forgive herself if she didn't ask. Tom sat on the bench, and she stood to face him. His lazy smile drifted over her midriff, before she heard a small breath of air catch in his throat. She entwined her fingers in his and he grinned up at her. "I can't believe I'm going to say this," she said. "Tom, I'm going to be at Bloody Mary's for dinner tonight at eight o'clock. I would love it if you'd meet me there. I realize you're here on a *date*, but if you can find a way to throw her overboard...."

Before he could answer, Tess turned to say goodbye to Mr. Rene. She stepped off the boat and sauntered backward down the pier, flashing him the sexiest grin she could muster. "I know you can't answer me right now, but I'll be there."

She wanted to kiss him goodbye, but it would be impossible to stop at one kiss. At this point, she might accidentally hurt him if she tackled him to the ground. Full of life and vigor she repeated, "Eight o'clock. Bloody Mary's."

CHAPTER FIVE

Tess had never been so audacious in her life. Asking Tom to ditch his date to meet her for dinner wasn't her style, but today, she didn't care. She wanted Tom more than she could've ever imagined. Loving another man was something she knew she'd never be capable of, and Tom Clemmins wasn't the kind of man who fell in love. But for the first time in her life, a carefree vacation full of passion, lust and great sex might be just what she needed.

The guilt she felt subsided. *I'm not cheating on Richard. Nothing I do now will change the fact that I was a faithful wife. Whether he meets me for dinner or not, I'm not going to be miserable any more. It's time to move forward and be happy.*

Anxiety kicked in as she took her time getting ready. She swept her dark brown hair across her eyes, and gathered the rest loosely in a sterling silver clip. *What if he doesn't show? He probably acts like this with every woman. He's a total flirt. What the hell was I thinking? Great, I just made a complete ass out of myself...again.*

She rummaged through her clothes, finally deciding on a scoop neck black dress showing off all those hours Tracy had dragged her out of bed to run. Thanks to the Tahitian motto, No Shoes Required, Tess usually went barefoot. She put on her cutest black sandals and silver hoop earrings before heading out the door.

Tess took the five-minute boat ride to the main island. She meandered down the barely paved road, passing several dive shops and restaurants. *I hope he shows. Then what? Will he come back to my bungalow? Will he ditch his date and stay with me? I haven't slept with another man in twenty-five years.* The possibility of a mere kiss, let alone going to bed with him, fueled a fire within her.

When she reached Bloody Mary's, several couples entered, but she didn't see Tom. She paced back and forth outside. *Should I wait outside or go in?*

"Tess."

The deep sexy voice came from behind and she turned to see Tom leaning against a palm tree, looking more gorgeous than she thought humanly possible.

"Hey." She beamed, sauntering over to join him under the palm tree.

"You look stunning."

"Thanks, handsome." She scanned over his flip-flops, jeans and nice black shirt. "I hoped you would show," she stammered anxiously.

He held her hands in his. "Before you say anything Tess, I need to ask you something, and I don't want you to get upset with me. All right?"

"Okay."

"Are you sure you're ready for this? I mean, are you really ready to be with another man because this isn't something I want you to regret later."

She gazed into his dark eyes and considered his question. "Yes, I'm sure. I want to stay with you, for the rest of my trip." She clarified with a slight nod.

His cocked his head to one side. "So if I told you right now, at this very moment, all of your belongings are being packed up and brought to another resort, you'd be okay with that?"

"That depends. Are all of your things being packed up and taken to the same resort?" she questioned timidly.

"Yes, whether you decide to stay with me or not. I sent my date home. I changed resorts and I'd like it if you'd stay with me."

"I'm sure."

"Are you hungry?"

Hungry for you. "Actually, I'm starving from all the snorkeling today."

"Do you have your heart set on eating here? I had something

a little different in mind."

Room service in bed? "Wherever you want to have dinner is fine with me."

"I was hoping you'd say that. I have a surprise for you." Tom led her across the street to a boat dock. "After you." He held his hand out to the side so she could step onto the boat before him.

"Where are we going?"

"I think you'll like it."

The Tahitian man introduced himself. "*Ia Orana*, I am Mr. Rene's cousin. My name is Tayia."

"*Ia Orana*," Tess said.

The boat skimmed across the lagoon, casting ripples through the reflection of the fiery sunset. Cool, moist spray tingled her warm face. She sat between Tom's legs and leaned back against his chest. *I haven't done this in so long. I hope he's a good lover. Please, please, please be good in bed.* She glanced over her shoulder and he grinned at her. *Crap! Is he sitting here wondering if I'm going to be a good lover? Tess sat up a little taller. Oh, I am definitely going to be good for him.*

With every draw of breath, her chest lifted and lowered. Tom must've noticed her nervousness. He placed his palm over her heart. She felt the hint of his smile as he nuzzled her neck.

She inhaled the scent of his skin. "You smell *delicious*."

Tom held her arm out to the side and lowered his nose to the inside of her elbow. "So do you."

Her gaze drifted to his profile, watching as his eyes closed, taking in the scent of her perfume. The heat from his breath tickled her skin as his lips pressed against her arm. Tess' lips parted and her tongue toyed with the corner of her mouth, wanting to taste his mouth.

The boat slowed, interrupting her gaze. Tess couldn't believe what she saw as they pulled up to a deserted *motu*. "How did you do this?" she whispered in awe.

Tiki torches surrounded a lovely table set with a white tablecloth and a bouquet of flowers. The setting sun cast a glow on the white sand, turning it nearly pink. She held up her dress a little so it wouldn't get wet, hopping off the boat.

Tom stood in the sand and wrapped his arms around her. "Do you like it?"

"It's beautiful." She turned to face him, reaching her lips up to kiss his.

"Not yet Tess, not yet," he whispered in a teasing tone.

Slighted by Tom's response, her eyes filled with disappointment.

"Awe, don't look at me like that."

Her expression didn't change, yearning to feel his lips.

His thumb coasted gently over her cheek. "Do you trust me? Hmm? I trusted you with the sharks. Remember? Will you trust me now?" He brushed his lips against her neck, causing goose bumps to cover her skin.

"Yes, I remember. But-"

"I assure you, I'll make it worth the wait." He toyed, whispering in her ear. "I promise I won't disappoint you."

She remembered how fantastic his hands felt. "I have no doubt."

Tayia finished setting the table with a bottle of wine and a delicious meal before leaving in the boat. Their conversation flowed easily all through dinner. They talked for hours discussing everything from places they'd both traveled to charities they supported. He spoke little of his career, and made it clear he was on vacation and didn't want to discuss work. She shared stories of her kids, but kept them to a minimal.

After dinner, they lay side-by-side on a white blanket Tayia left for them. Tess stretched out on her back with her legs crossed at the ankles, and Tom lie on his side with his head propped on his elbow. She hadn't felt sexy in a long time, but he made her feel unbelievably sensual. Every stroke of his hand on her arm or back, sent a current of blistering heat washing over her, filling the absence of longing and desire that had filled her life over the last year. The simple act of brushing the hair from her eyes caused her to lean closer into the warmth of his fingers. She wanted more, needing him to touch her, so she could set free the raw need she'd buried for too long.

Deep in her own thoughts, she tried to deal with a multitude of feelings. The sense of betrayal loomed heavily, but so did the burning ache between her thighs. She bordered on the edge of virgin-ish nervous. It might hurt. *Not to mention I might get off before we even get started.*

Shadows from Tiki torches flickered across Tom's face as he stroked her arm from shoulder to wrist. "Tess, are you still sure about this?"

"I'm sure. It's just…it's been a long time. I'm a little nervous." She smiled timidly. "How long do we have before he comes back to pick us up?"

"Did you forget already? You're supposed to trust me. No questions."

They stared up at the star-filled sky, listening to the waves roll onto the beach. He delicately traced her collarbone and neck. As his fingertip reached her lips, she rolled her tongue around it and heard him sigh softly.

Tom stood up, holding out his hand to Tess. They strolled along the beach and gazed out at the moon hanging over the ocean. He turned to face her and pulled her into his arms. Her heartbeat turned unruly as his head dropped, grazing his parted lips over her temple. Tilting her face toward his, Tess tensed and held her breath. He made a quiet sound of amusement and rested his palms on the sides of her neck. "Breathe, Tess, just breathe."

Tom's tongue drifted down her neck and back to her lips, playing slowly with her tongue. The warmth of his sweet mouth tasted so good that she instantaneously began to kiss him back. She had suppressed her need to feel desire for a man, hidden the longing of a man's hands on her flesh and buried her cravings in sleepless nights full of tears.

Taking pleasure in the heat of his mouth, she began to shake uncontrollably. All of her emotions came rushing to the surface, covering her in a tingling sensation. His fingers threaded through her hair and cradled her face with his thumbs. Teasing her, he plunged his tongue deeper, sending pulsating waves rippling through her very core. Craving more, she wrapped her arms around his neck and molded her body to his. Feeling his erection, she urgently thrust her hips forward searching for more. Her heart hammered violently in her chest as her fingers twisted through his dark hair. Tess pressed forward taking his mouth with hot, wet, indecent kisses, savoring the flavor of his lips.

He eased back and placed his palm over her pounding heart. "Easy," he whispered with a smoldering laugh. Both chuckled as she buried her face in his chest.

Tom led her away from the beach up into the palm trees. The darkness concealed a bungalow tucked between lush foliage and palm trees.

"Holy crap! Is this for us?" Tess gasped.

"Yes."

"It's beautiful," Were the only words she could utter before he drew her into his arms, kissing her fervently, keeping up with her hungry lips.

Standing under the starlit sky, he slid his hands down the small of her back, following the curve of her ass, grasping it with the perfect amount of tension. Tess softly moaned aloud, encouraging him to press himself firmly against her. He clutched her ribcage and brushed his thumb over the material covering her nipple, sending another set of ripples surging through her. "Oh, God," she whimpered.

Making their way inside, Tess unbuttoned Tom's shirt, exploring the details of his carved chest and stomach, letting her fingers play with the thin trail of dark hair leading into his jeans. Wanting to know the full extent of the force pressing against her hips, she unbuttoned his jeans with trembling fingers. Reaching in, she stroked the length of him and a low groan escaped his lips.

Nice.

He reached down, taking hold of both of her hands. "Trust me, Tess. Tonight is all about you." Tom chuckled. "You can make it up to me tomorrow."

"I trust you," she whispered under his lips.

He unzipped her dress, slipping it to the floor before laying her back onto the bed. Tom took his time, sliding his fingers from the hallow at the base of her neck to the center of her breasts, cupping one in his hand. His warm, wet tongue tickled her nipple. He fastened his mouth over the erect bud, taking it in and biting her tenderly before moving to the next.

Caressing her hips, Tom's lips traveled down between her thighs. She hung her head over the edge of the bed as his talented tongue explored the soft skin between her legs before sinking inside her. All of her worries faded away under the strokes of his tongue. Tess didn't take long, peaking almost immediately. Tears stung the corners of her eyes as her release came again and again. Gasping for air, she opened her eyes and lifted her head to watch him.

Rising up onto the palms of his hands, he pressed his body on top of hers. Tess slipped her thumbs into the waistband of his jeans, pushing them down past his hips. Raising her legs around his waist, her hands took hold of his firm ass while her toes wriggled his jeans to his ankles. She smiled up at him as she tossed his jeans to the floor with her toes.

Tom drew her leg up around his hip. Seeking admittance, he nudged her gently.

In one swift move, she flipped him over onto his back. "Do you mind if I drive for minute?" she grinned. "I'm a little nervous."

He let out a chuckle and quickly imitated her maneuver, pinning Tess to the bed. "I know it's been a long time for you. I promise I'll be nice, but I'll last longer if I drive."

Tess relaxed, granting him access. Ever so gently, he eased his ridge past her entrance, taking his time, slowly diving deep inside. What she thought might be painful felt more like full-blown heaven.

"Holy crap!" she cried out, peaking again five strokes in.

"You okay?" Tom asked, halting his movement.

"Oh yeah, don't stop."

He remained still. "Don't move, give me a sec."

She nodded in agreement, reaching up to kiss his lips. "Maybe you should come now so we could start again in thirty minutes."

"Give me just a minute, I'll be fine." His dark eyes stared into hers intently. "Okay, I'm good now."

He began to move again, slowly at first, then harder and faster, giving himself to her fully. Raising her hips to meet his, she matched him stroke-for-stroke. He spoke to her tenderly between eager kisses, "You feel so good...The taste of your skin...I want you."

Tess yearned for control. She'd been anxious at first, but didn't want him to be under the impression she was a timid lover. She wanted him to desire her without limits or boundaries, needing him to handle her passionately, like a lover, not like a fragile widow.

Without missing a beat, she rolled over on top of him. The moon shone brightly through the open doors, allowing them to see each other perfectly in the darkness. Her palms rested his chest as she stared down, admiring his fit body. Her hips took control rhythmically, flowing to the sound of the waves crashing against the outer reef.

Tom stared back just as attentively. "You are so beautiful." He cupped her breasts, gently squeezing her nipples.

Her passion laid dormant for over a year, but now she felt alive, powerful and sexy. She wanted to be beautiful for him. Tess gently removed his hands from her breasts and replaced them with her own. Raising her hips up high and then diving down, she crested waves of sheer pleasure. Her head dropped forward as she slowed down momentarily before the next set of breakers, building deep within her came crashing in again.

Tess lifted the damp hair from her neck, so the ocean breeze would cool the sweat trickling down her back. Tom gripped her hips and held her still, but she shook her head no, wanting to ride freely no matter what the cost. "You don't have to wait, it's okay." He released his grip, letting her have her way.

Knowing his gaze would follow hers, Tess eased her hips back and gazed down to watch their bodies connecting intimately.

Peaking together this time, he let out a low groan, "Jesus, Tess."

She collapsed on top of him, sucking in air, trying to catch her breath.

Minutes later she panted, "Whew. Thanks!"

"Thanks? You're seriously thanking me?" he choked, bursting into a shocked laughter. "If anything, I should be the one saying thanks. You're fucking amazing. Damn, Tess."

Completely embarrassed, she giggled. "Not like that! You know what I mean! Thanks for waiting."

"My pleasure." He laughed, pulling her tightly beside him.

Tess curled into the crook of his arm and hitched her leg up over his hip. Tom stared up at the ceiling, languorously playing with a strand of her hair. Her body felt heavy and sedated. Lying in the arms of another man was somewhere she never expected to venture again. This was the first time she'd ever engaged in casual relationship, a fling, a spontaneous affair. As she peered up at Tom, nothing felt casual. Feeling the weight of uncharted territory, she released a shaky breath of air she'd been holding. *He's just a rendezvous. He's just a vacation. You can't keep him.*

He smiled at her and gathered her closer into his arm, brushing a kiss against her hair. "When's the last time you had fun, Tess?"

"Other than the last few days? It's been awhile."

He turned on his side and propped up on his elbow, drifting the tip of his finger over the contours of her neck and collarbone. "That's about to change. Cause *we're* going to have a great time together. You up for that?"

She nodded. "I'm up for anything." *With you.* She added silently, settling into his arms and drifting off to sleep.

CHAPTER SIX

She woke to the sound of a boat in the distance, but Tom was nowhere in sight. She rose onto her elbows, marveling at the plush rustic interiors of the bungalow that she hadn't seen the night before. Woven bamboo paper covered the walls and several vases of freshly cut tropical flowers adorned the room. As she stood, a balmy breeze rustled the thatched roofing. Stiff, sore muscles brought a blush to her cheeks, remembering the night before.

The bungalow was completely exposed to the outdoors. Tess meandered toward the luxurious indoor, yet open to the outdoor bathroom. "Wow," she whispered. All of her things lay on a counter next to a stone basin, perched atop a smooth tree trunk. She brushed her teeth and climbed back into bed.

She spotted Tom walking down the beach with coffee and breakfast. He sauntered into the room, giving her a cheeky smile and a big kiss on the lips. "Morning, are you hungry?"

"I'm starving."

"I thought you might be." He chuckled. Tom set breakfast on the table and grabbed his camera, snapping a picture of her half-wrapped in the sheet and her hair blowing in the gentle breeze.

"Hey, you better erase that one," Tess complained.

"No way! You look scrumptious. I like this one."

After they enjoyed breakfast, Tom slid out of his jeans and they ambled naked down to the beach to swim in the lagoon.

"I never knew this place existed," she said in awe.

"I was counting on that last night. It's part of a new resort we'll be staying at the rest of the time we're here."

"We're not staying here?"

"Well, we could, although the bungalow I have for us at the resort is exceptionally nice. But it's a surprise."

"Are you always full of surprises like these?" She asked happily, already wanting to go back to bed.

"No, actually, I'm not. I wanted to do this for you. You said it had been a long time, so I wanted it to be nice for you. Not to mention you've been driving me crazy."

"I'm driving you crazy?"

"I find you incredibly sexy," he said, running his hands over her skin.

"You think so, huh?" A smile danced across her lips as she retreated from the water heading straight for bed, where they stayed for several hours until Tayia arrived.

Referring to their resort as 'exceptionally nice' was an understatement. The resort oozed elegance and luxury, putting a modern twist on traditional Tahitian style. Their overwater bungalow sat secluded at the far end of a pier.

When they stepped out onto the deck, Tess couldn't believe what she saw. "I've never seen a plunge pool in an over-water bungalow. Ever!"

Tom ordered an early dinner and a bottle of wine. She immediately undressed and headed straight for the plunge pool. She noticed him staring at her from the open doorway. Biting her lip provocatively, her fingertips skimmed over the water. He undressed to join her.

Three days went by before they actually left their bungalow. They spent the day's snorkeling coral reefs and skinny-dipping in the lagoon. Their bungalow came equipped with its own kayak tied to the bottom step of their deck and they paddled to a *motu* across the lagoon, in search of tropical treasures. He took pictures of exotic birds and landscapes fit for a calendar.

Tess' body was trying to make up for the lack of sex over the last year. Once they started, she didn't want to quit. They could finish after breakfast and she would be ready again before lunch and again after dinner. Tom didn't have any problem keeping up with her. *Thank God.*

Tess woke up early the following day wanting to run. She quietly slipped on shorts and a tank top, trying not to wake Tom, but he lay in bed, watching her.

"You're not taking off on me, are you?" he taunted.

"Yes, I am, the last couple days have been torture."

"It's been terrible for me, too. Maybe you should come back to bed so I can torture you some more."

"I thought about going running, but you make a very good distraction." She gazed at his naked body, deciding if she should stay or go.

"Do you mind if I run with you? How far are you going?"

"As far as you'd like to go. Come with me."

Tom dressed and grabbed his backpack. They ran for a few miles, taking a trail that ended with a magnificent waterfall, pausing long enough to skinny dip in the dark pool of warm water surrounded by lava rocks, lush green palm trees, and colorful wild flowers.

Heading back on the trail, it started to rain, followed by a downpour. "Who ordered the rain?" Tess joked.

He laid his hands on the sides of her neck and kissed her with fervor. Tess' heart pounded, drowning out the rain. She traced his muscles under the wet shirt clinging to his body. Drenched with rain, Tom's hair appeared darker, the gray hidden, making him look younger as he stared down at her, grinning wildly. "Do you trust me, Tess?"

"Yes."

He clasped her hand as they hiked through the rainforest to the top of a hill covered in grassy vegetation. Rain poured down on them. He wrapped her in his sodden arms and kissed her forcefully, stealing her breath. Before she could blink, he'd skimmed her shirt up over her head and untied her shorts. Caught up in the moment, their bodies entangled on a bed of ferns beneath them, colliding with the rhythm of the pounding rain, slowing as the heavy droplets turned to a drizzle.

They lay on their backs and stared up at the sky through the trees, gasping for air. Her long brown hair clung to her face, soaking wet with black mud and fern leaves sticking out of it.

"Holy crap," she panted bashfully.

"You're unbelievable, Tess."

Tom gathered mud on the tip of his finger and wiped it on her nose and cheeks. She laid still, letting him finish his artwork, drawing dots and lines down her arms, before she did the same to him. They received several glances walking through the resort, but Tess couldn't have cared less they were covered in dried mud. She was only interested in Tom.

Tom rented an electric car, stopping at a dive shop to purchase his own snorkeling gear. They hit a few beaches before stopping at The Freaky Tiki. The colorful bar set up high on a hillside and resembled a shabby run down shack ready to fall down at any moment. They relaxed in a hammock slung between two palm trees and gazed out over the pristine Pacific Ocean drinking *Hinanos*. She lay quiet, sipping the Tahitian beer.

"What's weighing on your mind?" he asked, running his finger across her forehead.

She sighed heavily. "I was just counting up the days I've already been here."

"Oh…oh," he stammered, struggling for words, followed by the same heavy sigh.

Tess didn't want Tom assuming he needed to coddle her or worry about their goodbye. They were having a wonderful time, but she was well aware that he didn't date long term. No matter how much it would hurt to say goodbye to this amazing man lying in the hammock next to her, she refused to dwell on it. Rendezvous. This is nothing more than a wonderful, amazing, incredible rendezvous.

She lifted her *Hinanos* to his and said, "Here's to the best vacation."

Tom drew back his face, and furrowed his brows. Nodding hesitantly, he clinked his beer to hers. "To the best vacation."

Later that night, they enjoyed a private dinner on the beach. A Tahitian man and woman performed a traditional Polynesian dance in grass skirts, asking Tess and Tom to join them. Tess loved to dance and knew this dance well, slowly moving her hips in a circle by barely moving her feet. The ocean blue pareo she'd bought that morning was tied in a knot low on her hip, exposing her bare leg to the top of her thigh as she danced.

Tom picked a pink hibiscus and slipped it behind her ear. They danced barefoot in the sand as tiki torches flickered beneath the palm trees. She relaxed into his arms and rested her cheek on his chest, hiding the tears that pricked her eyes. *How am I going to say goodbye?*

When she rolled over, Tess found a note saying, "Be right back." She threw on bikini bottoms to lie in the sun. Torn between the polar opposite emotions of guilt and pleasure, she forced herself to acknowledge the fact that this was undoubtedly one of the best trips she'd taken to Bora Bora and all because of Tom. However, the pleasure, passion, and happiness were overriding the guilt, which made the guilt even worse. She dove in the lagoon to cool off.

Tess turned over to float on her back and noticed Tom staring at her from the handrail. "How long have you been standing there?"

"I have breakfast and coffee, if you're hungry." He smiled, ignoring her question.

She slipped a sheer white swimsuit cover over her bikini bottoms. Tom's eyes strayed slowly over the damp material clinging to droplets of water on her breasts as she sipped her coffee.

"When do Tracy and JC come back from Europe?"

"They get home a week after me."

"Tess," he said in a voice so delicious, the mere sound made her go weak at the knees.

Even though playfulness lingered in his tone, she glanced into his dark brown eyes and realized Tom had something on his mind.

"Do you need to go home in three days or can you stay on vacation with me longer? I'll understand if you need to get back, but I'm not ready to let go of you yet." His brows creased slightly, revealing the indication of seriousness to his offer, as if it were uncharted territory for him.

Her mind raced. She didn't really need to go home yet, but the idea of Tom wanting her to stay longer filled her full of happiness. *If I stay, what will that mean to him? What does it mean to me? Nothing? Something? Everything? Are we dating now? Am I simply going to be able to just walk away from this amazing man when the vacation is over?*

She wanted answers to all of her questions, but one thing she knew for certain, if she pushed Tom, even the smallest amount, he'd be gone.

Lowering her gaze to the table, she dragged her hands through her hair and chewed nervously on her lip. "You really want me to stay longer? I thought-"

"I don't have any commitments for a few weeks." His lips caressed her neck. "I'm enjoying my time with you and I'm under the impression you're enjoying yourself, too."

Acting on a whim was completely out of character for her. This trip was the most unpredictable thing she'd ever done in her life.

"Come with me, Tess. I'll show you a great time. What else do you have to do right now back at home that can't wait for awhile?"

After every sentence he paused, giving her the impression he was waiting patiently for her response. She lifted her eyes, searching for reassurance that she wouldn't regret her decision. He gave her a sexy imploring smile.

"Why, Mr. Clemmins, are you trying to seduce me into staying here with you?" She teased with a quiet chuckle.

"Is it working?" he whispered in her ear.

"Yes, I believe it is. I can stay." She imitated his slow sexy tone, "I'm not through with you yet, Tom Clemmins."

Reality sunk in a few hours later.

"I should call my girls," she said apprehensively.

"Are you going to tell them the truth? Will they be upset you're here with me?" he asked honestly.

"Can I tell them I'm here with you, Tom?"

"What do you mean?"

"Everything we've done has been so discreet. I know you're worried about your privacy. And to tell you the truth, I don't have a clue what they'll say."

"Of course you can tell them you're with me. I trust you. I do enjoy my privacy, but that's not why we've been doing

56

everything *so discreetly*. I wanted to be alone with you. I want you to myself."

Tom grinned mischievously. "By the way, if it's all right with you, I'd prefer to stay somewhere else for the rest of our vacation."

"A different resort?"

"No. I'd like to take you somewhere else."

"Where are we going?"

He didn't answer.

"You're not going to tell me are you? I can tell by your devious grin you're up to something."

"It's a surprise."

Tess called John first. He didn't answer, so she left a message, explaining she was fine and having a good time, but wasn't ready to come home yet. She'd be switching resorts and would call him in a few days with the information. *That was easy.*

She dialed Tracy's number next. "Hello?" she answered in a sleepy voice.

Tess completely forgot it would be four in the morning in Europe. "Hi honey, crap, I'm sorry. I forgot about the time difference."

"Mom? What's going on?" She sounded concerned.

"I'm fine. Do you want me to call you back?" Tess asked.

"No, it's fine, I'm up now. Did you do your thing with Dad today? Are you upset?"

"No, I did that when I first got here and it went perfect." Tess paced nervously, realizing her girls might get upset with her news. "I need to talk to you for a few minutes."

"I'm up, JC's right here, too."

"Hi, Mom. It's amazing here, and European guys are *gorgeous*." JC sounded half-asleep in the background.

Tess chuckled, shaking her head at her youngest daughter. "JC you're not there for boys. My trip has been wonderful. I wanted to let you know I'm not going home yet. I'm staying another week, but I won't be in Bora Bora. I left a message with your brother, so if you talk to him will you fill him in?"

"What do you mean? Are you changing islands?" Tracy asked.

Tess' face turned beet red as she struggled to find the right words. "Well, actually I'm not sure where we're going."

Tom sat on the chaise, smiling, watching her pace around in a circle.

"*We?* Who's we? Who are you with?" Alarm sizzled through the phone line and JC uttered something in the background about a Polynesian fire dancer.

"It's kind of a long story, but I met someone. He's taking me somewhere else, but I'm not sure where exactly."

"What! You met somebody? Who is he? How do you know he's not some psycho?" Tracy shrieked, sounding more like a hysterical parent than a daughter. "Are you joking? Where's-"

Tess cut her off. "I'm not joking and he's not some psycho. In fact, he's quite wonderful." She turned redder by the second. "He's just surprising me, that's all."

"Are you out of your freakin' mind? Do you even know anything about this guy? What does he do? I can't believe you're telling me this. I don't think it's a good idea for you to be running off in a foreign country with some stranger! What the hell, Mom!"

"Come on, Tracy, I'd never do anything stupid."

"No offense, but it doesn't sound like the smartest decision. You don't even know this man." Tracy frantically repeated the conversation to JC at the same time she lectured her mom.

Tess took a deep breath. "I'm here with Tom Clemmins. We've been together for the last week. He's taking me somewhere else, but won't divulge that information because he wants to surprise me."

"Tom Clemmins? *The* Tom Clemmins?" Tracy exclaimed. JC shrieked with excitement in the background.

"Yes."

"*The* Tom Clemmins?" she asked again. "Hollywood hottie, *actor* Tom Clemmins?"

JC grabbed the phone from her sister. "Right on, you go, Momma. How'd you hook up with him?" She squealed before Tracy yanked the phone back.

"I just wanted to call and tell you what was going on."

"Wow! How'd you hook up with Tom Clemmins? I bet you

are having a good time." Tracy said with a touch of cynicism.

"We met on a shark excursion. Actually, he tried to steal my private tour, but it all worked out for the best. I'll tell you all about it later."

Tom raised his eyebrows. "I hope you're not going to tell them everything, and that's not fair, I didn't steal your tour."

"I'm just so…surprised. Isn't he supposed to be a total….*you know*….jeeze, Mom…doesn't he date a lot?"

"He's very nice," she chimed sweetly, winking at Tom.

Tom motioned for Tess to give him the phone. "Can I talk to her for a minute?"

Tess eyed him suspiciously, wondering what he'd say, but decided what the hell. "Hold on Tracy, he wants to tell you something."

After handing him the phone, she began pacing back and forth again wondering if it was a wise idea to let him talk to her girls. She'd never intended on needing a *Dating 101manual*.

"Hi, Tracy. I don't want you to worry about your Mom," Tom said in a sweet slow voice.

Tess couldn't hear Tracy's end of the conversation, however she could hear JC from across the room as Tom held the phone away from his ear, yelling in the background, "Hi, Tom! Tell him I said hi!"

He chuckled. "If it'll make you feel better, I'll get your number from your mom and text you in a couple of days when we leave, so you can have the address of where we'll be staying. I just want it to be a surprise for her."

Tom's grin turned sober. "I promise. I'll take good care of her. I understand. Okay. I won't. Yep. Thanks. It was nice talking to you. I can hear your sister in the background, tell her I said hi. Have fun in Greece, it's beautiful there." He handed the phone back to Tess.

"I hope you're having fun, I miss you and please don't worry about me I'm fine. Actually, I'm great. I'm sorry for waking you up, go back to sleep."

"Mom, we love you. Please be careful, he's supposed to be a total lady's man."

"I can see why they say that." Tess smirked at Tom. "Call

your brother for me. I won't be able to call him again. Love you, be safe." Closing the phone, she huffed out a big anxiety-filled breath of air.

"I'm sure they think I've lost my mind." Tess laughed nervously. "What did she say to you?"

"She seems a lot like you," he chuckled sarcastically. "Practically de-ja-vous of our first meeting on the dock."

She groaned. "Oh great! What did she say?"

"She said her mom had been through a rough year and was just starting to heal and I better not hurt you. Apparently, they're under the impression I'm a real "womanizer". I'm quite sure that's the term she used, but she said it in a nice voice." He stared into her eyes, running his finger under her chin. "Am I hurting you, Tess?"

"Yes, you're torturing me slowly," she teased, but realized he really was concerned.

"I'm serious. I don't want to cause you any pain. I care about you."

"Look Tom, I knew this was a vacation for both of us. I won't pretend that the last week hasn't been much more than I ever imagined it could be, but I knew where I stood when I agreed to stay with you. I'm not going to say goodbye now. It's still going to hurt just as much in another week."

His brows wrinkled apprehensively.

She rested her hands on his firm shoulders and confessed, "I've learned the hard way that every day is a gift. I refuse to waste one more moment of my life. I won't do it."

He frowned. "Tess, I don't-"

"Tom, you agreed with me when I asked if you believe everything happens for a reason."

"I do believe that, but this is different."

"No, it's not different. We were supposed to meet. For what reason I don't know. It wasn't by chance you came here with someone who was unimportant to you, or that you taking my tour led me to a perfect place to say goodbye to Richard and brought me to you. What about the manta rays? They miraculously found me after all these years of trying. I believe those things are meant to be. I'm not naïve. I realize that you don't have long-term relationships. I'm okay with it. Life is too damn short. I don't care where we go or what we do. I only want to enjoy my time with you, even if it's only one more week."

"I'm having a *great* time with you." He folded her into his arms and caressed her back, almost as if he was trying to tell her something that he couldn't put into words.

She attempted to control her emotions, but she'd been tucking these thoughts deep inside since their first night together. She paused, gathering courage to lower the wall that protected her heart. "If I'm being totally honest, and I can't believe I'm going to admit this to myself out loud, you're the best time I've ever had here. I've had some incredible times in Bora Bora, but the last week has been truly fantastic."

Tom's eyes smiled. His lips found hers as his fingers tenderly cupped her face. "I don't know what to say. I'm so flattered, but I don't want our time together to take the place of your trips here with your husband. I only want to make you happy while we're together."

"That's not exactly what I meant. Nothing can replace my memories here with Richard. I know you'd never intentionally do that, but this is supposed to happen to me. Right now. At this exact moment in my life." One tear trickled down her cheek.

"Please don't be sad, Tess. I don't think I could take it." He gently wiped away her tear.

"I'm not sad. You make me happy. I haven't allowed myself to feel anything in such a long time. I just want to live in the moment, Tom."

As the night lingered, he seemed unusually quiet. She couldn't even begin to guess what he was thinking and hoped she hadn't said anything to scare him off.

CHAPTER SEVEN

Tess tossed and turned in the early morning darkness, too anxious to sleep. For a moment last night, she worried she'd wake up and he'd be gone. She was afraid he'd literally run to the airport and catch the first flight to anywhere so he wouldn't have to use the word *relationship*.

Tom slept soundly on his stomach with the sheet covering him from the waist down. She nibbled on his back, moving her way to his ear. "I'm going for a run, do you want to come?"

He turned over, sitting up on his elbows.

Her heart raced just looking at him.

"No, go ahead without me, I've got a few things I still need to take care of for our trip. I'll order breakfast when you get back."

Running had turned into such a great outlet, and she needed to clear her head. Obviously, they were continuing their trip together, but one day soon she'd wake up and it would be over. Tom only got involved with a woman up to a certain point, and she assumed he had already gone way beyond his relationship limits.

I'm okay with it. She thought, rehashing the words that slipped so easily from her lips the night before. *Am I really okay with a casual fling? Who am I kidding? It doesn't matter if I'm okay with it or not. I can either accept Tom the way his is, commitment phobia and relationship hang-ups included, or I can go home.* She pushed herself into a full on sprint. *God, I like him so much. I'm so attracted to him it's ridiculous. All I really want to do is climb back in bed and kiss every inch of his smoking hot body.* She stopped to catch her breath before turning back to the resort.

Tess didn't want to torment herself for enjoying her time with Tom, nor did she want to become too attached to him. She decided to perceive their relationship as a rendezvous. Nothing more, nothing less. An amazing, once in a lifetime rendezvous. A time in her life that she could look back on with no regrets, having lived in the moment, sharing time with a remarkable man.

When she returned to the bungalow, Tom was gone. She showered outside, letting the sun warm her face as the cool water washed away her uncertainties. *No more wasted time. Don't worry about tomorrow. Enjoy him while you have him. Life isn't about tomorrow. Life is about today.*

"Tess." He peeked over the shower wall with the crooked grin she loved so much. "I have breakfast. How was your run?"

"Great."

"I wondered if you'd like to visit a pearl farm today. They grow vanilla there, too. We have today and tomorrow, and check-out the following day at noon to make our flight," he said.

"Sounds perfect." She stepped from the shower and pressed her lips to his neck, trying to decipher his mood. He seemed slightly pensive and a bit quiet, but still obligingly stripped her of her towel and assisted drying her off. Leading her to believe everything was fine between them.

Tom rented a jeep and they drove to a lovely pearl farm that lay nestled in a beautiful bay on the other side of the island. It was a small shack perched on stilts over the lagoon with a pier. They toured the farm, learning the extensive process of cultivating pearls.

Making their way next door, they meandered through the vanilla fields, taking in the exotic aroma that permeated the air. Tess picked vanilla beans to take home with her. The thin black beans made the best homemade ice cream. Tom took pictures of the pearl shack, the bay, even an old woman working in the fields.

"That relaxes you, doesn't it?" She nodded toward his camera.

"It does." He smiled with surprise. "I love taking snapshots. It's kind of a hobby."

"What do you do with your photos?" She asked curiously.

"I only do it for fun."

"Will you send copies to me? I haven't been taking any pictures, and your camera is a lot nicer than mine."

"Of course. I don't mind if you use your camera, Tess." He kissed her lips, but withdrew too quickly.

A small flutter trembled in her tummy sensing a slight wariness in him. "You okay?"

"Of course. Why do you ask?"

"You just seem a little preoccupied." She thought for sure he was turning paler by the second and his body language stiffened immediately. *Don't push him.* Standing in the middle of the field, Tess reached her hands over his shoulders and pulled his mouth down to hers. She kissed him and kissed him and kissed him. A long, sensual, indecent kiss that she broke only when the tension released from his limbs and she needed air.

"What's that all about?" He gasped, holding her willingly in his arms.

"I can tell you have a lot on your mind." She smiled timidly. "I just wanted to give you something else to think about."

A tinge of blush colored his cheeks as he let out a low chuckle and nodded his head, acknowledging her suspicions. He smiled, mumbling something about her being able *to read him like a book*. She said nothing in return, only bumping him playfully with her hip.

Heading back to the resort, they drove through several rural villages and stopped at an outdoor market where Tess picked up a few trinkets for her kids. Tom bought her a wooden bracelet with intricately carved flowers and earrings made of transparent beach glass. She would wear them to dinner that night with a white wrap dress.

"How can you wear something so basic and look so incredibly gorgeous?" she asked. The way she eyed Tom in his faded jeans and button down white shirt, they might not even make it to dinner.

"Funny, I was thinking the same thing about you. Are you ready?"

"I am, unless…" She slid her hand across the bed, inviting him to stay a little longer.

He grabbed her around the waist and kissed her enthusiastically. "After dinner."

They enjoyed a wonderful dinner on the water, watching the sunset. Tess sensed other couples studying them, wondering if Tom was actually Tom Clemmins.

"Is that hard for you? Having people know who you are everywhere you go?"

"Sometimes. My career is more than I ever dreamed it would be, but there are some definite downsides. No privacy is unquestionably one of them."

They chatted about his career. Tom told funny stories about actors he enjoyed working with, and a few who weren't so fun to work with. He supported several charities, and going green was on the top of his list.

Tess talked about her life at home. She'd been heavily involved in their contracting company until Richard took on a partner ten years ago. Since then she'd stayed home, raising her kids. Tess didn't need to go back to work if she was careful with her money. She considered going back to work, but had no desire to work fulltime. She'd traveled to Bora Bora searching for inspiration and direction in her life.

"Clearly, I've been inspired, but in a completely different way." She bit her lip and coasted her fingers across his thigh.

He laughed when she ogled over him. "Let's go. I hope you don't mind, but we aren't going back to our bungalow. I want to stay on our deserted *motu* until we leave."

"I'd love that."

A boat waited at the pier and dropped them off on the private moto.

The stars lit up the bungalow as they laid on the bed in the dark.

"Close your eyes," he said.

"Why? What are you going to do to me?" she flirted.

"Close your eyes, Tess."

She did as he asked and received what she hoped for, Tom's soft kisses on her lips. His fingers tickled the nape of her neck.

She opened her eyes, staring at the gorgeous Black Tahitian Pearl necklace. "It's beautiful. Thank you. When did you get this?"

"At the pearl farm today. I noticed you don't have one, or at least you're not wearing one. The colors in it reminded me of you," he said affectionately.

"I didn't see you pick it out." Heat spread through her body, surprised by his gift.

"I know. You were listening to the pearl farmer talk about cultivation or something."

"I love the color. It's so dark, but almost looks like it has swirls in it."

Tom stared at her adoringly, touching his fingers to the necklace. "The pearl is dark, but the dark brown overtone matches your hair, and tomorrow in the daylight you'll be able to see an iridescent blue sheen that reminded me of your eyes."

Her heart clenched, dreading their eventual goodbye. *Don't get attached, Tess. He said it himself, he only dates. He's just a vacation.* She whispered softly, "Thank you."

Tess allowed herself to surrender in the moment, letting go of her guilt, fears and doubts. The way Tom touched her that night seemed slower and more natural. They were getting to know each other better and she had to admit, she was crazy about him.

"What should we do with our last day in paradise?" Tess asked gazing out over the sunrise.

"I have plans, would you like to know what they are?"

"Hmm, surprise me. I lied, you can tell me."

"Nope, you said surprise first, so surprise it is. Let's eat so we can get out of here. It's a casual day, nothing extreme."

"Tom, every day is casual day here. I've hardly even worn any clothes or swim suits, and you can't get much more casual than this." She bit her lip and slid her hands down her naked body.

"You've got a point, but don't start trying to entice me back to bed. Not yet Tess," he said with a playful smile.

The boat picked them up and dropped them off at the dock in front of the resort. Tom led her to the very end of the property where a single bungalow jutted out over the lagoon. Special touches were placed perfectly around the resort spa, stimulating her senses. Freshly cut tropical flowers set on a table next to a bowl of fruit, scented oils sat on a shelf waiting to be chosen, and plush robes hung in the closet.

"Wow, just when you think it couldn't possibly get any more beautiful," she whispered in awe.

"I know." Tom agreed embracing her tightly.

"When you stopped me from seducing you this morning, is this what you had in mind for later?" Tess pointed to the Jacuzzi on the deck that baited her to undress and climb in.

"Maybe..."

One massage table sat in the center of the room with three rain-head showers hovering above it. "Are we getting massages?"

"We are."

"Do you want to go first?"

"No, I'd like you to go first." He fondled her breasts, raising her shirt over her head and slid her shorts to the ground before lifting her up onto the table. Tom pulled his shirt off. "Face down, please."

Tess couldn't quit giggling. "Mr. Tom, are you my masseuse?"

"Yes, yes I am. Do you think I'm up for the daunting task?"

"I'm not sure," she teased.

He picked an oil and started at her neck, kneading the muscles in her shoulders with the perfect amount of pressure. Using his forearm, Tom worked over her back and butt. Tess' body began to pulse as his strong hands rubbed down her thighs to her feet. Tom's long tapered fingers eased up her legs, caressing the inside of her thighs, making her sigh loudly. She wanted to wait for the Jacuzzi, but wasn't sure if she could hold out. Her body squirmed under the strokes of his strong hands.

"Tess, can you roll over please?"

Aroused and excited, she turned over and closed her eyes. Tom massaged her face, neck and breasts, stopping to feel her heart pounding beneath his hands. As his fingers traveled toward her thighs, she could feel the warmth of his breath on her tummy. Tess held her breath in anticipation.

"Breathe, Tess, just breathe." She rolled her hips toward his hands, but he whispered in her ear, "Not yet, lay still."

She exhaled loudly, nodding her head. He touched her affectionately, kissing and licking her nipple, teasing her with his tongue until she began to simmer. Tess wouldn't be able to wait. She was too close. Overcome by temptation, she couldn't lie still, writhing beneath his hands. Dipping lower between her thighs, his tongue and fingers moved as if he knew her body better than she did.

Tess had never been touched like this. Pleasure surged through her. He worked over her spot, her *favorite* spot, throbbing with the need for release. Her quiet moans climbed higher. Reaching down, she held him there, clutching her wrists to his temples. He was remarkable. His fingers glided in a tireless rhythm as her muscles frantically tightened and clenched them inside her.

The sounds coming from her throat sounded foreign and distant over the loud buzz ringing in her ears. "Yes. Oh yes. Oh God." She cried out as she peaked over and over again, cresting and crashing in violent spasms. Tom began to withdrawal his touch and her upper body thrashed back and forth, pleading, "Don't stop...please...not done." When she felt the heat of his mouth return, she released his head from her grip and arched higher, raising her hands above her head. Consumed by raw pleasure-filled emotions, tears stung the corners of her eyes as she shuddered uncontrollably. She whimpered and tugged him upward. He sat on the edge of the table and wrapped her in his arms, stroking and caressing until her breathing slowed. Tess couldn't move or get up.

"Holy crap," she panted.

He kissed her shoulder and nuzzled his smooth face against her neck. "Did you enjoy your massage?"

"Yes, I did. You make me so loud."

"Umm hum, just a little loud." Satisfaction hung on the curve of his smile.

"I know it's your turn, but I need a minute. Shit, my hands are shaking."

While she recovered, Tess noticed stones warming in a miniature oven. This was one of her favorite massages. Although, after the massage he just gave her, she definitely had a new favorite.

Tom settled facedown onto the table. She slowly drizzled oil over his back, causing his muscles to flex as he squirmed. Using the smooth stones with oil, Tess massaged his back and worked out the knots in his shoulders. She spaced the warm stones evenly down his spine before moving on to the rest of his body. Her eyes explored every inch of physic while her hands took in the feel of his fit body beneath her fingertips. She knead the chords in his forearms, moving on to manipulate the center of his palms, gently tugging on each finger.

Tess found herself moving instinctually over his body. Touching without thinking. She felt a connection to Tom, a bond. Her heart raced yearning to give him pleasure.

After removing the stones, she whispered in his ear, "Roll over."

Driven by the burning desire to please him, she was overcome with the urgency to be better than ever before. Tess loved going down on him, but longed to take him to new heights. Touching her hot, wet tongue to the length of him, she breathed a veil of moist heat on his engorged head. She waited, knowing he would open his eyes to watch her. Lying on his back, Tom sat up onto his elbows, staring down at her. Her lips tugged into a smile before she wrapped her mouth around him, taking in every inch.

A low groan escaped his throat as she began massaging him with her tongue. "Oh…my…God." he groaned loudly as his head dropped back. "Tess."

Without releasing him from the suction of her mouth, she climbed onto the table and kneeled between his legs. She set the rhythm, manipulating the length of him with strokes and flicks of her tongue. He clasped his hands to the sides of her face, twisted his fingers in her hair and tugged gently. He strained and his muscles went rigid. Tom moaned from deep within, calling out her name, shuddering fiercely as he came. She took him in, tasting his sweet release. Tess lay her head in his lap, smiling with contentment.

They rinsed off in the rain-head showers and lay on the chaises, munching on fruit. "Your hands should be registered or insured with the authorities. All of that womanizing you do paid off rather nicely for me today." Tess wiggled her eyebrows and plunked a grape into her mouth.

"What is that supposed to mean?" Tom choked on a piece of pineapple, acting as if she'd insulted him.

"You know what I mean," she said playfully.

"Actually, I think you bring out the best in me," he said seriously. "I just want to please you, and believe me, that's not something I usually worry about. I find you irresistible."

"Oh, I'm beyond pleased."

"Good. Me, too."

They grabbed lunch before heading back to their bungalow. They lay in bed, wrapped their arms around each other, and fell asleep. When Tess woke, she could see Tom floating in the turquoise water with his snorkel sticking above the surface. *He's hooked.*

They snorkeled and relaxed on their last day in paradise. She hated to think about leaving, but her excitement grew, wondering where he was taking her. She couldn't believe she was there with him. Not because of Tom's fame, simply because he was wonderful. Most of all, she felt happy. Tess thought she'd never be happy again. She figured she got so lucky being with Richard all those years. How could she ever deserve more?

"What's on your mind, Tess?" he asked curiously.

"I was just thinking how ironic this trip is. I expected this to be the worst thing I'd ever endure in my life, but it's turned into something completely different."

"It's turned out to be something entirely different for me, too."

She paused for a moment. "I want to tell you something, Tom."

His face mimicked a deer-in-the-headlights, scared to death of the words about to come out of her mouth.

Tess rolled her eyes and laughed at him. "I just want you to know…I didn't stay with you because of who you are, not because you're *Tom Clemmins*. I would've stayed even if no one knew your name and you weren't famous. I didn't want you-"

"Tess, I already know. You don't need to tell me. I'm sure

you've probably never taken advantage of anyone in your whole life and you don't have a mean spirited bone in your body. Unless you think someone's taken your tour." They laughed together.

Tayai dropped off a wonderful dinner. Tom kicked back, chilling in the chaise. Curious to know the whereabouts of their next destination, Tess tried to bribe the location out of him. "So, will it be hot were we're going?" she asked in her best sexy voice.

"Maybe, maybe not."

"What time zone will we be in?" She ran her tongue down his neck, tasting the salt on his skin.

"Different than here."

She took off the only clothing she had on, her bikini bottoms, and dangled them from her finger. "Will I need different clothes?"

"That's not going to work, Tess, but you can keep trying if you'd like." He stretched and yawned, pretending to ignore her.

She turned her back to him, sticking her ass out, bending over to pick up a speck of sand. "What country is it in?"

"I'm sorry, what did you say? I didn't hear you." He cocked his head to the side, definitely looking and grinning now.

"Come on, can't you give me one little hint?"

"Okay, I will give you one clue, but only one. You can do this all night, but that's all you're going to get out of me."

She pranced over to sit on his lap. "The clue please."

"You're meeting a good friend of mine and his wife, who I'm sure you will love. We'll be staying with them for a day or two before we go somewhere else."

"Who am I meeting?" she stammered.

"You might recognize them."

Tess almost wished she hadn't asked. "We're going to stay with them?"

Tom chuckled at her sudden apprehension, "Look, if I visit these particular friends and don't stay with them, it would hurt their feelings so-"

"Do they know I'm coming with you?"

"I've said too much already, no more questions. I can tell you're already nervous, don't be. They're going to love you. Don't make me regret my one clue."

"But-"

"You're supposed to be trusting me, remember?"

"I do trust you," she smiled thoughtfully.

"I believe there's a bribe that still needs to be settled," he said suggestively.

"I haven't forgotten."

The sun rising over Mount Otemanu shined in her eyes. Tess was on edge, wondering where he was taking her, who was she meeting and would they like her?

Breakfast was delivered and they were both starving. "All this time I've been going to the gym when all I really need to keep me in shape is you," Tess said.

Tom nodded in agreement.

"Tess, you were right the other morning when you asked if I had something on my mind. I understand how difficult it was for you to open up and tell me that this has been your best vacation here. This is hard for me to admit too-" He held her hand and stroked small circles over her palm with his thumb. "My trip here with you has been much more than I ever expected. I've been many places around the world and I've dated beautiful women, but you, are my best time. You're different, in a wonderful way. I don't want you to think this trip is normal for me. It's not."

"Thank you." She went to him and sat in his lap, kissing him slowly for a long time. Her heart started beating frantically again and she rested her head on his shoulder. "I don't know what's wrong with me. You are driving me so crazy, it's almost ridiculous."

"I'm not complaining." Tom chuckled.

"I've always been pretty…" She trailed off, searching for the right word.

He finished her sentence for her. "Sensual."

Tess blushed. "Yeah, but not like this. I can't keep my hands or lips or even my thoughts to myself. I keep thinking, we couldn't be better than we were last night, it couldn't possibly be better than yesterday, it couldn't be better than five hours ago. We went to sleep six hours ago and I just want to climb back in bed again."

"We don't have very long. Our boat will be here in two hours."

"I'll be ready by then." She tackled him on the bed, taking full advantage of him until it was time to leave.

Mr. Rene arrived right on time, serenading them the entire way to the airport. Tess didn't know the story the song told, but it sounded beautiful. Tom put his arm around her and she leaned back next to him.

"I hate leaving here, but I'm excited to see where you're taking me."

The wind whipped her hair around, so he tucked it behind her ear. "I don't want to leave either, but you're going to love my surprise."

Mr. Rene pulled up at the dock. He patted their backs offering each of them a warm embrace. "You two come back to see me soon. Don't stay gone so long, Mrs. Blue Eyes. I'm happy for you and Mr. Tom. You make a nice couple. See, I knew everything would work out for the two of you. I could tell from the first day on the shark tour. I even told my Mrs. how happy you look together."

Tom chuckled, clearing his throat. Heat rushed to Tess' cheeks. She considered stepping on Mr. Rene's toe to make him be quiet.

They started down the dock toward the airport. She glanced at Tom and shrugged her shoulders. "Sorry, he means well. I've known him over twenty years. I can't help but love him, but I thought I might have to kick him in the shin to make him quit talking." She chuckled awkwardly.

CHAPTER EIGHT

Upon reaching the airplane, she gawked at him and then toward the plane. "Is this what we're taking? Is this yours?" She'd never flown first class, let alone a private jet. "Show off! You're unbelievable."

A smile flickered in his eyes. "No, it's not mine, but I use it to travel occasionally."

The plush plane came complete with a bar, private bedroom and full bathroom.

"Hey, before I forget, would you mind giving me Tracy's cell phone number? I promised to text her the address of where we're staying. I don't want her to worry, and I don't want her mad at me either."

"I'm shocked you didn't already pay somebody at the front desk for it or search through my purse to find her number." She teased.

He appeared dumbfounded. "I thought those two things were cardinal sins, getting into a woman's purse and checking her phone numbers."

"Are you serious?" She could tell by the puzzled look on his face that he was. "Tom if I trust you enough to give you my body for the last two weeks, don't you think I should trust you with my cell phone? I don't have anything to hide from you. I'm not into secrets."

"Oh." He cocked his head to the side and added, "You're not upset with me for keeping our trip a secret, are you?"

"No, that's a surprise. That's entirely different. I simply don't like hiding things. First off, I'm no good at lying. You can totally see it all over my face. I don't play games Tom. I'd rather say it like it is. You know what I mean?"

His brows creased.

She explained. "So when you ask me if I trust you, I mean it when I say yes. I wouldn't have stayed with you, not the way we've been together, if I didn't trust you."

Tess gave him Tracy's cell number, and then opened her purse, asking if he wanted to take a peak. He pretended to begrudgingly stick his finger in her purse.

"It's going to be a very, very, very, long trip. I need to get some sleep, Tess. You're wearing me out," he yawned.

"Why, Tom Clemmins, are you complaining?"

"Never," he chuckled, heading toward the bedroom. "By the way, everyone on the plane knows not to tell you where we're going, so don't try to coerce it out of the flight attendant. No bribing the pilot either, you'd probably give him a heart attack if you used the same voice on him you used on me yesterday."

Tess teased using the same sultry voice. "Did you really expect to get some sleep on this plane?"

"Yes, actually, at least for a few hours." He pulled her down onto the bed, cuddling up to her.

"I'm only teasing. I'm tired, too."

Hours later Tess opened her eyes in the pitch-dark room, forgetting where she was for a moment. Her things waited in the bathroom. *How does he do this?*

Tom lay stretched out on the couch, watching a movie. "Hey, sleepy head."

"How long was I out?"

He glanced at his watch. "Ten hours."

"Man, I was tired. I need some coffee, I still feel wiped out."

"We have a few more hours if you'd like to shower."

Tess finished showering when a thought occurred to her.

"Hey, Tom, can you come here for a minute?" Lying naked on the bed, she reached for his hand. "I'm sure you've done this before, but I haven't. I can't imagine we would be any better in the sky than on a deserted island, but I'm willing to try."

"You're unbelievable, Tess."

"I'm glad you think so," she said between kisses.

After she joined the mile high club, they lay on the bed. She didn't want to think about how many times he laid there before with other women. She had no right to feel jealous, but didn't like the idea of him in bed with someone else.

"What are you thinking about?" He slid his finger down the tip of her nose.

"N..Nothing."

"What's up? You looked serious for a minute."

"I'm curious which you preferred, the sky or the deserted island with me?" she questioned coyly.

"This was wonderful, but nothing compares to the *motu* Tess. Nothing."

Tom hopped in the shower. His dark tan body glistened in the sudsy water. He caught her watching him. "Do you want to join me?"

"No, I'm enjoying the show."

He flexed his muscles, washing himself slowly. "Is that good for you?"

She laughed aloud. "Little slower please."

Tom dressed in jeans and dark blue-collared shirt over a T-shirt. Tess put on a blue dress, redid her makeup and blow-dried her hair straight.

"I love that dress. You had it on the first time I saw you. I've never seen you with your hair straight either, I like it."

"Do I look all right?" she asked, wringing her clammy hands. "I want to look nice to meet your friends."

"You look beautiful. I can tell you're getting anxious. I promise, they're nice people. Believe me, my friends are going to love you. Do you want a glass of wine? It might help you relax," he urged, holding up a bottle of wine.

"Sure, maybe just one." She sighed heavily. It felt as if she were going home to meet his parents.

"We need to go over a few things."

The eight little words spilled effortlessly from his mouth, however they sounded like words of warning to Tess, especially with the wine in his hands.

"Oh, great." She motioned for him to fill up her wine glass. "Okay, go ahead, what is it?"

"I just want you to be prepared. This will be a very different experience than Bora Bora. This was the first trip in a long time where people didn't recognize me, which is another reason why I love it there. When we're out, people will recognize me here. It won't be anything like the States, but it will happen. I don't usually stop for pictures or talk to people too much because it gets chaotic, so we need to keep moving."

Tess chewed on her cheek, taking a big breath of air.

"Are you all right?"

"Umm, yeah, just don't leave me, okay?"

"I won't, I promise. It'll seem weird at first, but it'll happen the entire trip, so try not to let it bother you. We'll lay low most of the time, but I want to take you a few places while we're here. So basically, keep your head down and keep walking. Got it?"

"Got it," she confirmed, pacing in circles. Tess never yearned to be in the spotlight and quickly realized stepping off the plane might feel like standing in the center of the Big Top next to the Ring Master.

Tom held her close, nibbling her neck. "Tess."

"Can you do that for the next hour? It really relaxes me."

"We'll be landing in Italy soon."

Her eyes lit up. "I've never been to Italy before."

"I know," he stated matter-of-factly.

"What do you mean, you know?"

He reached into his pocket, pulling out his cell phone. "Tracy," he said in a pleased tone. "She's warming up to me. Sort of. Okay, well maybe just a little. But JC was friendly."

"When did you-?"

"When you were sleeping. Oh, and I'm supposed to tell you something from JC, 'Good job, Mom, no wheelchair. Be safe.' Plus, they talked to John and he said the same thing. I'm not sure what the wheelchair comment was about, but she seemed happy with *your catch*. That's what she referred to me as." Tom laughed and cast out a pretend fishing line, reeling Tess in like a marlin and smooching her lips.

A car waited for them at the small airport when they landed. It wasn't nearly as bad as she'd anticipated. People definitely pointed, but Tom didn't take notice. He seemed comfortable and confident. She admired that about him.

Tom had been driving for an hour. Quaint vineyards and olive groves dotted the landscape in front of them. The longer he drove the prettier and more captivating the scenery became. Green rolling hills spotted with villas covered the countryside. Tess always dreamed of traveling to Europe, but after going to Bora Bora, she could never bring herself to go anywhere else. However, at that moment, she wished she'd made herself visit sooner.

"It's so charming here. The old buildings have so much character. Tracy would love it."

"She did sound a bit envious." He smirked with eyes full of mischief. Tom pulled over to the side of the road in the middle of the countryside.

"What are we doing?"

He jumped out of the car and opened her door. "I'm keeping a promise. Stand right over here." He pulled out his cell phone, taking a picture of Tess with the breathtaking Tuscan scenery behind her. Then he stood beside her, held the phone out, and took a picture of them together. "The first one is for Tracy, and this one's for JC. I think she'll like it, don't you?"

"Oh yeah, she'll love it. You do realize those pictures will be all over her Facebook in twenty minutes? There's no way of keeping that a secret."

Tom tapped his finger on her nose. "You're not a secret, Tess. You don't like secrets, remember? Besides, I think you're giving her way too much credit, I'll give her four minutes to have it on Facebook."

"How much longer?" She asked, climbing back into the car.

"Five minutes. Tess, relax please, for me."

"I'm trying." She sighed.

He held her face tenderly and pressed his lips to hers, teasing her with his tongue. "Are you ready to go now?"

"Umm hmm."

Ten minutes later, Tom stopped at a set of tall, ornate, black wrought iron gates, entering a code to pass through. Towering cypress trees lined the long meandering driveway, leading to a gorgeous villa.

"Wow, is this their house?"

"It is. You look amazing."

"Thanks." She waved her hands in the air to dry the moisture caused by nerves. "This place is more like an old castle." Fuchsia bougainvillea climbed the stone walls, highlighting the shutters made from aged timber.

"Actually, I think it might've been a castle. They just finished restoring the whole place."

"This is incredible."

As they approached the front door, he clutched her hands in his and pressed them to his lips. "Please don't be nervous. These are my *best* friends. They're *my* family. You just need to be yourself. Okay?"

She nodded. "I'm always myself, hence the nervous wreck," she smirked with a slight eye roll.

"You weren't nervous when you met me," he offered as a comforting gesture.

"I was mad at you."

"Did you want me to piss you off real quick."

This provoked a smile from Tess and she squeezed his fingers. Tom rang the doorbell. She sighed anxiously once again. He bent down to nuzzle her neck when the massive wood door flew open.

"Tommy! It's about time." The handsome man shook Tom's hand, grasping him firmly by the shoulder.

"Tommy!" Squeals of delight came from the gorgeous blond as she reached up to kiss Tom on both cheeks.

Tess couldn't believe it. They were Hollywood's IT couple Benny and Lisa Levi. *He could've warned me.*

"Hey, Benny. Lisa."

"Shit, Tommy, you look like you got stuck in a tanning bed," Lisa smirked flippantly, giving him the once over.

"Good to see you too. I want you to meet *my girlfriend*, Tess Mathews." Tom beamed, cinching Tess by the waist.

The expression on both of their faces mirrored the look on Tess' face. Shock! Benny and Lisa recovered from the word "girlfriend" faster than Tess did. She stared at Tom with her mouth gaping open.

Tess reached her hand out, but was quickly pulled in for a

big squeeze by Benny and kissed by Lisa on both cheeks. "Hi, it's nice to meet you," Tess squeaked, attempting to stay focused, however the word "girlfriend" still rang like a fire alarm in her ears. She didn't miss the unmistakable exchange of pure shock between Benny and Lisa either.

"Come in, get comfortable. How was your flight?" Benny asked.

"Jeeze Tommy, where the hell have you two been? You look great," Lisa said.

"Bora Bora. We flew straight from there to here."

Lisa's eyes lit up like Christmas. "Bora Bora! How was it? I've been asking Benny to take me there. Did you love it?" Lisa asked enthusiastically, throwing an eye roll Benny's direction.

"Oh great," Benny smirked rolling his eyes, "You're killing me Tommy. I'm never gonna hear the end of this."

"Oh yeah, we loved it!" Tom held Tess' hand entering into the house.

Tess wasn't sure where to look first. Benny and Lisa were both beautiful and she wanted to watch the expressions on their faces. Clearly, they weren't expecting Tom to bring his "girlfriend", however their villa was astonishing and Tess wanted to scope it out. *I can look around later*.

Lisa's eyes wandered from Tom to Tess, "Obviously you two have been together. You're browner than he is. Did you love it there?"

"I do love it there."

Benny gripped Tom's shoulder. "Let's bring in your luggage so you can get settled. You are staying here, aren't you?"

"Of course. You have to take Lisa to Bora Bora. You'd love it, too. I can't wait to tell you about our trip. It was amazing."

"Obviously," Benny murmured, glancing at Tess.

"The guest house is all set up for you. I'll put some more towels out there for the two of you." Lisa directed her statement to Tom, but her eyes fixed on Tess.

Tess could hear Benny whispering to Tom, "Did you just call her your girlfriend?"

Tom nodded. "It's a long story." He said in Benny's ear.

"Your place is incredible." Tess babbled, trying to hide her anxiety.

"Thanks," Benny replied.

Lisa put her arm around Tess, welcoming her into the living room. Tom and Benny headed toward the front door to get their luggage when Tom said, "Oh hey, wait a minute." He reached into his jeans to find his phone. "Benny go stand with Tess and Lisa."

Tom took a cell phone picture of the three of them together with Tess in the middle.

"Tommy if you wanted a picture I would've fucking given you one," Lisa rolled her eyes sarcastically. "We probably look like a reverse OREO cookie. I can't believe how tan you are."

Tom chuckled, raising his eyebrows. "JC will love this."

"Who's JC?" Benny and Lisa asked at the same time.

"My daughter," Tess replied, shaking her head, laughing at Tom. "They're going to freak out when they see that picture."

"You have kids?" Lisa choked.

Tess flushed, responding with a tongue-tied, "I do."

Tom was oblivious to their reaction, too busy forwarding his picture to Tracy and JC.

Lisa's beautiful full lips appeared to be speechless, which Tess assumed might be highly unusual for her. "Do...do they know Tommy?"

"No, but he's talked to two of them on the phone. I didn't know we were coming here or to Italy for that matter. Tom wanted to surprise me, so he texted my girls telling them where we would be staying. Now he's really going to torture them with that picture." Tess chuckled.

"How many kids do you have?" Benny asked, surprise still plastered on his face.

"Three." Tess was getting more uncomfortable by the second. His friends were undoubtedly stunned.

"No shit," Lisa said, glancing at Benny with raised brows.

Tom walked outside and Benny followed right behind him. Tess got the impression his friends thought Tom had lost his mind in Bora Bora, gone mad with island fever.

Lisa inspected Tess from head to toe, blatantly sizing her up. "Three? How old are they?"

"JC is eighteen, Tracy is twenty-one and John is twenty-three."

"No shit," she replied again with her mouth hanging wide open. "Wow."

If her mouth keeps hanging open like that, she's gonna have a bruise on her chin in the morning.

"Don't you have kids?" Tess knew the Levi's had children. It was plastered all over the tabloid magazines.

"Umm hum, two. Tommy is twelve and Kim is six. You really don't look old enough to have kids that age."

Tess sighed heavily, overwhelmed by her reaction. "Thanks."

"Hey, I'm sorry. I'm a little shocked. I don't think Tommy's had any dates who have kids. Let's go in the other room. I'm dying to hear about your trip. Would you like a glass of wine?"

"Please." Tess nodded, following Lisa into the kitchen where she poured them each a glass of wine.

When Tom and Benny returned Tess could've sworn Tom's face looked as red as hers. Watching the two of them laugh together, Tess thought they looked like brothers. Benny was younger than Tom and not quite as tall, but they had the same athletic build. Their facial shapes were similar, but Benny sported blonde hair and blue eyes.

Tom glanced at Tess, pulling his lip back to grin at her. She smiled tensely in return, so he stood behind her, resting his hands on her shoulders.

"Your villa is absolutely beautiful," Tess chimed, shaking off her nerves, comforted by his touch.

"Thanks, it took forever to finish," Benny stated.

Tom's phone rang. "It's for you," he smiled at Tess, answering the call. "Hey, did you get my message?" Tess could hear JC squealing in the background. "You liked my picture, didn't ya?" He asked sarcastically. "Yes, I think she's still in shock. We just got here fifteen minutes ago. She's right here, I'm sure she's dying to talk to you. You're welcome. Hi Tracy. Yep. Okay. I understand. Of course, I promise. You're welcome. Here she is." He handed Tess the phone.

She asked Lisa. "Do you have someplace private I can talk?

I'm sure this will take a few minutes."

Lisa waved her hand toward the guest hallway. "Sure. Pick a room. Take your time."

Obviously, Tom needed to talk to his friends. They seemed more shocked than her girls were. She entered the first room and shut the door behind her. "Hey, Tracy, how's your trip?"

"Mom, are you by yourself now?"

"I am. How's your trip going?"

"We don't want to talk about our trip. What the hell is going on?" Tracy exclaimed.

"I'm not even sure where to start." Tess plopped down on the bed, swinging her feet like a little girl.

"From the beginning would be nice." Cynicism sat on the edge of every word.

"Details Mom!" JC yelled in the background.

"Tracy, I need to know something before I tell you about Tom."

"Yes, I've been keeping JC out of trouble, but she has kissed a few cute guys and exchanged numbers...*a lot*. What else do you want to know?" She informed curtly.

"I....I need to know that you're not going to be *mad* at me."

"Do you really want me to answer that?" Tracy huffed harshly. "What do you expect, Mom? Do you know anything about him? Let me tell you, we Googled him, and it *didn't* paint a pretty picture."

"I know that he's been wonderful to me," Tess answered quietly. "That's all I care about."

"Do you have any idea *who* he's dated or *how many*?" Tracy warned. "Did you expect us just to say, *Right on Mom!*, just because he's famous?"

"I understand your concerns." Tess sat silent for a minute contemplating Tracy's attitude. "None of that matters to me. I don't care if he's famous or not. It's not fair for you to judge Tom without knowing him."

"So what? Is he your boyfriend now? Or...or are you merely *hooking up* with him for a couple weeks?" She spit out tersely, on the verge of yelling at her mom. "From what I saw online, quick and easy seems to be his style."

"I'm not sure what *this* is. I'm going to enjoy my time with him. I don't care if it's three weeks or three months." Out of all the different reactions she might've expected from her girls, this was not it.

"And then what? Are you gonna come home and go back to bed for eight months?" Aggravation and fear saturated Tracy's voice. "We're leaving for college. Who's gonna be there if you fall apart again? I'm not coming home from school to take care of you if Tom Clemmins breaks your heart."

Tess' throat constricted, absorbing her daughter's brutal honesty. "That's not fair Tracy. Don't you *dare* compare this to your father's death, and I *never* asked you to come home when he died. You have no right to talk to me this way." Anger welled up inside her. "This is *my* life, and I'll deal with the consequences of *my* choices however I see fit. I sure as hell don't need you beating me up about this. I'm doing a good enough job of that on my own. The guilt is…horrible."

The dampness of her tears burned as they dripped down her face. Tess could hear JC in the background asking for the phone and telling tell her sister she was out of line. Tracy snapped back at JC informing her to wait her turn.

"I'm sorry Mom." Tracy sighed with a touch of regret. "We didn't know if you would ever date again, and the first guy you meet happens to be a complete womanizer!" She sounded as if she were sniffing back her own tears. "I just don't want you to get hurt. That's all."

"It's not as if he's giving me false hope for the future with him." She admitted candidly, even though it hurt to say out loud. "But, h-he's actually very nice. For what it's worth, I think you'd like him and I've been really h-happy the last two weeks." Tess sniveled, wiping her tears on the back of her hand. "I never thought I'd feel this way again. I've already made up my mind. I'm going to enjoy whatever time I have with him."

After a long silence, Tracy sighed somberly, "Please be careful. I love you. JC wants to talk to you."

"Hey Momma." JC chimed with endearing tenderness. "Are you okay?"

Heat flushed her face at JC's understanding tone of voice.

Tess couldn't answer, but nodded with a sniffle.

"Great. Are you crying?" JC scolded her sister with a growl, *You made her cry Tracy*.

"I'm fine. Are you having a good time baby girl?" Tess wanted to change the conversation.

"Yes Momma, I'm having a great time, or at least I was, until Tracy turned into Cruella De Vil."

"It's all right. I understand why she's concerned. It's just...he's wonderful, and this is my choice, but I don't want you to be disappointed in me." Her voice steadied and she let out a small chuckle. "*You'd* really like him JC. The two of you could have an entire conversation about commitment issues." Her youngest daughter swore she'd never get married.

"Maybe he could help me write a couple chapters in my *Dating Rulebook*." JC laughed. "Seriously though Momma, we would never be disappointed in you. You're with Tom Clemmins in Italy with the Levi's. Have fun, it's good for you. Do we get to meet him?"

"I don't know if you'll get to meet him. I'm not even sure when I fly home. I told him I wanted to be home in time to pick you up at the airport."

"Well for the record, I hope so. Look Momma, I'm not going to give you a hard time, but I do have one question. Are you having safe sex?" JC's impish laughter filtered through phone.

"That's enough out of you missy." Tess snickered. "Love you. Be safe."

"No, you be safe." JC let out another playful giggle. "Love you too. Have fun."

Tess hung up and tossed her phone on the bed. She stood up and stared out the window into the darkness. Catching a glimpse of her tear-streaked reflection in the window, she blotted the dark smudges beneath her eyes.

Tom knocked lightly and cracked open the door. "Hey, are you all right?"

"I'm fine." She answered, without turning to face him. "I just need a few minutes."

The door shut. Her eyes closed and she exhaled heavily,

thankful he'd left her alone. She rubbed the tension gathered in the nape of her neck. Tess flinched when Tom rested his hands on her shoulders.

He brushed a soft kiss to the top of her head and gathered her into his arms. "So, it went that good, huh?" he asked gravely, turning her to face him.

She nodded and rested her cheek on his shoulder, unable to see through a slick of tears.

"I wasn't sure if they'd approve of you being with me," Tom admitted quietly.

"It's not that they don't *approve*. JC certainly did." She sniffed out a chuckle. "Tracy has…questions and concerns."

"What kind of questions." He swayed a little bit with her as he stroked her hair.

"Questions I don't have answers to." Her frayed emotions began to calm, wrapped in the reassurance of his warm embrace. "Relationship questions. Tracy's not thrilled that her mother's hooking up. Apparently they've spent their spare time on the computer doing *research* about you."

He stiffened. "Tess, I-"

"It's okay Tom. I don't care about *yesterday's* or *tomorrow's*." She nuzzled into his neck, resting her lips against the rasp of his stubble. "I don't expect anything more than *today*."

"Most of that stuff online is complete bullshit. I wish I could've talked to her. I don't want her to worry about you." He began to sway again. "What can I do to make it better?"

She clung to him, taking in the scent of his skin, the comfort of his strong arms, and the rise and fall of his breath. "This works perfect for me." It was true, she was completely at peace.

After a few minutes, Tess placed her hands firmly against his chest, pushing away to see his face. "Did Benny and Lisa know I was coming here with you? Because they seemed completely shocked to see you with someone."

"They were shocked," he smirked contently. "They aren't upset, Tess, they're happy you came with me. It's just that I've never brought anyone here before, that's all."

"Oh," she stammered in surprise. "You could've warned me who I was meeting."

"I was worried you'd say no, so I thought surprising you would be best. That way you would only freak out for a few minutes, not three days."

"Even though I hate to admit it, you're probably right." Tess grinned as they walked out the door.

CHAPTER NINE

Tom led her down the hall into the enormous dining room. Stone covered the walls and a massive dark wooden table big enough to seat twenty sat in the center of the castle-like setting.

"This can't possibly be where they eat dinner every night," Tess questioned curiously.

"No, I only wanted to show it to you." Tom drew her close, easing her tension with a kiss.

Benny cleared his throat, smiling from ear-to-ear. Lisa peered at them from over his shoulder.

"You did an amazing job restoring this place," Tess said in admiration.

"Thanks." Benny replied, still grinning at Tom.

Lisa walked directly toward Tess, licked her thumb, and gently wiped away some remains of tear-stained mascara. "How are your kids?" Her head tilted to the side with a hushed sigh of empathy. "You okay?" she asked, rubbing Tess' arm.

Tess nodded dabbing the corners of her eyes. "They've been in Europe while I was in Bora Bora. We were, we were just catching up." Tess floundered and glanced at Tom, unsure of what to say.

"Her girls have been online," Tom responded honestly with raised brows.

Benny and Lisa both cringed. "That doesn't sound good." Benny shot Tom a sympathetic look of discouragement.

"Oh shit. Did you tell them not to believe everything they read?" Lisa asked Tom.

"I didn't talk to them." Tom reached down taking hold of Tess' hand.

"They're fine now." Tess knew as the words left her mouth, they didn't sound remotely believable.

"Where are your kids?" Tom asked, changing the subject.

"They had a busy day and crashed early. Kim can't wait to see her Uncle Tommy, so be prepared. She's been talking about you for two days."

Benny and Lisa took them on a tour of their villa. The aged architecture mixed with modern elements intrigued Tess. Current paintings of Italy adorned the walls, fitting perfectly with the design of the villa. Everything was on such a massive scale; the rooms were big, the furniture built large, even the marble tiles were cut in huge squares. However, the fireplace made a statement all by itself and instantly became her favorite piece. It was original to the villa and encompassed an entire wall, built of massive light colored stones and a huge wooden mantel.

"Your place kind of reminds me of an incredibly nice wine cellar, it has the same character. I love the aged stone exterior mixed with a rustic modern interior." All three of them stared at her again. "Not the size of a wine cellar, but the ambiance of a wine cellar," Tess clarified.

"That's exactly what Lisa wanted it to feel like," Benny said in amazement. "We were vacationing here in Tuscany, visiting a few vineyards and wineries. Lisa loved it here, so we wound up buying this villa and restoring it to have that same vibe."

"It's beautiful. I love the hand hewn beams and the mantel, too." Tess dragged her hand over the dark wood.

Tom's brows furrowed. "I didn't realize you knew anything about architecture."

"I used to do quite a bit of design work. I love old architecture though."

"I knew I was going to like you." Lisa put her arm around Tess. "Don't look too surprised, Tommy. How much can you truly know about her? You've probably had her in bed for two weeks." Her blue eyes sparked playfully as she winked at Tess.

"Actually, I think it was the other way around," Tom muttered.

Lisa and Tess wandered into the kitchen. "It sounds like a great trip. Tommy seems really happy he went." The bright lighting exposed faint freckles covering Lisa's nose and cheeks.

"I am, too." Tess smiled, finally able to unwind.

"I hope it doesn't upset you, but when you were on the phone Tommy told us that you lost your husband. It must've been horrible for you?" Lisa said quietly.

"I don't mind. It's been very difficult, almost brutal, but the last three or four months have been a little bit better."

"How long were you married?"

"Twenty-five years."

"Twenty-five years? Shit, that's a long time" Lisa's eyes were full of sadness.

Tess had seen the familiar expression so many times over the last year. "It's been hard." Tess admitted openly, feeling an instant bond with Lisa.

"What do your kids think about you being Tommy's *girlfriend*?"

"Well, my youngest daughter JC was fine, but Tracy acted like I was running off with Lucifer himself." Tess rolled her eyes. "Last year was horrible for all of us."

"Tommy worried that they might be upset. I don't mean to be nosy, I'm just curious. Tommy hoped your conversation would go well."

Tess realized immediately it was Lisa's personality to say whatever was on her mind. "She's concerned and all of my kids are very protective."

Lisa's eyes narrowed into a squint, as if contemplating Tess' situation. "So, have you dated anyone else since you lost your husband?"

"No." Tess shook her head.

"Are you telling me that you haven't been with another man in twenty-five years until you met Tommy?" Lisa asked candidly.

It was beginning to feel like twenty questions. Tess figured Lisa wondered what Tom was getting himself into. "Nope."

"Wow." Lisa filled their wine glasses. She raised her glass to Tess. "I hope they give Tommy a chance. He's a great guy. And he *obviously* cares about you."

Unable to utter one word, Tess' gaze drifted to the counter. She didn't want assume anything from Lisa's opinion, *cares about you.* No doubt she looked pathetically confused as she took a long sip of her wine and then another. She eventually raised her eyes, only to see Lisa staring at her with a wide smile. It suddenly became very apparent to Tess that their vacation was completely outside the norm for Tom.

"Let's go in the other room." Lisa draped her arm around Tess, leading her out of the kitchen.

The four of them hung out in the living room for hours talking about work and what roles they were looking at. Tess and Lisa chatted about her restoration project. Tom and Benny were discussing agents and publicists. Tom sounded unhappy with his. Tess curled up next to Tom, almost falling asleep on the couch, so they said good night.

Tom held her hand as they walked outside to a private cottage at the back of a beautiful hidden garden. The guesthouse came complete with a gorgeous rock fireplace tucked in the corner and a wrought iron headboard with grapevine scrolls running through it.

They undressed and climbed into bed. "Did you have a nice time tonight? I knew you'd like Lisa."

"I had a great time and I do like her. She's very outspoken. You and Benny seem like brothers. Lisa called her boy Tommy. Is he named after you?"

Tom smiled proudly. "He is named after me. I love their kids. Benny's closer to me than my brother is. We met on set about sixteen years ago and we've been friends ever since. I'm sorry about your girls. I don't want this to be a problem for them, or for you."

"*My kids* will be fine. I think my biggest problem is *me*. I feel so damned guilty sometimes." Relief flooded over her as she said the words out loud.

"I can tell when you're feeling bad," he said despondently, delicately tracing the curve of her face with his fingers. "I see it in your eyes, Tess."

"Tom, please don't be upset if I'm struggling with this, with us. It doesn't have anything to do with my feelings toward you." Tess smiled, biting her lip. "I'm enjoying myself with you."

"I'm enjoying myself too, but I don't want you to feel guilty when you're with me. You try to hide it with your smile. As a matter-of-fact, you're doing right now." He touched his hand to her heart as they laid on their sides, staring at each other. "I can feel your sadness."

"Sorry. I'm not very good at hiding my emotions," she admitted.

"For the record, I'm not very good at sharing my emotions. Although, I seem to have no problem being open and honest with you. Our discussions over the last two weeks are probably the deepest conversations I've had in I don't know how long. Maybe ever. All I'm saying is that I want you to be happy with me."

"I am happy." Tess blushed, pausing as she played with his fingers. "It's more as if I never expected to date again. I thought I had my good luck. I never expected to find anyone who even turned my head. After being married for so many years, sometimes it feels like I'm being unfaithful. Like I'm cheating on Richard. Believe me, I don't want to feel that way, but I can't help it."

Tom wrapped his arms around her, pulling her to his chest. "Richard was a lucky man."

She nuzzled his neck, taking in the scent of his cologne. "Thank you for understanding."

Tess' eyes were getting heavy, but she wanted to ask him about the girlfriend comment. She sat up and turned on the light, wanting to see his eyes. Her arms folded across her chest, waiting for an answer to a question she hadn't even asked yet.

"What?" Tom said innocently, struggling not to smile.

"You know what I want to know. Don't act all coy with me. You know exactly what I'm thinking." She couldn't hide the playfulness that filled her heart.

"What?" he repeated, sitting up beside her.

"Your poor friends, I thought I was going to have to pick their mouths up off the floor myself. They probably think you've gone mad from extreme heat in Bora Bora."

"Do you mind if I introduce you as my girlfriend?" he asked with a sexy grin as he unfolded her arms, holding her hands in his.

"No, I rather like it. I don't think they were ready for it."

"Tess, I feel like you're my girlfriend, and you're right, I'm sure they were never expecting you."

"Tom, can I ask you something?"

"Yes."

"Have you ever dated anyone with kids?"

"No, I haven't."

She hesitated, unsure if she wanted to hear the answer to her next question. "Do you date women my age?"

"Honestly, I haven't in a long time, but I don't want it to hurt your feelings. Your age doesn't matter to me. Look at you. You look fantastic. I find you incredibly sexy, not to mention witty, sarcastic, smart, athletic and adventurous, but as we learned tonight there's obviously a lot I don't know about you." Tom gazed into her eyes. "You're younger than me, Tess. I'm forty-nine."

"I don't mind being forty-four. I'm feeling exceptionally good about myself at the moment. Besides, I'm much better now than I was in my twenties or my thirties." They snuggled in each other's arms, drifting off to sleep.

Tom was up early and out of the guesthouse. When Tess woke up she headed over to the villa and could hear music playing down a long stone corridor. As soon as she got close enough, the thumping music sounded familiar. Lisa and Benny's kids were playing Rock Band. Tess loved to play with her kids and their friends. It dawned on her, they hadn't played in over a year. *When I get home, things are going to change.*

Tess peeked into the room. Tom, Tommy, and Kim each had their stage roles down. Tom jammed out on the guitar, Tommy sounded good on the drums and Kim stood on the sofa singing, swinging her long black wig around. Tom wore a pink headband, which she assumed Kim put on him because she was dressed in a rock-and-roller costume. Probably something she wore on Halloween. It was comical and a side of Tom she didn't know existed.

Tess caught Tom's eye as she stood in the doorway. Without missing a stroke on his guitar, he motioned her inside, introducing her to Tommy and Kim. Tommy resembled Benny with blonde hair and blue eyes, but Kim sported Lisa's long blond hair and freckles on her nose and cheeks. Tom held Kim's hand as she jumped down off the sofa. Tess smiled at the little girl when she beamed up at Tess batting her long dark lashes.

"Come rock out with us." Tom snickered as if it were a challenge, assuming she wouldn't play along.

"I'm usually the vocals at my house. Only because I can't play the drums or the guitar," she admitted.

Kim handed Tess the controller and she picked her favorite classic rock song. The little girl jumped up on the couch next to Tess to share the microphone. They sang together and Tess showed Kim how to beat the tambourine by tapping the microphone. Tess' heart melted when Kim climbed up on her hip so they could dance while they sang.

They were rocking out to their third song when she noticed Benny and Lisa standing at the doorway. Both looked completely stunned and very amused. The song ended and Benny and Lisa clapped loudly, mainly for Kim's benefit. Tom teased Tess about her lovely vocals, calling her 'superstar' and Tess applauded his mad guitar skills. Tommy took a bow while Kim jumped on the sofa.

Tess grinned, shaking her head at Tom. "I can't believe you don't have kids."

From the corner of her eye, Tess saw Benny and Lisa each glance at Tom for one split second and then carry on clapping.

Tess wasn't sure what it meant, but there was definitely an unsaid glance shared between them. She acted as if she didn't see anything, but curiosity saturated her thoughts. *Maybe he does have a child. I never asked if he had children. I just assumed he didn't have kids.*

After finishing their last song, Tess gave Kim a piggyback ride to the end of the hallway. The little girl squeezed her around her legs before bolting down the hall.

Tom and Tess sat in the kitchen with Benny and Lisa. "Do you have plans today, Tommy?" Benny asked.

"I might take Tess shopping." He looked her over nicely. "She came prepared for Bora Bora not Italy."

"I thought the same thing when I was getting dressed this

morning. I didn't even pack any jeans, only shorts, tank tops and flip flops."

"Shopping? I'll take you shopping. I love this great little boutique I found about thirty minutes from here. You'll love it!" Lisa offered.

Tess' face showed a hint of disappointment, and Lisa didn't miss it.

"Jesus, Tess, I promise we won't be gone all damn day. I'll have you back in time so you can have him for dinner," Lisa scoffed.

"Thanks." Normally Tess never got embarrassed, but she blushed. She didn't want to give up a day with Tom. Tess tried not to count how many days until she went home and longed to be with him as much as possible.

"I'm going to hop in the shower," Tom said.

"I'll change." Tess chimed, holding his hand. "Lisa, I'll be ready to go-"

"In about three hours." Tom cut her off as they walked out the door.

"Fine, but you better not be too worn out to go shopping with me, Tess." Lisa and Benny laughed.

Tom and Tess strolled back to the guesthouse. As soon as the door shut behind them, Tom pressed his body tightly to hers, pinning her against the wall. His lips fastened around hers, stealing the breath from her lungs. He raised her arms above her head, holding her wrists tightly with one hand. The pleasure of it sent her pulse rocketing through her veins.

He released his grip on her wrists and fervidly tugged at her clothing. "Were you afraid you'd miss me today?" he whispered before bearing his mouth down over hers.

Caught up in the heat of his hungry lips, she couldn't answer, but nodded yes. She gently stroked his face with her fingers and kissed him deeply in return. Tom buried his face in her neck and she could feel him trembling beneath her fingers. Moans climbed from her throat and he greedily took her cries of longing into his mouth.

His dark eyes locked on hers and he grasped her upper arms, holding her to the wall. "I *want* you," came a possessive growl from deep within him. His words spoken so powerful, it was as if he were trying to tell her something.

To her own surprise, the strength of his intense desire, flooded her with a fierce wave of arousal. She vehemently gripped the hair at the nape of his neck. "Then *take* me."

Glancing at the bed, she stretched her leg to the side, her toes searching for the bedside table for support.

"We're not going over there," Tom flirted in a low rumble.

Clutching her firmly by the ribcage, he bent down taking hold of her nipple tenderly between his teeth and drawing it into the heat of his mouth. She balanced on her tippy toes as he squeezed firmly along the outside of her thigh, grabbing hold of her leg and drawing it up over his hip.

She fumbled blindly with the button of his jeans as his kisses became tender, brushing over her cheek, neck and throat. "I want you," he whispered again, softly this time.

The gentleness of his voice made her tremble even more, making it nearly impossible of her to get his jeans off. "I'm trying."

One brow bent into a touch of a frown as if she didn't understand what he was trying to tell her. He reached down to help her with the fastening of his jeans. He nudged his hips forward and the hard length of him slid along the wetness of her skin, only teasing her with his ridge.

On the edge of peaking, she whimpered softly, "Please."

He did it again and again, sliding against that one throbbing spot. Holding back, paying no attention to her pleads for more. "Not yet, Tess." His deep sexy voice rumbled low in his chest.

Her fingers dug into his shoulders as she lifted her other leg around his hip, sinking onto him fully. Hot kisses trailed up her neck as he grabbed her ass. The strength of his hands and vigorous thrusts made her cry out with pleasure, securing her hands behind his neck for support.

Tess felt a connection with him like no other. Tom handled her tenderly, yet powerfully at the same time. *How can this be? Oh God. He touches me just right and his mouth tastes so fucking good. I've never felt like this. I didn't think it could be so good. Kiss him, Tess. Kiss him like you want to.*

Letting go of her fears, guilt, and the sheer desire she'd been holding back, Tess planted her lips on his and kissed him with passion and hunger. Plunging her tongue deeper as she played with his, she ignited a new energy in him. The louder she moaned, the more dynamic he became, driving deeper into her very soul. A tear spilled down her cheek as she crested her peak again. Tom kissed her tenderly as his body convulsed and slumped heavily against her.

He wiped the tear from her cheek. "What's wrong, Tess? Did I hurt you?"

"I don't know what to say."

"I'm sorry. You should've stopped me."

"Stopped you? Are you kidding me! No, Tom. I'm not hurt. I just....I don't even have the words. It keeps happening again and again and again."

"I've never felt like this." He pulled her onto the bed with him. "You are amazing."

"I'm still shaking all over. My ears were ringing so loud I thought I might pass out." She kissed his shoulder that glistened from sweat, tasting the salt on his skin.

He touched her body intimately, tracing every detail of it. "You'd better get ready or I'll never hear the end of it from Lisa."

She was getting dressed when she heard Tom say, "Tess."

She waited for him to finish but he didn't say anything. "Yes, Tom?"

"Nothing. I...I just wanted to say you look beautiful."

It seemed as if he had something else to say, but again he held back.

"Thanks, I'm probably glowing."

They ambled toward the door. "I want to give you some money to go shopping." Tom handed her a stack of one hundred dollar bills.

Tess glanced at the money in shock. "No, thanks. I have my own money."

"Tess, I'm not going to take no for an answer. I want to do this for you. Please take it. I had every intention of taking you shopping myself, but there's no way Lisa will step aside."

"Your money doesn't matter to me. I don't want you to

think-"

"Tess, I understand what you're saying, but I already know you're not using me for my money." A smile crossed his face. "You're using me for my body!"

"Well, at least you know where you stand." She grinned playfully. "That's a lot of money, Tom."

"I know Lisa and you'll probably need it. Please take it! I want to do this for you. Get whatever you want. Okay?"

"Thanks, but I still feel strange taking it."

"One more thing, Tess, don't let Lisa pressure you into doing anything you don't want to. I love her to death, but she can be a little overbearing sometimes. She may try to bring you back with new lips, new boobs and a new ass," he said, grabbing her butt.

"Hey, I like my boobs!"

"I do, too. And your lips and your ass. That's why I'm warning you. I like you just the way you are."

Benny and Lisa lounged on the sofa when they reemerged. "Bout time, I thought I might have to come down to the guest house and get you myself," Lisa teased Tess and winked at Tom.

"I'm ready," Tess said.

"Um hmm, I bet," Lisa scoffed.

CHAPTER TEN

Tess and Lisa headed out the door, shopping for new attire fit for Italy. Restaurants, shops and boutiques lined the streets of the charming village, as well as several specialty shops. Tess bought a couple of pairs of jeans, several cute tops, and heels too. They enjoyed lunch at a great little sidewalk café and then ducked into the lingerie boutique across the street.

When they returned to the villa late in the afternoon, Tom and Benny were playing football in the yard with the kids. The different time zones were taking a toll on Tess. She needed to crash for an hour. Tom followed her to the guesthouse, telling her about his day playing with the kids and catching up with Benny.

"I love coming here. I can't believe it's been eight months since I've seen them."

"Why did you wait so long to visit?"

"Work. My agent's been keeping me too busy. Benny and Lisa do it right, they take time off. I haven't had this much time off in years, probably since I first started in the business."

"Why? I mean if you want time off, why not take it for yourself? Life's too short Tom. You should enjoy it. I never wanted to wait until I retired to take time for myself. Vacations are much more fun when you're able to get around without your wheelchair." Tess grinned, thinking about JC.

"It's not that easy sometimes. Anyway, enough about work. How was shopping?"

"Great!" She cupped her boobs. "Still the same, no changes. I'm teasing. I had a great time." Tess handed him back his change, kissing his cheek. "Thanks for taking me shopping. Lisa mentioned something about the four of us going to dinner."

"Yep. You don't mind, do you, Tess? I have plans for us in a few days, but I like spending time with them. We don't get to see each other very often."

"No, I don't mind at all. I like them. They seem normal. Kind of like you."

"Are you going to show me what you bought?" he asked in a wishful sort of way.

"Nope, maybe later," she yawned.

Tom wrapped his arms around Tess and they both fell asleep.

Later that evening, Tess was about to slip into her black strapless dress. She could feel Tom watching her from the bedroom.

"You're not really going to put that dress on, are you?" Tom sauntered into the bathroom and stood behind her.

"What's wrong with the dress?"

Peering into the mirror, he wrapped his arms around her, skimming over her abs and dipping his fingers into her panties. "I like the dress. However, I love your new black lace thong and the heels, too. I'm so used to seeing you naked, I didn't realize how good you'd look like this."

"You're going to have to hold that thought. We're already late." Tilting her head to the side, she smooched his neck.

"I will." Tom teased, slipping the dress over her head and zipping the side as he fondled her breasts.

"Thanks."

"My pleasure."

Tess loved the way Tom looked that night in casual dark jeans and a light gray sweater. They enjoyed a scrumptious dinner at a quaint, romantic Italian restaurant. She had never eaten authentic Italian food before, and the wine from a local vineyard was the best she'd ever tasted. It had been a long time since she'd been on a date with another couple and Tess had a great evening. All of them had a passion for skiing, so they laughed and joked and shared their best stories.

Returning to the villa, Tom and Tess said goodnight, then meandered back to the guesthouse. "They like you," Tom said.

"I like them, too. They're gorgeous together."

"That's funny. Lisa said the same thing about us."

"Thanks for bringing me here." Tess let out a big yawn.

"Sleepy?"

"I think it's all the wine. Maybe the pasta too, but yes, I am tired."

Tom lay next to her propped up on his elbow, touching the outline of her body with his fingertips.

Tess drifted off. The next time she opened her eyes, Tom lay in the same position, staring at her and gently tracing her curves.

"Morning. Sorry, I didn't mean to fall asleep." She slid her leg around his waist.

"You don't need to apologize to me. I knew you were tired. I have to run an errand. When I get back we're going to have some fun today."

"Do I have time to go run?"

"Yep." He grinned ear-to-ear.

Tess knew he liked to surprise her, so she wouldn't ask where they were going. She threw her hair in a pony and walked over to the villa. The sweet aroma of muffins filled the kitchen.

"Morning, Tess. Are you hungry?"

"Morning. I'm going to go for a run before I eat. Is there a good direction to go or a trail I can take?"

Lisa smiled her wicked little smile, "Tess, you go down the second hall to the last door on the right. If you can give me five minutes, I'll work out with you."

"Sure. I'm going to see if I can get a hold of John first. I'll be back as soon as I'm off the phone."

Tess went back to the guesthouse to call John, dialing the house phone first. It rang and rang, so she started to leave a message, but he picked up.

"Mom! Hey, hold on. Let me turn the machine off. What's going on? I can't wait to talk to you."

"I wanted to call you again. Did you get my message?"

"Yes, I've talked to Tracy and JC, too. So…you're in Italy with Tom Clemmins?" he taunted. "I don't know what to say. I knew you'd call me back and I had fifty questions to ask you, but I just can't believe you're with him."

"You mean because he's Tom Clemmins or because I'm

with a man?"

"Well, both, I guess. The girls told me the whole story of how you met, and JC forwarded me some pictures of you with him and with Benny and Lisa Levi. Is she as gorgeous in real life as she is in the movies?" His voice full of envy.

"She's prettier actually and they're very nice, too." Tess chuckled.

"I miss you, Mom. You sound great! So where are you anyway?"

"Somewhere in Tuscany. I'm not sure exactly. I'd have to look at a map. I miss you, too."

"*Sure* you do. Do you want me to pick the girls up at the airport?"

"I should be home by then. Tom cancelled my flight, so I'm not sure when I get home."

"Do you think maybe you could get me Lisa Levi's autograph?"

"Sure, I'll try." Tess laughed.

"I don't want to upset you, Mom, but how did it go with Dad? Do you feel better?"

"It went perfect. It couldn't have been a more beautiful spot. I'm happy with my decision."

"Dad would've wanted to be there. All right, my friends just walked in the door and they're standing here staring at me."

His friends yelled in the background. "Hi Mom!"

"Mom, promise me you'll be careful with this guy. Have fun, but be cautious, okay?"

"I will. I promise, but I don't need to be careful John. He's wonderful. And tell your friends hi for me."

Lisa was waiting for Tess when she returned to the villa. "Holy crap! This is an entire gym. I expected a tread mill." The gym came complete with every weight machine imaginable. Two bikes, two treadmills, two elliptical machines and a flat screen TV with surround sound.

Lisa smiled. "What's your favorite?"

"I like to run, but I do Pilates, kick boxing, yoga."

"I usually spin. Do you want to box after?"

Tess got the feeling she missed something by the haughty

smirk covering Lisa's face, but she agreed. "Sure."

After they finished their cardio, Lisa asked, "Do you do the Wii?"

"I know what the Wii is, but I've never played it."

"Do you want to try it?" Lisa flashed her devious grin.

Shrugging off the distinct feeling she was about to get pummeled "Don't kick my ass too bad."

Lisa snickered, giving her instruction. Tess began to get the hang of it, but Lisa had done this before, a lot. Tess was down two rounds, and covered in sweat from the intense workout. They were getting ready to start another round. Tess had caught up and Lisa wasn't very happy about it, mumbling something about, *Sure you've never played.*

Tess noticed Tom and Benny standing at the doorway. Tess smiled at Tom, motioning him to come into the room. She raised her eyebrows, holding her fists up in the boxing position. "Come on in, Tom. You wanna play?"

Tom and Benny laughed their asses off. "I don't think so," Tom said.

Tess motioned to him again, laughing aloud while he shook his head no.

Lisa waited impatiently. "Let's go, sweet cheeks."

Tess couldn't quit giggling while trying to finish their last round. Lisa beat Tess and jumped up and down like Rocky, thrilled to have won. Tess recognized right away Lisa was extremely competitive.

"I knew you were going to kick my ass. I could see it written all over your face. You totally set me up!"

Lisa huffed. "I thought I might lose for a minute there at the end."

Benny chimed in. "Tess, if I would've known she was bringing you in here, I would've warned you. Seriously! I hate to play with her because if I win, she gets so mad. But I usually lose, which is even worse because then I have to listen to her gloat for days."

It felt wonderful to laugh so much. Tess thoroughly enjoyed her new friends.

Heading back to the guesthouse, Tom flipped her ponytail

through his fingers. "I liked watching you box, Tess. I had no idea you worked out like that. Very impressive."

He made her feel on top of the world when he complimented her. "Lisa's pretty good."

Tom narrowed his eyes suspiciously. "You let her win didn't you?"

Tess chuckled.

"You did let her win!"

"Please don't tell her. Don't tell Benny either. He'd probably rat me out one day when she was kicking his ass at boxing."

"That's awfully nice of you to take the loss."

"Yeah, well I sure as hell don't want her mad at me. She would've been pissed if I'd beaten her."

Tom watched her step into the shower.

"Are you getting in here with me?"

"Nope. Not yet."

Tess showered, dried her hair and did her make-up. She threw on dark jeans with a white shirt and a pair of cute wedges.

"I like your outfits."

"Thanks. This extremely attractive man bought them for me." She kissed him appreciatively.

"Let's go," Tom scoffed.

The peaceful ride put Tess at ease. She stared in awe out the car window. The landscape appeared as if it came straight out of the pages of a fairytale. Several art galleries and shops offering gourmet foods, wine and cheese lined the streets. Tess loved the paper mache masks adorning the windows of one of the specialty shops. The dramatic dark green, red, purple, and gold masks resembled exquisite theater masks.

An abundance of historical richness filled the small village. Friendly locals came with their own special blend of character, too. People recognized Tom, but only waved, calling out, "Hey, Tommy!" in their Italian accents. Tess chuckled every time.

Tom and Tess spent the day at a charming vineyard, tasting delicious wines, warm bread, and scrumptious cheese. They held hands and meandered through the grounds, admiring perfectly aligned rows of vines covered with flawless grapes.

Tom arranged an early dinner in a cellar of the winery. Tess was blown away by the ambient scent of earthy spices mixed with a smoky hint of oak exuding from the dimly lit cellar. Stone covered the walls, curving into a barrel arch ceiling and bottles of wine wrapped an entire wall at the far end of the room. Dinner tasted delectable and the wine was by far the best she had ever had.

They left the vineyard driving on a quiet dirt road, zigzagging their way to the top of a hill where a modest villa waited for them.

"Where are we?"

"We're staying here tonight. It's an old farmhouse turned into a bed and breakfast and supposed to be great for watching sunsets. We only have a few minutes." Tom held a bottle of wine in his hand and handed her two glasses to carry. He clutched her other hand, quickly heading up the spiral staircase leading to the rooftop overlooking the valleys below.

They cuddled on a gliding loveseat, watching the sunset in silence. Low misty clouds came in and lay between the valleys of each rolling hill below. As the sky darkened, villas dotting the hillsides came to life as twinkles of light cast out from their windows.

"This is one of the most beautiful moments I've ever experienced. Top ten for sure," she said in a soft voice. "It's mystical, like a fairytale."

"Tess?"

"Umm hum."

"You know the other morning when we were playing rock band?"

"What about it?"

"You said to me, 'I can't believe you don't have kids'."

"I remember." She tilted her head, searching his eyes as he stared past her.

He sighed, furrowing his brows deeply. "I can't have kids, Tess."

Her brows creased, making the same frown. "I'm sorry, Tom."

"Me too, sometimes," he replied despondently, avoiding her gaze.

Her heart ached with sadness. Tess rose to her feet and stood behind him, tenderly running her hands through his hair, massaging his neck and shoulders.

"I've wanted to tell you for a while, since the day on the boat when you said goodbye to Richard. I felt such a strong urge to confide in you, but I couldn't make myself. I wanted you to know that day that I understood a little bit of the pain you were feeling."

"I'm so sorry, Tom, I had no idea." Tears stung her warm cheeks, sensing the hallow affliction hidden in his heart.

"I haven't had anyone close to me die, but for a long time and still sometimes now, it feels that way. Like I've lost someone or as if somebody has stolen something away from me."

"Have you always wanted kids?" she asked poignantly.

"Maybe when I was younger. All these people around me were having kids and I couldn't. When I was in my thirties, I started drinking too much because I was angry and frustrated. I didn't know how to handle my emotions. When Benny and I were making our first film together, I got drunk one night and I told him I couldn't have kids. I didn't even remember my liquor induced confession, but he did and we've been like brothers ever since. Benny helped me through a lot of shit back then. He forced me deal with my anger and resentment. He helped me try to make sense of it. Benny and Lisa are the only people who know. I've never told anyone else."

"Does it bother you that I have kids, Tom?" Tess knew this hurt him deeply.

"No." He chuckled softly, tugging on her fingers so she would sit beside him again. "I like the fact you have kids. I like everything about you." He gazed into her eyes. "Do you remember when you asked me if I believe everything happens for a reason?"

"I do."

"Good or bad?"

"I remember. I'm not a very religious person. I think some people refer to it as *His plan*. I prefer to think of it more as luck or fate or destiny. It makes more sense to me if I look at it that way," Tess said sorrowfully. "That's how I had to look at it when

Richard died. I was lucky to have him as long as I did, but for some reason, he had to go."

"I felt like I had been ripped off, short changed. You know what I mean? Why me? I had so much going for me except this *huge* flaw. Why wasn't I supposed to have kids? Was there something *wrong* with me? *Would* I have even been a good father? You know, all those inner demons that feed off your insecurities. I definitely had my share when I was younger. I'd date women and within a week, they were hearing wedding bells and wanting babies. I wasn't even sure if I liked them yet. It seemed like everyone around me was either having babies or wanting babies. Women just did not want the right things from me. I couldn't deal with it. It used to freak me out. I couldn't wrap my head around it. I think that's why I never wanted to get married."

She nodded trying to understand his pain and hurting.

"Benny told me those exact words, 'Everything happens for a reason Tommy, good or bad'," Tom said quietly. "It helped me see things in a different light. For whatever reason, kids weren't in the cards for me."

Tess affectionately placed her hands on his face. "You are not *flawed*. Some things just aren't meant to be. I *know* you would've made a great father."

"I think so, too. I can tell you're a good mom. I haven't even seen you with your kids, but your girls seem crazy about you."

"Well, I'd like to think I'm a good mom, but they sure as hell didn't come with instructions or a manual. Most of the time, I felt like I was doing a great job, but other times I felt like a complete failure. It's not easy raising kids into fun, responsible, well-rounded adults. It's a lot of work, and you never know if the decisions you make are the right ones."

"I can't picture you being a failure at anything. Did you enjoy staying home with your kids?"

"It was a difficult adjustment for me. Even though I've been lucky enough to be home with my kids, I don't want that to be what defines me as a woman. I'd like to think there's more to me than being a mom. Right now I'm just not sure what that's supposed to be," she said softly.

"Oh, I think there's a lot more to you than being a mom." Tom slipped his finger into her shirt, skimming the lace on her bra.

"I hope there's more to me than that, too," she smirked.

"I'm teasing you, Tess. You have a lot of good in you. You're a strong woman, but very playful, and you've been very passionate with me. The last three weeks have been more than I ever expected. I've never met anyone like you."

"I don't remember being quite this passionate ever. Seriously, you drive me crazy," Tess admitted.

"I feel the same way," Tom agreed.

"Speaking of that, you said we're staying here tonight?"

"Yes, we are."

"Are all my things miraculously here already?"

"They're in the trunk of the car." He grinned immensely.

"Oh, man, did you pack my stuff?" She hoped to surprise him with the lingerie she bought.

"As soon as Lisa found out we were coming here she gave me strict instructions. 'Don't touch or even think about peeking into a white bag with pink ribbon on it.'"

"You didn't peek did you?"

"Nope. I wanted to though. I'll get our things from the car for you."

Tess reached for his hand. "Hey, Tom, thanks for sharing that with me tonight. It means a great deal to me that you trust me."

They smiled at each other as he repeated the words she said to him earlier. "If I've trusted you enough to give you my body for the last three weeks, don't you think I should trust you with this?"

Tom retrieved their things from the car. After rinsing off in the shower, Tess stared into the mirror nervously adjusting her boobs and panties, wanting to look perfect in her skimpy midnight blue negligee. It seemed silly because Tom had already seen every inch of her body, but she wanted to impress him.

Tom sat in a chaise on the rooftop sipping wine. She quietly snuck up behind him, bending down to nibble on his ear. He leaned his head back, she kissed him softly, gently tugging on his bottom lip. Releasing his lip from her teeth, she raised her head and stood in front of him.

Through the darkness of the night, moonlight exposed her taut nipples and perfectly manicured tuft of dark hair through the sheer negligee. He admired her, not saying a word. Her heart pounded violently, waiting for him to say something, hoping he'd like it. His jaw tightened as he swallowed hard, sending a shiver over her skin.

"Damn." He paused, swallowing hard again. "You look beautiful."

Tom tried to stand up, but she laid her hand on his hard chest. "I like it up here," she purred.

She straddled him, sitting backward on his lap. He caressed her back, unraveling the tension in her spine. He reached around to fondle her breasts through the sheer material. She drew in a hissing breath and whimpered at the soft tug on her nipple. She unzipped his jeans and slipped her fingers into the waistband, arching forward seductively to remove his jeans with her hands and teeth.

His searing breath tickled the small of her back. She moved out of reach of his wandering tongue, repositioning herself to face him.

"Do you remember what you told me our first night together?" she asked, leaving a trail of wet kisses down his neck.

"Yes."

Her lips pulled to a smile as her tongue slid over her lips. "Tonight is all about you."

Her mouth descended and she dragged her tongue over the taut bands of his rippling stomach. She explored every contoured detail, before wrapping her lips around the full length of him. Teasing him with delicate, moist strokes and flicks of her tongue, she peered up to find his dark eyes locked on her. She grinned going down, taking in inch-by-inch until she heard a low groan in his chest as he tugged at her arms.

Working her way back up to his mouth, she kissed him passionately. Her emotions rose to the surface and she stared through the darkness into his shadowed face, wondering if she had ever felt so powerful before. She didn't know if it was the novelty of a being intimate with someone new, or the exploration and discovery of sensual need she thought would be gone forever, but this man unlocked something deep within her, a fervent connection that was empowering.

Tom's long tapered fingers firmly gripped her hips, seeking admittance. She sat up high, wanting to make him wait, needing him to desire her as much as she craved to feel him. Her long hair fell down around her face as her eyes fixed on his. He stared at her in a way that made her feel as if he saw clear down into her soul. Her chest ached with a longing and the need to open up to him, but she couldn't even explain her feelings to *herself*. She feared that if she tried, he'd disappear.

Tess knew she shouldn't do it, telling herself repeatedly, *he's just a vacation. He's just for fun. He's just for incredibly good sex*. She wouldn't deny it anymore. She wouldn't waste one more minute pretending. Tom wasn't just a rendezvous and it wasn't just sex. The passion and desire she felt for him was too intense. Tess made love to Tom. She knew it would cause her pain in a few days, but at that moment, it was perfect.

CHAPTER ELEVEN

Tess slept face down on the bed. Tom gently slipped the sheet back kissing the back of her thigh moving up to the small of her back.

"That tickles so much. Do you want me to put my outfit back on?" She twitched and giggled until goose bumps covered her skin.

Tom laid his body on top of hers, nuzzling her neck with his unshaven face. "I'm quite fond of it, but we have to get ready, sleepyhead. I have a meeting I need to take care of, so we need to get out of here. We can't be late, Tess."

A permanent grin covered her face as they drove toward the airport. She had no idea where they were heading and didn't care, as long as she was with Tom.

"Are we leaving Italy?"

"We are."

"I should've said goodbye to Lisa and Benny," she said regretfully.

"You'll see them again, I think. Otherwise, we would've both said goodbye."

"Oh, I'm not meeting anyone you should warn me about, am I?"

"No. I need to take care of some business, so we're going to have a quick lunch and then leave again."

Tess thought Tom seemed a bit anxious boarding the plane. He fidgeted with his fingers and rubbed his knuckles over his jaw. "Is this really the first time you've taken off work for a long vacation?"

"For the most part. I take a week here and there all the time, but I needed to get away."

"Why don't you take time for yourself?" she asked curiously. He gave her an odd glance, as if it was the first time someone had ever asked him the question. "You don't have to talk about it. I'm just wondering,"

"When I was younger, I took every script thrown at me because I never knew how long I would be on top. Now, after all these years, my agent and publicist are used to me taking on a heavy load. They're accustomed to pushing me. I want to be more selective now, and they aren't on the same page as me at the moment. It's not them. It's me. I've changed. They just haven't caught up yet."

"Doesn't it really come down to your decision? I mean, they work for you right? What may have been ideal for you earlier in your career may not apply to you now. I know nothing about it but-"

"You make it sound so easy, but trust me, it's not. It is my choice though, in the end."

"Could it be, Tom Clemmins that you don't know how to say *No* to someone? It can't possibly be that you *need* to work. It's obvious you love acting but-"

"But what?" he asked with intrigue.

"I mean, my financial theory has always been, give some, save a lot and have fun with the rest. You can't take it with you when you go, Tom."

"You are one of the most laid back people I have ever met. I like that theory. Give some, save a lot, and have fun with the rest."

"It's true, isn't it? I mean, I don't have to go back to work if I don't want to. What's it going to get me? More money! But if I truly don't need any more money, why do it?" Tess joked. "Maybe I should just go buy a shack on a beach somewhere."

"You're funny, Tess."

"I'm glad you went on vacation. I'm having a wonderful time."

"I am, too." They both grinned. "We should be landing in a few minutes."

"That was quick."

Tess wasn't sure where they had landed because the window shades were closed on the plane. Tom held her hand as they walked to the car, and she kissed him as the driver opened the door.

"Hi, Mom." Tracy smiled softly.

"Hey, Mamacita!" JC giggled with excitement.

"What are you doing here?" She pulled her girls in for an airtight hug. Tess already knew the answer, looking at Tom. "I can't believe you," she said to Tom with a huge smile. "Seriously, how did you do this?" Tess shook her head, completely shocked to see her girls.

"Well, Tom called Tracy to see if we could meet for lunch before leaving on our cruise in three hours. Our chaperone said no at first, but then Tom spoke to her on the phone and she agreed to let us go, so here we are," JC said.

"I can't believe you're here." She was utterly stunned, but worried to see how her girls would react to Tom.

Tracy and JC's faces flushed, as he extended his hand. "I feel like I already know you, but I'm Tom."

Tracy reached for his hand. "Thanks for bringing her here to see us before we leave."

JC threw her arms around him, squeezing Tom as if she had known him for years. "Thanks for the pictures, too."

"No problem. I'm glad we're able to have lunch together before you leave on your cruise."

Tess sat next to Tom in the limo, leaning forward to hold her girls hands while they talked. Tom rubbed his hand across her back.

"So tell me what's going on. I don't even know what to say. You're unbelievable. Thank you." Tess leaned back into the crook of his arm and he tenderly kissed her cheek.

She tensed under the pressure of his lips and her girls tentative gaze. Tess was fully aware that her girls were examining their every move together and they probably saw her kiss Tom before getting in the car. She didn't want to hide her feelings, but she didn't want to upset her girls. The discussion of dating had never come up, not a serious conversation anyway and she didn't know how they'd react to Tom.

"You look great, Mom. You're both so tan. I love your necklace," Tracy reached forward, delicately touching the pearl hanging from Tess' neck.

"Thanks, I love it, too. Tom got it for me."

"How was Bora Bora? Were you nervous to swim with the sharks," JC asked Tom.

"I was a little anxious at first because your mom led me to believe the sharks don't attack people...very often, but it was indescribable. I loved it."

"That's what our parents always said when they came home." JC laughed.

"It was intimidating at first, but I'd definitely do it again."

The car stopped along the waterfront. Walking into the café, Tess held Tom's hand. The girls talked non-stop about their trip while they ordered lunch.

"So, how was the Coliseum, Tracy?" Tess asked. "I still can't believe you did this." She poked Tom in the ribs.

"We've seen so many cool things. We don't have enough time to talk about most of it, but the Coliseum was unbelievably impressive."

"I liked it better than Tracy. It was awesome! Did you know it could hold 50,000 people and they used to flood it with water to hold mock sea battles, not to mention gladiator games, and executions, too? That place was definitely one of my favorites," JC declared.

"What was your favorite?" Tess asked Tracy.

"Definitely Venice. It's surreal how the waterways are the streets. I love how the buildings rise up straight out of the water. And the bridges, I loved the bridges. They were beautiful, but I'm saving my excitement for the cruise."

"She liked the gondoliers', Mom. Don't let her fool you." JC held her hand over her heart theatrically mocking her sister. "She's in *love* with Venice."

"I'm not even gonna lie, Mom. They were all pretty cute. Even the old chunky ones were adorable, in a grandpa kind of way. I loved it there."

Tom laughed. "Are you taking a lot of pictures?"

"A ton. I had to buy another memory card for my camera,"

Tracy replied.

JC giggled uncontrollably. "We took some really funny ones of David."

"The statue of David." Tracy chortled, holding her hand over her mouth to cover her laughter. JC joined in, laughing so hard she got the hic-ups.

"Anyway, we've both been taking pictures, but some of them aren't turning out right. The pictures I'm taking in the middle of the day are too shadowed from the sunlight, so I'm kind of pissed. Hopefully they'll look better when I get them printed," Tracy said.

"What kind of camera do you have?" Tom asked.

She pulled her camera out of her purse and handed it to Tom. "Just one I picked up before we left."

He examined her camera. "Here, look, if you change this setting, they'll turn out better with the sun behind them."

"Thanks." Tracy gave Tom an appreciative nod.

Though Tom hid his apprehension well, Tess sensed it. She could feel a trace of rigidness in his frame and he rubbed his knuckles across his jaw several times throughout lunch. She gave Tom's leg a gentle squeeze and shot him a smile of appreciation. He pulled her closer and draped his arm over her shoulder.

"Hey, since you have the camera out, can we take some pictures before we leave? It's pretty down by the water." JC looked at Tom when she asked.

"Sure," he replied.

All four of them chatted as they headed across the street to take a couple of pictures. Tess hadn't noticed the vivid surroundings because she'd been so preoccupied with her girls. "It's beautiful here. The white buildings are incredibly dramatic, but the water, I had no idea the water was so blue."

"It is beautiful here. You girls are going to have a great time." Tom assured Tracy and JC.

"Have you been here before?" Tracy asked.

He nodded. "I love Greece. The islands are amazing." Tom put his arm around Tess' waist and she wrapped her arm around his.

Both girls stared at them. "Wow, you guys look really good

together," JC acknowledged with a bent eyebrow. "I can't believe you're with Tom Clemmins, Mom. You seem so *normal*," she said to Tom.

"I am normal, aren't I?" he asked Tess with a sarcastic grin.

"I don't know if I would say normal," Tess teased and they all laughed.

After taking several pictures, they drove toward the port where their cruise ship docked. The girls discussed Greece with Tom. He told them about a great little café they should try, an art gallery to stop at, and several other places they might like to see.

Tess appreciated the tremendous effort Tom was making for her girls. She knew the only reason he brought her to Greece was to make her girls comfortable with the idea of them dating. But what surprised Tess the most, was how at ease he acted around the girls.

The car pulled up to the docks, and JC and Tracy's tour group waited for them.

"I'm glad I got to see you. Have fun and be safe. I'll pick you up at the airport," Tess assured.

Both girls glanced at Tom, grinning with their beautiful smiles.

"Actually, Momma, you have *plans*. John's picking us up at the airport," JC mumbled, attempting to bolt out of the car as quickly as possible. Tess caught her by the wrist.

"Plans?" Tess scowled with intrigue, refusing to release JC from her grip.

"*Plans, surprise*, whatever he calls it. Have fun." Tracy rambled, trying to shove past her sister. "Seriously, Mom. We have to go."

"Before we cave," JC muttered.

"What? You! I knew you were up to something," she said to Tom. "What's going on? Spill it."

Tom exited the car and then ducked his head back inside. "Tess, I'm not going to tell you where we're going yet, but I think, and your kids agree, you'll be excited. But right now I have to make good on a promise I made." He gave her a heart-stopping smile before striding over to schmooze their chaperone.

"Hey, what if I would've said no?" Tess beamed, calling

after him.

"You wouldn't." He turned back shooting her a haughty grin, making her blush.

Both of the girls still sat in the car with Tess. "It's all right, isn't it? He called and asked our opinion and we told him yes. You're going to love his surprise, and please don't ask us what it is. We promised, promised, promised, swore up and down not to tell you." Tracy said.

"Yeah, we had to take it to the grave," JC grumbled. "And it's killing us not to tell you."

"He's unbelievable!" Tess shook her head.

"He's really nice. I like him," JC squeezed her mom. "You're gonna freak!"

Tracy and JC took off after Tom. Tess followed, snapping pictures of him with the tour group. The chaperone could barely contain her excitement when she met 'The Tom Clemmins', that's the term she kept using. Tess thought he was a good sport about the whole thing, but it occurred to her that he was used to it. Tess didn't see him as famous Tom Clemmins. She saw him as her incredibly wonderful, handsome lover, Tom.

Tracy shook Tom's hand and thanked him for stopping in Greece. She followed it up with a leery half-hug. She casually reached for Tess' fingers and the two of them sauntered toward the dock. "He's nice." Tracy admitted. "And you're smiling, a lot. I'm sorry that I threw a fit about Tom and I never should have said that about-"

"It's okay. You don't have to apologize." Tears of appreciation welled in Tess' eyes. "For the record, I know it was a huge sacrifice for you to move back home after your dad died. You'll never know how much it meant to me."

"I wanted to come home. It was really hard for us to see you in so much pain." Tracy pulled her mom into an embrace. "I don't want you to get hurt. He better not screw you over." Tracy stated stiffly, inconspicuously wiping her own tears.

Glancing over her daughters shoulder, Tess watched JC give Tom a hug goodbye and then mosey toward her.

JC rolled her eyes as she approached Tess and Tracy. "I can't leave you *delicate flowers* alone for a minute. Did you two make up?"

Tess and Tracy both nodded and wiped their tears. Tess motioned for both of them to get going. "Go have fun. Love you."

Tom joined her, snuggling her in his arms from behind. "Are you okay?"

She nodded, laying her head back against the hard planes of his chest.

His lips moved against her temple. "Are they okay?" She nodded again and he exhaled a heavy sigh of relief into her hair. "Do you think they liked me?" he asked earnestly.

"Back up! You're not getting off that easily. I can't believe you did this for me and I'm sure Tracy feels better." She turned to face him. "What are we doing that you had to go through all of this trouble for?"

He drew her closer and kissed her lips. She forgot about the people still standing on the ship watching them until she heard JC yell. "Have fun, Mom!"

They waved back and Tom asked, "I'm serious Tess, are your girls okay with us being together?"

"Is that why you were uptight on the way here? I thought you were stressed out about work."

"Work is an issue for me right now, but what did they think?"

"I think yes, they liked you. What's not to like? You're wonderful!"

"Let's get out of here."

They drove up a winding road, leading into a little town. "Do you like ice cream, Tess? We don't have very long, but I know of a great little place. If I can find it."

"Sure."

The driver parked along a cliff and they roamed the narrow streets. "This place is just so..." Tess couldn't find the words to describe it.

"It's mesmerizing. Greece is one of my favorite places. I love it here."

"The buildings look like they're sculpted right out of the rock face and I love the bright white houses." She sensed him staring at her and tilted her head to stare back. Busted, he grinned timidly in return.

They entered an ice cream shop and ordered when a woman recognized Tom. She ran straight toward him, telling him how much she loved his movies and how cute he was. Tess' hand covered her mouth, trying to contain her laughter. He politely let her take a picture. Tess winked at Tom, offering to take the woman's picture with him, she became overly excited and called her husband over, so Tess took another picture.

Tom led Tess by the hand across the brick street. She kept pace, sprinting several blocks before stopping to check out the magnificent view of the Aegean Sea. Tess sat on a white curved wall. Tom stood between her thighs, so she wrapped her legs around him. The volcanic cliffs, golden beaches and vibrant colorful flowers were stunning.

She rattled on about how beautiful it was, but he only stared at her again. Tom slipped his fingers into her hair, kissing and nibbling on her neck. She dropped her head back and her hair hung down to her waist. His hot breath tickled her collarbone as he kissed it from one side to the other, making her nipples tighten and her pulse accelerate.

"I don't want to tell you to stop, Tom, but people might start gawking if I take my clothes off right here."

Tess struggled to keep herself under some kind of control, because even though no one was around, it was a very public spot. Nevertheless, she didn't stop Tom as his hand traveled up her waist and caressed her breast. He pressed himself against her, revealing his arousal. Fixated on her face, he kissed her passionately, sucking on her bottom lip, stimulating her hunger. She slipped her fingers into the top of his jeans to touch him.

Tess raised her eyebrows asking, "Is there somewhere we can go, cause in about thirty seconds, it's going to get very embarrassing."

He held her hand, darting down several side streets, stopping outside of an inn. He grinned. "Will this work?"

"Yep." The words were barely out of her mouth and he was inside getting them a room.

By the time the key unlocked the door, Tess had her shirt half off. Both scrambled out of their clothes before Tom tackled her to the bed. He pinned her hands beside her head, kissing her fervently, on the verge of being forceful, robbing her of air. Turned on by his zealousness, she could barely breathe. Fully aware the balcony door was wide open, Tess tried to contain her moaning, but she was beyond excited. At this point, she didn't care who heard them.

An hour later, they lay on their backs, covered in sweat staring at the ceiling. "I like Greece!" She giggled with a sultry smirk.

"I had something I wanted to ask you before you seduced me back there on the wall." Tom teased innocently.

"What? Me? Oh, I don't think so! You totally started it. I thought it was me lusting after you this whole time but-"

"It's not just you. I didn't care where we were. Thanks for stopping me."

"I certainly didn't want to stop." They laughed for a few minutes. "Okay. What did you want to ask me?"

Tom rolled over on his side, gazing intently at her. He grinned with excitement, but seemed serious and a bit self-conscious, too. "I want to know if you'll you come back here with me, to Greece on vacation?"

"Do you mean like, tomorrow or next week or when? Is this the surprise?" Her heart raced at the idea of spending more time with him.

"Look, Tess, I haven't figured out when yet, but I'm crazy about you. I think you're amazing. I don't want to be without you, or you to be without me, like my girlfriend."

Tess nervously chewed on her cheek, overcome with sudden urge to guard her emotions. She climbed out of bed and stared out at the sea with her arms folded across her chest. Secretly she wished for this moment, but there were still so many unanswered questions running through her mind.

Being Tom's girlfriend would come with numerous drawbacks. He lived an entirely different lifestyle than her. The media, his career, and the list of women he dated prior to her. Questions she refused to let herself ask previously, started stacking up like poker chips on a hot Las Vegas casino table. Tess wasn't foolish, if she bombarded him with twenty questions, she risked the chance that he might panic. This was a huge step for her, but an even bigger one for him. She couldn't be happier, but she didn't want to get hurt.

She didn't realize he was standing right next to her until he reached down and took hold of her fingers, pressing them to his warm lips. His eyes fixed keenly on her face and she knew he was waiting for her reply.

"Yes," she whispered softly. "I would love to come back here with you."

"Are you sure? Because you're not as excited as I hoped you'd be." Tom asked quietly, unable to mask the rejection in his voice.

"Sorry, actually I'm elated. It's just that I...I've been telling myself I couldn't keep you, so to speak. At the end of three weeks, I'd have to give you up and try not to be devastated. I've been attempting to convince myself you're just a vacation."

"I've never found someone I can put up with for two weeks, but I can't be without you for ten minutes. You're the best time I've ever had. I want us to be together."

"I think you're the best time I've ever had, too." She confided in a hushed voice.

Tom's eyes filled with skepticism.

"Please don't look at me like that. It's difficult for me to admit aloud. I feel bad enough when I admit it to myself inside my own thoughts, let alone confessing it to you. I feel like I'm saying Richard wasn't as good, but that's not how I mean it. What I had with my husband was wonderful and anyone should be as lucky as I was to have the marriage we had. But you make me feel like I've never felt and I'm not even talking about the sex yet."

He smiled deliriously. "I have a job coming up my agent committed me to, so in a week or two I have to leave for a film. If I can figure out a schedule, will you come see me until I can make time to come back here?"

"Yes." Staring into his dark brown eyes, she knew there wasn't anything she wouldn't go through or give up in order to be with him, except one.

Monogamy.

"But Tom, I need to know your definition of a *girlfriend*. I refuse to set myself up to be hurt," she stated bluntly.

"I'm not sure what you mean. I want to be with you, like the last three weeks. You *are* my definition of a girlfriend." He pulled her onto the bed playfully.

She realized he was oblivious of what she asked him. "Tom, I'm asking you if you're going to go on "dates" while I'm your girlfriend. I'm not going to see anyone else, not that I would have many options, but I know you have a hundred different options anywhere you go. So if you want to sleep with other women, or even just one other woman, then my answer is no! I'd rather say goodbye to you now." She spoke directly. "I wouldn't even be able to deal with that crap. I don't care who you've been with, but it would hurt me if you sleep with someone now."

"Tess, I don't want to see other women."

She straddled him, sitting on his stomach. "'*I don't want to…*' is still a little vague, Tom. I want your word. I want to be with you, but that's what I need. Your word."

He sat up onto his elbows, looking her in the eye. "Tess, you have *my word* that I won't date or sleep with or kiss another woman. No one else would compare to you. I promise." He curled his lip in disgust. "And I don't want you to date other men. I wouldn't like that. At all!"

"I won't. You have my word." She smiled, kissing him. "Please don't freak out in the middle of the night and leave me here, okay? If you change your mind and want to see other women, just tell me. First. Please."

"Do you trust me?" he asked in a slow sexy tone.

She recognized a serious question underneath that steamy voice. "I have been trusting you, haven't I?"

"That's a little vague," he said, mimicking her. "I've never denied the fact I've dated a lot, but I didn't find you until three weeks ago. Now, I want you. Only you. The thought of you sharing yourself with another man, might hurt me more than I could possibly even imagine. So, Tess, do you trust me?"

She swallowed hard. "Yes, I trust you."

"So it's official. You're my girlfriend. And I am your boyfriend."

It sounded silly, almost juvenile coming out of his mouth, but in fact, Tess understood it was a huge commitment for him.

"Tom, just so you know, I'm very excited." She hopped off the bed and danced around the room. "Was that the response you were hoping for?"

"No, this was." He grabbed her from behind and planted a big kiss on her lips. "I have to make some calls. Let's leave early in the morning."

"Oh! I'm not sure if I'm going to like it here," she replied sarcastically, gaping out the sliding glass door. Tess slipped on his shirt, stepping out onto the balcony. "No wonder you like Greece so much."

The inn perched on a cliff with a view of the clear, blue sea. Whitewashed houses with blue shutters lined the brick street below them and fuchsia bougainvillea grew everywhere. *Gorgeous!*

"I like it." Tom snapped a photo of her wearing his shirt.

"Are we really coming back here together?"

"Yes, we are and you haven't seen anything yet. I know you'll love it here; the islands, Athens. We can go hiking and go to an archeological site."

Tess threw her arms around his neck. "I can't wait."

That night, the streets bustled with artists selling their work and people out shopping. Several recognized Tom, only a few approached him, most just pointed. Tess chuckled to herself.

"What's so funny?" he asked with his crooked smile.

"I see you so differently than all these people." Tess glanced around at the people in the streets.

"What's that supposed to mean?" He pretended she offended him.

"I see you as a person; smart, charming, funny, adventurous, gorgeous and very confident. They see you as Tom Clemmins the famous actor. I just think it's ironic. I understand my fascination with you, but I don't get theirs. No offense. Not only you, famous people in general."

"I'm glad you feel that way because everything changes tomorrow, Tess."

"Don't tell me. I actually don't want to know yet. Right

now, I simply want to enjoy this place. Okay?"

"All right." He agreed

CHAPTER TWELVE

Tom and Tess grabbed breakfast at a café before heading to the bottom of the hill to meet the car. He informed her it would be a long flight so she changed into comfortable clothes, lounged on a couch, and watched a movie while Tom stayed in the bedroom on the phone. He sounded unhappy about something, but finally joined her when she finished her second movie.

"All right, Tess," he smiled nervously. "We have about five hours left, so we need to go over some things."

"Okay."

"First off, we're going to my home in Malibu."

"Great," she paused. "It's not a castle, is it?"

He shook his head and continued. "Did you know Benny has a new movie coming out?"

"No. Well, maybe. Lisa mentioned a film he'd finished recently."

"We're going to his movie premier. That's one of the reasons I took you to see your girls, because you won't be able to pick them up at the airport."

"All right," she agreed with a casual nod, not fully aware of what a movie premier entailed.

He wore an enormous grin. "Tess, it's a big deal. There's going to be a lot of people there, including reporters and photographers. Plus a little red carpet you'll be walking down with your *famous* boyfriend, remember?" he teased sarcastically.

"Are you kidding me? Red carpet? No way! What am I going to wear? Holy crap!"

"It's going to be a great time. Lisa will be there too, not at my house, but you'll get to see her. She said she'd help you get…prepared." His voice faltered.

"Prepared?"

"I have to tell you one more thing. There will be paparazzi everywhere when we land." He rubbed his knuckles against his jaw.

"Why? What is it? What's wrong?" She knew something was wrong by the way he scratched the rasp of his unshaven face. *He would never win playing poker.*

"Apparently, there's a picture of me kissing a beautiful woman in Greece circulating on the Internet today. I don't know if you can get a hold of your kids, but you might want to try, especially John because when the paparazzi get your name, and they will, they'll want to know who you are."

"How could that happen? Are you sure?"

"Oh yeah, I'm sure."

"Have you seen the picture?" She knew the answer by the look on his face. "Let me see it."

He pulled up the picture on his phone and handed it to her. "That's when we were on the wall last night!" Utterly dumbfounded, she stared at the picture in astonishment. "Who took this?"

"Tess, it doesn't matter who took the picture, probably the lady from the ice cream shop. They're going to want to know who you are. They'll be waiting when we land."

"Let me see that picture again. Shit, we do look good together."

Tom chuckled uneasily. "Tess, you need to call John. He's going to see this, and we're all over each other in this photo. Your girls might see it, too."

Her eyes glued to the photo of Tom standing between her legs while she sat on the white curved wall. Her head hung back and Tom kissed the base of her neck. One hand squeezed her ass and his other hand rested right under her breast.

"How much money do they get for these pictures? I would've paid for this one. I can't believe we look so sexy."

"Tess, you should call," Tom reiterated, sounding baffled by her lack of response.

"I need to think for a minute. What exactly is the problem?

Photographers? Aren't they going to be taking pictures in a couple of days anyway? Seriously, is there really going to be a red carpet?"

"Are you delirious?" he asked in confusion. "You don't seem very upset."

"They're going to find out who I am anyway. Why not just tell them? I don't get it. I'm proud to be with you Tom."

"I thought you would be pissed, Tess. It's an invasion of your privacy."

"Well, at least it's a good picture. I might be pissed if it were a bad picture. We look like we could be on the cover of a smutty romance novel."

"Tess, why don't you get ready? I have to make a phone call."

"Is this picture a problem for you, Tom? You sounded upset earlier on the phone."

"It's not a problem for me at all. My publicist is unhappy with me, but I'm not going to hide you."

Unsure of how to respond, she stammered, "I'm going to get ready, and then I'll call home." Tess headed for the bedroom, but turned back around. "I don't want this to be an issue for you. Just walk me through it so I know what to expect and I'll be fine. I don't want to hide. I promise I won't embarrass you."

She turned toward the bedroom. Tom grabbed her by the wrist and pulled her into his lap. "Wait a minute, Tess. I'm not embarrassed of you at all! That's not what I meant. Sometimes in my business, there's a certain way people like to handle things. I wasn't going to take you out until the premier so you wouldn't get anxious and be a wreck that night. I want to be seen with you. That's why I brought you here."

She smiled. "I was referring to the picture of you with your hands all over my body." She grasped his hands and placed them over her boobs. "What I meant was, I will try not to do *this* in public. But I can't make any promises."

"Oh, well, please don't promise me that." Tom chuckled.

Tess paced in circles, trying to decide what to wear. She wrapped a towel around herself and ambled out to Tom who was still on the phone and didn't sound any better. "Can you help me pick out something to wear when you're done?" she whispered to him.

He nodded, hanging up the phone, trying to peek under her towel.

"What should I wear?" she asked, standing in a white lace thong.

"That looks perfect," he said, inspecting her half-naked body. She shook her head at him. "What are you comfortable in?"

"I thought about my blue dress with the leopard pumps. Or should I wear jeans?"

"The blue dress is my favorite, but I love your jeans, too. Which is more comfortable?"

"Please, will you pick? I want to look good next to you."

He pulled the picture of them back up on his phone. "You look beautiful next to me. I like the blue dress."

"Thank you!"

"Call John, please. I don't want your kids to get mad at me," he sighed uneasily.

She called John's cell.

"Hello?"

"Hi, son. How's it going?"

"Well, hi, Mom. I thought I might hear from you today," he scoffed.

Crap. He already knew. "I saw your sisters yesterday. I'm sure they've talked to you about picking them up at the airport."

"Yes, I talked to them yesterday, but I'm sure I'll be hearing from them again soon."

"We're still in the air. I called-" Tom stretched out on the bed watching Tess pace around the room.

John cut her off. "So, Mom! How was Greece?" he asked sardonically.

"Okay, go ahead. I can tell you've obviously seen the photo I'm calling to warn you about."

"I haven't, but my friends and girlfriend have."

"I'm sorry. You haven't actually seen it though?"

"No, but I heard about it. Blow by blow."

"Sorry, I didn't know someone-"

"You don't need to apologize. And *please* don't try to

explain anything. That's a little too much information for me. You're obviously having a great time."

"More than likely, there will be more photos," Tess forewarned.

John groaned. "Please tell me you're not naked or topless! I'll never hear the end of that shit from my friends. They've already been telling me, *'Dude your mom looks so hot'.*" he mimicked with irritation.

"No, I'm not naked or topless in any photos." Tess glanced at Tom. He reassured her, shaking his head no. "Sorry about your friends giving you crap."

"I appreciate you trying to warn me, but you were too late. Everybody said it's a great picture."

She gave a slight chuckle. "That's what I said. Tom wanted me to get a hold of you before you saw it."

"Well if he wasn't *groping you in public*, maybe he wouldn't be feeling guilty right now. Sorry. I'm fine. It's just weird. You're my mom, but it sounds like, or should I say it looks like, you're really into him. My only concern is that you're happy." Annoyance sat heavy in his voice.

"I am happy."

"I'm gonna go. This conversation's a little too weird. Love you."

"Love you, too."

"He's upset?" Tom asked, after she hung up.

Tess could tell it bothered Tom. He wanted her kids to approve of him. "Well, I'm not sure about mad, maybe embarrassed. However, he did request you not grope me in public. Please tell me there won't be pictures of us from Bora Bora? They would die. I would die if there were topless photos of me."

"No, there aren't." He attempted to be convincing.

"Lovely," she smirked, falling straight back onto the bed.

Tom touched the Tahitian pearl necklace hanging around her neck. "If you don't mind, Tess, I'd rather you didn't wear this right now."

She frowned with hurt feelings. "Why?"

"I don't want them to have any idea where we've been. This

necklace would be a dead giveaway. They probably assume we've been in Greece the whole time, and I'd like to keep it that way."

"Okay."

"I'm sorry. It won't be near as crazy after our public interest wears off, but it'll be an ordeal for a while. I'd love to sit here and tell you that it won't be a nightmare, but it will. If I could make them go away I would, but the media doesn't work that way. So, we can either go out and get it over with or lay low until the premier. Either way, they're still going to line up outside, hide in the bushes, and follow us everywhere. Waiting will only delay the inevitable."

"I think I'd rather get it over with."

"I'm not going to sugarcoat it, Tess. This might be very overwhelming for you. The paparazzi can be brutal. A few of them are decent, but some will say anything to piss you off so they can get their pictures."

"Lifestyles of the rich and famous..." she smirked.

"Get dressed. We'll go over some things." He taught her how to stand. *Don't fidget, it shows weakness. And don't ever look pissed. Move slowly. Don't rush when you walk.* "And, Tess, no matter what you do, be very careful getting in and out of the car." He reached his hand under her dress, snapped the top of her thong, and raised his eyebrows. "I'd like to keep that out of the photos."

She listened carefully, absorbing his instructions.

"I'm friendly with some of the paparazzi, so what we do will depend on who is here. Just follow my lead. If I stop, then stop with me."

"Is there a problem with your publicist? I get the feeling I'm an issue of sorts."

"Just a small one, but it's fine." He acted nonchalant, but obviously, there was a definite problem.

Tom's phone rang. He smiled, handing it to Tess.

"Hi, Tracy. How's your cruise going?"

"Hey, Mom. We are loving Greece! Apparently you did, too!" Tracy and JC giggled hysterically.

"Oh, great. I didn't think you'd see it."

"When we got into port, JC had eight photo messages from all of her friends. So yeah, we've seen it!"

"Did you have a message from your brother, too?"

"Oh, yeah. He was quite peeved."

JC snatched the phone away from Tracy. "We had to explain to our brother the effect Greece has on you." JC laughed. "We can appreciate how you could get caught up here. Greece is incredibly romantic. At least it was a good picture."

"That's what I said."

Tracy had the phone now. "We can't talk long because we're getting off the ship. We told John he should bring his girlfriend here on vacation then maybe he wouldn't be so judgmental. Europe is magically romantic. Anyway, we have to go. He's fine now and we all want you to have fun. Do you know where you are going yet?" she asked enthusiastically.

"Yes, I do."

Both girls chimed, "Have fun. Love you."

"Bye. Love you, too."

"Your girls seem awfully sensible. I knew they'd love Greece." Relief covered Tom's face.

"They are very responsible, but apparently they find Europe incredibly romantic. I hope they come home."

Tess sat anxiously waiting for the plane to land.

"I wouldn't have brought you here if I didn't think you could handle it. If we want to be together, this has to happen at some point. The sooner we get it over with, the sooner the cameras will go away. Somewhat."

Paparazzi loomed when they exited the airport. Tom held her hand. She followed behind him casually doing everything he told her to do. *Walk smoothly. Don't fidget or look directly at them.* He slid his arm around her waist, smiling at her. Tess focused so hard on concentrating, she didn't hear much of anything, but a rush of mumbled voices. Tom moved toward one of the men with a camera, but kept his distance.

"How was Greece Tommy? Let me take your picture! Who's your new date, Tommy?" the man asked.

Tom stopped for five seconds and pulled Tess in next to him. "Hey, Joey. This is my girlfriend, Tess Mathews. Greece was especially nice."

Flashes popped off. Before she could duck her head from the strikes of light, Tess caught glimpse of the stunned look on the man's face. He resembled Benny and Lisa's when Tom used the word girlfriend. The paparazzi were still taking pictures as Tess slipped into the car carefully.

"I hope you're ready for this." He kissed her on the cheek.

"That wasn't bad."

CHAPTER THIRTEEN

The car pulled up to a large black wrought iron gate. Lush, tall landscaping exposed only a very small portion of the garage doors from the road.

Entering Tom's home, she whispered in awe, "It's beautiful." Drawn to the mesmerizing view of the Pacific Ocean, Tess walked straight past the modest, modern décor. "Wow." She stared out the floor to ceiling glass panels that created a frame for nature's finest canvass of coastal artwork.

Tom stood behind Tess, embracing her. "Come on, you can look around later." He led her to his room, turned on some music, and opened the glass doors, letting in the moist ocean breeze.

"The view is spectacular." She wandered out onto the balcony and leaned over the stainless steel railing, taking in the smell of the ocean. He stared at her and tucked a strand of hair behind her ear. "What? Why are you looking at me like that?" She blushed.

"I like looking at you, Tess, you're beautiful." He placed his palm to hers and his other hand grasped her hip, dancing slowly gazing into her eyes. She laid her head on his chest, gently swaying to the music.

"Do you want me to show you around the house?" he whispered in her ear.

"Not right now. I feel so relaxed."

Tom kissed her lips tenderly, until they heard the front door open.

"Tommy? Hello! Hey, where are you?" a woman shouted.

"We'll be right out!" He replied and then brushed his nose to hers. "It's my assistant."

A very young, attractive woman stood in his living room. "Tommy! I'm glad you're back. I tried to knock, but you didn't hear me." She gave him a welcoming embrace. "I have some things for you. I hope they're the right size," she said to Tess, setting several bags atop the driftwood coffee table.

"Tess, this is my assistant, Shayla," he said, arms still wrapped around the striking, blond haired girl with hazel eyes.

Tess consciously made an effort not to show any emotions on her face as a rush of jealously surged through her. His assistant looked as if she could've stepped right out of a surf magazine. Very California. "It's nice to meet you." Tess reached for her hand.

"She's my assistant and my niece," Tom clarified.

Shayla embraced Tess. "It's nice to finally meet you. Tommy's been talking about you on the phone for weeks. He said you needed a few things."

"I do?"

"I had her pick out a couple of outfits for you so we wouldn't have to go out shopping right away. I wasn't sure how this morning would play out. Lisa helped me with your sizes, so hopefully they'll fit." Tom said.

"They probably will. That woman is gifted when it comes to shopping." Tess peeked inside the bag.

"If they don't fit or you don't like them, let me know and I'll exchange them for something different. Tommy can give you my number. If you need anything, Tess, call me. By the way, two guys are lurking around out front."

"I'll call you later so we can go over plans for tomorrow," Tom confirmed.

A shudder trickled down her spine as she wondered what it would be like to go shopping in public with Tom. Tess smiled appreciatively. "Thanks for the clothes."

"No problem. Call me with whatever you need. See you tomorrow."

"Hopefully you'll like the things she picked up. Lisa set the whole thing up for me."

"You're spoiling me," she murmured. Tess treasured everything Tom did for her, but she was used to taking care of herself.

"I enjoy doing things for you and don't give me any trouble over it, please, because you're going to have a great time the next few days."

"I'll just say thank you then." She kissed him appreciatively.

"Tess, I want nothing more than to take you to bed right now, but I hoped we could wait until later."

Tess realized she didn't need to rush all of her feelings into three days. They were together now and she could enjoy him for a long time. "I see a pool out back. Or do we have plans?"

"I want to take you to dinner later, but we can unwind for a few hours. I'm going to unpack and make some calls."

They both unpacked. She casually glanced around his thoroughly organized closet, slightly satisfied to see there weren't any other woman's things hanging in his closet. The outfits Shayla picked out for her were perfect in fit and style, even the shoes fit right.

Tess put on her bikini bottoms, heading out to the pool. He slipped his fingers around her wrist turning her so he could observe her. A huge grin spread across his face. "I didn't think you wanted topless photos of yourself on the Internet."

"But your back yard is so private."

He handed Tess the top to her bikini. "You should probably put this on, but it's up to you." He winked.

"Thanks."

Large white stone tiles bordered the long narrow rectangular pool. Perfectly manicured trees and shrubs lined the property so not to block the view of the ocean. Tess swam laps in the warm water and lounged in the sun. Tom eventually joined her. "I brought this back from Bora Bora for you." He handed her a bottle of the monoi oil she loved so much.

"Thanks. That was sweet of you." She rubbed oil on his back. He wanted to wait until later to take her to bed, but just the scent of the oil turned her on.

"Roll over, I'll do you," he said.

"I was hoping you'd say that."

"Play nice, Tess." He swatted her butt playfully.

Her thoughts kept wandering back to Bora Bora and the

massages her gave her. "I give up. I'm going inside."

She retreated back inside, trying her best not to tackle him on the bed, couch, counter or anything else that looked like fair game. He wanted to wait and she knew it would pay off nicely in the end.

Tom showed Tess around his home.

"Your place is so…"

"Bachelor pad? I don't have much design skill."

"I was going to say contemporary or modern. I like the clean lines." Dark brown leather sofas looked rich against the light gray walls and several pieces of colorful artwork hung on the walls. "I love the artwork. The colors add a lot of warmth." The painting extended the full length of the sofa it hung over. Midnight blue faded into purples, reds, oranges and yellows, mimicking a sunset.

"Do you like art?"

"Sure. Not strange pieces, but I appreciate unique things." She stood in front of his fireplace, admiring the pallid mosaic gray-blue glass tiles surrounding it. She suspected the glass tiles came from Italy.

"Tell me about your house, Tess."

"I have a nice house, but I'd rather show it to you."

"Would it be hard for you to have another man in your home?" Tom asked softly as they ambled down the hall to his room.

"I'll get past it. Is it strange for you to have me here?"

Both stretched out across his bed. "Yes, a little bit. Truthfully though, I couldn't wait for you to come home with me, and that's nothing I've ever wanted before."

"I know you leave soon to start your film, and I'm not sure what your plan is, but if it works out, can you stay with me for a couple days when you take me home?"

He fidgeted with his fingers. "Stay with you?" His brows creased and he cleared his throat.

Sensing his hesitation, Tess started to ramble. "If you have the time. Plus you could meet John."

Tom ran his tongue over his teeth, sucking air through them as he folded his arms across his chest.

I've never seen him do that before. He's freaking out.

"You don't have to stay with me if you don't want to." Caught off guard by his reaction, Tess tried to swallow her insecurities. "Tom, I don't want this to be weird. Our relationship should be easy for both of us. I'm not looking to get married again, so I don't want you to think that's where my head is." She tried to be light hearted so things wouldn't be awkward between them. "I enjoy spending time together. You make me happy. You're fun, not to mention I can't keep my hands off you."

He may as well have stamped *panic* to his forehead.

Tess didn't do well with sweeping things under a rug or hiding from reality. "Look I understand this is new for you, but please don't trip out because I asked you to come home with me."

He remained silent.

"Seriously, come on, Tom. I'm here with you at your home, and I have no idea how many women have laid in this same spot, but I really don't care. I'm not going to let it bother me because right now, I'm in your bed. It shouldn't bother you to stay with me."

Tom sat silent as the grave, letting her rattle on while he squirmed in his seat.

So much for Benny curing those inner demons. Apparently they still linger.

Irritated by his lack of confidence in their brand new relationship, Tess huffed. "Look, I need our relationship to be straightforward and uncomplicated for both of us. I don't like drama and I don't do well with bullshit. If there's something you need to say, just say it. Okay?"

She turned her back to him. "I'm taking a shower."

As the hot water rained over her, Tess' thoughts were spinning. *One little, 'Will you come home with me?' and he freaked. I shouldn't be surprised. This is obviously new for him, but jeeze it wasn't as if I asked him to move in with me.*

A few minutes later, Tom stepped into the shower and wrapped his arms around her. He stood behind her, placing affectionate kisses on her wet shoulder and tenderly stroked her arms.

Heat and tears stung her face beneath the steamy veil of the hot water. She turned away from him, hiding her frustration. "I'm pretty much *willing* to blindly throw myself to the wolves lingering outside your front door with a camera in their hands. You should be willing-"

"You're right. I'm sorry. I panicked for a minute. Uncomplicated. That's how I want us to be, too. No drama."

"No games, no bullshit. Okay?"

He turned to face her, slipping a sodden lock of hair from her face to look into her eyes. "I promise Tess. No bullshit."

Tom lifted her up a bit, nudging his hard-on between her legs.

Feeling his, *I'm sorry* searching for forgiveness between her thighs, she said, "Not yet, remember?"

"I changed my mind."

"I know you have something planned later, so not yet, please. I like it when you surprise me. I've waited all day. I can wait a little longer." She grinned stepping out of the shower.

"Is this when I'm supposed to turn the water to cold?"

"Umm hmm. Let's save *that* for later." She laughed suggestively.

Tess dressed for dinner, checking herself over in the mirror. The dark straight jeans and sheer lavender top fit flawlessly. She loved the tan wedges with a silver buckle across the top, too. "Thanks for the outfits."

"You're welcome. You'll probably meet some interesting people. There'll be camera's here tonight. That's one of the reasons I want to go out. I don't want you to be surprised."

Tom drove them to a well-known restaurant where they had dinner and drinks. Tess met several of his friends, most were very nice, and a few were slightly pretentious. She became quite bored with the 'Holy Shit' expression people wore on their faces when he introduced her as his girlfriend. It made her proud to be by his side, though.

She'd had several drinks and was having a hard time staying focused. She whispered in his ear as she gently bit his earlobe. "Tom, I can't wait any more. Can we go?"

"Let's go."

Cameras flashed like strobe lights as they left the restaurant.

Tom smiled nonchalantly, letting them get their shots as they rushed toward the car. Tess sensed his annoyance with the paparazzi, but he hid it so well, no one else noticed. She tried not to look nervous until one of them said, "So, Tommy, is this one of your date's moms?"

Tess remained unruffled, but Tom was pissed off. His stance turned rigid and she could feel his anger reverberating through his hand as he squeezed her fingers. He stepped toward the guy, swearing under his breath through gritted teeth, giving him the reaction he so badly wished to get a photo of.

She gently tugged on Tom's hand, smiling up at him, changing his demeanor instantly. Tom brushed his cheek against hers, nuzzling her neck, whispering, "Thanks." He turned to the man who made the comment, leaning in next to him to say something in his ear.

In the car Tess asked, "What did you say to him?"

"He's lucky I didn't rip his fucking head off." He shot her a look of remorse. "I'm sorry. They're such assholes sometimes. That was really shitty."

"Can we let it go, Tom? I don't want it to ruin the night."

"I might've been thrown in jail if you didn't look at me that way."

Tess had his shirt unbuttoned by the time they pulled in the drive. All the lights were off inside, but the moonlight casting its reflection on the ocean beamed in. Music echoed softly down the hall as Tom led her to his room. Several vases of flowers were set around his room and rose petals lay scattered on the bed. Candles flickered in the cool ocean breeze blowing in from the open glass door.

"Oh, my God. How did you do this? You're going to make me cry."

Tom reached for her fingers, taking her in his arms, slowly dancing her around the room.

"You are really spoiling me. Thank you, I love it." Bending to take in the fragrant scent of red roses.

"I've never done this for another woman and I want you to be comfortable here. I'm sorry about earlier."

"Here I thought it was because you're incredibly,

ridiculously attracted to me," she said bashfully.

Color rose to his cheeks. "That, too."

"Tom, just so you know, no one has ever done this for me before."

"It's a first for both of us then."

Tess kissed him hungrily, unable to get enough of the smoky wine lingering on his breath. He swayed her, dipped her, and undressed her. Standing in front of Tom with nothing left but heels and panties on, Tess' heart raced as she sank to her knees. Staring down, his dark brown eyes devoured her as she wrapped her lips around him, taking him in, craving for him to desire her more than any other woman.

Attempting to raise Tess to her feet, Tom cautioned, "Wait. Stop."

She backed off momentarily and peered up at him as she rolled her tongue around him. "I want to taste you."

His hands touched the side of her face, twisting his fingers in her hair as he gazed down watching intently, giving her what she wanted.

Laying her back on the bed, Tom's warm, open lips brushed against her nipples. Slipping his thumbs into her panties, he pulled them off, tossing them over his head. Gripping his hair between her fingers, intuitively, she guided him down between her thighs. He ravished her body as if reading her every thought. Relinquished all control, Tess let her arms fell behind her head as her hair hung over the edge of the bed.

Tess couldn't hear the music. She could only hear what she thought was a voice sounding somewhat like her own, moaning loudly as waves of pleasure overcame her.

CHAPTER FOURTEEN

Tess rolled over in bed, reaching for Tom, but found only his pillow. Dangling her feet over the edge of the bed, she smiled softly, glancing at rose petals scattered over the floor.

Ambling down the hallway, she recognized voices talking in the living room.

"It's about time you woke up. Rough night?" Lisa chimed sarcastically.

Tess tried to keep a straight face. "No, actually I had a lovely evening."

"Are you excited about the premier or are you nervous?"

"Both," she admitted, grateful to see Lisa.

"There's coffee in the kitchen. Shayla brought by a basket of fruit and bagels."

As she helped herself to breakfast, it dawned on her that Shayla fixed the room last night.

"Go throw something comfortable on. You have a date with me today. Oh, and I have something for you." Lisa handed her several magazines.

Tess tossed the magazines on the coffee table. She didn't want to fall into the trap of caring about what complete strangers thought of her.

"You're in those magazines. I thought you'd like to see them."

"I'm not sure if I want to look. The pictures don't bother me, but I'm not interested in what they have to say."

"I looked through them, there's nothing bad," Tom reassured her.

"What are we doing today?" Tess asked Lisa.

"We're having a girl's day."

Lisa took Tess to several shops. This time a driver and a bodyguard went with them everywhere to make sure Lisa wasn't hassled.

"Do you have any idea what you'd like to wear?" Lisa asked enthusiastically, almost as if she hoped Tess would let her pick the dress out for her.

"I have no idea. I'm assuming it has to be a dress, but it doesn't have to be long, does it?"

"You don't have to wear a dress at all, but I would. You two are the next biggest news second to the actual premier."

"What do you mean?"

"It's a big deal for the two of you. Most of the time, Tommy comes to these things alone, and if he does bring someone, it's for publicity. You two are the buzz right now. He's been calling you his girlfriend since he got into town."

Tess' stomach fluttered with flickers of excitement and apprehension. "I know you're dying to help me find the perfect dress, and I would be very appreciative if you would. I want to look amazing."

"Yay! Thanks, Tess, I knew you'd let me help. Believe me, when I'm through with you, they won't even notice Tommy. I know you're not big on attention, but you're under the spotlight, Tess. You might as well shine."

"Hopefully that light isn't shining too brightly when I fall on my face," she mumbled.

Lisa took Tess to a posh dress boutique. She tried on a dozen dresses, finally finding the perfect, strapless, royal blue dress. It was stunning with pleats at the top, making the silky fabric flow to one side of her waist, molding to her curves like a glove.

They stopped at a café, enjoying lunch outside on a patio. Tess felt like a goldfish sitting in a fish bowl. Leaving the café, several paparazzi called Lisa's name, asking for her picture. Tess recognized a photographer from the airport. He approached Tess, calling her by name, asking nicely if he could take a photo. Masking her surprise, she stopped and smiled.

"You handled that well!" Lisa nonchalantly took her hand, guiding her into another boutique.

"That was the same guy from the airport. Tom was friendly to him, and I think he called him Joey. Hopefully I didn't look like an idiot. Should I have stopped?"

"You did great. You're very photogenic. You need a strapless bra for your dress, don't you?"

"Yes."

They were trying on lingerie when Lisa entered Tess' dressing area, which resembled a dressing room suite. "So, Tess, I thought I should give you some pointers. If you don't mind."

"Please do, I'll take all the advice I can get."

"There will be dozens of movie stars coming out to support Benny's film, so you're going to see a lot of familiar faces. You don't seem too hung up on that, but you still might get overwhelmed. Tommy will know everyone there. People adore him, so be yourself and stick next to him. Whatever you do, don't drink too much. If you're going to drink, have water in between. I don't want to be your hair holder while you're wrapped over a toilet."

"Okay. I never drink too much."

Lisa hesitated for a minute. "Tess, on a scale of one to ten, how confident are you?"

"Maybe an eight. It depends on the moment. I don't know. Why?"

"I know Tommy is crazy about you, but you need to be a ten at the premier."

"What do you mean?"

"I'm not trying to upset you, but I think I should warn you. It's no secret that women constantly pursue him."

Tess gave a begrudging shrug and folded her arms across her chest.

Lisa patted the tuft silk dressing bench, encouraging Tess to sit beside her. "You're different, Tess. He's been chasing you since the moment you two met. He's probably been chasing you his whole life, he just hadn't found you yet."

Tess smiled biting her lip. "Am I really that different for him?"

"You have no idea." Lisa said sarcastically.

"He makes me feel incredible." Heat flooded her cheeks.

"Good, you're going to need to be incredible, Tess. You need to be prepared."

"What are you trying to tell me Lisa? Just spit it out. You're making me nervous."

"There will be a lot of women at the after party, a few he's probably dated. Not that it means anything to him, believe me it doesn't, but you need to be confident. A ten in confidence, Tess." Lisa held up ten fingers. "These women don't care who you are. They want to go home with him and they won't be shy about it either. They don't play nice, and you're almost *too* nice."

Merely the thought made her angry. Tess' eyes narrowed.

Lisa pointed at Tess' frown. "That's what I'm talking about, that look right there. This is why we're having this conversation now, because it won't do you any good to get angry with these women or pissed at Tommy. They'll sense it like a shark smells blood and it'll make it worse. They'll notice your jealousy and play off it. They're going to flirt with him and paw on him and try to dance with him. It's pathetic, but they do it, so you need to be able to handle yourself."

Tess nodded as she absorbed Lisa's advice.

"Tommy's not going to want you being all pissed off and jealous. It will ruin your night and his if he has to constantly reassure you. Babysitting someone's hurt feelings all night is a complete drag, especially when you haven't even done anything wrong. He wants to show you off. That's why he brought you here. He's proud to have you with him and this is a huge, huge, *huge* deal for him. So basically, don't fuck it up. Benny and I like you. I've never seen Tommy this happy. He's been on cloud nine since the day you two met, and from what I can see, you're just as crazy about him."

"I am," Tess agreed.

"Check your emotions at the door and claim him as your own. You need to be confident. A ten, Tess."

"Are they really going to be that bad?" Her palms started to sweat and she waved them in the air.

"Yes, Tess. Some of them are. Look, he's been pursuing you, right?"

"I guess. He likes to surprise me all the time."

"Turn it around, seduce him for the evening. Everyone there is going to be beautiful, so don't be insecure. You are the incredibly gorgeous woman he wants to be with. The way he ogles over you constantly, he probably won't notice any other women."

"Ten, I'm a ten." Tess straightened herself very tall, looking into the mirror. "I can do this. You're right. I won't freak out. No babysitting."

"Can you dance?" Lisa asked.

"Oh yeah, I can dance."

"I mean can you really dance?"

Tess tried to keep a straight face as she showed Lisa her best moves in the dressing room in her thong and strapless bra. "Running man, the sprinkler, I can even do the superman."

"You had better be fucking with me," Lisa groaned, looking scared to death.

"I am." Tess showed Lisa her best Las Vegas style dancing and they both laughed so hard they had tears. "How do you do this?"

"You have to tune it all out and ignore the negative. Benny and I learned the hard way. It took many ruined evenings to figure it out, and that's why I'm warning you. Now Benny's a ten in confidence and me... I'm an eleven! No other woman in a crowd of hundreds is going to get Benny's attention over me."

"They wouldn't stand a chance," Tess agreed, hugging Lisa, unconcerned that she was half-dressed. "Thanks. Seriously, thanks for everything."

Lisa sauntered on her tippy-toes back to her own dressing room. She turned back to Tess, flashing her ten fingers, mouthing, "Ten."

They headed to a spa across the street. "What are we having done?" Tess asked.

"Everything."

They got massaged, waxed, rubbed and scrubbed. Lisa even hooked Tess with someone to do her hair for the premier, declaring, "Thank *God* I came a few days early. You'd be walking the red carpet in shorts and a ponytail."

It was late in the afternoon by the time they returned to

Tom's house. Benny and Lisa left to have dinner with the producer for photo ops. Tess curled up next to Tom on the sofa.

"Are you going to show me your dress?" he asked wishfully.

"Nope, I'm going to make you wait." She smirked, biting her lip, thinking of being a ten. "You're going to like it."

Sunshine gleamed through the windows, warming Tess' toes poking out from under the sheets.

It was a beautiful day. Tom took her for a ride through the verdant wooded canyons near his home. The cool, fresh air whipped through her hair while they listened to classic rock, talking about California and places he loved. They stopped for lunch at a bar all but hidden in the dense pine trees. Row after row of motorcycles lined up perfectly in front of a red neon sign, blinking *Mom's*. Bikers dressed in full leathers gathered in small packs, checking out the latest and greatest motorcycles.

Tess shook her head and let out a snicker. "Well aren't you just full of surprises?"

His eyes glimmered with boyish charm. "This is one of my favorite bars. No one takes pictures here."

As they stepped into the dimly lit bar a deep husky voice hollered, "Well, look what the cat drug in!"

Tom chuckled, heading straight for the end of the bar. "Hello, Codge."

"I wondered if I'd be seeing you soon. Rumor has it you finally got yourself a girlfriend." Codge stroked his long braided goatee and brushed his hands down the front of his chest, as if smoothing out wrinkles in his sleeveless black Harley T-shirt. He gave Tess a polite once over. "Hell, you look more like a woman to me. Bout time, Tommy." He grabbed Tom by the shoulder, giving him a firm whack on the back.

"Tess, I'd like you to meet Codge, short for Old Codger."

Codge stood at least 6'4" with broad shoulders and biceps most men would consider guns. She leaned forward over the bar to see if he was standing on a step. Tess stared up at the man who had to be at least seventy and extended her hand. "Holy crap, you're tall," she muttered in amazement at the sheer size of him. "Nice to meet you."

"He only looks tuff, Tess. Codge is a big pussy cat."

Codge let out a deep thunderous laugh as he took Tess' hand and seated them at a booth. "Let me get somebody to cover the bar. I'll be right back, honey."

Tess giggled, catching a glimpse of a tattoo covering his arm of a biker pin-up girl with *Mom* scrolled in a halo above her head.

"*Mom* is Codge's wife. He swears she's a saint for putting up with him. He looks intimidating, but looks can be deceiving. He's a great guy."

"Looks *can* be deceiving," Tess agreed. Codge looked like a Hell's Angel but seemed more like an adorable grandpa, dimples and all. "I thought you were going to be a complete ass the first day we-"

"He has asshole written all over him, till you get to know him." Codge interrupted from behind, roughly clasping Tom's shoulder and scooting next to him at the booth. "It's cause he's so *pretty*." He cut loose another boisterous laugh. "Nah, this guys all right, Tess. He's one of the best friends I got. I'll vouch for him."

Tom cleared his throat and rolled his eyes. "I don't need you to vouch for me old man. I just wanted her to taste one of your famous turkey burgers."

"Turkey burger my ass. Don't let him fool you honey." Codge eyes him suspiciously and then raised a wary eyebrow. "Some people go to church to find solace, Tommy comes to *Mom's*."

Tom smirked. "Comparing church to *Mom's* is a bit of a stretch, don't you think? They might not let you into heaven if you keep talking like that."

"Hah! Hell, Saint Peter will be guarding those pearly gates with a shotgun the day I die, Tommy." The two men gripped in another manly embrace, both wearing huge smiles. "I'll go put your order in."

Amused by their camaraderie, Tess' smile broadened across her face as Codge left the table. "Are you two related?"

"Not by blood, but he is like family to me. I've known him for thirty years."

He went on to explain that Codge had helped him out of more than one bind when he was younger, including bailing he and his brother out of jail after a fight in his bar. Tom's older brother left home in Tennessee and moved to Hollywood to be an actor. Two years later Tom followed. His brother had a knack for drinking too much, fighting too often and finding any trouble in a thirty-mile radius.

Unfortunately, his brother's bad choices ultimately ended what could've been a promising acting career. Tom got lucky and landed a roll in film that started his claim to fame. It drove a wedge between them that only got worse over time.

"Shayla's his daughter?" she asked, and he nodded in reply. "How did she wind up working for you?"

Tess couldn't help but notice a change in Tom. He was relaxed and openly talking about his family. He had only mentioned his brother once before, briefly saying he was closer to Benny than his own brother.

"My brother wasn't any better at acting like a father than he was in front of the camera. Worse actually. I went back home to visit my parents before they died and spent time with Shayla. She was a senior in high school and-" his lips drew taut with anger. "I told her if she ever needed anything, money, a place to stay, a job, to call me."

"So she called?"

"I'd been out of town for a month, and when I got home, she'd been waiting for me for three days. My neighbor took her in until I showed up." Tom frowned. "My brother's a piece of shit. Anyway, I put her through college and gave her a job. She's a great girl."

The waitress brought out their lunch. Tess ran her hand over the top of his. "That was a really nice thing for you to do. I'm sure she appreciates all you've done for her."

"I wish I could've done more for her, when she was younger." Tom climbed out from his side of the booth and sat beside her. "Speaking of brothers-" he flipped her hair behind her shoulder. "Do you want to have John pick us up at the airport or do you want me to arrange a ride?"

Her glance drifted down to the table and she smiled to herself thinking her heart might beat right out of her chest. When she lifted her gaze, his dark eyes stared back intently. "Did you bring me all the way out here in the middle of nowhere to tell me that you're taking me home?"

"I was working up the courage," he admitted self-consciously with a smirk.

She planted a big kiss of appreciation right on his lips. "When do we leave?"

"Sunday afternoon. Three days," he said regretfully.

"I'll call him later, just to make sure he can pick us up."

"If it's going to be uncomfortable or too difficult for you once we get there, and you change your mind, we can stay downtown. But, I want to stay with you."

"I'm not even going to try to convince myself or you that it won't be difficult, but I don't care what it takes, I still would like you to stay."

After enjoying one of the best turkey burgers Tess had ever eaten, they said their goodbyes to Codge. He advised Tess with a gentle bear hug, "You be careful of that one. He's always up to no good." Codge followed with a warning to Tom. "You'd better be good to her, Tommy. I'd hate to have to have to come looking for you."

"Yes, sir, old man."

"Old man? You ain't gettin' any younger Tommy," Codge roared as they strolled out the door.

They drove back through the canyon and stopped at a fairly private beach. The strong surf kept them out of the ocean, so they spread out a blanket on the warm sand.

"You don't ever get to do this, do you? Chill, relax, go where you want."

"No, I don't, not in a long time. I miss doing this kind of stuff out in the open. It's nice to be normal."

"Are you referring to me as normal?" she teased.

"You know what I mean, and you are *far* from normal." He traced the small of her back with his fingertips to tickle her. She giggled, covered in goose bumps.

"I'm sure you get to do a ton of incredibly fun, interesting things that make up for missing out on some of the normality's of life."

"True. I've had some great opportunities. I like being able to use my celebrity to help charities. I enjoy taking advantage of the media to benefit an organization that needs help. Plus, I've been able to travel places I never thought I would ever see."

"Out of all the things you've gotten to experience and all the places you've traveled, what's your favorite?" Tess played her fingers along his ribs.

"You, Tess. *You* are my favorite," he answered sincerely.

Tess held her breath, holding back the tears stinging her lashes. "I don't want to do this now. I don't want to cry and dwell on saying goodbye to you, Tom. I'll cry and miss you later, but not yet."

He kissed her shoulder, stroking away the single tear sliding down her cheek. "Tess, I promise we'll be together. We'll work it out around our schedules."

"I don't have a schedule," she scoffed. "I don't care where my life is headed any more. I only want to be happy and you make me ridiculously happy. I'll do whatever it takes to be together."

"I do have to leave, though. I'll be on set for a while, but after filming gets started, it'll be easier to stay in character and I'll have you come see me."

Tess looked away, laying her head on the blanket to hide her sniffles. At this point, she couldn't imagine not seeing him for a day.

"Tess, I gave you my word. Please, trust me. I don't want to go, but I don't have a choice. When this film is done, we'll be together."

"I do trust you. It's just going to be hard to say goodbye, and I have this fear. I don't want to lose you. It's difficult for me. Do you understand?" She'd couldn't go through another loss like Richard, nor did she want him to break her heart.

"I understand." He rolled her onto her back, studying her face as he caressed the contour of her abs.

Minutes passed, Tess and Tom simply stared at each other, letting unspoken words pass between them. "I can't do this, Tom. I don't want to talk about saying goodbye. I feel like I'm wasting moments with you when I'm lying here crying. Life is short and I don't want to cry anymore," Tess finally admitted.

He lay quiet, caressing her shoulder.

"What are you thinking about?"

"Life is short. I just want to be happy, too." He grinned the crooked grin she loved so much. "Let's get out of here before we caught in another indecent photo."

They returned to Tom's as the sun sank into the ocean. He made martinis and they swam. The warm pool felt wonderful, but the drinks were even better. Tess had never drank martinis, and they were making her randy.

Tom rattled on, seemingly having a conversation with himself, because she wasn't paying attention. Tess watched his lips move, but could only focus on the urge to gently suck on them and run her tongue down the muscle on his neck that fluttered when he talked. All she wanted to do was make love to him. Eventually, Tess stepped out of the pool in the middle of his sentence, never turning back to see if he followed. Her bikini hit the ground before she made it inside the house. She only made it as far as the top of the stairs.

He grabbed her from behind, his hot breath traveled over her shoulder and back. Twisting her neck, she searched for his mouth. He turned her to face him, and she clung to him, kissing him with hunger and desire unlike anything Tess had ever experienced before. He guided her down to the floor, taking her right there on the stairs. She wanted to tell him to make love to her, but feared to say the words out loud.

"Are you okay, Tess?" He watched her face intently.

"Umm hum."

"You're thinking about something else. What can I do to change that?" He placed her hands above her head.

She inhaled deeply, holding her breath before exhaling loudly. She was dying to say the words so badly, but scared he would bolt out the door.

"Tell me, Tess. What do you want?"

That voice! She breathed deeply again.

"I'm listening," he coaxed.

She blurted out. "I don't want to have *sex* tonight."

"I think you're too late." He smirked, tugging gently on her nipple with his teeth.

"I want this to be more than *just* sex." She yearned for him to realize what she needed from him. "I'm not asking you for *words*, Tom. I'm not ready for that, but I want this to be more than just sex."

He stopped mid-thrust, cocking his head to the side, understanding exactly what she meant. He pulled away from her to stand up.

Panic set in and regret filled her eyes as she reached for his hand to pull him back. *Shit, I shouldn't have said anything.*

Tom took her hand and led her to his room to start over. Tilting her chin up toward his. "Tess, I'm not sure if I've ever had just sex with you. It's been much more than that for me from the beginning."

"Me, too."

Tom kissed her lips softly, nuzzling her neck, burying his face in the scent of her skin. Their bodies moved slower, more deliberate, connecting as one, touching each other tenderly. Neither felt compelled to impress. They simply took pleasure in one of the most intimate nights either had ever experienced. That night they made love together.

CHAPTER FIFTEEN

Tom grinned from ear to ear. "I need to take care of some things this morning. I know you like to run when you get anxious. There's a treadmill and a few other things downstairs if you feel like it."

"I think I'm going to swim for a while instead."

"Keep your top on today, because there's probably someone watching." He planted a kiss on her lips then headed for the door.

"I don't mind the pictures when you can see the guy taking them, but hiding in the bushes is creepy. More like stalking. It shouldn't even be legal." She cringed in disgust.

Tess enjoyed breakfast on the balcony. She reflected on the past few weeks, and accepted the fact that it was okay to look forward to the future. Richard was gone and she missed him terribly, but she wasn't going to feel guilty being with Tom. She'd been inconsolable for over a year, but not anymore.

Tess dove into the pool's warm water. She strived to embrace her inner ten. *No eye rolling, no silly smiles, try not to turn red, no thong shots when exiting the limo, but above all don't get jealous.*

Tom returned, joining her in the pool. "Do you get nervous at all for these things?" she asked curiously.

"I used to get really nervous, almost ill, but now it's more exciting than nerve racking. You always hope a movie will be successful, but until you actually see it, you never know. It certainly makes it easier when your friends are there, or at least it does for me. Are you excited?"

"Very."

"Good. There's a huge after party later. You are going to

have a fantastic time."

"Lisa mentioned it when we went shopping. I'm excited."
Ten. Ten. Ten.

"By the way, I left our flight information on the counter."

"Okay." She needed to get ready, but wanted to call John first.

"Hi, Mom."

"Hey John-"

"I was just getting ready to leave for the airport. You didn't need to remind me to pick up the girls. Are you nervous for the red carpet tonight? I still can't believe you're dating Tom Clemmins." He mumbled the last sentence.

"I am nervous, but excited too. He's very nice, John. You'll like him," she rambled.

"You say it as if I'm going to get to meet him."

Tess immediately recognized the hesitation in John's voice. "Well, I wasn't calling to remind you to pick up your sisters. I knew you'd remember. I'm calling to tell you that Tom's bringing me home on Sunday and I'm hoping you'll pick us up at the airport."

There was silence on the other line, then a soft exhale. "He's coming here? With you?"

"Yes. He has to leave the next day to start a new film, but I asked him to bring me home."

"Umm…"

"He can have a car pick us up, but I'd prefer it if you would," Tess said softly, feeling slightly crushed by his hesitation. "I'll understand if you don't want to."

"I'm just a little surprised, Mom, that's all. I'll pick you up. I take it that he'll be staying here with you at the house?"

"Yes."

John had no response.

"Look, John, I've been with him for three weeks. I want him to be a part of my life, and my kids and my home are a big part of that. It won't be easy for me either, but I'm happy and it's because I'm with him."

She loved her kids, but wouldn't change the way she felt about Tom. She wanted them to accept Tom and hopefully like him. It would not be simple with John, as he was as protective as a father when it came to his sisters and Tess. If a man so much as checked her out in passing or attempted to approach her, John would shut him down with a death stare. He was only twenty-three, but was as wise and responsible as any man she knew.

"You're right. I want you to be happy, and I will always support your choices. It's just difficult to think of him staying here at the house. Give me the flight information. I'll be there."

"Thanks, son. I know you'll like him."

"I'm going to tell you flat out, Mom, I don't like everything I've read about him online. He'd better not trample on you."

"I'll see you at the airport."

"Have fun tonight. It is pretty cool, all the stuff you're getting to do."

"Thanks, I will. love you." She hung up, exhaling loudly and blowing the air from her lungs. She tossed her phone on the bed and turned toward the shower.

Tom leaned against the doorway. "Are you okay?"

"Yep." She attempted to smile, but he wasn't buying it. "Have you been standing there the whole time?"

"Long enough."

"He'll pick us up. He's fine." She tried to be convincing.

"Tess, I won't come between you and your kids. If it would be better to wait for a while, then I'll wait to come home with you."

"It's not like that. He's not like that. This is a huge change that my kids will have to adjust to. I have no doubts, John's just being overprotective. Stupid Internet."

"Oh, great," he groaned. "No wonder he's protective."

"The funny thing is, I know he'll like you and I know you'll like him. He has the same kind of confidence as you. It might take him a little longer, that's all."

"Sounds like he gets it from you."

"Not really. He's just like his dad." She smiled.

He began untying the strings on her bikini. "Do you want some assistance in the shower?"

"No, you can assist me later," she teased. "I'd rather wait. So, in case I forget, will you remind me, please?"

"You're asking a lot of me, Tess, but I'll try."

The hair and makeup guy, Marco, arrived right on time. Tess immediately adored his flamboyant, entertaining attitude. Marco brought out her blue eyes with smoky dark colors. The fake lashes took some getting used to, but he only made them a bit longer than her natural lashes, so they worked perfectly.

"Okay, Miss Tess, let me see your dress."

She retrieved the dress from the closet and laid it on the bed.

"Damn girl, you are going to give that poor man a heart attack." Marco spoke lively with his colorful accent. "How do you want to wear your hair?"

"I want to wear it down." She gave a pleading look of desperation.

"Straight and sleek or half pulled back? Give me some clues here, girlfriend."

"No, not straight, kind of messy."

"*Tussled*, girlfriend. We refer to that as tussled. Like I-just-got-laid-on-a-Saturday-night kind of hair! You are a naughty one! I know what to do. You leave it to Marco."

Tess always considered herself to be a fairly simple, no frills woman. She never indulged in extravagancies unless it included airplane tickets and a vacation. *Oh, who am I kidding? I'm having a blast!* Peeking at her reflection, she knew that she looked better tonight than she'd ever looked in her life. *Eleven!*

Marco had just finished Tess' hair when Tom entered the room. Marco pointed toward the shower, warning Tom, "Get in there, and don't be peeking at her."

Standing in her bathrobe, she said goodbye at the front door. Marco air-kissed her cheeks. "Um hmm, get laid for me too, honey. You look irresistible."

Tess sat on the bathroom counter in her royal blue strapless bra and lacy thong, waiting for Tom. She leaned back with her palms on the counter, spreading her legs barely enough so he could stand in front of her. Her dark hair swept to one side revealing her smoky eyes. She felt empowered and provocative, ready to take on the night.

Tom stepped out of the shower and rounded the corner. His mouth gaped open. "Damn, Tess. You look fucking incredible."

Standing between her thighs, his hands traveled up her waist. "I can't believe how beautiful you are."

"I kind of like it, too. Marco did a great job. It's exactly what I wanted." She nibbled on his neck, feeling the blood pulsing through his veins.

"Tess, I thought you wanted to wait to make love to me until after the premier."

Tom spoke those words for the first time, and Tess' heart went into overdrive. Wanting to make love to him right there on the counter, she pulled him tightly against her, kissing him passionately.

His towel now lay on the floor, driving each of them very close to a point of no return. "I do want to wait to make love to you. I don't, but I do." He nudged gently, but she wiggled out of reach. "Tom, you're supposed to be telling me," she imitated his sexy voice, "'Tess, you wanted to wait, remember?'"

"That's right." He chuckled, "Tess, you wanted to wait until later, remember?"

"Thank you. You can think about this moment all night long until we get back."

"That's not very fair." He grinned.

"Oh, yes it is. Because this is what I'm going to be thinking about all night long."

"You did this on purpose, didn't you?"

"I would never."

Tom stepped into his closet to get dressed. Tess slipped her dress over her head and ambled into his closet, so he could zip her up. She quietly waited for him to turn around, but when he did, heat rippled through her core. "Holy crap." He looked so gorgeous. Tess had never seen Tom in a suit before. She wrinkled her nose and squished her eyebrows together with her mouth gaping open. They had gotten too close on the counter.

"You need some help?" Tom asked, reaching to zip her dress. "Your dress is gorgeous. I'm not going to be able to take my eyes off you tonight. Blue is my favorite color on you."

"Uh, huh," she stammered, staring at him from head to toe.

"You don't like the suit?" he asked in surprise.

"You look....beautiful."

"Beautiful?" he snickered, rolling his eyes.

"Yeah. Beautiful, smoking hot, fan-fucking-tastic. Holy shit, I need a minute." She turned and walked briskly into the bedroom, pacing in circles with red cheeks. *How did I get so lucky? He's so handsome! Maybe I should undress and climb into bed. No! Pull it together Tess.*

He finished getting ready and found her lying on her back on the bed. "Tess, are you okay?"

She tried to compose herself, but he looked way too appetizing in his black suit and crisp white shirt. He had left it unbuttoned, revealing a peek of his chiseled chest. His hair appeared darker, as if he'd just run his hands through it, making him look younger and his eyes darker, too. "Yep, I'm fine."

She stared at him lustfully, making him laugh.

"Later, Tess. Come on, it's time to go."

"But you look really delicious."

"Later, I promise." Tom tugged on her hand and pulled her off the bed. "I have something for you." He casually handed her a long narrow box.

She glanced down at the box timidly.

"Tess," he said. "Open it, please."

She opened the box to find a gorgeous choker-length diamond necklace. "Holy crap, I don't know what to say." She didn't want to tear up and ruin her makeup.

"Say, 'Thanks, Tom. I love it', and please don't cry. Turn around so I can put it on you."

"Thank you. I love it." She smiled up at him.

"You're welcome. Come on, the limo's waiting."

"Wait one sec." She glanced at herself in the mirror, touching her fingers to the breathtaking necklace.

He whispered over her shoulder, "You look beautiful. Let's go."

Tess carefully climbed into the limo. She nervously chewed on her cheek.

"Look, Tess, it'll be easy, just follow my lead. When I stop, you stop. I'm not signing autographs, because it's not my film. I won't let go of you or leave you standing by yourself. Lisa will be busy at the premier, but we'll sit with them later tonight at the club."

"Okay. I'm ready."

"Good because we're here."

Opening the limo door was like flipping the On switch of a radio that was stuck on three AM stations at once. Fans lined up twenty rows deep to see the stars. People screamed Tom's name, as well as several other actors who were in front of them. Voices muffled together, making Tess unable to focus clearly. Tom slipped his arm around her waist. Nuzzling her neck with his warm, smooth cheek, he whispered, "You okay?"

Filtering the voices now, she inhaled deeply, taking in the scent of his cologne. "Yes."

Once they passed the bleachers full of fans, Tom sauntered past photographers, pausing every few feet for another set of pictures. Each time Tess mimicked his controlled pose and smile, instinctually bending her elbow, resting her fingers on the dip between her hip and abdomen.

Tess caught a glimpse of Joey, the photographer she recognized with Lisa and at the airport. Tom paused, leaning in closer to her face, brushing his cheek to hers. She understood, he liked Joey and gave him the better photo op. Several reporters worked the carpet. Tom introduced Tess as his girlfriend, followed by an immediate statement of how happy he was to be there supporting Benny's film. He moved on to the next reporter so quickly, they didn't have the opportunity to ask any further questions. Everyone told them how great they looked. A reporter commented on Tess' dress, asking *who* she was wearing. She had no idea, but Tom did. "Versace," he said, squeezing her waist.

Inside the theater, Tom mingled with everyone, introducing Tess to movie stars, producers, even a band who had written several sound tracks for the movie. He was ridiculously charming. Men and women both wanted to talk to Tom or be near him. She recognized when he genuinely liked someone or was merely being polite by the way he greeted them.

The film was an action movie with a lot of comedy, targeting young adults. Tess enjoyed the film, as she wasn't a big fan of drama and didn't like to cry at movies.

As they left the theater, more reporters, photographers and fans waited to snap pictures and catch a glimpse of their favorite stars. Tom stopped to talk to a reporter who asked him what he thought of the movie. He then turned his attention to Tess. "How did it feel to land Tom Clemmins?"

Tom squeezed Tess' hand, glaring sharply at the reporter. Turning to leave Tess said, "I feel wonderful this evening."

At the after party, the club exploded with Hollywood's young, rich, and famous. Tess found this to be quite intimidating, but she merely went with the flow, concentrating on keeping her gawking to a minimum.

Tom sensed her distraction, so he bent down briefly kissing her neck and lips. "Better?" he asked with his crooked grin.

"Yes."

They mingled their way through the club. Plush circular couches with low tables created secluded and private seating areas. Similar to the Vegas nightclubs, the atmosphere was very modern, very loud and very, very sexy. It seemed absurd how many beautiful young women and just as many, if not more, gorgeous young men filled the club. Some people were nice, some were ostentatious, few were complete asses, and most were very clingy and pawed on everyone.

The music was loud and pumping. She knew most of the songs the DJ played because her kids listened to them, but the DJ mixed the music so it thumped erotically along with the bass. She watched people dancing in the crowd, and grinned thinking of her three kids. They definitely loved to shake their groove thing and teased Tess because she would dance with them no matter what kind of music they listened to. Rave, rock, rap or country, it really didn't matter.

"I need a drink," she told Tom.

"Would you like a martini?" A haughty grin plastered his face.

Blushing in return, she recalled how aroused martini's made her the night before. "Yes. Yes, I would."

They found Benny and Lisa at a lounge area. Lisa and Tess shouted to each other over the loud music.

"Tess, how are you holding up?"

Tess sipped her drink. "Great."

Lisa squinted as if she were analyzing her. "Do you remember what we talked about?"

"Yes. I'm trying. It's a little distracting with so many people here. I'm fine."

"If you're distracted, then he's distracted. Be better than fine. You're here with Tommy and he's taking you home tonight," she smirked wickedly.

Tess drank her drink and started to loosen up. Tom continuously stroked and caressed her shoulders, arms and back. He gently squeezed her thigh and she sank in next to him, changing her demeanor instantly, comforted by his touch. Another drink came and Tess felt much more comfortable. Lisa slyly held up her fingers. First, a six, working her way up to an eight.

Tess' body grooved to the music. She slid her hand inside Tom's jacket, stretching her arm across his abs, gently stroking his side. "What did you say to me earlier? What do you want to do when we go back to your place?" She put her lips around his earlobe sucking on it gently.

He peered through her long brown hair. "I said, I want to make love to you."

"Oh that's right, for a minute I thought you said you wanted to fuck me real slowly." Tom's back stiffened and Tess knew she had his full attention. "But I like the way you said it better. I want to make love to you too," she flirted.

He swallowed hard and locked his eyes on hers. "That's not even fair Tess. You're cheating."

"I haven't even started with you yet." She gripped his side firmly. Tess knew she'd keep his undivided attention all night. Out of the corner of her eye, she noticed Benny and Lisa watching them. Tess shot Lisa her best saucy smile, and Lisa slid a glass of water toward Tess.

She mouthed the words *'Thank you'* to Lisa.

Lisa held up nine fingers in return.

People continuously stopped by to see Benny. Tess noticed several women looming near their table. She got the distinct feeling they were coming by for Tom. No way in hell would he notice them that night, or any other night.

Lisa reached over and touched her leg, motioning toward the powder room. Lisa gripped her hand, weaving through the crowd. Tess' ears rang from the loud music.

"Hey I told you no hair holding," Lisa joked.

"I'm fine. I feel incredible."

"You need to stay that way for about three more hours, okay!"

They laughed together fixing each other's hair and makeup. "Thanks for the advice. I'd feel extremely uncomfortable right now if you hadn't talked to me, or should I say, inspired me. I truly appreciate all your help."

"We like you Tess. You need to be able to hold your own in Tommy's world, and you are certainly managing perfectly. You're about a nine and a half at the moment. If you keep kissing him that way, you'll be leaving in an hour."

"Oh no. I want to dance with him."

"I can tell. I see you over there grooving in your seat."

"He does dance, right? I mean, like this. I know he can dance formally."

"What do you think?" Lisa answered sarcastically.

"I think he hasn't danced with me yet," Tess squealed confidently.

Lisa weaved her way back through the maze of people heading for their table. Tess' eyes narrowed when she noticed a woman in her seat. She stopped in her tracks practically yanking Lisa's arm out of the socket. Lisa spun around following Tess' gaze.

"Don't make that face Tess. He goes home with *you* remember."

Lisa took her place next to Benny. Tess waited for the young woman to get up, but she didn't budge. Tom squirmed uneasily in his seat, but Tess simply smiled at him. She recognized the girl from Bora Bora. Mariah. As Tom scooted away from her, Mariah slithered closer, sliding a hand up his thigh and whispering closely in his ear. Tom asked the young woman to leave, but her hand continued to travel further up his thigh.

Tess started to lurch toward her, but stopped herself midway when she noticed Benny and Lisa observing her reaction. *I can do this. Be calm.* She took a deep breath, restraining the urge to rip the girl out of her seat by her hair.

Tess winked at Lisa and stepped toward Mariah, standing directly in front of her. The young woman acted completely oblivious to Tess' presence, but Tom didn't. His eyes widened and he started to stand up out of his seat. Tess' brow raised to a point in defense, giving him *an I got this* grin. She could've sworn he turned a shade paler as he settled back into the seat.

Tess bent down, putting her lips to Mariah's ear, twirling a piece of her long, blond hair through her fingers. "You're in my seat."

Mariah shot Tess a condescending sneer and turned her head, barely acknowledging her presence.

A jolt of red hot molten surged through Tess' veins. *Oh, Hell no!* She bent down to her ear again. "Those thighs you're rubbing and everything in between belong to me now. If you touch his leg again, Mariah, I'm going to break your fucking nose and anything else I can get my hands on."

Mariah sat up straighter, flung her hair over her shoulder and glared at Tess.

Tess pulled back so the girl could see the fiery look in her eyes and understand exactly how serious she was. Mariah didn't budge. Tess leaned back into her ear, "I'm counting to three Mariah, and if you don't move, I swear to God, I'll kick your ass." She stood tall, looked down at Mariah and mouthed, "One."

Mariah glared at Tess and slid out from under her. As the young woman raised to her feet, Tess warned, "Don't bother coming back." Mariah sneered at Tess as if she were insane before slinking away from the table.

Tess collected herself and started to giggle. Benny, Lisa and Tom stared at her with a look of *What the hell did you say to her?*

Tess shrugged innocently. "I just asked her to move. Nicely."

Tom whispered in her ear. "What did you say to her?"

Tess raised her hands up like a boxer. The whole table erupted in laughter.

The look on Toms face. Priceless.

"Tommy, you've got your hands full," Benny teased.

"Hey!" Tess complained, as if he had insulted her.

"That's a good thing, Tess. He needs his hands full. Believe me, it's a compliment."

Tess' confidence boosted to a full-blown ten. As she sipped her martini, the urge to dance overwhelmed her, and she could hardly resist the beat pumping through her veins. A young woman sauntered to the table and leaned over her.

"Hey, Tom. Susan said I should sit with you."

Tom shook his head. "She's mistaken."

The young woman obviously wasn't going anywhere and Tess couldn't threaten every woman in the club. She had sat in her seat long enough. Recognizing the song, she stood up, her body automatically flowing with the rhythm. The poor young woman thought Tess stood up so she could sit by Tom. She was wrong! Tess shot Tom a come-hither look and rolled her ass in an invitation. He followed right behind her, heading for the dance floor.

Tess smoothly rolled her body, lifting her hands above her head and then let them fall to her side. Her hips pumped to the music that had taken over. By the end of the second song, Tom no longer grinned at her. His eyes now fixed on her body. Tess danced on the edge of being provocative, mixing it with a Tahitian flair.

People crowded the dance floor, many of whom scrutinized every move she made, dissecting her piece by piece. Aware of the onlookers, Tess only smiled, knowing she captivated Tom. The DJ mixed a rap song and her rhythm instantly changed, adding a little bounce to her movements. Tom smiled changing his groove to match hers. Tess sang a few of the dirty lyrics and his smile widened across his face.

A slower song started and her movements became smoother and more deliberate. She turned her back to him and his hands followed the curves of her waist and hips. Her heels made her taller, so her ass fit Tom's body perfectly. Their hips swayed together, flowing with the music.

At some point she noticed Benny and Lisa dancing not far from them. Lisa smiled and Tess flashed her ten fingers.

Tom took Tess' hand in his. She let him take control, dancing slowly, squeezing her hip pulling her tightly against him. Before the music stopped, he headed for the door. "There's going to be people out here. Are you ready?"

"Do I look okay?" She glanced down to make sure everything was in the right place.

"You look better than okay. You're everything a woman dreams of being." He kissed her hard before exiting the club.

Photographers lined up outside. Bright flashes popped off, blinding them after being in the dark club and white noise hummed in her ears. Tom held her hand dashing to the car with their heads bowed.

In the limo, Tess couldn't keep her hands off him, wanting him right there and then. She unbuttoned the rest of his shirt, kissing his chest, running her tongue down his abs and trying to unbutton his pants. Taking hold of her hands, he wrapping is lips around hers with such intensity it side tracked her roaming fingers.

"How much longer?" Heat gathered under the material of her dress. She tugged it up to the top of her thighs and straddled his lap.

"We're almost there."

Her head dropped straight back, as she reached behind to unzip her dress. He remained calm, cool and collected as he gently took her hands kissing her again. She frowned realizing this obviously wasn't going to start in the limo.

"Not in here. Not with you." He brought her fingertips to his warm lips.

His words of rejection stung, almost bringing a tear to her eye. "Why not here?"

"Because…." He stammered struggling for words.

"Why not with *me* in here?" she asked again with hurt feeling.

"Because I want to…I have something different in mind." Nuzzling her palm to his cheek, he smiled his crooked grin as they pulled into the driveway. "Not yet Tess."

Tess bit her lip smiling self-consciously, heat turned into madness as she remembered the words he spoke earlier.

"Next time, I promise."

"Damn straight. Next time we are so having great limo sex," she whispered exiting the car.

Tom led her to his bedroom and turned on some soft music. Taking his time, he unzipped her dress, sliding it to the floor. Tom's mouth tasted exceptionally good as he pressed his soft hungry lips to hers, teasing the corner of her lips with his tongue. His palms coasted over her arms as her head fell back allowing his tongue to travel down her neck to her breast. Skimming over her shoulder with his warm parted lips, he asked softly, "Where were we before we left?"

Tom sat on the edge of the bed, maneuvering Tess so she stood between his thighs, clutching her hips firmly with his fingers. She gazed down, taking in every soft line surrounding his dark brown eyes as he stared up at her. His eyes fell away from hers hesitantly as he rested his head against her tummy, only looking up to find them again. "Make love to me Tess," he asked bashfully.

Tears bit the corner of her eyes, and words remained strangled in her throat. Tess tried to speak, but her voice failed her. She had no way to convey the emotions rising in her chest. Bringing her knees up onto the bed, she crawled on top of him and ever so slowly rubbed her nose to his chin. Gazing down at the gorgeous man beneath her, her heart beat violently in her chest. She caressed his jaw and cradled his face in her hands, tenderly stroking his neck and ears with her fingertips. Savoring the martini that lingered on his breath, she possessed his mouth with sensual, wet kisses.

Relinquishing his lips, her eyes and hands wondered over his chest and abs. She dragged her fingers down the muscular chords in her arms, firmly entwining her fingers in his.

Tess hadn't realized until that very moment how much she yearned to bear this part of her soul with Tom. Staring into each other's eyes, they made love together, sharing the intimate bond of their bodies connecting to the rhythm still playing in her head. His dark eyes devoured her, revealing a part of himself she wasn't even sure he knew existed.

CHAPTER SIXTEEN

Tom lay in bed next to Tess with his hands behind his head, looking up at the ceiling. She snuggled up next to him.

"Good morning, Tess."

"Morning. I had a fantastic time."

"I did, too. How'd you learn to dance like that? Every woman in that club wanted to be you last night."

"Every woman wanted to be me because I was going home with you."

"No, that's not why. Jesus, Tess, I can't believe you can move like that."

"The martinis helped. I always dance at home with my kids. Well, not quite like that, but probably close."

Tess attempted to get out of bed, but her body felt stiff and sore. "Oh, shit."

"What's the matter? Do you have a headache?" he taunted.

"No, I didn't drink too much. My body hurts."

"I'll take care of that for you a little later."

"Promise?"

"Yep. I'm impressed by how well you handled yourself last night. You were a natural on the carpet."

"I couldn't hear much of anything when we got out of the limo. It seemed garbled or in slow motion."

"That's somewhat normal." He nodded. "I have a question for you."

"Shoot." She lay in bed, stretching.

"Do you ever get jealous? Because I thought you were going to be pissed at me when you came back from the bathroom with Lisa. I asked Mariah to leave as soon as she sat down."

"I can be jealous, but possessive might be a better word. Mariah's lucky she got up, I think I might have hurt her. Actually, Lisa warned me what it would be like. It helped a lot."

"Speaking of Lisa, she left something for you." He helped her out of bed and gave her a card. It contained twelve single dollar bills and a huge happy face drawn on the card.

> *Positively a twelve, Tess!!!*
> *Thanks for coming last night.*
> *I know we'll see you soon.*
> *If you're missing Tommy and get bored, come visit us. I*
> *mean it!*
> *Most of all, thanks for making Tommy smile.*
> *See you soon sista,*
> *Love, Lisa*
> *P.S. Tommy put my number in your phone, so call me!*

Tess smiled to herself, plopping down on Tom's bed. They talked about the premier, the after party and all of the different people he introduced to her. Tess was curious about something, but uncertain if she wanted to know the answer. "Who is Susan? That woman who wanted to sit with you said Susan sent her over to see you."

Tom narrowed his eyes, shaking his head in anger.

"If I'm not going to like the answer, don't tell me. I shouldn't have asked."

"Susan is my fucking publicist," he seethed. "I'm not happy with her right now. We've worked together for years, and this time she went too far. I don't want to talk about her."

"I forgot, what were we talking about?" she asked innocently.

"I feel like running. Are you up for it? Or are you too sore?"

She could tell he was beyond furious. "I'll go, but can we run outside?"

"As long as you don't mind getting your picture taken."

They drove to the beach and ran on a trail that wound its way up the tops of the cliffs and back. A mile from the car, they took off their shoes to stroll along the ocean, letting the cool water relieve Tess' aching feet from dancing in heels the night before. When they reach the end of the trail, they noticed three photographers. Ignoring the onlookers, they wrapped their arms around each other, staring out over the ocean.

"Better?" she asked quietly.

"Yes, I am."

They went back to his place. Tess helped him get rid of his frustrations and Tom massaged her sore body. They crashed for a couple of hours and it was almost dark when they woke up.

"We have reservations for dinner."

"Great. I'm starving," Tess said with astonishment. "I can't believe how hungry I've been."

Tess actually recognized the restaurant. A famous actor opened it the year before last, and it was supposed to be the big thing in Hollywood. As soon as they pulled up, paparazzi started snapping pictures. The hip, trendy restaurant had an intimate nightclub vibe to it. Tess had already met several of Tom's friends, and they stopped by their table to say hello to him. A producer talked to Tom about an upcoming film he thought Tom would be perfect for.

"Thanks, but I'm taking Tess on an extended vacation when I'm done shooting this next film," Tom replied.

"If you change your mind, Tommy, let me know. I didn't know you ever took a vacation."

"Things have changed."

Driving back to his place, Tess realized it would be their last night together at his house. They wouldn't be able to be as open at her house because of her kids. No more walking around naked. They'd have to be much quieter.

They lay across his bed for a long time talking. Tom gently touched Tess' shoulder and played with her fingers. He stood up and pulled her off the bed to dance with her, but it was unlike previous times they'd danced. He wasn't seducing her. Tom held her close, placing his cheek next to her neck, inhaling the scent of her perfume. Tess got the distinct feeling he wanted to say something, but never did. That night felt entirely different. They made love with a new desire, full of passion, but unhurried or hungry, just slow and deliberate and wonderful.

Tess woke up at four in the morning. Unable to quiet her thoughts, she slipped out of bed, put on her shirt and shorts, grabbed her shoes and quietly headed downstairs for his treadmill. She started off slowly, because her body still ached, but before long she was running from the feelings of anguish that would come when Tom left.

Tess thought about the way they confided in each other. She loved his grin, his confidence, his humor and sarcasm, his generosity, and most of all, the way he made her feel about herself. She felt phenomenal with him, confident, smart, funny and sexy. Tom made her a better woman. *I love everything about him. Holy crap! I'm in love with him.*

She ran harder and faster. How long have I been in love with him? *Why didn't I just admit it days ago, weeks ago?* She'd guarded her heart, protecting herself from heartache. Tess told Tom she trusted him, but did she truly trust him? She wanted to. Tess needed Tom to be faithful and it scared her. Deep in her heart, it seemed as if she knew him so well in such a short amount of time, but would he really stay committed to her? Tess would have no problem being faithful to Tom, but being monogamous might be difficult for him. *Can I really trust him not to hurt me? I have to trust him.*

Tess wouldn't tell him she loved him. Later, not yet. Love was a whole new ball game for Tom and she didn't want to lose him now. Love would be hard enough for Tess to deal with, and she had loved her entire life. *I won't tell him. Not yet.*

She ran for a long time, but suddenly the treadmill quit working. Tess poked and pressed buttons, trying to turn the instrument panel back on. Tom casually stood in the doorway with his arms folded, holding the plug in his hand. She started laughing, but his eyes filled with worry.

"You climbed out of bed over an hour ago, Tess. Do you have something you want to talk to me about or are you going to run until the sun comes up?"

She put on her best lie face. "No, I'm good. I couldn't sleep."

"Um hmm. Really? I think you're full of shit. What's going

on?"

"I couldn't sleep. That's all." She knew he wasn't buying it.

"Did you want me to plug you back in or are you done?"

"I'm done." She tried to be convincing, but Tess sucked at lying.

They went back to bed and he wrapped himself around her. Finally, she slept.

When Tess woke up late in the morning, Tom was in his closet, so she peeked in to see what he was doing.

He was packing.

He'd be leaving straight from Vegas for his film. She smiled immensely at him. *Yep, I'm in love with him.*

"What?" he smiled back.

"Good morning."

"Sleep well this morning?"

"Umm hmm. Are you almost done packing?"

"Almost."

A sense of relief came over Tess and all her anxiousness disappeared, leaving her calm inside. Tom, however, was not calm. She'd never seen him this edgy, squishing his brows together and rubbing his index finger on his chin.

"You seem a little high strung," she teased.

"I am not," he smirked. "Look who's talking. What was the deal this morning? I watched you run for a long time. You were flat out sprinting on the treadmill."

She only laughed and didn't answer. It seemed easier than lying.

A few hours later, they stood against the railing on the balcony, gazing out over the ocean. "Tess, I've liked having you here with me."

"I love it here. I've had an incredible time."

"There are so many places I want to take you. Places I've been and places I've always wanted to travel."

"There are places I'd like to take you, too, but right now, I just want to take you home with me. I'm excited and a little nervous," she admitted.

"I thought it was just me."

"Why are you nervous? Is that why you're so tense?"

"It's not like I go home to meet someone's family every day, Tess. I don't. Ever. I'm anxious to meet John. I know his opinion is important to you, and I don't want it to be an issue for us. It's a big deal to me."

"It might be awkward for all of us at first. I've never done this either. For that matter, neither have my kids. I'm sure it'll be fine." She had no idea how John would react to Tom or how she'd handle having him in the bed she had shared with her husband, but none of that mattered because she was in love with Tom.

"I hate to say it, but it's time to go."

There were no paparazzi to be seen when they boarded the plane for their short flight to Las Vegas. "What's the deal with you and Joey? How does he know where you are all the time?" she asked inquisitively.

"Well, I like him better than most of the others. He's not out to be a jerk and get me pissed off or sell bad pictures of me. I've known him for years and we have a decent working relationship."

"But how does he find you? Does he follow you all the time?"

Tom wore a shitty ass grin on his face. "I know if I give Joey the opportunity to get pictures before anyone else, he'll be decent, like today, and not follow me to the airport. Plus, he'll take flattering shots."

"That's flat out weird. I actually liked most of the pictures he took."

"Good because I put the magazines in my suitcase for your girls. So, is there anything you want to tell me before we get there? Fill me in. Is there anything I should know or do?"

"My, my, my, how the tables have turned. This is a whole new side of you I haven't seen."

"Me either. I'm way out of my comfort zone."

"Just be yourself. Please don't be uncomfortable. Easy, remember, it's supposed to be easy. The girls like you and I'm sure John will, too." She straddled his lap. "I'm crazy about you and I'm positive my kids will like you. If they have a problem with us being together, then it's their problem. Not mine. I'll be happy to explain our relationship, but this is my life, not theirs.

They're my children. You're my partner." She wanted to tell him that she loved him. *Not yet!*

"Partner? I like the sound of that."

"I need you to be self-assured and confident like you always are. Not for my kids, but for me. It will help me through this." She chewed on her cheek, knowing it would be difficult, to say the least, having him in her bed.

CHAPTER SEVENTEEN

As Tess and Tom exited the airport, John welcomed them with a huge smile. He threw his arms around Tess, picking her up to squeeze her and kiss her cheek.

"Hey, Mom! How was your trip?"

"It was outstanding. John, this is Tom."

They shook hands. "Nice to meet you," Tom said.

"Great to meet you, too. So how was the premier? We can't wait to hear about it."

"We had an amazing time."

"I can't believe how tan you guys are. How was Bora Bora? My sisters said you were pretty terrified of the sharks," he said to Tom.

Tess appreciated John's attempt to make conversation with Tom.

"I was petrified because your mom scared the shit out of me. She told me the sharks only attack *occasionally*. It was the craziest thing I've ever experienced, but I loved it."

"That's what I hear. I prefer to keep my feet on the ground more than the water. I don't know if I could do it."

John unlocked the car to put their luggage in the trunk.

"Nice car. I haven't ridden in one of these yet," Tom said to John.

"This isn't my car." John's laugh filtered through the parking garage as he pointed at his mom. "This is her ride. My truck's dirty and covered with mud."

"Nice, Tess. I would've never guessed." Tom smiled, scoping out her new black Camaro.

John threw his mom a questioning glance, waiting for her

response.

"I just went down and bought it one day."

John drove while they caught up. He'd been working hard and playing hard. He rattled on about biking in Utah and all the great trails there. Tom asked him about snowboarding in Utah. That was all it took. They talked non-stop. Tess eased back into the leather seat smiling, hoping it would be this easy for the rest of the night.

Tess' home sat nestled at the base of the mountains surrounding the Las Vegas valley. Pulling into the drive, Tess sighed heavily as anxiety began to set in.

"Your home is beautiful," Tom murmured, taking in details of her home. He stepped out of the car, heading toward the trunk to retrieve their luggage.

John opened Tess' car door and whispered in her ear, "Did he expect you to live at home with your parents like some of his other girlfriends?"

Tess' eyes widened in shock. Glaring back at John, she rumbled through gritted teeth, "John Richard Mathews, you're not funny. Knock it off." She wrinkled her nose at her son who just made her feel all of forty-four years old. *Jerk. It's not like Tom dates women in their twenties. Maybe thirties.*

He mouthed, *"Sorry"* while helping bring in their luggage.

As they entered her home, Tom's eyes casually glanced around, taking in the rich, brown woodwork and walls painted the color of beach sand. Light travertine floors ran through the entire house. Ocean blue pots filled with tropical plants soaked up the desert sun that streamed through the windows.

Tess and Tom strolled out back to find Tracy and JC hanging out by the pool. John followed behind them.

"Hey, Momacita," JC chimed.

"Hi, Tom," both girls chorused as they stood up to give Tess and Tom hugs hello.

Block walls encompassing the property disappeared behind the lush palm trees and flowerbeds surrounding the pool. The entire house and yard was drenched in an island ambiance.

"Holy crap, it's hot. Let's go inside and look at your pictures," Tess suggested. Tom agreed with a nod, noticing a thermometer on the wall reading a sizzling one hundred and eight degrees.

They gathered on the dark, brown, leather sofas topped with colorful pillows and throws, surfing through pictures while her girls recounted their trip. Tracy thanked Tom for his advice about the camera, and he showed her how to use all of her settings. They talked about their vacations, and Tess gave a full detailed report of the premier. All three of the kids asked Tom dozens of questions about Hollywood.

After an hour, her kids went back out to the pool. She took Tom's hand and moseyed to her bedroom to unpack some of her things. She didn't want to even bother unpacking until tomorrow, but needed to hang up her dresses.

Tess' bedroom and bathroom still held slight traces of Richard. She glanced at a picture of her and Richard on the nightstand. She dreaded the idea that Richard was watching her with Tom. Her eyes quickly fell to the floor, evading the photo. She drew in a deep breath of air, B-lining through the bedroom, past the bathroom and into the walk-in closet.

Tom leaned against the dark granite counter in the bathroom while she hung her dresses in her closet. He rattled on about her house, holding a conversation with himself.

Feelings of betrayal began to overwhelm Tess, turning her deep sighs into hyperventilation. She inhaled deeply again, trying to collect enough air to fill her lungs, afraid she might pass out from the lack of oxygen.

"Tess?" he called out tenderly.

She emerged from the closet in tears.

"Come here, Tess." She threw her arms around his waist, holding back sniffles. He wrapped his arms around her, running his fingers through her hair. "Do you want to go for a ride?"

She laid her head on his chest, trying to calm down.

"Tess, if it's easier for you, we can stay someplace else. Or if you'd rather that I go, so you can be alone, I will. I would understand," he offered sweetly.

She pulled her head back in surprise. "Go? No, I don't want you to go. I don't want to be away from you for one night." She bit her lip, asking, "I just said that out loud didn't I?"

"Yes, you did. Tess, I feel the same way. You don't have to hide how you feel. I promise I'm not going to take off. You act like I'm going to bolt out the door running and screaming."

She chuckled through sniffles. "Well, I do worry." The desire to tell him she loved him seemed unbearable. *Not yet.* She lifted her chin, hoping he'd kiss her so the words wouldn't accidentally slip out.

"Do you have a different room you'd like to stay in tonight? You don't have to stress out. We'll do whatever is easiest for you. Okay?"

"Let's go for a drive."

Tom followed behind Tess, rubbing her shoulder as they walked back into her room. He stopped to admire the headboard made from an ornate hand-carved door from Mexico turned on its side. "Did you do all this yourself or do you have a decorator?"

She wiped the smudged mascara from under her eye. "No, I don't have a decorator. I'm too much of a control freak to let anyone else pick things out for me." As soon as the words left her lips, she realized she'd abandoned those idiosyncrasies from the moment they'd met. And oddly enough, it didn't bother her. "Usually, I'm a little neurotic about control issues, but I seem to be living on the edge the last few weeks."

Tom pointed to the photo next to her bed. "Do you mind?" asking if he could pick it up. "Where was this taken at?"

"We were skiing over Christmas at Lake Tahoe two years ago."

"Your son is a splitting-image of him." Tom smiled sweetly. "It's a good photo. You looked good together." He set the picture down, but she picked it up and carried it with her, setting it on a glass top table in the hallway.

She peeked outside. "Hey, we're going to drive through Red Rock. I'll be back in a while and then I'll make dinner."

"Sounds good," John said.

Tess tossed the keys to Tom. "Do you want to drive?"

He tossed them back, flashing her a glance of sexy mischief. "I'd rather see you drive."

She liked to drive fast, but didn't enjoy getting speeding tickets. They cruised through Red Rock scenic loop at the base of the mountains. Tess hadn't hiked there recently, but she'd driven this loop many times over the last year. Huge boulders stacked on top of each other and the clay colored mountains etched with veins of white, yellow, purple and black created a beautiful portrait in the middle of the desert.

Tess stopped at an overlook and they sat on a rock to relax. She told him about the Indian petro glyphs on the rocks, desert tortoises and wild donkeys in the area. She had a relaxed babbling going on as they watched rock climbers off in the distance.

He glanced at her car. "So what's the story behind the Camaro?"

"We always wanted to get an old one to fix up, but never did. A week after Richard died, the day before what was supposed to be our twenty-fifth anniversary, a salesman from the dealership called and left a message on Richards's phone. He had ordered this car, but never got the chance to give it to me. So, I went down that day and picked it up." She smiled. "I actually, really do like it."

"It suits you." They sat on the rock, holding hands when he asked softly, "Do you think you'll ever marry again someday, Tess?"

Tess reeled her head around in sheer shock.

"I was just asking. No. I mean. That's not what I'm asking. I...I was just curious. I didn't mean-"

"I understood what you meant. Sorry. Was the look on my face that horrible?"

"Yep. It was," he said in astonishment. "You always sound so happy and fulfilled with your marriage, more than anyone I've ever known. I'm a little shocked by the *Hell no!* expression on your face."

"I never expected to date again, so it's not something I've even considered." She paused, gathering her composure. "You know, when you're young you think, 'This is what I'm supposed to do. Get married, have kids and life will be perfect'. At least that's what I thought life was going to be. No one warns you about the challenges that lie ahead or how difficult being a parent is going to be. My marriage was great, but it wasn't easy. It takes a lot of work having a family and being on the same page as your spouse. You're a team, but you don't always agree on everything. Now that I've raised my kids, I don't want them to be under the impression life is going to be a fairytale. I want them to go out and be adventurous. I always tell them, 'When the right person comes along, then great, but until then, don't settle.' I've seen a lot of messy divorces that leave deep scars."

"I wasn't asking about your kids and you didn't answer my question."

She shrugged her shoulders poignantly. "I don't know. It's just a piece of paper."

"You sound like me. 'It's just a piece of paper.' I never got past *date* until I met you. I've never even remotely considered the *"M"* word."

She straddled the rock, looking him in the eye. "If you're afraid I'm hearing the ding dong of wedding bells in the future, Tom, you can quit worrying. You can relax." They grinned at each other and kissed. "Your word is all I need. I trust you."

"I trust you, too. Ding dong of wedding bells? That's pretty funny."

She rested her cheek on his shoulder. "I feel better. This was a good idea."

"Let's go."

Tess tossed him the keys.

Tom drove the shit out of her car, pushing it to its limits. He obviously was not concerned about getting a speeding ticket.

"Perfect timing," Tracy said as they walked through the door.

"You didn't have to make dinner. I planned on grilling," Tess said, catching a whiff of sizzling steaks.

"Don't get too excited, Mom. We're just hungry." They all laughed.

Tess opened a bottle of wine and everyone sat down for dinner. It was nice to visit with her kids. Tom was himself, and John even acted pleasant.

"Mom, we're taking off. We're staying over at JC's friend's house tonight," Tracy said.

"You don't have to lea-" she started to say.

"We already had plans. Honest. Did you forget we've been

gone for a month and leave in two weeks for school? I need to catch up with my girls and show them all the hotties we found in Europe," JC chimed.

"Tom, you're not leaving early, are you? We want to see you before you take off," Tracy said.

"I leave late in the afternoon." Tom beamed, noticeably happy by Tracy's comment.

"Oh, good cause I'm leaving, too," John informed as he kissed Tess on the cheek and shook Tom's hand. "I'll be by before work or for lunch, but I'll see you before you take off."

Tom and Tess sat out back and drank a glass of wine, enjoying the city lights and view of the Strip.

After Tess worked up the courage to take him to bed, she led him down the hallway and they entered her bedroom. Her chest felt tight, making it hard to breath. Standing frozen at the foot of her bed, she cringed with embarrassment, wondering if she could go through with it. *For God's sake, Richard's not coming back. This wonderful, amazing man wants to make love to me. In my own home. In my own bed. Yesterdays are gone, but today is standing right here beside me.*

Tom remained understandingly silent, gently clasping her nape, turning slow circles with his thumb. "You okay?"

She nodded and approached the bed, hoping her knees wouldn't buckle before she got there. Sitting on the edge of the bed, she patted the comforter and Tom sat next to her. He reached down and slipped her tennis shoes off before removing his own.

He tugged her toward the center of the bed and they laid side-by-side, staring at each other in the quietness of the dimly lit room. Tucking an arm beneath her neck, his other hand coasted over her spine as he brushed soft kisses across her forehead.

It was after four in the morning when Tess sat straight up in bed. She stared at Tom lying on her bed in the dark in only his shorts. At that moment, she could think of nothing she'd ever desired more. She quietly took off her shorts and T-shirt, snuggling up next to him, kissing his neck to wake him up.

"I think I fell asleep."

"Me too, but I'm awake now."

He slid his hand down her side. "You undressed?"

"Yes." She crossed her leg over his hip, pressing herself against him. He gazed into her eyes inquisitively through the darkness. "I'm with you now, Tom." She unbuttoned his shorts, slipping them off with her toes, kissing him softly, touching his body lovingly. "I've never wanted anyone the way I want you. The way you kiss me and touch me drives me absolutely crazy."

Tom looked as if he wanted to say something, but only kissed her. Finally, after a very long, intimate kiss, he murmured, "I never thought it was possible to feel this way."

The next morning, Tom was out of bed. Tess could hear him in the other room. When she came out, Tom sat on the sofa with her girls, laughing, rolling actually.

"What is so funny this morning?" Tess asked, smiling.

"Oh, nothing!" her girls chimed sarcastically.

"What? Spill it. Come on. What's so funny?"

Tom peered down at the floor, evading her eyes as if trying to hide another chuckle.

JC held a magazine in her hands and turned it so Tess could see a steamy picture of them dancing at the after party. Tracy and JC burst out laughing.

"I happen to like that picture." Tess held her head high, but pink cheeks gave away her embarrassment.

"I bet," Tracy snickered, jumping up to mimic her mom's best dance moves.

Tom's face turned as red as Tess'.

"You! I can't believe you ratted me out. I'll get you back for this." She poked him in the side.

"Hey, I just brought out all of the magazines. It's not my fault they like this picture the best."

All of them laughed until their sides hurt and just as it was almost over, John came in and it started all over again. Even he imitated her dance moves.

"Very funny. Ha, ha, ha." Tess acted mad, but was only teasing.

After the laughter died down, John stood tall and folded his arms across his chest. His demeanor turned blatantly protective. "So, where are you flying today for your film?"

The frank tone of John's voice made Tess flinch.

"Right outside of Germany. It's a war movie, not the typical type of film I do."

"What's it about?" Tracy asked

"I haven't read over the script too much." He smiled, but his creased eyebrows gave him away. Tom didn't want to leave. "I'll be doing a crash course of the script on the airplane."

"So how long will you be gone for?" John questioned in a harsh manner. His eyes narrowed apprehensively, waiting for Tom's reply.

"Several months." Tom's eyes darted uncomfortably between John and Tess. "I've asked your mom to come see me. It would be too distracting at first, but once it starts rolling, it'll work."

"Are you going to go, Mom?" John asked cynically.

"Yes, of course," she replied, glaring at her son who was on the verge of stepping into her personal business.

The mood in the room turned strained. Even Tracy and JC gawked at their brother, surprised by his forwardness.

"So you two are a couple then?" John asked Tom skeptically.

Tom appeared a bit uncomfortable being put on the spot, but grinned at Tess. "Yes. Partner is the word your mom used. I've told her that I don't want to see anyone else. I'm sure that was your next question, John."

"Do you have any more questions? Actually, don't answer that. If you do, you can discuss it with me later. You're out of line," Tess said firmly to John.

Seeming impressed with John for asking, Tom had no hesitation answering his questions. "It's okay, Tess, I understand. Your kids don't want to see you get hurt. I don't have anything to hide. Even though my entire life story appears to be online, most of it is untrue, so if you could keep that in mind, I'd appreciate it," he stated to John.

Tess thought he'd handled that well. Better than she did.

John hesitantly extending his hand toward Tom's. "Sorry, man."

Oddly enough, Tom acted like he completely understood.

"No problem."

"Sorry, Mom." He kissed her cheek. "Hey, man, wanna come check out my bike?"

Tom winked at her, following John to the garage.

"What the fuck was that?" If Tess was mad enough to drop F-bombs, somebody was in trouble.

"We don't know. John's just being protective. He's worried Tom will *crush you like a bug*," JC mocked her brother, pretending to squish a bug with her toe.

Still stunned by the whole confrontation, Tracy whispered, "John looked exactly like Dad when my dates would come pick me up."

The three girls laughed. "You're right! He did," Tess agreed.

Thirty minutes later, John and Tom emerged from their male bonding session in the garage, seeming completely fine together. John had to go back to work. The two men shook hands and John told Tom to have a good trip and hoped he'd see him soon.

"I'll see you when you get home from work," she said.

Tracy and JC headed out the door behind John. "We're going out for lunch. We'll be back before you leave, Tom." Both girls bowed their heads attempting to hide their giggles.

JC whispered to her mom, "You're welcome."

"See you later," Tess said with a flushed face, knowing they were leaving so she and Tom could say their goodbyes in bed.

"I like your kids, Tess. They're funny, nice, polite and very protective. Like a mini version of you. The dancing thing was hysterical this morning. It's refreshing to see how open you are around each other. It's nice."

"I have a good relationship with them. They're good kids. Do you want to go for a swim?"

"Nope." He led her to the bedroom. "I want to talk to you and then I'm going to make love to you again before I have to leave."

They lay across her bed and she told herself, *Don't cry.*

"Tess, I don't want you to think this is goodbye. For the first time in my life, I have no desire to go to work. I want you to come see me, but I won't be able to take days off while we're filming. I'll find fun stuff for you to do while I'm busy."

"You won't need to entertain me, Tom, I can keep busy. It'd be nice to come see you and sleep next to you."

"I've totally blown this job off for the last month. I'm not complaining, I merely want to explain my situation to you. When I get on the plane, I have to go to work and I need to try to concentrate. If I call you and talk to you all the time, it's going to make it extremely difficult for me to focus. I already know I'm going to be a wreck because I don't want to leave you, Tess, but I need to finish this job so we can go have fun."

She understood, nodding her head. Tess had been avoiding this conversation like it was the black plague. She didn't want Tom to leave, but she refused to make him feel bad about having to go to work.

"You have no idea how hard this is for me."

"I do understand." She choked, trying not to cry.

"Look, Tess, I need to know you're not going to be here falling apart. To think I might be hurting you…it's tearing me apart."

"I promise I won't be here crying all day." She smiled. "You have my word, Tom. I'll miss you beyond desperately and I'm not going to tell you I won't cry, but I'll be okay. I'll be busy the next two weeks getting the girls off to school in Colorado."

"Oh, that's right. I forgot. When do you leave?"

"I might leave earlier than I originally planned, maybe next Friday. I'm taking my car so I won't have a lot of room, but I'll go shopping for all the things they'll need when we get there."

"One more thing, Tess. I know you take care of yourself, but-"

Tess raised her eyebrows and giggled.

"I didn't mean physically." He gave her a playful smile. "I meant financially, but if there's anything you need or something I can do for you, will you please tell me?"

"I appreciate the offer, but I don't need anything." A naughty chuckle filtered through the silence of her room. "And just so you know, without a doubt, I will definitely be taking care of myself and I expect the same from you. So when you're lying in bed, remember our first night together in Bora Bora, or the rain storm, or the wall in Greece," she rubbed her cheek against his neck, whispering in his ear, sliding her tongue around his earlobe, "or every time I kiss you like this," she kissed him passionately. "But most importantly, I want you to remember right now." She undid the button of his shorts with her teeth. "I want you to wait for me right now." She looked up at him. "And when we're apart. Wait for me, Tom."

He tried to pull her up toward his lips to kiss her, but she grinned up at him seductively, running her tongue over his skin. "I'll always wait for you, Tess, I promise."

A few hours later, Tess found Tom in the hall studying family photos that adorned the wall.

His eyes filled with admiration. "You have a very beautiful family. You all look so happy." He examined all the photos, stopping to point out an old picture of her and Richard. "How old were you in this one?"

"Twenty-five maybe."

"You're even more beautiful now."

"They're my favorite vacation pictures from over the years."

They kicked back on the couch, teasing each other and being playful. Neither of them heard Tracy and JC standing in the kitchen watching them. Tom noticed them first and smiled, nodding his head as if to say hi. Tess glanced over and for one split second, worried, until she saw their faces. They were giggling. Her girls were happy for her.

They joined Tess and Tom on the sofa like it was no big deal. Her girls didn't seem bothered by the fact he had stayed in their home. Tracy and JC were back to asking him questions about his career, films he had been in, and actors he had worked with. They made him feel comfortable.

"Well, I hate to say this, but it's time for me to go," he announced sadly.

The girls stood to walk them to the car. Tess reached the garage first with JC right behind her, but Tracy pulled Tom off to the side in the hallway.

Tess suspected Tracy was up to something. Minutes later, she observed them as they entered the garage. The girls hugged Tom and said goodbye.

Tom and Tess climbed into the car. As he backed out the driveway, she stared at him and watched his face turn redder by the minute.

"Well?" she asked. "Are you going to tell me what Tracy said that's putting that big smile on your face?"

"She's warming up to me." He shrugged, flashing her an innocent smile. "She even apologized for judging me, and calling me a womanizer, and not liking me."

But then his face smile softened and he dragged his knuckles over his jaw.

"What?" She could've sworn he had tears in his eyes.

Reaching for her hand, he squeezed her fingers. "She thanked me for making you smile." His voice turned hoarse. "Your kids are pretty amazing. You should be really proud of how you've raised them."

The adoration in his voice damn near made her fall apart. Tess suspected not many people would talk to Tom the way her kids had and he respected them for it.

As they parked at the airport, Tess was determined not to break down. "I can't go in, Tom. I don't want to do this in front of people."

He opened her car door and lifted her onto the hood of her car. "I've had the best time. I'm going to miss you, Tess," he said, running his fingers through her hair.

"There are so many things I want to say to you."

Tess learned a year ago that tomorrow isn't written in stone. She yearned to tell him she loved him, but panicked, wondering which scenario she feared more. She could choose *not* to reveal her feelings and risk the one in a billion odds of losing him in a tragic accident, never to see him again. Or, she could gamble, admit her love, and lose him to his own commitment phobias, never for him to *return* again.

Don't say it, Tess. You'll lose him. Don't roll the dice. Don't be scared. Be patient.

"I have so many things I want to tell you, too, but there's not enough time for me to get it all out. I wouldn't even know where to start. We belong together, Tess. Everything happens for a reason, including this. I'm not sure how I could be any fonder of you than I am right now, but as they say, 'Distance makes the heart grow fonder.'" He grinned, tilting her chin up to kiss her lips.

"Your right. We do belong together."

"I've given you something that I've given to no one else."

"What's that?" she asked playfully.

"My heart," he said sincerely. "I'm crazy about you. When I'm done with this job, we're going on vacation. Don't be sad. Let's look forward, okay?"

"I can do that."

"Be good while I'm gone." Tom smirked roguishly.

Tess bit her lip. "I'll be good. You don't have to worry, Tom. I'll wait for you."

Tom embraced her tightly one last time. "My word, Tess. You have my word. I won't disappoint you."

Her heart raced. "I trust you, Tom. You've never disappointed me. Don't forget what I told you in bed today."

"You don't have to remind me. I remember. My favorite was the night you asked me to make love to you. Or it might've been at Benny's house against the wall. I'll replay them in my mind and let you know." He kissed her sensually, tugging on her bottom lip.

They talked across the parking lot while he walked backwards away from her. "Mine was today or maybe the rainstorm. Actually Greece, definitely Greece!"

He flashed her the grin she loved so much.

"Hey, will you please try to save those for me? That one is my favorite."

He smiled even bigger. "I'm never gonna be able to leave you."

Ditching his luggage in the middle of the parking lot, he jogged back and secured her tightly in his arms. She struggled to get closer, wanting this moment to last forever in her memory. The sweet taste of his mouth. The infinite gentleness of his hands as he cradled her face. The spicy scent of his skin. He brushed his nose to hers and walked away.

Tess climbed into the car and watched him disappear through the doors. If they created this many unforgettable moments together in a month, what would the next six months be like with him, or the next year, or the next few years? If her heart held this much love for him now, how would she feel after spending a year together? She couldn't wait to see what was next for them.

Tess was certain that Tom loved her, too. He simply wasn't ready to say it. Love would be hard for him to admit to himself, let alone admit out loud.

Pulling into the driveway, she received a text from him.

"Are you smiling?"

"Yes, I am! No more tears, Tom."

"I miss you already!"

"I miss you, too! Go to work so I can come see you! Call me when you can."

"I needed that. Bye, Tess."

CHAPTER EIGHTEEN

When Tess arrived home, her kids waited on the couch with their supportive faces on.

"Are you okay?" Tracy was the first to ask.

"I'm fantastic."

"Did Tom drug you when he left?" JC asked flippantly.

"Very funny."

"Wow." Seemed to be the only word John could sputter.

"We thought you were going to be a mess." Tracy exhaled in relief.

"So did I, but it won't be long until I see him again. While you're all sitting here ready to take care of me when I fall apart again, I want to tell you something." Tess steadied herself. *No tears!* "I realize how much of a complete wreck I've been for the last year. I should've handled it better when your dad died, but I didn't know how to. Thank you for taking care of me. It should have been the other way around. I love you."

"It's nice to see you smile again," John said.

"Thank God. We thought you were going to be *weeping* for days." JC rolled her eyes.

Tess needed to stay busy. Putting her things away, she examined her closet and decided to gut her side. Richards's things still hung in the closet. Tess hadn't been able to bring herself to get rid of his clothes. She contemplated it now, but she wasn't crying about saying goodbye to Tom and didn't want to cry about Richard either. *I'm through crying.*

For the next week, Tess ran, worked out and spent as much time as she could with her girls. She felt energetic and alive, but dreaded the fact her girls were leaving. The house would be much quieter, and Tess needed to find a project.

Tom texted her almost every night, but when she didn't hear from him, she refused to sit around waiting and wondering. Doubt was a place she would not allow herself to go. *Trust. I need to trust him.*

Tess thought it might be fun to leave for Colorado a few days sooner. Tracy loved the idea and thought it would be good for JC to get her bearings around campus.

Three days went by faster than Tess thought possible. The girls were up early straightening their rooms and getting ready to go. Tess was happy to get the hell out of the house. It would do her good to have some fun with her girls. Colorado couldn't be any more different from Las Vegas, and Tess looked forward to getting out of the heat and into the cooler weather.

The car was packed full and the girls were ready to take off when John finally showed up to see them off.

"Morning," Tess said.

"Hey, Mom," he said quietly. "Where are the girls?"

"We're right here. Are you going to miss us?" They teased, but quickly realized something was wrong. John stood in the kitchen with his fingers clenched tightly into fists, bracing himself against the counter.

"Did you break up with your girlfriend?" Tess questioned.

"Umm, no," he huffed, shaking his head.

"You look terrible. What's going on?" Tracy asked.

"Mom, I need to tell you something," he said hesitantly through pursed lips.

Tess sank down on the sofa. Tears instantly stung her eyes and her hands started to sweat. Tom hadn't called her in two days. "What? Just tell me. What is it?" At first, she thought that Tom had been hurt or died. It was a feeling that crept into her thoughts way too often. *What if I lose him? What if he dies like Richard? Every time she didn't hear from him, she worried she'd never see him again.*

"I don't want to be the one to tell you this, but I don't really have a choice." The dreadful look on John's face told the story. His eyes filled with anger and rage, not pain. John handed Tess a magazine. "I'm sorry, Mom."

Tracy and JC stared in confusion. "What is it?" JC asked.

"This issue just came out today," John informed reluctantly.

Tess unrolled the crumpled pages of the magazine to see a photo of Tom walking through an airport with his arm wrapped around another woman. She could only see the woman's long blond hair, but recognized her immediately.

Mariah.

Tess' hands trembled and her face flushed with anger. Hot tears burned as they slid down her cheeks.

She shook her head, clenching the magazine in her hand. "Fuck!" Snapping her head up from the magazine, Tess saw the distress on her kids faces. Tracy had tears streaming down her face.

At that moment, Tess made a conscious decision not to break down in front of her children. They'd experienced too much pain over the last year. *No way in hell am I going to put my kids through this. Tom Clemmins is my mistake, not theirs. I will not sit here and fall apart in front of them. They will not carry this burden for one second.*

She stood quickly and wiped the tears off her cheek. "We leave in one hour. Be ready to go. If my stupid phone rings, don't answer it." She spoke to all of them, but looked straight at John. "Got it?" She grabbed two waters out of the fridge and was running before she hit the door.

Anger flowed through her veins as she pushed herself harder and faster into a full on sprint. Tess was hurt, confused, and pissed off. Her thoughts spun out of control. *He totally played me. I trusted him and he gave me his word. I was in love with him. I'm so stupid. Urggg. Jerk!*

Ignoring the scorching heat, she ran and ran and ran. How could I be so foolish to think he could truly love me? *I was just a piece of ass to him. A damn good piece of ass. He was so incredible. He was so wonderful to me. How could I have gotten him so wrong?*

She stopped and paced back and forth under a shade tree, going over all the times and places they made love, how he'd made her feel when he kissed her and how they laughed together.

That grin. That stupid fucking grin. She wanted to wipe that grin right off of his face.

Maybe he's like this with every woman he sleeps with. *No way! He couldn't possibly be like that with anyone else! Bullshit. I know he felt the same way. What the hell am I doing? Never again Tess. You will not sleep with him ever again. Never again.*

It was too much for her to comprehend as she stood under a tree, sobbing, gasping for air, trying not to hyperventilate.

What have I done? Pull it together Tess. Your girls are at home waiting for you to be a responsible mother. Not a shit on, fucked over lover.

When she bolted through the door, her kids simply stared at her. None of them had ever seen her this furious. Not once.

"I'll be ready in five minutes."

"Mom, maybe you should wait until tomorrow," John said. "I can take off work if you want me to drive you."

"Nope, I'll be fine. Five minutes."

"Mom, really, we can wait," Tracy agreed.

"Five minutes," she snarled through clenched teeth.

As they headed out the door for Colorado, Tess glanced at John sadly. "I would appreciate it if you would not tell me *I told you so*. Please! Not now! Not tomorrow! Not ever!"

"I would never do that to you," John said sorrowfully.

"I don't have any idea when I'll be home. I love you, John, and I'm sorry you had to give this piece of shit magazine to me."

"Drive careful."

The girls sat quietly in the car. Tess talked to herself as she drove. The fact that Tom would simply throw her away was killing her. She felt used, as if he never really cared about her at all. They'd been driving for three hours when she stopped so her girls could get something to eat. She wasn't even hungry and thought she might get sick. It was a long drive and Tess needed to reach their hotel before she broke down into the tears she locked away in front of her girls. It was all she could do to concentrate enough to drive.

Two hours passed when her phone rang.

It was Tom.

She let it ring.

He called four more times and when the phone rang again, she could see an off ramp coming up in front of her. She answered the phone. "Can you hold on a minute?" She pulled off the highway, parked and stepped out of the car.

"Hello?"

"Hey, Tess, I've been trying to call you."

"I know. I didn't answer."

He was silent.

"What do you want, Tom?" she seethed.

"It's not what you think."

"Now you're going to try to tell me how I should think? You're not that smooth, and I'm sure as hell not that stupid!"

"Tess," he said painfully.

"Don't fucking talk to me like that! It won't work. You did this! Not me."

"Tess, it's not like that."

"Really? How is it, Tom? Let me tell you how it is. My son brought me the magazine this morning. Jesus, Tom, I brought you home with me. I introduced you to my kids."

"I'm not with her, Tess."

She cut him off. "Really? It looks like you're at an airport with your arm wrapped around her. You're not even close to the man I thought you were." She fumed, hoping the insult cut like a knife.

"Tess, will you please listen to-"

"No, I won't. I don't want you to be all charming with me. Why would you do this to me? How can you be so heartless?"

"Please listen to me. Have you even looked at the photo? It's-"

"Did you just ask me if I've looked at the fucking photo? I looked at it! Great shot. Did you call your buddy Joey so he'd take a nice picture of her? I can't even begin to understand how you could hurt me this way. I trusted you. You gave me your fucking word, Tom. Your word is worth nothing. Zero. Zilch! I thought you were as crazy about me as I am about you. You're killing me!" She bawled.

He sounded completely distraught, which made her even more upset. "I *am* crazy about you Tess, the pict-"

"Don't call me again, Tom. It hurts too much."

She hung up on him.

Tess paced around her car in circles. He called back, but she didn't answer. She got back in the car and took off.

Her girls each wore the distinct look of *Oh shit!* across their faces. "I can't believe he'd do this to you. Fucking jerk." Tracy seethed. "I never should've apologized to him."

"What an asshole." JC sniffled. "He's not good enough for you Momma."

Even though they were right, she bit back the urge to defend him. Tess shook her head and wept out a half-disgusted laugh. "So much for dating."

All three of them were torn between an odd mixture of tears and bitter laughter. JC started to share her philosophy of hooking up, swearing that it beat the hell out of having a boyfriend.

Five minutes later, he called back. She pulled off the road again and got out of the car.

"Tess, please! Will you just look at the picture, it's-"

"I cannot believe you're asking me to look at that shit. Maybe I should rip my fucking heart out so you can run it over. You want me to look at the picture?" She left the phone open and set it on the ground in front of her tire. Tess yelled at the phone on the ground. "Are you listening? Because this is what you've done to me, Tom! I hope you're fucking happy! Actually, screw you! I hope you're fucking miserable!" She got in the car, raced the engine, and ran her phone over.

"Do you want me to drive?" Tracy suggested.

"Did you seriously run over your phone?" JC asked in pure shock.

"Yep! *Just look at the picture, Tess*," she mocked. "Fuck him!"

As Tess drove down the highway, her head was a mess. She'd run her phone over and was freaking out, realizing she wouldn't be able to talk to him or even hear his voice. *I'm so pathetic!* Now she was furious with herself for still yearning to hear his voice. She was so hurt and angry, but still wanted him and missed him and loved him. Nevertheless, seeing him again was not an option.

They were an hour from the college when Tracy's phone started chirping. "It's him."

Tess answered the phone. "What do you want?"

"Jesus, Tess, did you really run over your phone? I need to talk to you."

"Yep, I did. You know what, Tracy is awfully fond of her phone and I'd hate to have to run it over, too."

"I need you to listen to me for one minute."

"I can't, the pain I feel right now is more than I can take. I can't believe you would throw us away." She hung up and turned off Tracy's phone.

When she arrived at their hotel, Tess asked for two rooms.

"Mom, why are you getting two rooms?"

"I need to be alone tonight."

Tess lay wide-awake inside her own personal nightmare. *Why didn't he just let me go? Why did he ask me to stay with him, to be his girlfriend and then screw me over? Fucking pussy. So scared of commitment, this is how he handles it. Inner demons my ass, he's chicken shit! He should've just said goodbye.*

Tess' mind was exhausted, her body numb, and her heart damaged. The heartache she endured over the last year almost killed her, and this wasn't going to be any easier. She cried herself to sleep.

The next morning, Tracy arrived at her door with muffins and coffee. Tess was supposed to be having fun with her girls and she was angry at Tom for ruining her time with them. They went shopping and Tess pretended to be much better, but it was only for show. They set up the girl's dorms so they could sleep in their rooms that night.

Back at her hotel, feelings of anger, pain and confusion consumed her. How could she still miss him after what he had done to her? Tess had loved him deeper than she realized.

She drove to the dorms the following morning. "Tracy, do you want to run with me?"

"Mom, I'd love to, but I can't. I have too much to do." Tracy said regretfully. "There's a track and gym on campus you can use."

Tess ran, pushing past her limits, punishing herself for being a fool. She hoped kicking her own ass would make her feel better, but it didn't. She found the campus gym, in hopes of finding a way to pound out her rage. As Tess looked around, she spotted a heavy bag hanging in the corner of the gym. *Perfect. I need something to beat the shit out of.*

Tess hit the bag, kicked it, kneed it and punched it again and again until her hands were numb and sweat ran down her body. She was furious at Tom for hurting her, and even more livid with herself for trusting him and allowing herself to fall in love.

Her mind and body were completely worn out. Tess headed to her car to drive back to her hotel so she could shower and crash before taking the girls to dinner. People glanced at her strangely as they walked past. She must've looked like a complete disaster.

She reached for the car door.

"Tess," Tom said in his slow, deep voice that made her stomach lurch.

Enraged that he would still use that tone on her, Tess spun around to see Tom leaning against a tree next to her car. He wore dark sunglasses that hid his eyes from hers. *Chicken shit can't even look me in the eye.* Anger rocketed through her core.

"Don't say my name like that anymore. What are you doing here?" she snarled at him. "What do you want from me?"

"We need to talk." He stepped toward her, but she pulled away from him. Tom looked devastated by her reaction and reached out to touch her again.

Tess backed away, shaking her head. "Don't you fucking touch me." Her lip quivered as she growled.

Tom's face drained of color as he raised his hands and stepped back a half a step.

"How long have you been here waiting for me?"

"I don't know. Hours. Can we please go for a drive? People have been coming up to me since I got here, and I can't deal with that shit right now. I need to talk to you. Alone."

Through broken sobs Tess choked, "I don't want to go with you. I don't trust myself and I sure as hell don't trust you."

"I only want to explain. Please. I promise I won't try to touch you." He sounded sickened by his own words.

She couldn't bear the tenderness in his voice or her aching need to feel his arms around her. Adrenaline sizzled through her veins and her chest heaved up and down. She began pacing with heel-digging strides.

Hesitantly, he stepped toward her and held his hand out asking for the keys.

Before she realized what she had done, she was sitting in the passenger seat.

Tom drove as they sat in silence.

"Tess, it's not what you think. The picture isn't real."

"Again with the fucking picture! Why don't you just pull it up on your cell phone so you can rub it in my face? I told you in Greece, if you change your mind and want to see other women, then tell me. You didn't have enough respect for me to tell me first!"

"Tess, stop and listen to me."

"No, maybe you should listen to me. I would've let you go, but you asked me to be your girlfriend. I wouldn't have chased after you. It might have killed me, but I would've let you go. You gave up on us after one week. One fucking week. The photo looks damn real to me!"

"Will you just look at the magazine, maybe-"

"No, I won't."

Tom's phone rang, and he handed it to her. "It's for you."

Tess could hear Tracy on the line. "Tom, she's really pissed, you-"

"It's me, Tracy."

"Oh. I heard kids saying they saw Tom on campus. I wanted to warn him you're upset. Are you okay?"

"We're going for a drive. I'll call you in a while." Tess looked at Tom and her heart beat faster, fueling her with rage. She didn't want to be attracted to him. She didn't want to be in love him.

"Wait, Mom! I need to tell you something. John left a message on my phone."

"What's wrong with him?"

"Tom went to our house two days ago, and...well... John kind of kicked his ass."

"What did you just say?" Tess asked in shock.

"Well, actually it wasn't a fight, Tom wouldn't hit him back. John's message said you need to listen to Tom."

"Great, just great! I'll call you or find you later."

No wonder he looks like shit. Her fingers trembled, afraid to touch him because she still wanted him so badly. She carefully reached over and lifted Tom's sunglasses off his face, revealing a huge black eye.

"I've been dreaming of doing that for two nights," she snarled, shaking her head in disgust.

"Very funny, Tess. Are you going to let me explain?"

"What we had was special. Something *you* just wouldn't understand. How could you even want to be with her? She's nothing but an irritating, play-toy."

He tried to talk, but she cried harder now.

"You know, Tom, I made my husband deliriously happy for twenty-five years, twenty-five long years, and you can simply throw me away-"

Tom jabbed himself in the chest with his finger. "*I* understand *exactly* what we have together. More than you realize." His voice raised, full of pain and anger. "And don't you *dare* compare me to your husband."

"There is no comparison," she snapped.

Toms face fell heartbroken as the words left her lips. They had come out different than intended, and Tess colored with shame, watching Tom turn ashen white.

"I was better with you. You don't fucking get it, do you? If I made him incredibly happy for twenty-five years, I sure as hell know I could make you happy because I was better with you! You made me a better woman! You brought things out in me I didn't know existed. I'm different with you. I didn't think that was possible. You let me go. For her? You've got to be fucking kidding me. You're a fool."

"Are you going to be quiet now?" Tom asked rudely, almost yelling at her. "Tess, I'm begging you, look at the damn picture. I haven't thrown you away. I didn't do anything wrong." He tried to hand her the magazine again, but she refused to touch him or look at the picture. He reached for her hand, but she yanked it away.

The pain in his eyes made her stop resisting. He held her hand, but she stared straight ahead with tears streaming down her face. Tom tried to kiss her and she turned her head. "I want to kiss you so badly, but I can't."

"Damn it, Tess, I wasn't with her. Yes, I was in the picture with her. Yes, the picture is real! The fucking picture is old."

"What? Oh bullshit! You really expect me to believe that shit? How gullible do you think I am?"

"If you were quiet for one fucking minute, I could've explained this to you two days ago." He held up the magazine in front of her face, poking it with his finger. "Do I look familiar to you in this picture?" He sneered through gritted teeth.

"I don't understand." She sniveled, frowning through wet lashes.

"Jesus, Tess. Look how white I am in this picture. Look at me. Tess…look at me. I'm as dark as you are. I've been trying to tell you for three damn days. The picture is old," Tom explained, his voice full of hurt and angry sarcasm. "Did I look like this the first time you saw me? Do you even remember the first time you saw me? Because I remember everything about you, from the very first moment I saw your beautiful blue eyes at check-in. I know exactly what you were wearing, the curve of your lip when you smiled at me, and how you wore your hair that day." He asked indignantly, "Do you remember what I looked like at that moment? Hmmm? Do you, Tess?"

"I remember everything about you!" she cried out, sobbing. She knew exactly what he looked like that day in Bora Bora. Dark straight jeans, a white shirt and flip-flops. Tess gasped staring at the magazine. She turned her head, staring at Tom and how tan he still looked. He wasn't tan at all in the picture. Tess realized instantaneously that the photo had been taken the day he left for Bora Bora over a month ago.

"I tried to tell you, but you ran your phone over," he said painfully.

"I think I might be sick." Everything started to spin. Tom rolled the windows down. "I don't understand. Why did you let them put this picture in this magazine then? Who fucking did this?"

"I sure as hell didn't do it! I would never hurt you. My publicist, or I should say my former publicist, purposely released the picture out without telling me."

"I think I'm going to puke."

"I'm almost there, Tess. Two minutes, can you wait?"

"Where are we?" she asked. "Why would anyone do this to you? Tom, you really haven't been with her?"

"No, I haven't. I wouldn't do that to you. To us."

"I'm so sorry." She began bawling. "I feel like I've been dying for three days." Her hands covered her face. "I'm such an idiot."

"Yeah, well, I feel like I got the shit beat out of me. Oh, that's right, I did." He smirked. The car stopped and Tom opened her door. "Tess, you're breaking my heart. Can I please touch you now?" She nodded her head. He wrapped his arms around her, embracing her shivering body. "You're a mess. Come on."

"Where are we?"

"This is my cabin. Let's go inside."

She sat on a bench on the porch while he found a hidden key.

"Are you feeling better? You're not going to throw up are you?"

"I'm not sure. I think I need to eat." She trembled. "I really thought you were with her. I felt so used. I've been really pissed at you," she snarled.

"I'm sorry. I know I hurt you, but I haven't done anything wrong. I could never be cruel to you. I was already on my way back to see you when all this shit happened."

"What do you mean on your way back?"

"We need to talk, but I need you coherent and you look like you might pass out." He led her upstairs to his room.

"Did you just buy this place? Why don't you have any furniture?" she asked deliriously.

"Take a shower, you'll feel better. Jesus, what the hell have you been doing to yourself?" he questioned sadly. "Running for three days? You're all sweaty and salty." He touched the dry salty residue on her collarbone.

She sniffled and nodded.

"You look like you've been in a fight." Tom glanced down at her red swollen hands, one knuckle split open and bleeding. "Please tell me you didn't lose your temper and hit a door or wall."

Tess rolled her eyes. "Just a heavy bag I found at the campus."

"Get in the shower. I'll see what I can find you to eat. Do you want me to text your kids to let them know where you are?"

"Yes. Did John really do that to you?" She cringed.

"Yeah, he did. Get in, you'll feel better."

She sat on the shower floor, crying as the hot water rained down over her. Everything she'd said to him replayed through her mind. Tess didn't want to lose him. She loved Tom. After she saw the picture, she was glad she hadn't told him she loved him, but now it was all she wanted to do.

Tom made her some pasta. They sat on his bed, which was the only thing in his room, and ate. Emotionally drained, she lay back on the bed and passed out.

Tess could hear the rain on the tin roof during the night and it was still raining when she woke before sunrise. When she opened her eyes, Tom lay on his side, staring at her through a big purple and yellow shiner.

She gently touched the dark bruise surrounding his eye. "What happened with John? I can't believe he hit you."

"Believe it. I assumed you'd be home when I knocked on the door. I hadn't realized you'd left early for Colorado. John was so furious when he answered the door, I couldn't even get three words out of my mouth. I think he has your temperament. Thank God Lisa jumped out of the car and started yelling at him. Once John saw Lisa, he stopped instantly. I'd probably look a whole lot worse if she hadn't been there."

"I don't have a bad temper, but my kids have never seen me that furious. John showed me the magazine, Tom." She paused as heat rose to her face. "That's the second time my son has had to deliver the worst news of my life to me." Her lip quivered as she remembered the moment John told her Richard had died. Each time she remembered that instant in the hospital, all of the air drained from her lungs. Tess could almost taste the antiseptic odor of the hospital that still made her queasy.

Tom's dark eyes filled with sorrow. "I didn't know. I'm so sorry, Tess."

She sniffled, waiting for her breath to catch. "Did he let you explain? Are you two okay now? Why was Lisa there?"

"It's a long story. Yes, we're fine now. John felt horrible when he realized I hadn't cheated on you. He tried to call you, but you ran your phone over and Tracy's phone was turned off."

"Sorry he hit you."

"I'm the one who needs to apologize. Susan, my publicist, totally screwed me over with the picture. She was pissed that I wanted to go on an isolated vacation, and sending Mariah back the first day didn't make her any happier. When I told her I was bringing you home with me, she went ballistic. She tried to convince me it would be the most ridiculous, career-crushing mistake of my life, blah, blah, blah... I didn't care what she thought, so I started handling things the way I wanted them handled."

"You mean with Joey and all the pictures of us?" she asked. "The premier?"

"I wasn't going to hide you. I want to be with you. I'm proud to have you with me and I don't care that you're not famous. It doesn't matter to me."

"Wait. Did you just say you sent Mariah home the first day you were in Bora Bora?" Tess asked suspiciously.

"Shit," Tom muttered. "Okay, I have to tell you the truth. I was never going to admit this, but I have lied to you. I stole your tour on purpose so I could meet you."

"I knew it, you little thief!" she said with satisfaction, but then puzzlement. "What do you mean, so you could meet me?"

"Tess, when I turned around and saw you in the lobby during check-in, you were so beautiful in your blue dress, and the smile you gave me totally sent me over the edge. You were kind of shy and blushing. I had goose bumps all over. I couldn't even talk straight. That *never* happens to me," Tom said softly. "I sent Mariah home the next day and moved to the resort you and I stayed at the very first night I arrived. I never should've let her off the plane."

"I could've told you that at check-in."

"After I 'threw her overboard' I went down to…*steal your tour*…as you like to put it. I asked about you, and they said you were vacationing alone. I am truly sorry I intruded on your time with Richard. I felt awful, but was captivated by you and only wanted to make you feel better."

"Actually, you made me feel better, and I'm glad you were there."

"You got so furious with me for going on the boat with you. You didn't care who I was." He paused for a minute. "That's one of the things I love about you. You liked me for me, not for my name or my money or my career. You didn't care about any of that." He caressed her. "Tess, I want to make love to you, but I need to know, are we okay now?"

She sat on top of him and kissed his bruised eye. "I'm not mad anymore. I feel horrible about everything I said to you. I should've let you explain."

"I don't want to fight with you. Ever. Not like this. Not at all." Tom rolled her onto her back, his eyes were drenched in hurt and anger. "I don't want you to compare me with Richard again. That really irked me."

Her lip quivered. "I wasn't comparing you to him. I wanted to throw it in your face that I'm more passionate with you and you were really, really going to miss me. It was going to destroy me not to be with you, and I wanted you to realize exactly how miserable you'd be without me," she said softly. "I know that we have something special together and it hurt me to think you'd let me go so easily."

"It doesn't bother me when you talk about Richard. I think it's nice you feel comfortable enough to share things about him without it being awkward." Then he said sincerely, "I have no doubt you could make me happy for twenty-five years."

Rain tapped on the window as Tess lay wrapped in a blanket on the couch while he lit a fire in the big stone fireplace. "Why were you on your way here, Tom? Aren't you supposed to be at work?"

He smiled at her from across the room. "I'm not doing the film, Tess. I was there three days and was worthless. And to make it worse, I didn't care who they got to replace me, or what it cost me, or who I pissed off. I only wanted to be with you. I knew you were coming to Colorado to drop your girls off. I had a plan to surprise you, but the whole thing fell apart when the magazine came out."

"Did they find someone to replace you?"

"Benny. He's wanted to take on a more serious role and he offered to do it. The producers were happy, he was happy and I'm deliriously happy." Tom paused for a minute. "To tell you the truth, I think he might've taken the role just for me. Benny knows how much I want to be with you. They're happy for me."

"You don't have to go back to work?"

"Nope. I'm taking time off with you."

She grinned, but raised her eyebrows in question.

"Yes?" he asked.

"Trust me, I want nothing more than to spend time together, but the last thing I want to do is interfere with your career. I know you love what you do and I don't want you to give anything up for me."

"I'm not giving anything up, Tess. If I never want to work again, I don't have to. I simply need time off, I don't know how long, a year, two years, I don't know."

"No regrets?"

"Not one regret. This is undoubtedly the best decision I've ever made."

CHAPTER NINETEEN

Tess and Tom drove back to the girls campus to say goodbye. She checked-out of her hotel and headed back to his cabin.

"Did you buy this place recently?"

"No, I bought it two years ago. I haven't been able to get back here again."

"Seriously? That's terrible Tom. I can't believe you have this beautiful cabin and don't come here." His traditional log cabin came complete with a river rock fireplace and a wraparound porch with black wrought iron hand railing. The gorgeous interior had so much potential, but sat bare and naked with only a couch and tiny table sitting in the huge dining room.

"I was here skiing over Christmas and met a man on the lifts who needed to sell this place, so I bought it." They pulled into the driveway and he pointed to an area in the trees. "In the winter we can cut through a trail right over there and you're on the slopes."

"It's ski-in and ski-out?"

"Yep."

Tom opened the door and put their things on the kitchen counter. He inhaled heavily dragging his fingers over the stubble on his face. Tess grimaced wondering what could possibly be wrong.

"Tess, can you sit down for a minute?" he asked, nervously holding his hand out toward a bench on the porch.

"What's wrong?"

"Nothing is wrong. I have something for you."

"Okay," she replied hesitantly, taking notice of a box Tom held in his hand.

He opened the box, revealing a key inside.

She smiled with bewilderment. "What's the key for?"

"This cabin. I don't want to be without you. Not now, not in a year, not ever. I've stayed here one time, by myself, alone. I want this to be our place."

A surprised smile crossed her lips. "You do?"

He tucked her hair behind her ear. "I do."

"What about my house? I love my house." She was ecstatic, but couldn't wrap her head around what he'd just said.

"No, Tess, you'd keep your house. I still have my house in Malibu and I have another one also. I want to be with you all the time." He played with the key. "I bought this place on a whim. It felt like home as soon as I stepped through the front door, but after I left, I had no desire to get back here. I knew buying it wasn't a mistake, I just didn't feel compelled to come back and dive into it. Now, I know why. We can go wherever we want, here, Malibu, or Vegas, but this is supposed to be our home. So, I have this key for you. I want this to be ours, Tess. Officially. On paper."

"What do you mean? Officially?"

"I want to give you half of this cabin, legitimately. Don't say no simply because I'm trying to give you something monetary. It would hurt my feelings. If you don't want to live together then I'll understand. Not really, but I'd try to understand. I want this to be a commitment. It's something I've never made to another woman, Tess, *a commitment*." He smiled his crooked grin, attempting to charm her.

Tess sat on the bench overjoyed, staring at him, looking slightly bemused.

"I love you, Tess." He pulled her to her feet and held her hands in his as he gazed into her eyes. "I love you. I have been crazy about you since the moment I first saw you. I've been struggling to tell you for a while. It tore me apart to leave you. Life is short, and I want to share mine with you. Just you. I don't want you to be with another man, Tess. Just me."

Tess beamed. "I love you, too. I almost told you at the airport, but I was afraid you'd leave and never come back. I don't want anyone else, Tom. I only want to make you happy."

"You make me happier than I ever thought possible. I love everything about you."

Tess understood how difficult this was for Tom. She was thrilled, happy, and excited but he was beyond that and more. This was a first for him.

"So is that a yes?" he asked.

"Of course it's a yes! I love you. I want to live with you, but I don't legitimately want half of your cabin, Tom."

"That's the deal, Tess. Take it or leave it. Partners, remember?"

"Partners...Okay, deal, but I'm not really comfortable with it. I don't love you because of all of this." She looked around the cabin. "None of this matters to me. I'm not going to lie, I've had a ton of fun, but I love you no matter what you have."

"I already know, Tess. You don't have to tell me." He smiled at her. "You can decorate the whole cabin, or we could do it together."

"Together. I like that."

"It has six rooms, so your kids can come here whenever they want. We could all spend Christmas here together," Tom suggested with a lot of enthusiasm, but then quickly backtracked, appearing as if he might've crossed an unseen line. "Well, I mean, do you think we could all spend Christmas together? You can spend it with your kids if you'd rather."

"Tom, I'm going to be with you for Christmas. Thanksgiving and New Year's Eve too. If we're going to be a couple, then I don't want to lead separate lives. That won't work for me." She waited for him to let out a big heavy sigh but he only smiled. "Are you sure you're ready for all this? I come with a family."

"What do you mean exactly?" he asked with hesitation.

Tess giggled at his response. "My kids are my family, and if you and I are a couple, you're part of that family too. I can already tell they like you, even John. So holidays, college graduations, weddings, you get to share in all those family traditions with your girlfriend. Are you ready for all that? I come with a few...accessories."

He acted as if he were mulling it over, tilting his head from side to side as he led her upstairs. "Yep, I'm sure."

"You said you stayed here for Christmas two years ago. What do you usually do for the holidays?" she asked curiously.

He stopped and chewed on his lip furrowing his brow. "Truthfully, I spend Christmas alone. I usually drink too much, wherever I am, and try to figure out what the hell is wrong with me and why I don't have someone special in my life. It's actually somewhat pathetic." Tom chuckled, trying to make light of his situation.

"Not any more, Tom. Christmas is my favorite holiday and this is going to be our first together. I promise, you won't be wondering, *What the hell am I doing?*" Tess laughed. "You'll probably wonder, *What the hell have I gotten myself into?* I guarantee you're still going to drink too much, but happily. How about martinis?"

"I love you, Tess."

"Do you think Benny and Lisa would come here for Christmas?"

"Maybe! That would be a good time. I texted both of them to tell them we're fine, but I'm sure Lisa might want to talk to you soon. She seemed very impressed with your determination to ignore me, and had you been standing in front of her, she might've actually high-fived you for running over your phone."

Tom looked around at the empty cabin. "So, Tess. Do you want to stay *home* and decorate this place or would you like to go back to Greece first?" He grinned saying the word home.

"Those are some incredibly tough decisions you're asking me to make." She put her arm around his waist examining the cabin. "You do realize you're spoiling me?"

"I like spoiling you. Right now I know you're tripping out because I'm being generous to you, aren't you?"

She exhaled heavily and smiled. "Maybe. It makes me feel like I'm taking advantage of you. I do struggle with the whole money issue. I love that you're so good to me, but I feel awkward about it. I'm used to taking care of myself."

"Starting now, you need to get used to it. I know you're not taking advantage of me. I want to give you things and I just want you to enjoy them. Do you remember when you told me your theory? Give some, save a lot and have fun with the rest, you can't take it with you."

"Yes, that is my theory."

"I happen to agree with you. Tess, I've saved a lot, for a long time. You need to get over those feelings and simply say 'thanks' or 'great' or 'that sounds perfect'. It would make me happy."

"Thanks, great, that sounds perfect."

"Now let me start spoiling you. Pick one. Greece or the cabin?"

"Can we stay here until Thanksgiving, then go to Greece?"

"We can fly there, eat dinner and come back if you want. We can do whatever your little heart desires."

Tess glowed. "Well, I don't know about dinner, but there's this great little Inn I'd like to go back to."

"Let's do it and be home in time for Christmas."

A few hours later, Tom and Tess pulled into the first shop in the quaint mountain town near their cabin. Equipped with pictures and a tape measure, they set out to furnish their home.

Tess asked, "So what's our budget?"

"We don't have a budget. Let's just get what we want." Tom shrugged nonchalantly.

"I'm better with a budget. It's a big cabin," she sputtered.

He whispered a number in her ear with way too many zeroes at the end of it. "Whatever it takes, Tess. It doesn't matter."

Her mouth hung open and her eyes blinked in astonishment. "Are you serious?"

"Yep! Dead serious. I told you, I've saved all my life and I'm very good with my finances. Wipe that look off your face and let's go shopping."

The cabin was coming together nicely. They decorated each room with elegant, rustic furnishings and ordered the dining table and leather couches. Several other pieces that would be waiting for them when they returned from Greece. Tess wanted to repaint one of the bedrooms. If Benny and Lisa came to stay over Christmas, it would be their room, and the lovely hunter green walls needed to go.

Tom had wanted to hire someone to come and paint, but she assured him it would be more enjoyable to do it themselves. Tess quietly slipped out of bed, prepped the room with plastic and taped off the trim. She rocked out to the music playing on her Ipod, soon sensing Tom's lingering eyes. *Game on! I knew he'd help me paint.* After several minutes she said, "Good morning, Tom."

Holding out his hand for a paintbrush, he scanned the length of her body. Tess wore nothing but her unbuttoned flannel shirt, revealing her bare breasts. She had a roller in her hand, but he pushed it off to one side and wrapped his arm around her waist to kiss her.

"Is this how you always paint?" He slowly examined her body.

"Nope!" She grinned.

"We're not going to get much painting done!" he chuckled, flicking her nipple with his tongue.

"Really? I thought we'd get it done faster." Tess pulled her shirt to the side to expose her other nipple, not wanting it to miss out.

Halfway through painting the second wall, Tom was distracted, watching her dance and sing to the music. He stood behind her and said in her ear, "Tess, you've got paint all over your back."

She glanced over her shoulder. "I do?"

Tom pinned her back to the wall, kissing her passionately as he eagerly fondled her body. "You do now."

Before Tess could get one word out of her mouth, he had her shirt off, covering her bare back with wet paint.

"Wait, let's finish painting first," she said under his lips.

"I don't think so." He drew her thigh up around his hip, pulling his face back to look at hers. "You don't really want me to stop, do you?"

She giggled. "No, I don't."

He made love to her right there up against the wall. Paint covered his hands as well as her back and butt, changing the tips of her hair to creamy white. They both burst out laughing as they tiptoed into the shower.

"Are you sure this isn't how you paint all the time?" he teased her curiously.

"No, this is definitely a first!"

"I love firsts with you, Tess."

CHAPTER TWENTY

Tess and Tom had spent October and November settling into the cabin and their new relationship. Thanksgiving was a week away, and Tom was expected in Malibu. He and every other A-list actor were invited to attend the fiftieth birthday party of Hollywood's top movie director.

Upon arriving in Malibu, Tess suddenly realized she was home and smiled from ear-to-ear.

"What?" Tom asked.

"It just dawned on me, I live here with you! Can I go unpack and hang my stuff in the closet?"

"Yes, you can, but I have to warn you, I have a bit of OCD with my closet. Well, I guess it's our closet now. This could be difficult for me." He said it jokingly, but she knew he was serious. His closet was as big as a bedroom and everything in it hung perfectly organized, color coded and sorted.

"I'm not that...particular. If it makes you feel better, I can take a different closet or I can even let you organize my clothes for a while."

They both laughed. "I know it's ridiculous, but it might help me adjust."

She poured them each a glass of wine while Tom made room for her clothes and helped put her things away. She didn't mind. Whatever made it easier.

"Are you going to be the same way with the bathroom? Or can I put my own things away in there?" she teased.

He smirked with embarrassment. "No, you can do whatever you want in there, smartass."

Tom went to pour another glass of wine. When he returned,

her clothes lay scattered on the closet floor and Tess was wearing his tie. Only his tie.

"That happens to be my favorite tie." His eyes slowly drifted up her body.

"Hmm, it's my favorite, too. I'm hoping you might find a new appreciation for it."

"Oh, I think I can." He set the wine on the bathroom counter, took her hand, and headed for the bedroom.

"I had something different in mind." Tess sauntered back into the closet.

"I don't think so." He stopping at the closet door.

She sat down, flipping one leg over a bench in the center of the closet. "Oh, I know so."

"Tess."

"Tom, if you want me, you'll have to come in here to have me." She leaned back on the palms of her hands, exposing every inch of her body.

He gave her the crooked grin she loved and strolled over to sit on the bench. She took his shirt off and tossed it on the closet floor.

"That doesn't bother me, Tess."

She took off his jeans and threw them on the floor, too.

"Okay, I lied. It bothers me."

They straddled the bench, facing each other. "Am I going to need to do this every day so I don't have to keep your closet perfect?"

He swallowed hard. "I promise I won't be upset if you don't keep your side perfect."

"I promise I will try to be neat in our closet." She climbed onto his lap.

"Can we go in the bedroom now?"

"Nope. Right here. Right now." She made love to him right there on the bench.

As they headed for bed, Tom confessed, "Tess, I love the way you get your point across."

His tie still hung around her neck. She smiled as her eyes closed. "My side won't be quite as perfect as yours, but I'm definitely willing to compromise."

Tom took Tess shopping to get a dress for the party. People recognized him everywhere they went, and paparazzi followed him relentlessly. At times, she felt similar to a fish in a fishbowl. In Colorado, people were much more laid back, and nobody seemed to care who he was, but in the land of the lifestyles of the rich and famous, everyone was watching.

That night, limos lined the drive as they pulled up to the house. Tess chuckled nervously, turning to glare at Tom.

"What?" he asked innocently.

"This is *not* a house. This is a *mansion*. It looks more like a resort, or a spendy re-hab facility."

"Judging by the guest list, you probably nailed it on the head with re-hab facility." They both laughed. "Trust me, Tess, you're going to have a great time."

She shot him a humorous glance of disbelief.

Entering the ostentatious foyer, many faces looked familiar as her eyes scanned over the crowd of several hundred people. Guests dressed in everything from cocktail dresses to birthday suits. Tess exuded modern elegance in a slinky, one-shouldered black dress, and Tom looked outrageously sexy in jeans and a charcoal grey V-neck sweater. She wondered how long she'd be able to keep her hands off him. She grinned to herself. *We are definitely having great limo sex on the ride home.*

People loved Tom. Women followed him everywhere. For that matter, so did men. They all needed to touch him when they spoke, placing their hand on his arm or shoulder. Some turned red merely saying hello. Tess became acutely aware of people watching their every move. Tom loved introducing her as his girlfriend and Tess smiled proudly, standing by his side.

Weaving their way through the sea of partygoers, he led her through the house to the backyard. Tess mingled outside while Tom went to the bar to get drinks. The merrymaking obviously started much earlier because a number of guests were very intoxicated. Several men introduced themselves, but as soon as 'Tom Clemmins' girlfriend' slipped her lips, they miraculously disappeared quickly.

Two men approached Tess. She made polite conversation,

but fidgeted uncomfortably at their audacious leering. She scanned the room again, searching for Tom, and jumped when he laid his hand on her bare shoulder, handing her a drink. Judging by the concern in his eyes, he recognized her uneasiness and pulled her close, kissing her cheek. Tom knew both men, and by his greeting, didn't care for either.

Both men snickered when Tom introduced Tess as his girlfriend. "Tommy, when you're done with her, give her my number."

Tom remained unruffled. "You're drunk. Maybe you should get a ride home."

She couldn't hear their response because Tom's arm cinched around her waist, walking her away abruptly. "Sorry, Tess. The guy is a jerk whether he's drunk or not."

They found a spot under a pergola. They were having a good time hanging out with a comedian and his wife and several other couples. The comedian was hysterical. Tess laughed so hard she needed to find a bathroom. She excused herself and told Tom she'd be right back.

Exiting the restroom, the two men who'd hit on her earlier stood in the hall, waiting for the bathroom. Tess tried to walk past, but one guy stepped directly in front of her and stretched out his arm, placing his hand against the wall so she couldn't pass by.

The man towered over Tess, even in her high-heels. Cocking his head from side-to-side disdainfully, he brazenly gawked at her boobs. Slumping his head, nearly resting it on her bare shoulder, he mumbled something. She could only make out the words *lucky bastard* through his garbled speech. Tess flinched with alarm. He was too close. Close enough that the heat from his alcohol saturated breath rustled her hair. Her lip curled in disgust.

"The bathroom is open now." She stood taller, raising her hands and gesturing for him to move so she could pass by.

He continued talking shit, slurring his words. "Tommy won't last long. Why don't you come home with me tonight instead? He's probably outside hooking up with some other chick as we speak. Tommy Clemmins *girlfriend*. What a fucking joke!"

Annoyed and unappreciative of the way his eyes blatantly examined her body, Tess attempted to maneuver around him.

"Tom's waiting for me," she seethed.

He cut her off again, blocking her exit. Tess felt cornered, causing her heart to race as panic started to build.

He tapped the center of her chest with his pointer finger. "Maybe you should join me?" Roughly clasping her boob, he belligerently pinched her nipple.

Tess winced in pain as he twisted, automatically slapping his hand off her chest. He grabbed her by the wrist, his face inches away from hers. Frightened by his crazed sneer, she cringed away from his lips so he couldn't kiss her.

Tess squirmed back and forth to loosen his grip. Through gritted teeth she snarled, "Tom's waiting for me. Get your fucking hand off me. Now!" Adrenaline coursed through her veins, causing her to break out into a sweat.

"You don't need him. I'll take care of you, baby." He squeezed her wrist, dragging her toward the bathroom. Tess thrashed about, yanking her arm violently, trying to get free of his grip, but he was too strong. She struggled, digging her heel into his foot, but gained no ground.

Tess could hear his friends' voice in the background as he laughed, making rude remarks about Tom. She moved into a position to kick her attacker between the legs, but feared losing her footing. The bathroom door seemed three seconds away as he forcefully dragged her by the wrist, laughing with a horrid grin on his face. Nothing she did worked and they inched closer to the door.

Panicking, she slapped him as hard as she could across the face with her free hand, but it didn't even faze him. It only pissed him off more. He slammed her back against the wall, thrusting his entire body against hers as he growled, "Bitch!"

Tess screamed, jabbing her fingers into his face. "Let me go! You're fucking hurting me!"

Out of the corner of her eyes, she saw a couple coming down the hallway. They had been sitting together outside. The man's name was Teddy.

The next thing she knew, the guy toppled to the ground, knocked out cold. Tess heard a scuffle and fists connecting, but it happened so fast it was all a blur. Teddy must've broken her assailant's nose because blood covered his face as he lay sprawled out on the floor. His asshole buddy stood with his hands held high, *saying don't hit me.*

Teddy shook his hand, inspecting his knuckles. "Damn, are you all right?"

Tess cradled her wrist, shaking uncontrollably. "Th…Thanks. He wouldn't let go of me."

Teddy sent the next person who entered the hallway to find the host of the party. People began gathering in the hall to see what was going on. The guy still lay unconscious with blood spewing everywhere.

Tess saw Tom pushing his way through the crowded hall. He looked horrified, embracing her in his arms. "Tess are you all right? What happened?"

When Tess replayed the scenario, Tom flipped out. He lunged toward the other jerk standing in the hall, hitting him two or three times before Teddy pulled Tom off him. "Tommy, not now. You can't do this here."

She thought Tom was going to kick the guy on the ground as he lay unconscious. Tess had never seen Tom so mad. Full of rage, his dark eyes burned black with hatred.

Teddy insisted, "Tommy, get her out of here. Take her home. You shouldn't be here."

"I don't think so, Teddy. I'm going to fucking kill that prick when he wakes up." Tom's fists clenched, reeling toward the man left standing.

Teddy stepped between the two men, grabbing Tom by the arms. "Tommy, you need to go. She's white as a ghost. Take her home. I'll take care of him."

Tess' hand covered her aching breast, trying to ease the burning sensation throbbing in her nipple. Fearing she might puke right there in the hall, she choked, holding back tears. "Take me home."

Reaching around Teddy, Tom jabbed his finger into the second guy's chest. "You're done. You and your friend. You're fucking done. You won't ever work again!"

Tess turned abruptly, walking down the hall, nodding respectfully at Teddy's wife as she passed her by. Tom caught up to her, clasping her by the waist. She trembled uncontrollably, still in a terrified daze.

Tom kept saying repeatedly, "They're done. They'll never fucking work here again."

She wasn't sure who was more upset, her or Tom. Normally Tess wasn't a vindictive person, but she hoped Tom would be able to carry out his threats.

The entire ride home, Tom spewed apologetically while holding her in his arms. "I'm so sorry, Tess. I should've been with you."

"It's not your fault. I'm just glad Teddy and his wife showed up. Teddy h...had him on the ground s...so fast I didn't even see what happened."

When they walked through the door, Tom immediately made her an ice pack for her wrist. It was already turning purple. He wanted to have it looked at, but she refused. It was only bruised.

Tom paced vehemently back and forth like a caged animal.

Her body was exhausted, but her mind would not rest. "I can't go to sleep. I'm going to take a hot bath."

Tess soaked in the hot tub. Tom sat behind her, rubbing her back for comfort, but she couldn't stop shaking. As she stepped out of the tub, Tom caught a glimpse of her red, swollen left nipple. He automatically reached out to cup it, but she flinched fearing it would hurt if he touched it. Seeing tears build in his eyes as rage set in again, she took his hand and gently placed it over her nipple. "This might need an icepack, too. Definitely some tender kisses." She smiled affectionately, trying to ease his fury.

Tess didn't fall asleep until morning.

Tom never did go to bed.

Tess awoke to the sound of Tom's enraged voice. She tiptoed into the living room and could see him angrily pacing back and forth on the balcony, screaming into the phone. Tess watched in agony, chewing on her lip until he hung up. Tom turned and saw her standing inside. He exhaled deeply between pursed lips, before coming inside.

He gently reached for her wrist, inspecting it with concern.

"I'm fine, Tom."

"Tess, don't give me that shit. You're not fine. I'm sorry. I know I'm furious. That asshole's going to pay for laying a finger on you. I'd like to beat the shit out of him, but I won't stoop that low. Killing his career will have to suffice," Tom seethed, shaking his head. "Thank God Teddy was there."

"I really am okay, but I'll admit, I hope the creep does get what's coming to him." She couldn't allow herself to think about what would've happened if Teddy hadn't been there. It scared her too much. "I hate seeing you so angry. I mean, I understand why you're so mad. I'm furious, too. But I don't like seeing you like this, Tom."

"It would kill me if something bad happened to you. I've waited all my life to find you, Tess. I couldn't take it if I lost you. I should've been with you. I know it's ridiculous, but the thought of losing you-"

"It's not ridiculous, I understand more than you realize. Don't you think it's difficult for me? You don't have any idea how many times I've almost asked you to get a physical, so I know you're not going to have a heart attack and die on me, too. Do you know how long it took me to let my kids out of my sight after Richard died? Even then, I didn't want them driving in the same car together? Just in case…"

He tucked a loose strand of hair behind her ear. "I get a physical every year. I'm not going anywhere."

"I need to ask you for a favor, two actually." She paused, cradling her wrist, willing away the throbbing pain. "This will probably be the only time I ever ask this of you, but I need you to lie for me, Tom. I don't want to tell my kids about this."

He obliged with a slight nod. "And the second favor?"

"I don't want to dwell on this. I can't look back anymore."

Tom tenderly stroked her jaw with the back of his fingers. "No looking back."

The crisp mountain air pinched her cheeks and snow blanketed the ground. Tess couldn't be happier to be back in Colorado. Thanksgiving was in two days. John, Tracy and JC would all be there the next day ready to hit the slopes. "Are you looking forward to spending Thanksgiving and Christmas together?" she asked him one day.

He smiled coyly. "You know I am. I don't remember the last time I had a real Thanksgiving dinner. I'm excited to get a tree, too."

She stared at him in astonishment. "You don't usually get a tree?"

"No. I might've gotten one once but...I don't remember buying it. The tree was lying on the floor in the middle of the room the next morning when I woke up." He chuckled.

She couldn't envision his Christmases. This was her favorite time of year and Tom's worst. "I've always bought a tree in Vegas. I've never cut one down out of the woods. We could start our own family tradition this year. If you'd like."

"I would love that. Another first," he said warmly, looking at her mouth, sliding his thumb over her bottom lip.

John flew in from Vegas the next day. Tom picked up Tracy and JC from college while Tess made pies and a few other dishes for Thanksgiving Day. She was happy to have everyone under one roof, and was disappointed that Shayla couldn't make it. She was spending the holiday with her boyfriend's family.

Tess' kids had been looking forward to spending time with their mom and Tom. He appeared to have no problem adjusting to having her kids around and enjoyed skiing with them. That evening, everyone played pool and watched movies. Her kids unwound from school and work.

Tess crashed early, and when Tom climbed into bed it was after two in the morning. He snuggled up to Tess, rubbing her back until she curled up next to him.

"Happy Thanksgiving, Tess," he whispered in her ear.

"Happy Thanksgiving, Tom," she murmured, falling back to sleep with her body tangled with his.

The sun barely crested over the mountain as Tess prepped the turkey. The scent of fall candles mixed with the fire burning in the hearth hung in the air. John headed out to get a half a day of snowboarding in before dinner and Tom watched football downstairs. Tess took snacks downstairs and found Tracy and JC kicking back on the couches in their long underwear, watching football with Tom. She grabbed Tom's camera to take a picture of the three of them.

"What the heck Mom, I just woke up," JC protested.

"New memories. That's all. No complaining, JC." Tess smiled, taking another picture.

Thanksgiving was never a day to be formal, not for Tess. It was a day to enjoy her family and treasure the things in life she appreciated. Her last Thanksgiving had been awful. She couldn't even get out of bed. This year, however, was a brand new beginning and she had a lot to be thankful for.

Tom had been in high spirits all day. Every time he came upstairs, he'd comment on how good it smelled, how hungry he was, or how beautiful Tess looked.

She pulled him into the kitchen. "Will you help me carve the turkey? I'm not very good at it." Richard had always done this for her in the past and she hoped Tom would carve the turkey for her now.

"Umm. Sure. I hate to even touch it. It looks too pretty," he pointed out before diving in.

For their first Thanksgiving together as a family, they enjoyed a delicious dinner of turkey, ham, mashed potatoes and sweet potatoes, salad, rolls, and pumpkin pies. As they sat gathered around the dining table, her kids shared funny or embarrassing stories from previous holidays when they were younger.

The next morning, everyone piled into the car in search of the perfect Christmas tree. It took a while to find the perfect big, fat, fluffy, blue spruce, but they did. John and Tom cut the tree down while the girls made snow angels.

Tom admitted, "I haven't had a tree since I was your age, JC."

"Aren't you glad you're with us now? We love Christmas," JC replied.

He smiled and put his arm around her shoulder. "Yes, I am glad."

"Okay, this is the new Clemmins-Mathews Christmas tradition. Every year we're cutting a tree," Tess declared. Her kids cheered and made a big deal out of it.

Later that night after everyone decorated the tree, Tess opened a bottle of wine for her and Tom. They lay on the couch with all of the lights off except the Christmas tree lights and the fire crackling in the fireplace. Tom ran his fingers through her hair while they listened to music. He stood, holding out his hand, and they danced to the music. He gazed at her with such adoration she started to blush. Tom bent down to kiss her and a flash went off. They both squinted. "Who is that?" Tess said.

"It's me. Go back to what you were doing. I'm just getting even for the other morning. Oooh, it turned out nice, too," JC giggled, setting Tom's camera down before trotting back down stairs.

"Another first, Tess. First Thanksgiving weekend together. First tree," Tom said happily. The fire burnt burned out and Tess and Tom headed upstairs. Both were asleep in five minutes.

John left in the morning, and Tom and Tess drove the girls back to school. The girls sang and danced in the back seat the entire ride. Tom even sang along, smiling at Tess.

Saying their goodbyes, JC hugged Tess. "Love you, Momma, Thanksgiving was great." Then she hugged Tom and said, "Thanks for everything, and taking us skiing, too. Love you."

Tess' heart damn near beat right out of her chest and she tried to contain her huge smile and waterworks long enough to reply. "Love you baby girl."

Tracy did almost the exact same thing. "Love you. Thanks for everything," she said, squeezing both of them.

"Love you, too. You're welcome." His cheeks turned bright red as he put his arm around Tess, watching the girls walk away.

"I knew they liked you," she chimed matter-of-factly. "I'm impressed, Tom. You've been saying those three little words a lot the last few months."

He chuckled, still red in the face. "I do love your kids. They're fun."

It was after dark by the time they returned home.

Tess sauntered down the stairs looking for Tom. She found

him lying on a blanket in front of the fire. "I always love it when you surprise me," she exclaimed.

Her long brown hair fell to one side as she looked up into his dark eyes. Tom's hand slid down the small of her back and over her ass, making her stand up a bit straighter onto her toes. His thumb slid over her lips. "I'm going to keep you in bed until we leave for Greece in a few days," he whispered in her ear. Tess rolled her tongue around his thumb and he pressed himself against her. "I couldn't wait to be alone with you."

"I love it when my kids are here, but I like it when they leave, too."

CHAPTER TWENTY-ONE

The house Tom rented in Greece sat alone perched on top of a sheer cliff with dramatic views of the Aegean Sea. It was plush but not over the top, very casual. Grey flagstone ran through the house, continuing through to the patio surrounding the pool.

"Wow. This is beautiful."

"Wait till you see the sunsets. They're famous here."

The lovely kitchen came stocked with food and wine. "Hey can we get stuff to make martinis? We don't even have to go anywhere! I could stay here the whole time."

"Everything is already here."

Tess explored the four bedrooms, each with its own bathroom. The hand textured white walls made the pops of cobalt blue, canary yellow and cherry red stand out against the natural wood furnishings.

She wrapped her arms around his waist. "This place is beautiful."

"Thanks," he said with a sly grin.

She realized, "Is this your other house?"

He nodded. "Umm hmm."

"No wonder you love it here."

Tom and Tess explored several beautiful islands, each blessed with unique beaches. One had pebble sand, another had golden sand, one even had soft black sand, but the water was a beautiful azure blue no matter where they went. They strolled through villages, stopped at cafés, and browsed through art galleries. Locals knew Tom and would wave to him saying, "Hey Tommy!"

Late in the evening Tom said, "Tess, I want to take you someplace nice tomorrow."

"Are you going to tell me where?" she asked curiously.

"I'd rather not, but I will tell you that we're not coming back here tomorrow night. We'll be back the next night."

The next morning Tess found Tom swimming laps. She slipped into the pool naked and reached her hand out to touch him. He flinched lifting his head out of the water.

"You scared the shit out of me Tess." Sighing heavily, he wiped the water from his face.

"I didn't hear you get up. How long have you been out here?"

"A while." He inhaled deeply again with bent eyebrows.

"Is everything okay?" She frowned. Tess hated to see him stressed out.

Tom grinned. "Everything is perfect. Come swim with me."

Tess teased him, floating on her back, kissing him, and wrapping herself around him.

"Tess," he said in a steamy voice.

"Yes."

"Not yet." He kissed her quickly on the lips.

She stepped out of the pool and stretched her arms above her head. "Okay."

"You're not being fair." He called after her, watching her saunter inside.

Tess showered and Tom peeked in at her. "You're going to be happy later Tess, I promise."

"I'm only teasing you Tom," she said seductively.

He instantly quit peeking. "Yeah, I know exactly what you're doing."

"Hey wait, I don't have to wear heels do I?"

"Nope, just wear something cute, and what you had on in the pool doesn't count."

Full of excitement, she danced around the closet searching through her things, finally choosing the little blue dress Tom was fond of. She couldn't decide if she wanted to torture him. *Yep!* She giggled to herself in the closet as she slipped her dress on with nothing underneath of it. When she turned around, Tom

225

stood with arms folded watching her.

"Crap! You scared me." Heat rose to her cheeks, turning her face scarlet red.

"Please tell me you're forgetting something."

"Actually I'm going to wear this today." She struggled to keep a straight face.

Tom fumbled through a drawer for her panties. "Jesus, Tess. Please don't do that to me today. You're gonna drive me fucking crazy. I already...I...I have something planned for you and there is no way in hell I'll be able to concentrate if you're naked under that dress."

"I was only going to mess with you a little. Okay, maybe a lot, but I thought it would make for a *revealing* day." Her hand covered her mouth to stop laughing.

Panties hung from the end of his finger. "Here, please. Take these with you at least. I love the idea of you not wearing anything under your dress, but I-" He was completely flustered.

"Give them to me, I'll put them on."

He pulled them out of her reach. "No, I'm fine. Maybe you should put them in your purse or something."

She took the panties from him, whispering in his ear, "You know I'm going to tease you all day, Tom. Every time I get out of the car, sitting at lunch...should I go on?"

He rolled his eyes, regaining his composure as he reached his hand under her dress. "Careful, Tess. This could back fire on you."

"Shit! I'll put them on." She attempted to squirm away from his wandering fingers.

He kissed her passionately, touching her just for a moment. "No way. Are you ready?"

"Yep," she squeaked.

During their short flight, Tess' excitement grew, wondering what Tom had planned. They'd had a late lunch under a private veranda at an olive grove. It had the best food Tess had eaten in Greece and delicious wine, too.

Tom seemed content as they roamed the stone streets of another quaint village, holding hands while browsing through shops.

"I love you, Tess," he said in a quiet voice, playing with her fingers.

"I love you, too. This has been a beautiful day. It's going to be a gorgeous sunset," she said.

"Yes, it is." He looked down at her and raised his eyebrows. "Maybe the best I've ever seen."

Zigzagging down a hill, the view became more and more breathtaking with every turn. The scenery began to look a little familiar as she gazed out over the water. Tess kept glancing around and Tom wore an immense grin.

"Where are we?"

He ignored her and continued walking. The little road turned and she knew exactly where they were. Tess smiled up at him, meandering toward the curved white wall they'd stopped at the first time they visited Greece.

"I didn't know where we were until just now," she said with a soft smile.

"I wanted to surprise you."

"Are we staying at the inn?" she asked enthusiastically.

"Yes, we are."

They reached their spot on the curved white wall. Tom sat next to her as they watched one of the most vivid sunsets Tess had ever seen.

"I have something for you, Tess." Tom held out his hand with a ball resting in the center of his palm. It resembled a perfectly round golf ball made from wadded up strips of paper.

"Where did this come from?"

"My pocket," he flirted, pulling back his lips to flash the smile she loved so much. Tom hopped off the wall and stood between her thighs, placing the ball in the palm of her hand.

"Awe. Thanks," she snickered sarcastically, looking down at the paper ball. "What is it?"

"It's a piece of paper," he said very sexily, watching her face intently. His lips traveled down her neck, whispering in her ear. "It's a funny thing, this piece of paper. I never thought much of it before."

She grinned, knowing he was toying with her.

"Open it up."

He stared at her face adoringly as she began pulling at the wadded up pieces of paper. Tom waited for the precise moment, until she had completely finished unwrapping. "Tess. It's not just a piece of paper to me anymore. Will you marry me?"

A very beautiful ring lay in the center of the crinkled up strips of paper. Tess set the ring on her lap and placed her shaky hands on the side of her neck. Her entire body trembled. She stared down at the beautiful ring in her lap.

He reached down and took both of her hands in his.

"What?" she asked in confusion.

Tom held up the ring between his fingers. "Tess, I love you. Marriage was always just a piece of paper to me. I never understood why people bothered to get married. I get it now. I've been waiting for you for a long time." He bent down, looking into her eyes, "Marry me, Tess. Be my wife. I want to make you happy for the rest of our lives together. Forever."

"I…I just…I never thought you'd want this," she choked, tripping over her tongue.

"Tess, that's not an answer. You're making me nervous."

"I'm sorry." She was so stunned she had no words.

"Tess?" he asked again trying to read the answer in her eyes.

Tess nodded her head.

"Are you nodding yes?"

"Yes, I will marry you."

He slid the ring on her finger.

Tears streamed down her cheeks as she buried her face in his chest. The man had a true gift for surprising her. "You really want to marry me?" She lifted her gaze and the sunset silhouetted his face, almost hiding his broad smile.

"Yes. I love you. I love the way you look at me. I love how funny and sarcastic you are, yet incredibly grounded and responsible. I love the fact you'll go anywhere with your hair in a ponytail and lip-gloss on. I love how you think you're taking advantage of me if I buy something for you. You're so cute every time you say 'Holy Crap'. You're so confident and happy with yourself. I love everything about you."

They kissed for a moment.

He inspected her finger with the ring on it as he spoke. "You're the most amazing woman I've ever known."

"I love you, Tom. I didn't think you would ever want to get married. Actually, I didn't think I ever wanted to get married again. Are you-"

"Please don't ask me if I'm sure. I'm positive."

She bit her lip and smiled. Tess had no idea he paid so much attention. "I love the way you say my name. It literally makes my heart thump faster. I love the sarcasm between us," She said quietly. "You make me a better woman. You make me feel incredible about myself."

"It's unbelievable, isn't it?" They kissed and laughed. "This is what I love the most, we laugh. And that everyone calls me Tommy, but you don't, you call me Tom." He lifted her finger. "Do you like your ring, Tess?"

"I'm sorry, I didn't even look at it." She stared down at the gorgeous, brilliantly cut diamond with a wide, platinum band. "It's beautiful, Tom. Holy crap!"

He chuckled at her *holy crap*. "Do you really like it?"

"I love it. It's perfect."

Tess gripped the hair at the nape of his neck, kissing him enthusiastically. She slid closer nudging her body against his. Both were acutely aware she didn't have anything on underneath her dress. Tom struggled to gain some restraint, but it wasn't working.

"What is it with this wall? I want to make love to you right here. Maybe we should put one of these in your backyard."

"*Our* backyard." He pulled away from her so he wouldn't embarrass himself in public. She wrapped one leg around his side and brought him back in front of her. "Speaking of not waiting-"

"I agree. Let's go."

"Actually, I'm referring to our wedding."

She could've sworn a bead of sweat dripped from his temple as he uttered the word wedding. "Was that hard for you to say?" She teased.

"Not at all. You are going to be my wife. I'm going to be your husband. See? I'm more than fine. I've waited for so long to finally find you, and I really don't want to wait to get married," he said sincerely.

"When do you want to get married?"

"Let's get married now, here, in Greece." He nibbled on her neck.

"Tom, I can't get married without my kids. And what about Benny and Lisa? I'd love to, but I don't know if they'd be able to just leave and come to Greece." She contemplated. "Maybe?"

"Tess, what if I told you that your kids already expect this? Would you be upset with me?"

Her mouth dropped open. "Did you tell them?"

"I asked John for his blessing over Thanksgiving, so I'm assuming he mentioned it to his sisters. I wanted to ask him in Vegas, but he was too busy knocking my lights out, and I didn't know if you'd say yes."

"You've known for that long?"

"Yes." Tom nodded his head. "I've known that I've loved you since the shark tour…it just took me awhile to figure it out. When you got attacked in Malibu, it scared the hell out of me. The thought of losing you made me crazy. I don't ever want to be without you."

"I've known that long, too, but I never expected you to want to be married."

"There is nothing I want more." Tom nuzzled her neck. "Back to my question. If I can get everyone here this weekend, in four days, will you marry me here in Greece?"

"Of course, I will. Well, how many people are you talking about? Are you okay with a small wedding?"

"I don't need a big fancy Hollywood wedding, if that's what you're asking. I love it here in Greece and we're here right now. Life is short, and I want to spend the rest of mine with you as your husband. What kind of wedding would you like?" he asked sweetly.

"One where you're standing by my side, Tom. That's all that matters to me. If we can get everyone here, let's get married. Please tell me they're not already here."

"No, I'm not that good, Tess. Besides, what if your answer would've been no?"

"Did you really think I might say no?"

"I didn't think so, but I wasn't positive. Do you remember when I asked you in Vegas if you would ever marry again and you said-"

"It's just a piece of paper." Tess peeked down at the paper wrappings in her lap. "I love the ring."

"I knew it was the right ring as soon as I saw it. Just like the first time I saw you."

"If we stay here much longer, this wall is going to have some stories to tell." The night grew darker and the wall became a little too tempting. They headed toward the inn.

Collapsing onto the bed, Tom held up her hand, inspecting the ring on her finger. "It looks nice on you." His hand barely skimmed her dress, "What do you want to wear, Tess?"

Her heart raced with eagerness. "I'll find something tomorrow. I can't wait anymore. I've wanted to be with you all day."

He slid his hand up her thigh. "You've been waiting all day? I've been waiting all my life for you, Tess."

CHAPTER TWENTY-TWO

Tess expected the next few days to be hectic and stressful, but they weren't. She called her kids to tell them the good news and Tom called Shayla to help arrange flights and hotel rooms for family.

They flew back to Tom's house, which he kept reminding her was their house now. On the dock by his home, Tom found a little old man with a boat to take them to an island. Tom retold stories, claims of an ancient ruin left on an island, he was right. Rubble lay scattered on the ground, but three and a half majestic marble pillars remained mostly intact. Marble stairs leading up to the pavilion remained in good shape despite their age. There were no trees, but beautiful vibrant red, deep violet and pale yellow wild flowers surrounded the ruins. It overlooked the Aegean Sea as well as the surrounding islands.

"Do you like it?" he asked, hoping she'd say yes.

"I love it."

It was late by the time they returned home. Tess was so tired, she didn't even feel Tom climb into bed with her.

"Again?" A deep chuckle rumbled in his chest. Tess snuggled on top of his back while he lay sleeping face down in bed. She had already reached for him in the middle of the night to make love. "Tess, you're unbelievable."

"Thanks, but that's not why I woke you up."

"You're still unbelievable. What's up?"

"You need a ring."

Tom chose a platinum band with five diamonds spaced evenly around the ring. When the jeweler asked Tom why he favored that particular ring, he replied, "This band represents my new family. One diamond for each of us."

Tess buried her face against his chest and started bawling right in front of the jeweler. "We'll t...take this one." She managed to sniffle before wrapping her arms around Tom's neck and crying again.

After leaving the jewelers, Tom pointed to the top of a cliff. "There's a restaurant right over there on top of the hill, can you see it? A little old man and his wife own it. We'll go there after the wedding. His wife is going to make the cake for us. I just need to tell her what kind you want. What's your favorite?"

"I love any kind of cake, but chocolate is my favorite. What about you?"

"Believe it or not, I'm not big on cake, so chocolate is fine."

"You don't like cake? she asked in surprise. "Any kind of cake?"

"Nope, I'm more of a cookie guy. Chocolate chip is my favorite."

"Let's have dinner there tonight so you can check it out."

Old-world ambiance filled the restaurant. Crisp white table clothes with blue napkins dressed the tables and pictures of Greece hung on white textured walls. The older couple sat with Tess and Tom, drinking a glass of wine while they discussed the menu. The small, dark-haired man had weathered skin and his eyes smiled when he talked. He spoke to Tess in his heavy accent, suggesting several special dishes for the wedding. The woman's long, gray hair was pulled back into a bun and her eyes twinkled as they discussed the cake.

They enjoyed a wonderful dinner on the patio.

"This is perfect, Tom," she said softly. "It's incredibly romantic."

By now, they were the only couple left sitting outside. White lights were strung from one side of the patio to the other, creating a starry canopy. Tom rose from his chair. Tugging gently on her hand, he pulled her into his arms. Laying her cheek to his chest, he danced her across the floor.

"Just think, Tess, in forty eight hours, we'll be standing here doing this exact same thing, only you'll be Mrs. Mathews-

Clemmins."

She tilted her head, gazing into his dark eyes. "I was thinking Mrs. Clemmins."

"Really? Are you sure? I assumed you'd want to keep Mathews."

"I'm positive. I have wonderful memories as Mrs. Mathews, but I want to make new memories as Mrs. Clemmins. I'm one hundred percent yours, Tom."

He stopped dancing, touched by her decision. "I don't know what to say."

"You're supposed to say, 'Thanks!', 'Great!' and 'That's perfect!'"

"Good morning. How long have you been up?" Tom kissed Tess' cheek.

She sat by the pool going over her checklist. "Not very long. It seems impossible, but I think everything is taken care of."

"It's going to be perfect. Let's just take it easy today. Your kids don't fly in until this evening and Benny and Lisa will be here tomorrow morning. What would you like to do today?"

"It's our last day single. What do you want to do?"

Tom picked her up and tossed her in the water. She automatically wrapped her legs around his waist, which is exactly what he wanted.

"Let's wait," Tess suggested.

"Let's not."

"Seriously. Let's wait. It's only one day," she laughed.

He walked up the pool steps with her legs still wrapped around his waist, carrying her to their room. Tom kissed her with so much desire she didn't even pretend to stop him.

"Tess, this is going to be the last time we make love while we're single. Forever."

"It's not going to be different tomorrow, Tom."

"Actually, I have a feeling it'll be better tomorrow, but I'd like to think I tried my best today, Tess."

"Umm hmm." Tess understood his last day of being single marked a significant moment in his life. Tom was on a mission to make this the best *last time* he'd ever have before getting married.

"You mean you want to have incredibly great sex before you get married? Is that what you're trying to say?" She wiggled her eyebrows, settling deeper around his hips.

"Yes, I do." He gripped her ass as she unfastened her legs from his waist, lowering her toes to the floor.

Her hand fell to the center of his chest and she shoved him onto the bed. "Do you want me to make this day memorable for you, Tom?" She moaned with exaggeration, teasing him as she climbed on top of him. Tess caressed her breast, extending fingers downward to touch herself. Her head dropped back, brushing her hair against her back. She squeezed her legs against his sides, only rubbing against him, not letting him have what he desired.

Tom stared intently. "I want you to feel me," he said, gripping her hips, attempting to shift her body.

Tess kept control, needing him to be hungrier for her. She'd never really cared for talking dirty, but knew he'd like it. Her long hair fell around his face as she brushed her nipple over his wet lips. She moaned in his ear, "You want me to feel you? What else do you want?"

Releasing her nipple from his mouth, Tom's lips pulled to the side in a grin. "What was my second option the night of the premier?"

Tess rolled her tongue over his earlobe, whispering in her sexiest voice, "You want me to fuck you real slowly? I believe that was your other option."

At that exact moment, he flipped her onto her back, staring into her eyes, teasing her once before diving deep inside. *Oh shit. How the hell did he do that so fast?* Turned on more than ever by the sheer lust in his eyes, she said words she'd never said before, sending both of them into overdrive. Tess moved aggressively, sinking her fingers deep into his shoulders, keeping up stroke-for-stroke.

Tom sat back on his knees, rolling her over onto her tummy, lying on top of her, giving her just the tip. "Is that what you want?" he toyed.

She raised onto her knees and elbows, probing for control, and he backed off. "Don't stop. I want to feel you," she whimpered.

Tom gave in to her desires. Leaning over her, grasping a handful of hair, he took command of her entire body. "Can you feel me now?"

Distantly, she was aware of her own voice crying out. "Oh, yes! Holy crap!"

The strength in his fingers loosened, giving her freedom to ride freely. Reversing the roll of her hips, Tess stretched her arms out flat on the bed, dropping her cheek to the sheet, allowing him to plunge deeper. As she felt his body contract, her zealous need intensified, vigorously thrusting against him to climax again.

Tom groaned deep in his throat. "Oh, shit." He collapsed on top of her, shuddering with his own release.

Reaching around, Tess grabbed his hair in her fingers. "You've been holding out on me, Tom Clemmins." Her ears were ringing as blood surged through her veins. She peeked over the edge of the mattress that had scooted two feet away from the box spring. "We need a sturdier bed," she panted.

Tom chuckled while trying to suck in enough air to catch his breath.

"What's so funny?" she questioned, her voice still shaky.

"I'm thinking maybe we could make love Monday through Friday and have incredibly great sex on Saturdays and Sundays."

She laughed with him. "Weekend sex. I love that idea."

"I thought you might. I'm so lucky. I get to take you home every night. No matter what we're having."

As they drove to the airport, Tess couldn't wait to see her kids and Shayla. When their plane landed, she enveloped them in her arms. Joey the photographer was there, as well as Marco the stylist and his partner, Rick.

That night, they ate dinner at a restaurant by the beach. Tess hadn't seen her kids much since the middle of summer. She enjoyed sitting back and relaxing with her kids and Tom, wanting to share him with them so they could be a family. It was important to her that they like him and it was important to Tom, too. All of the pieces of her life were coming together.

After dinner, Tom and Tess trailed behind her kids and Shayla, strolling hand-in-hand down the narrow cobbled streets.

"Are you happy, Tess?" Tom whispered in her ear.

She leaned her head on his shoulder. "I hoped it would be like this."

"Me, too. They seem thrilled for you."

"For us, Tom. They're happy for us."

When they returned home, Tess and Tom lay in bed and Tess said, "Thanks for bringing Marco here to do our hair and makeup."

"Marco is fond of you. He was more than willing to make the trip."

"I was surprised to see Joey. The two of you seem friendly, but not that friendly."

He hesitated for a minute. "I need to talk to you about that. We'll need to release a statement and pictures from our wedding."

"What? Oh shit!" Tess suddenly realized, "It's a big deal, isn't it? You getting married. That didn't even cross my mind."

"Yes, it's going to be a very big deal for the media. If we put the story out ourselves, it'll be much easier. We can release photos we want the public to see and I think we'll need to do some interviews with a few reputable magazines. I hate doing interviews, but if we don't do anything, the media will be brutal."

"So how does that work? I'd rather the press be positive. I don't want to see lies about us on the cover of a magazine."

"Well, if I pay Joey an obscene amount of money to take pictures for us, he'll keep his mouth shut. Then, we can release them however we decide."

"How much money is an obscene amount of money?"

"It doesn't matter. When we release the photos, we'll make it back, plus some."

"That's just bizarre."

"It's the business, Tess. I was thinking we could take the money from the photos and give it to your kids and Shayla. It'll be a nice amount for each of them. You can give it to them now or in increments, however you decide. It will be enough money that, if they wanted to buy a condo or put money down on a house, they would be able to."

Her eyes narrowed. "Are you serious?"

"Trust me. They'll pay a lot of money for these pictures.

You don't need the money and I don't need the money, so why not?" He smiled nonchalantly, shrugging his shoulders.

"That's extremely generous of you. Are you sure? My kids aren't going to think more of you if you give them monetary things, Tom. They're not materialistic like that. Don't get me wrong, I'm sure they'd love it, but you don't need to buy their love. My kids love you because you're a good person. Not because of your money."

"I already know that. They're exactly like you. Trust me, we don't need the money and it would give them a nice start. Shayla, too."

"Speaking of money, Tom..."

"Yes," he said very slowly, as if he knew what was coming.

"Don't you have some papers for me to sign? Something that says that I promise not to take you to the cleaners or something to protect yourself and all of your millions from me? Like maybe a prenup?" she said, playing with his fingers.

"Nope." he replied smugly.

"What do you mean 'nope'? You're supposed to, aren't you? I was expecting one," she muttered in confusion.

"I mean, no. I trust you. And better yet, I trust myself," he proclaimed proudly. "I don't plan on divorcing you. I don't even like saying the word."

"I don't want anything from you." Panic-stricken, she sat straight up in bed.

"That is not entirely true, Tess. You do want something from me. You want *my word* that I'll never be with another woman. That I'll never be unfaithful, right?"

"Well, yeah, of course. That's not an option, Tom." Her tone turned serious.

"I know. I'm one hundred percent positive you'll be faithful to me, and I'll always be faithful to you. I'm so sure of myself and how I feel about you, I don't need a prenup, Tess," he boasted, ridiculously satisfied with himself. "Divorce isn't an alternative."

"I'm flattered, Tom, really, but I'd feel better if you had one. I don't want people to think that-"

"Tess, I'm not going to argue over a prenup. I love you more than you realize. I don't give a *damn* what anyone else thinks. *I* trust you. I'm not doing it. So please don't ask me about it. And if you sit here and get all stressed out the night before our wedding over a stupid prenup, I might just get pissed at you."

"We can't have that now, can we? I don't think I'd like it if you were pissed at me, and just so you know, if I thought there was a chance in hell we'd get divorced some day or if I had one doubt about us, I would've said no to you." She curled up next to him. "Can we have one rule Tom? No going to bed angry or upset with each other."

"Did this rule help you over the last twenty-five years?" he asked inquisitively.

"Yes."

"Then I agree. No going to bed angry. I'm not mad, Tess, I just believe in us. So much that I won't go into this marriage thinking it might fail someday down the road."

"You're right." Tess giggled with excitement. "Tomorrow, we're getting married."

CHAPTER TWENTY-THREE

Tom was sound asleep, sprawled out naked, lying face down. A smile broadened across Tess' face. *I get to wake up next to his fine ass every day for the rest of my life.* She lightly ran her fingers down his back.

"Morning, Tess. Today's the day." Tom rolled over and asked, "Are you ready to marry me and be my wife until death do us part?"

"Yes, I am. Would you mind if we say, as long as we both shall live?"

"Absolutely. That would be perfect."

There was a knock on their bedroom door. Tess reached down to the end of the bed, pulling the sheet and down comforter over them.

"Are you decent? Can we come in?" JC called through the closed door.

Panic spilled over Tom's face, appearing unsure of what to do, stay in bed or run for the bathroom. He tucked the covers up over his chest.

"You can come in." Tess laughed at Tom and shook her head.

Tracy and JC stood at the door with two cups of freshly brewed coffee. "Hey, you two! Today's the big day!"

Both girls danced into the room and sat on Tess' side of the bed. Neither paid attention to Tom, who was practically hiding under the covers.

"It's gorgeous outside!" Tracy said.

JC started singing. "Going to the chapel and we're gonna get married, going to the chapel and we're gonna get married."

The fear in Tom's eyes softened as he laughed out loud.

"John's making breakfast, so you'd better get up. Let's go, sleepy heads. Today is your big day!"

"Thanks for the coffee," Tom said.

"What's he making?" Tess asked.

"Your favorite!" JC danced out the door with Tracy right behind her.

"Banana pancakes." Tess glanced at Tom. "Are you all right? Don't worry, they always knock first. You might want to try to relax. This won't be the last time they come talk to us while we're in bed."

"Seriously? It seemed a little awkward."

"Yes, seriously. They're used to having their dad around, Tom. It's not a big deal to them. They're obviously comfortable around you."

He nodded, mulling it over in his head. "You think they see me differently because I'm going to be your husband? Is that what you're saying?"

"Yes. You're part of their family now. My kids see you as a good man, not Hollywood hotshot, Tom Clemmins. The same way I see you. Don't worry. They're not going to call you Dad or anything, but they're going to look up to you in a Dad-like way. Does that make sense? It'll get easier, Tom."

"I guess I never looked at it that way." A huge smile crossed his face. "Family. I like that."

"Good because in about seven hours, you're going to be a big part of one." She kissed his cheek. "Let's eat before I decide to stay in here and lock the door."

"Not until tonight when you're Tess Clemmins."

"I can't wait!" She danced around the room.

After breakfast Benny, Lisa, Tommy and Kim arrived. Tom smiled in relief, ecstatic to see Benny. Tess introduced her kids to the Levis. John had already met Lisa, and when Tess introduced him to Benny, Benny put up his hands as if they were going to box.

"So you're the guy who kicked Tommy's ass? It's nice to finally meet you." Benny smirked, high-fiving John.

"I still feel horrible. Thanks for reminding me," John

laughed, rolling his eyes.

"You feel horrible? How do you think I feel?" Tom asked.

Everybody laughed.

While Tom and Benny were outside catching up, Tess filled Lisa in on wedding details. Tess also told her how much she appreciated Benny doing the film for Tom.

"Tommy was going out of his mind. He only wanted to be with you. He was so cute. I didn't think that man would ever be able to utter the word *love*, but once he finally admitted he was in love with you, look out! He's head over heels for you. Benny and I knew from the moment he showed up at our villa with you, that you were the one."

"Seriously?"

"Of course! We went to bed that night saying, 'Thank God! Finally!' He's such a great guy, but nobody ever seemed to fit with him. You two are perfect for each other. How are your kids getting along with him? You heard about my first introduction to your boy John."

"They're great. John likes him, and my girls do, too. It feels like we're a family when we're together."

"Wow." Lisa's eyes widened with a look of surprise, maybe disbelief.

Tess clarified, "My kids are older. It would be entirely different if they were your kid's ages. Mine aren't looking for a father. All I'm saying is, it's comfortable when we're all together. Tom fits right in."

Lisa understood, nodding her head.

Tess and Lisa went to find Benny and Tom. They were in the kitchen talking. As Tess entered the room, she heard Benny telling Tom, "I don't think that's a very smart decision, Tommy. You should protect yourself. You never know what may happen in the future."

Tess fidgeted uncomfortably, realizing she'd walked in on a conversation about herself. As the men spotted her, a weighted silence filled the room. She chewed on her cheek, unable to mask the uneasy look on her face.

Benny touched Tess' shoulder. "No disrespect, Tess. Lisa and I love you, but I was just asking Tommy why he's not doing any kind of a prenup with you."

Tom scowled at Benny, narrowing his eyes, looking more pissed with every second of silence ticking by slowly. The tension so thick you could cut it with a knife

Tess finally responded nonchalantly, "Hey, I asked the same question. Actually, I'd feel better if he did, but do you see that face right there?" She pointed to Tom. "He got pissed at me. It's not worth arguing over. I don't want anything from him. Nothing monetary anyway." She chuckled, hoping to lighten the atmosphere.

Tom still glared at Benny.

"Tom, he's your best friend. He's supposed to be watching out for your best interests. Come on. If someone you knew were getting married like we are, you'd ask the exact same thing. So don't be angry with him." Tess smiled and kissed him on the lips. "You should be happy right now. We get married in five hours."

Benny squeezed her shoulder. "Truly, Tess, I didn't mean anything by it." He shook Tom's hand. "I love you, Tommy. Come on, don't be pissed at me. I only want you to be happy man."

"Benny, I told you, I know what I'm doing."

Shock covered Lisa's face, and she stepped outside to check on her kids. Benny followed behind her.

Tess reached for Tom's hand, playing with his fingers. "He's simply looking out for you. If he were marrying Lisa now, you'd be telling him the same thing."

"You're right. If Benny were getting married, I'd be dragging him to his attorney's office."

"I don't want to come between the two of you. You should be thanking him for being such a good friend. If anyone should be offended, it should be me and I'm not. So put a smile on your face. This should be one of the happiest days of your life."

"It is the happiest day of my life, Tess."

Tom wasn't over it, so she hopped up on the counter, wrapped her legs around him, and kissed him affectionately. She didn't want him to think about anything else but her. It worked until her girls walked in on them.

JC giggled, rolling her eyes as she muttered under her

breath, "Great, I feel like I'm back in high school."

"We're going to start getting ready, Mom. Marco and Rick should be here in about an hour."

Tess needed to loosen up, so she went to her room and turned on her music, loudly. She danced and sang in the shower.

Tom stood watching her with a martini in his hand. "I thought this might help you loosen up, but I see the music beat me to it."

"Thanks," she said, taking a long sip of her drink.

Marco and Rick arrived to style the girls' hair and makeup. Marco styled Tess' hair perfectly, sweeping her long bangs to the side and pinning the rest back loosely in pieces. He wanted free reign over her makeup, assuring her, "I promise, it will look even better than the premier. You'll be beautiful. Come on, girlfriend, you can trust me. Tom will love it, too."

Marco accentuated her blue eyes, giving them a smoldering, smoky look. "Marco! It's exactly what I wanted."

"Miss Tess, you're a perfect canvas. I love working on you. I usually have to work with bitchy, rich women. Not you, girlfriend. You're special. Any time you need something, you call me and I'll take care of it for you." He air-kissed her cheeks. "You look H.O.T. Hot. He is one lucky man. Take some pictures for me."

"What do you mean? You and Rick are coming today, aren't you? You have to come."

"Are you serious?"

"Absolutely!"

"Girl, you know we love weddings. We'd love to come."

Marco rushed out the door to tell Rick when Tom entered the bedroom. "I invited them to the wedding, I hope you don't mind."

"Jesus, Tess," He swallowed hard, looking her over. "You look…beautiful. I mean really, really gorgeous. Damn, I'm the luckiest man in the world."

She blushed. "Thanks!"

Tom shut the door before untying the belt on her silky robe, exposing her naked body underneath. Tess shuddered under the touch of his hands fondling her breasts. He began kissing her, sucking on her bottom lip, traveling down her neck.

"Tom." Tess' heavy breathing turned into a loud sigh. "Wait. Tom, wait."

Tom pressed himself against her. "I want you right now. No more waiting. I've waited way too long for you." He kissed her again. Both were on the verge of giving in when someone knocked on the door. Tom let go of her and backed away. "Shit."

"Just a second," Tess answered. They smiled at each other, neither wanting to stop. Tom rolled his eyes, heading for the cold shower that awaited him. She tied her robe and answered the door.

Tracy stared at her in awe. "Mom! You look beautiful!"

"You look like a movie star," JC exclaimed.

"Thanks. You two look stunning." Both wore a beautiful azure blue dress that resembled the color of the sea. They had their hair pulled back in a bun, reminding Tess of a flower. Loose curls framed Tracy's face and JC wore a French braid weaved on both sides into her bun.

"Rick is awesome! Where's Tom? We wanted to tell him thanks for the hair and makeup," JC said.

"He's in the shower."

"Oh! Okay then, just tell him thanks for us. We're out of here. Come see us when you have your dress on."

Tess checked on John, who was already dressed in black pants and a black shirt with a white tie hanging around his neck. Shayla sat in a chair, talking to him.

"Son, you look so handsome in black. You remind me so much of your dad," Tess said, thinking of Richard for a moment. "Hey, you don't have to wear a tie. Tom's not." Tess turned to Shayla. "You look absolutely beautiful. I love your dress." Her long, blonde hair hung down to the middle of her back, and Tess thought Shayla looked like she should be sitting on a surfboard, with her golden skin, hazel eyes and beautiful white smile.

"Thanks." Shayla squeezed Tess tightly. "Thanks for making Tommy so happy. You're lucky to have found each other. He deserves to finally have somebody nice in his life."

"You better go get dressed, Mom." John chuckled, glancing at her robe.

Tess smiled hugely and headed back to her room.

Tom stood in the closet getting dressed. He was barefoot with black pants and black shirt, which was still unbuttoned. He gave her a quick peck on her cheek. "I'm gonna go out in the other room. I can't watch you get dressed or we'll never get out of here."

"Chicken," she said with a smile.

Tess turned on her music and slipped into a white, lace thong and exquisite bra. Simply putting them on made her feel sexy and confident. She laid her dress on the bed and unzipped it when her girls knocked on the door.

"Mom, can we come in?"

"Yes."

Tess pulled them through the door. Thirty seconds later Tom walked in. He stopped and stared at Tess from head to toe in her panties and bra, then noticed her girls standing in the same room, watching him inspect their mother. Tom turned three shades of red. "I was, umm, shit, never mind, I don't remember what I wanted." He turned and walked out.

Tracy, JC and Tess burst out laughing. "Okay, stop! I have to get dressed before he comes back." The giggles started all over again.

Tess still chuckled as she slipped into her exquisite creamy white dress. The strapless dress had a sweetheart neckline accented with soft pleating at the bust, and cascading layers of tulle flowed from her waist. The delicate dress was stunning and fit Tess' body perfectly.

Tracy switched her mom's Ipod for her own, turning up the volume. "Come on, Momma, you know how to do this dance. We think this song is appropriate for today."

Tracy and JC turned on Beyonce's "Single Ladies". They tried to teach the dance to Tess earlier in the year, but Tess had been miserable then.

John chatted in the kitchen with Tom, but when he heard the song come on in the other room, he chuckled. "Oh, I gotta go!"

Tom warned, "Last time I went in there she was in her underwear."

John turned and smiled. "Come on, Tom. She's my mom.

246

I've seen her in her underwear."

"Not these underwear, you haven't," he said and followed John.

John reached the room first and started dancing with his favorite girls. Tom stood in the doorway with a huge grin covering his face, watching.

Benny and Lisa came to see what was going on. "Just fucking great! They all dance like her. Even John," Lisa huffed.

Tess grabbed Tom's hand, dancing in front of him.

"You've been holding out on me Tess," he whispered in her ear.

JC sang to Tom, "'If you like it then you should've put a ring on it.'"

Tears ran down his cheek from laughing so hard. "I'll never forget this," Tom said to Benny, shaking his head.

Benny turned to Tom. "Tommy, we are definitely coming for Christmas."

CHAPTER TWENTY-FOUR

Everyone arrived at the dock an hour before sunset. Two boats waited; one would take Tess and Tom to the island, and the other would ferry the rest of the wedding party.

Tess pulled Joey aside, advising him on what kind of pictures she wanted. Joey assured the pictures would be beautiful, explaining he used to photograph weddings.

Everyone boarded the boats. The little boat Tom and Tess rode in had been cleaned and freshly painted. They rode in silence, holding hands as the little boat skimmed across the flat, calm sea. They reached the island and took off their shoes, leaving them on the beach next to everyone else's. John waited for Tess with an exquisite bouquet of red roses.

Tom touched the side of her face. "I love you, Tess. Are you ready to marry me?"

One tear ran down her cheek. "Yes, I am."

"I'll see you up there in a few minutes." He kissed Tess and shook John's hand before dashing up the hill.

Tess gazed around at the beautiful surroundings. The whole place had been cleaned and raked smooth with rocks lining the pathway on both sides.

John kissed her cheek. "Are you ready?"

She could hear somebody playing an acoustic guitar. "I'm ready. Who is that?"

"Benny's boy Tommy."

John wrapped his arm in hers, escorting her up the steps leading to the beautiful pavilion of ruins. The priest stood directly in front of her. Tom and Benny stood to the right side of him, and Tracy and JC stood to the left. Massive ancient pillars rested behind them, creating a stunning backdrop. The vibrant red bouquets and azure blue dresses were dramatic against the paleness of the aged marble.

Tom wore a striking black suit and black shirt with his collar unbuttoned. A single red rose adorned his jacket. Tess could only focus on his handsome face. Everything else faded into the background.

As the guitar played softly, she kept stride with John, glancing down only for a moment to notice red rose petals Kim scattered on the aisle in front of her.

John smiled down at her, stopping in front of Tom.

"Who gives this woman to this man?" the priest asked.

John nodded toward his sisters. "We do." Each of her kids kissed Tess on both cheeks. John took his place next to Benny and the girls stood beside Tess.

Tom clasped Tess' hands in his. It took every ounce of her concentration to listen to the priest as he spoke of love and commitment. He knew a little bit about Tom and Tess' story and he spoke about how blessed they were to have found each other. Tom slid the wedding band on her finger, staring straight into her soul as he recited his vows in the deep sexy tone she loved so much. She reached up to kiss his lips without thinking. Tom grinned and said in a whisper, "Not yet, Tess." Everyone giggled.

"Sorry." Tess placed the ring on his finger and recited her vows of love and commitment, staring into Tom's eyes with every bit of love she held in her heart.

The priest said the words they both waited to hear. "I give you Mr. and Mrs. Clemmins. You may kiss your bride." Tom laid his hands on both sides of her face. He knew it was of no use to try and stop Tess from kissing him passionately, but she didn't embarrass them. Their lips connected for a perfectly long, intimate kiss.

Everything moved in slow motion. Rose petals rained down over them, dancing in the breeze across the aged marble under their bare feet. Flashes popped as Joey snapped pictures, and family and friends clapped in celebration. Tess knew she would cherish this exact moment, captured in time, forever in her memory.

Tom wore the biggest smile with a tear in his eye as Tess glanced up, kissing him again. Tess wasn't sure who had more tears: Lisa, Tracy or Marco. Overcome with love and happiness, Tess shed no tears now, only sheer bliss.

The sun began to sink into the sea, casting a luminous glow across the ruins, creating the perfect backdrop for the memories and photos of their wedding day.

Everyone ambled back to the ferry, but Tom and Tess stayed behind. He put her hand in his dancing with her slowly. Tom showed her exactly how much he loved her. He embraced her tightly, kissing her with enthusiasm and desire, giving her the kiss she wished for. Now tears stung her eyes and her heart beat wildly in her ears. Finally, he said, "God, I love kissing you Tess Clemmins."

Tom and Tess moseyed hand-in-hand down the sandy path to the little boat. Tess draped her legs across his thigh. He rubbed her bare feet as they watched the fiery orange sun dropping into the Aegean Sea. "For some reason, Mrs. Clemmins, sunsets seem so much better with you," Tom said quietly.

"We're going to make the most of every sunset."

The reception was on the patio overlooking the edge of the cliff. The fiery sky had turned to dark blue with the smallest amount of soft pink swirling over the sea. Everyone gave a round of applause, even people they didn't know, as they walked through the restaurant. Their family and friends stood as Tom and Tess entered the patio hand-in-hand with flush cheeks. The party had already started. Greek music played outside and bread was set on the table. Locals enjoying their dinner came out to congratulate them. Tess could feel the love and warmth of everyone there.

White candles were placed in groups of three around the tables and red rose bouquets sat in clear vases as centerpieces. The wedding cake turned out beautiful, made with three tiers and perfectly placed delicate red roses. Tess had asked the older woman who made the cake to make chocolate chip cookies for Tom. She placed them on platters around the tables as well as traditional Greek candy-coated almonds.

"Mrs. Clemmins, would you like wine or martinis?" Tom

asked Tess in her ear.

"Definitely martinis."

Dinner was wonderfully delicious. As the party grew louder and the night went on, the couple moved in close for their first dance. Reaching for her hand, Tom led her to an open area on the patio to dance with her. The couple who owned the restaurant joined in and led Tom and Tess by the hands to teach them the Greek wedding dance. Everyone joined in, creating a big circle. Tess had never experienced anything like it. All of their family and friends danced together, celebrating their love for one another.

It was getting late and Tom and Tess were still dancing.

"Tom, you need to take your wife home," Tess hinted.

John stood beside her. "You can't bail out of here before you dance with me."

As John stole Tess away, JC claimed Tom as her dance partner.

It made Tess beam to see him having a good time with her kids.

Benny cut in so he could dance with Tess. "Tommy loves your kids. I think he's always wanted a family, but he never really believed true love existed. A *nonbeliever* so-to-speak," he said matter-of-factly.

"They like him too."

He smiled mischievously. "You know it's going to be crazy when you go home?"

Tess turned crimson red and dropping her eyes to the floor.

"Not *tonight*," Benny chuckled. "I mean when you go back to the States. Prepare yourself, Tess. It's going to be outrageous. When Lisa and I got married, it was pure chaos, but you and Tommy? No one was expecting this."

"I remember seeing your pictures on the cover of every magazine."

"Laugh now, you'll be on the cover next week." Benny grinned.

"What? Holy crap! Seriously?" Tess nearly stopped dancing.

Tom cut in. "Don't be freaking out my wife on my wedding night, Benny."

Benny gave her a big smooch on the cheek. "Welcome to our family, Tess."

Tom danced her over to the edge of the patio. Her back rested against his chest and his arms embraced her as they swayed together. He bent down, nibbling her neck and she turned her face to kiss him. "Weren't you saying something about leaving, Mrs. Clemmins?"

"Let's go home, Mr. Clemmins."

They began saying goodnight. A tear pooled in Lisa's eye. "We have to leave early in the morning. The wedding was one of the most beautiful I've been to. I can't believe you pulled this off in four days. Take care of each other. We're coming for Christmas. I hope you don't ski as well as you dance, Tess." She smirked.

"See you at Christmas. Talk to you soon."

Grateful they didn't have far to drive, Tess already had Tom's shirt unbuttoned and her dress off by the time they pulled in the driveway. The moon shined brightly as he spun her around, studying her silhouette in the moonlight. "Mrs. Clemmins, you look beautiful in those. I couldn't wait to see you in them again *without your daughters* in the same room."

Tom glanced over his shoulder up the stairs at the front door. Swooping Tess into his arms, he carried her up the steps and across the threshold.

She giggled. "Have you always wanted to do that?"

He laughed as if she were delirious. "Hell no. Never! Not until today."

Tom set her feet on the ground and she sauntered toward their room. He slipped his fingers around her wrist, turning her to face him. "Not yet, Tess. I want to dance with you for a little while longer." Holding her close, Tom stared adoringly into her eyes. "I've never wanted anything in my life more than I want you right at this moment."

He kissed her slowly and passionately for a long time. Flooded with emotion, Tess had never felt so connected in her life. She felt as if they were one, linked together by love and passion, sharing a bond that was unlike any other love she'd experienced before. *Soul mate, he's my soul mate.*

Already aroused, her body pulsed from his insatiable kisses. His talented tongue sent spasms rippling through her core. She panted aloud, "Not yet, Tess."

"Really?" he said with a smothered laugh.

"Yes, really." She backed away from him. "I need to rinse off first. I want this to last more than fifteen minutes."

"You don't have to worry about *me*." He grinned immensely. Reaching out, he clutched her around the waist, sinking his tongue deep into her mouth.

"I'm referring to myself," she mumbled under his greedy lips.

Tom kissed her differently than ever before. His tongue traced her mouth, gently sucking on her lips while tugging with his teeth. Her hips writhed against the hard length of him, encouraging him to kiss her ravenously, turning her on to the point of being right on the edge.

"Holy crap, Tom. Wait," she panted.

"This would definitely be a first." He kissed her again, refusing to release her from his arms.

"Yes, it would be." Trembling, she slid away from him, deciding if she wanted to stop or not. "I need a minute. Jesus, Tom. Where did that come from?" He was proud of himself, wearing an impish grin that made her rethink her decision to stop him. "Can you make us a drink?"

"Yep."

Her body smoldered and still trembled as she stepped into the shower. *Maybe I should've let him keep kissing me? I was so close. No, not tonight.* That had never happened to Tess before, not from just kissing.

She was drying off when he brought her a drink with a roguish grin still plastered across his face. "Tess," he said suggestively.

"I'll be right out," she said anxiously. She rubbed monoi oil all over her body and downed her drink in one sip. She put on sexy, white lace lingerie that hugged her curves down to the bottom of her butt cheek. No panties needed.

Tom lay on their bed, waiting for her. He reached for her hand, but she shook her head no, pulling him up to her lips.

"Tess, you look incredible." His eyes fixed on her body as his hands coasted over her glistening skin.

"I'm curious," she said sexily, running her tongue over her lip. "Will you kiss me, like you were before?"

Tom's fingers twisted in her hair and gently pulled her head back. Tess' lips parted, allowing his mouth to seize control, rocking her to the core, leaving her only able to whimper beneath his kisses. He drew in her bottom lip and tugged with his teeth, instantly turning her heavy breathing into a low moan. Every time he sucked on her bottom lip, drawing it into the burning heat of his mouth, it sent a wave of pleasure spiraling through her body. Tom was on a mission now. Refusing to give up or give in, he plunged deeper into her very soul.

Tess had no idea she could get off just by making out, but it was happening. She rubbed against him eagerly, holding back the urge to take him in. Cresting a wave of sheer pleasure, she cried out softly, melting over him repeatedly as she clung to his arms. Tess thought she was finished, but Tom eased her back on the bed, sinking his tongue deep between her thighs, tasting the sweet rewards of his efforts.

As Tom raised himself atop her, Tess was overcome with the urgency to feel him inside her. She dug her fingers into his shoulders, thrusting her hips forward, only to be unsuccessful. Holding back, he teased her, wearing a haughty grin.

"Please don't make me wait. I want-"

"Shhh. I know what you want. That's the thing about being on top. I get to drive."

Tess flashed him a naughty smile, attempting to flip him onto his back, but he refused to relinquish the driver's seat. Pinning her hands to the bed, he bent down to brush his lips over her nipple. Just when she thought she could take no more of his toying, he thrust himself inside, driving deeper as her hips rode along, taking him in.

It was the beginning of a very long night, and Tess was far from being finished. They made love as their hands and bodies moved in ways new to both of them.

"Morning, Mrs. Clemmins. Or should I say good afternoon."

"I'm not ready to wake up yet."

"Your kids and Shayla leave in an hour so I thought we should go to the airport to say goodbye." He grinned impishly, looking at her lips. "You might want to look in the mirror."

Tess touching her fingers to her lips. "Why? Do I look that bad?"

"Oh no, you look beautiful." Tom's laughter filtered through the room. "I think I might have given you a...umm, go look."

She jumped out of bed, staring in the mirror at several purple hickeys surrounding her lips. "Oh, great! I can't go to the airport like this."

"You sound like you're complaining," he said, being a smartass. "No one will even notice them with some makeup."

"Oh, bullshit. They are definitely going to notice these. Crap, I'll never hear the end of this."

"Was it worth it?" he asked gently, kissing her bottom lip.

"Yes."

John, Tracy, JC and Shayla gathered at the airport to say their goodbyes. JC eyed her mom skeptically. Tess knew what was coming.

"Rough night, Mom? Makeup doesn't cover those very well." JC laughed uncontrollably, causing all of them to survey her lips.

"Ha ha ha very funny. Okay, get out of here. Love you."

"We'll be home in a few days, but we'll be in California before we go to the cabin," Tom said.

Shayla glanced at Tess' lips and smiled sweetly, whispering to Tom. "I wouldn't come back to California until those are gone."

"Definitely," he agreed.

The following day, Tom scheduled a meeting to hire a new publicist, Andy Johnson. Tess saw an entirely different side of Tom, very firm and assertive. He knew what he wanted and expected Andy to have the right answers for him. She loved seeing him so businesslike and learned a lot by sitting in on their meeting.

After Tom's meeting, Tess asked apprehensively, "What

exactly is going to happen when we get home?"

"It's going to be an onslaught of media when we go home." He admitted hesitantly, stroking her arm in reassurance. "Hopefully, you might actually enjoy some of it." Tom smiled self-consciously, continuously spinning his wedding band with his thumb.

"Crap, do my lips look any better?"

"A little better, but the first time we have a few days in private…" He kissed her enthusiastically, giving her a promising taste of what would come.

"We need to go over our wedding photos and pick our favorites. Do you want to release photos with your kids or of just you and me? How will they feel about their pictures being in magazines?"

"I don't know. I have no idea. I hate to leave them out. I'm proud of my kids, but I don't want people bugging them either. I should've talked to them about it before they left." Tess shook her head in frustration.

"Sorry, Tess. I didn't want to bring it up before the wedding. I guess I probably should've, but I didn't want to stress you out. I didn't want it to be hectic with the press. I wanted it to be easy for the both of us."

"I'm ready to go home as soon as my lips look better. I don't care what people say. Bring on the madness. I'd prefer to release photos with the kids, too. If we don't, they're just going to try to get their own pictures, and that, I won't like *at all*. I'll discuss it with them first, but I would rather put all the cards on the table and get on with our life together."

"I agree. We're always going to be under a microscope. That's just the way it is. But I actually think you have a knack for it."

"I sure as hell wouldn't go that far, but I did have fun at the premier."

"This will be more entertaining than the movie premier, trust me."

That night they went out for dinner and walked the streets of the village. Tess noticed Tom continuously spinning his ring with his thumb. "You'll get used to it." She smiled, watching him play with it.

He glanced down at his hand. "I love it. I've never worn a ring before."

She was admiring her own ring when a bright flash blinded her. A young man had taken their picture. He wasn't paparazzi, but he wasn't an idiot either. Tom instantly approached the man, offering him money, but the guy acted like a jerk saying, "I heard you got married here. Nobody will believe this." The damage was done. The man hurried away, muttering something about how much money he'd make off the photo.

"Maybe he doesn't realize what we were doing." Tess tried to be convincing.

"Come on," Tom fumed. "He knew exactly what we were looking at. Our rings! We'll have one day, maybe two. I wanted to do this my way, on my own terms. If Andy can move up an interview we might need to leave early."

"It is what it is, Tom. So what? I don't care. Bring it on! Nothing is going to ruin our honeymoon. The paparazzi can line up in front of the house. I'd be perfectly happy staying in bed for three days. I don't care what we have to go through when we get home. I have what I want: you. That's all that matters." She threw her hands on her hips at the end of her little speech.

A slow smile spread across his face. "First off, this is not our honeymoon, second, we might have to go home early, and third, I could definitely stay in bed with you until we leave."

"What do you mean this isn't our honeymoon?"

"I mean this is unquestionably *not* our honeymoon."

Returning home, Tom phoned Andy. They'd definitely need to leave early to go back to Malibu.

CHAPTER TWENTY-FIVE

On the flight back to Malibu, Andy called. Rumors had already started circulating online. Tess seemed more relaxed about it than Tom. He acted tense. "Tess, the paparazzi will be relentless when we land. It'll be entirely different from before. I might phone Joey. It'll give me a better idea of what to expect."

Joey informed Tom it would be crazy when they landed. Tess thanked Joey for doing such a great job on the photos. He said it had been a long time since he shot a wedding, but enjoyed doing it.

"His pictures are amazing. I don't know why he doesn't do weddings instead of chasing movie stars all over," Tess told Tom.

Tom smirked, "He probably makes more money."

"Maybe he's not shooting the right weddings."

"You're going to plug him aren't you? Give his name out?" Tom asked her curiously.

"Of course. He's wasting his talent hiding behind trees, taking pictures of stars."

"Hey, don't be stealing my *'in'* with the paparazzi," he joked.

"You can get a new one. He's very talented."

Tom continuously spun his ring with his thumb.

Tess frowned suspiciously. "You're not going to ask me to take my ring off, are you?" His face confirmed her suspicions. "Let me rephrase that: I'm not taking my ring off. Don't ask me to pretend for one second that we're not married. I'll put my hand in my pocket if that's what you want, but I won't take it off, Tom. I don't care who is looking or what kind of hell we have to endure. I don't want to play games."

"I hope you're ready for this." His eyes filled with concern and his face strained as he rubbed his jaw anxiously.

The plane landed and Tom was back to his confident-self. As they hurried through the airport, everything passed by Tess in a blur. It was so frenzied, and she wasn't sure how many paparazzi surrounded them. Several pushed their way next to her shouting, *Did you get married? How was Greece? Show me your ring.* Tom squeezed her fingers, striding in front of her to block them from getting too close.

More paparazzi awaited at their house in Malibu, snapping pictures of them in the car. It irritated her they would come to their home. It seemed more like stalking when they lurked in the driveway.

Shayla waited for them inside. Tess was relieved to see her, but she stayed only long enough to go over their schedule for the next week. They would be doing nearly a dozen interviews, starting the following day with *People* magazine, which changed their lead story to cover Tom Clemmins' wedding. They'd have one day off so the magazine could release its issue. After that, the entire week lined up with interviews and talk shows.

Tess plopped down on the couch next to Tom, chewing on her lip and waving her sweaty hands in the air. Tom teased, "Weren't you the one who said, *'It is what it is, Tom. I'm ready. I'm fine. We'll simply go with the flow.'* You were all tough two days ago. One little magazine cover and you fall to pieces. Come on, Tess, you're tougher than that."

"I was only being positive about the whole photo incident, not *People* magazine. Holy crap. I read that magazine at my doctor's office."

"It's only the beginning." he taunted. "They'll be here tomorrow at one."

Mary from *People* magazine showed up right on time, introducing herself cordially, appearing enthusiastic about the interview. Tom welcomed her into his home, showing her around, breaking the ice. They chatted outback before heading inside. Tom and Tess sat barefoot on the couch together.

Mary congratulated both of them on their nuptials. The interview went off without a hitch, going over the typical questions: How did you meet? How long have you been dating? How do your kids feel about Tom?

As the interview progressed, Mary's questions became more direct. "Tom, there are going to be a lot of people out there who are betting your marriage will never last. They say you'll never be with one woman. You'll never settle down. What do you say to those people?"

Tom shifted his head from side-to-side, him-hawing. "Well, you can't print what I would really say. So, I will say, I'll take that bet. I wouldn't have asked Tess to marry me if I wasn't one hundred percent certain of how we feel about each other. Obviously Tess is beautiful, but she's the most amazing woman I've ever known. I'm proud to be her husband."

Tess bit her lip and nudged Tom.

"Tess, Tom has dated numerous women prior to you. That doesn't bother you?" Mary asked innocently, as if it wasn't an insult.

Tess turned to Tom thinking, *Who the fuck would ask that? Tess snickered and a saucy smile expanded across her face. No way in hell is she going to get the best of me.* Tom's face turned a slight shade of pink as he closed his eyes, cringing as if he knew what she was going to say.

"No, not at all. I'm putting all his experience to good use."

Mary's face and neck flushed, hiding a smile. "Do you want me to quote you on that?"

Tess and Tom laughed aloud and Tom responded, "*No*, she doesn't."

Mary repeated her question. "Tom has dated many women prior to you. Does it bother you?"

Tess restated confidently. "No, it doesn't bother me. Who he's dated in the past, is exactly that: in the past. I'm the woman he loves and married. I'm the one he comes home with every night."

"Well, I will say, and I'll put this in the article too, you are a gorgeous couple. I'm pleasantly surprised. You act as if you've been together for years. If I had gambled on your relationship, I would've given you six months to a year. After meeting you and seeing the two of you together, I'd change that bet."

Tess handed Mary a piece of paper with Joey's name on it for photographer and Marco's name for hair and makeup. "I'd appreciate it if you'd include their names in the article. They did an excellent job for us."

"The photographer always gets listed," Mary responded feebly.

"Mary, it's important to Tess that they get credit in the article. She'd like *both* of them *mentioned*. Not just listed." Tom reiterated nicely, but firmly.

Mary glanced at Tom. "All right. I'll take care of it. Thank you for welcoming me into your home. You'll be happy with the article and the photos will look beautiful in the magazine. It was a pleasure meeting both of you. Tess, you're nothing like what I was expecting. Congratulations again."

"Thanks," Tess mumbled as Tom shut the door. "I think."

"She meant it as a compliment. Trust me. She wouldn't have been nice at the end if she didn't like you."

The different time zones were catching up to Tess and it was noon before she climbed out of bed. A copy of *People* sat on the bathroom counter. Tom sat on the couch, waiting for her. Covered with goose bumps, she jumped on the couch next to him.

"It's surreal to see us on the cover. This is wild. I love this picture, it's my favorite." In the picture, Tess stood with her back against the pillar with Tom facing her, gazing into each other's eyes as the sun sank into the sea.

"The article is very nice. I knew she liked you. Read it. I had copies delivered to your kids, too."

"They're going to freak out." She read over the article, smiling with excitement. He seemed just as happy. "Did you ever think you'd see 'this' picture of yourself on *People*? I know you've been on here for sexiest man or best-looking bachelor, whatever they call that issue. But *married* Tom Clemmins?"

Tom slipped his finger under her chin. "This means more to me than all the others. And no, I never expected to see wedding pictures of myself on the cover of People or anywhere else for that matter."

The next week was wild. Tom and Tess did dozens of

interviews. Paparazzi followed them everywhere, and most of the press was positive. Tess refused to watch any entertainment TV programs, but her kids filled her in on several shows they'd seen. Tess thought it was ridiculous for complete strangers to analyze their relationship: What was Tom Clemmins thinking? Would he cheat? Was she after his money? Was she pregnant? People even stooped as low as taking a poll, asking how long they expected the marriage to last. The whole thing seemed idiotic. Tess asked her kids not to watch them, and if they did, she didn't want to hear about it.

"I'm ready to go home soon, Tom," she said one day when she woke up at one o'clock in the afternoon. "I've had about all the *fun* I can take. I'm wiped out."

"I am, too. We can go whenever you're ready."

"Can we stop in Vegas first, so I can get some of my winter clothes and my ski stuff? Plus I need to take care of a few things."

"You can get new gear if you want."

"I like my stuff. It's almost brand new. I don't need to stay there long. I'm ready to go home, to the cabin."

"You're home right now too, Tess, in Malibu."

"I know," she paused. "I want to make my home our home. I need to go through my closet. When Richard died, I couldn't bring myself to go through his things, but I'm ready now."

"Are you sure you're ready for that?" he asked nicely.

"You're my husband now. You keep telling me, 'What's yours is mine.' I want to be able to say the same thing. I'm mentally ready to go through his things. I simply haven't had the time yet. I don't mind staying there for a night or two, and I need to change a few things. It's important to me, Tom. I need to do this. I want you to feel as comfortable there as I feel here."

"I know it won't be easy for you. I'm assuming you'd prefer to go through his things by yourself, but if you'd like some help, even if it's just for moral support, I'll help you."

"Thanks."

They flew to Vegas two days later. It comforted Tess to be home, but at the same time, it seemed awkward. This had always been her home with Richard.

As they walked through the door, John beamed. "We have a surprise for you. All of us wanted to be here to give this to you, but we weren't expecting you to come home yet. It's a late wedding gift." John led them to the hallway where Tess' favorite family pictures hung. "We thought it was time to add to the wall."

Fifteen pictures from their wedding, Greece and Bora Bora hung on the opposite side of the hallway. Most of the photos were of Tess and Tom, but they added several of all of them together as a family. Tears immediately stung her eyes and Tom stared in awe at the wall.

"I can't believe you did this! I love it. How did you get these?" Tom asked.

"Shayla helped us get the pictures. We pretty much stole them, but we put them back," John admitted.

Tom put his arm around John, squeezing his shoulder. "I don't even know what to say," he choked.

Tess could see how moved Tom was by the gift, he was speechless. Her children understood how important family snapshots were to Tess. The gesture of adding Tom to the family wall meant more to her than words of acceptance ever could.

"New addition to the family, new addition to the wall. We thought you'd like it." John said matter-of-factly.

Tess put her arms around John. "I'm truly touched." She brushed away the tears leaking from her eyes.

"We knew you'd love it. I have to get back to work. Maybe we can go out to dinner together." He shook Tom's hand, hugged his mom and headed out the door.

Tom and Tess stood in the hallway with their arms around each other. "This might possibly be the nicest thing anybody has ever done for me," Tom said quietly, staring at the photos.

Tess could only smile. It was exactly what she needed. Home would be wherever she and Tom were together. They'd left her Camaro at the cabin, but Richard's truck sat parked in the garage. She grabbed the keys and tossed them to Tom.

"Would you mind getting me some boxes?"

"Right now? Are you sure?"

"I'm one hundred percent sure. I'm ready." She smiled poignantly. "I'd feel better if I could do this alone though."

Tess knew Tom would never push the issue, however relief flooded his eyes. He seemed to appreciate that she was taking another step in letting go and moving on with him.

It didn't take nearly as long as she expected to go through Richard's things. His clothes lay on the bed ready to be boxed up. She placed his wedding ring in her safe. It would eventually go to John. After twenty-five years of marriage, all that remained in her bedroom was his cologne.

For months after Richard's death, nighttime had turned into Tess' weakest, most vulnerable moments. When it felt like her tears and the darkness would never end, Tess would step into her closet, spray cologne on one of Richard's shirts, curl up with it on the closet floor and cry herself to sleep.

She stared down at the glass bottle. It was the only tangible possession she had left of Richard. Hesitantly, she raised the half-empty bottle of amber liquid to her nose. The exotic scent reminded her of an island breeze, spiked with cedar and vanilla. Drawing in the familiar scent, she remembered the last time she smelled it. Tess had been shopping at the grocery store when a man passed her in the isle wearing Richard's cologne. She stopped in her tracks whispering, *Richard?* As her head turned, following the scent, anticipation rose in her chest, hoping to wake from the nightmare she'd been living. Staring at a stranger, she realized it was only the ghost from her dreams, haunting her again.

Tess slumped to the bathroom floor, clutching the bottle in her fingers. Sitting cross-legged on the cold tile, she rocked back and forth as tears streamed down her face. Her throat tightened around her painful cries.

She looked up through wet lashes to see Tom standing in the doorway with boxes in his hands, turning whiter by the second.

She stared up at him and then down at the cologne clasped in her hands. "I...I...I don't know w...what to do with it." Tess sniffled through sobs, clutching the bottle closer to her chest.

Tom dropped the boxes and knelt in front of her. He wrapped her in his strong arms, stroking her hair as he rocked back and forth with her. When she stopped sniffling, he pulled Tess to her feet. Tom held out his hand, silently asking her to relinquish the cologne. Her fingers tightened their grip momentarily before she hesitantly set the bottle into the palm of his hand.

Tom gently set the bottle on a silver tray alongside her perfumes. "You keep it, Tess. You hold on to anything that's important to you." He pulled her tight against his chest and pressed his warm lips to her temple. When she calmed down and quit shaking, he walked out to the living room, leaving her to finish.

They loaded six boxes into the truck, dropping them off to Goodwill. When they returned, a black SUV was parked in the driveway. "I wonder who's here?"

"It's ours. I bought it while you were busy. They delivered it for me."

Tess looked at him like he was crazy. "What? Why?"

"We're going to need four-wheel drive at the cabin. I figured we'd drive from Vegas to Colorado. It's big enough so if your kids and Shayla, or any of their friends are with them, we'll be able to go out together. And it's a green vehicle."

CHAPTER TWENTY-SIX

When Tom and Tess drove from Las Vegas to the cabin, they picked up Tracy and JC, who were just starting their winter break. John, Shayla and the Levi's, all arrived the next afternoon and everyone was ready to hit the slopes.

The picturesque, ski town was decked out for the holidays. Carolers performed in the park, wreaths adorned the light posts and white lights lit up every tree in town. Everyone took full advantage of the mountain terrain. They went skiing, snowboarding and even sledding.

The night before Christmas Eve, after dinner, Tess and Tom gathered her kids in the living room. John, Tracy, JC and Shayla all knew they wanted to discuss something, and they all looked a bit nervous.

JC smirked. "You're not pregnant, Mom, are you?"

"No! I'm not pregnant. What kind of question is that?"

"An obvious one. Plus, I read it on the cover of a magazine at the grocery store. Apparently, you're having twins in six months. You even have a baby bump." John snickered patting his belly.

Tom paced behind the couch, grinning at Tess, but probably didn't find it funny. Her kids had no idea he couldn't have children.

Tom joined Tess on the couch. "Tom had a great idea of what to give all of you for Christmas," she said.

"Actually, we decided together," Tom clarified, squeezing her knee.

"We planned on giving this to you whether it was Christmas or not, the timing just worked out right. We still have gifts for you to open under the tree. This is different."

"You're both acting all secretive and nervous. What is it?" JC asked.

Tom held four envelopes in his hand. "All of you know after the wedding, we sold our story and photos. We want to give the money to the four of you. Your mom and I don't need it and it would be a nice start for your futures."

They sat frozen.

Tom held Tess' hand, "Open it! Merry Christmas."

Tracy was the first to say anything. "There are way too many zeros at the end of this number. This can't be right! You made this kind of money from your wedding pictures? That's absurd. What am I supposed to do with this?"

Each had an account with over two hundred and fifty thousand dollars in it.

JC's smile lit up like Christmas morning. "No freaking way! Are you serious?"

Tears rolled down Shayla's face through her big beautiful smile. "Are you sure? This is a lot of money. A whole lot of money. Thank you!"

John frowned at the paperwork, shaking his head in disbelief. "I can't accept this. This is your money, not mine."

"No, John, actually, it's yours," Tess assured.

John jumped up out of his seat, handing the envelope back to Tom. "I appreciate the offer, man, but I can't take this." He trudged outside into the snow, wearing nothing but socks on his feet.

Tess stood to follow him, but Tom said, "Do you mind if I talk to him?"

All three of the girls hugged Tess with squeals of delight, along with a ton of questions, especially from JC. Could she buy a car? Could she quit school? Could she go to school in Europe?

"Well, you can't have a car at school. Hell no, you can't quit school, JC, and yes, if you keep your grades up your first year, you could go to school in Europe. If that's what you truly want, but you'd have to explore all of your options first."

"I can study my last year in Europe?" Tracy murmured softly.

"Absolutely," Tess said with a huge smile.

Shayla searched out the window for Tom and John. "Do you think I should go check on them?"

"No. They can't stay out there too much longer. It's freezing cold."

When they came back inside John held his envelope in his hand. He didn't look thrilled when he shook Tom's hand. He ambled over to Tess and hugged her. "Thanks, Mom. I don't know what to say."

"Thanks will work just fine, John." She kissed his cheek.

Tracy and JC hugged Tom, nearly tackling him on the couch. Tom asked if they wanted to watch an old movie so they headed downstairs. John plopped down on the couch next to Tess.

"John, are you okay? He, we, thought this would be a good start for all of you. I thought it was unbelievably kind of him to even offer."

"Mom, he explained why the two of you gave us the money. It doesn't make it any easier for me accept."

"Why? It's not like he's trying to buy your respect or anything."

"He doesn't need to *buy* my respect. I already respect him." John looked her straight in the face, studying her eyes as he asked his next question. "Are you going to try and convince me that you don't have issues with his money? The truth, Mom."

"Yes, I do, and I probably always will have issues regarding his money. Tom knows I don't love him for his money. Money doesn't matter to me. If anything, it makes me extremely uncomfortable."

"That's why he knew I wasn't going to want to take the gift. Tom thinks I'm a lot like you. Stubborn."

"John, you can save it for when you're ready to have a family. You could buy a house, but truthfully, I'm not going to be home much."

"It's hard for me to take this. Dad drilled into me, into all of us, you have to work hard for your money. Nothing comes free. That's how he had to do it. That's how you had to do it, too, Mom. *Work hard, play hard.* Dad's favorite motto."

"If this opportunity was given to your dad and I when we

were first married, do you think he would've turned it down? A gift, from his family the people who loved him? No. You're a good man, John, your dad was very proud of you."

"Tom's just so freaking nice. He even offered to help invest some of it."

She teased. "Are you complaining because he's too nice?"

John grinned, nudging her shoulder. "No, I'm not. I don't think you could've picked a nicer man to be with. He's fun to hang out with and I've had a great time skiing with him." John paused for a moment, "You know, I really miss Dad, but when I'm around, Tom, he fills that void a little."

The fire crackled and popped, filling the silence that hovered heavily in the room.

She knew that John accepted Tom, he even liked him, but his strong words of admiration meant the world to her. "I know you miss him. We all do." She draped her arm around him and they headed downstairs.

It was after midnight when they finally went to bed. "What did you tell him outside to change his mind?" she asked Tom.

"I told him I wanted him to have the money and that I wasn't doing it with an alternative motive behind it. I don't need to buy their love. They either like me or they don't." Tom paused. "Plus, I told him I wasn't able to have my own children and that he and his sisters kind of feel like my family now. I wanted to do this for them and it means an awful lot to me that he accepted it."

"You told him you couldn't have children?" She asked in hushed surprise.

"Yes, I did. He gave me his word it was between the two of us." He grinned. "You guys come from a different mold than anyone I know. You're all so honest."

"You didn't have to tell him. I know that's a difficult subject for you." She couldn't imagine the pain he carried, never being able to have children.

"I know, but for some reason I needed him to know."

She observed him quietly, knowing he had more to say. He grinned again, but the sadness he'd gotten so good at hiding from everyone else didn't work on Tess. She waited patiently for him to open up.

"Listening to you and your kids share family stories makes me feel like I've been missing something. I would've loved being a part of your life a long time ago."

"You're a part of their lives now, Tom. My job as a parent is entirely different than it used to be. It's easier now. I get to be myself again." She paused, trying to put herself in his shoes. "In five, ten, twenty years from now, when we're all here at the cabin having Christmas, they're going to be telling family stories about you, too. I know you would've been a great father. But just think. In a few years, you'll get to be a grandpa." She chuckled.

A smile touched his lips. He ran his hand over her tummy and kissed her stomach right above her jeans. "I would've liked to have had children with you."

She lay silent, stroking her fingers through his hair, contemplating. "Tom, if you really want a child, I'm sure there are ways we could have one. I'm not going to lie to you, I've never thought of having any more kids. It's not something I truly want, but if it means that much to you, I would. We could find a way. People adopt babies all the time."

Tom swallowed hard, turning his typically tan cheeks ashen white.

She uttered a soft laugh. "Or you can simply enjoy being a grandpa someday. I think it'll be nice to be a grandma years from now. You get to give them back when they're crying or being ornery."

Tom stared at her in astonishment. "So you are telling me, if I want to have a baby, you would do that for me?"

"I really wish I could do that for you, but unfortunately my body won't have any more babies. If you really want a child than, yes, we could find a way." Her voice cracked and her eyes dropped away from his gaze. Regret rushed through her veins like fire. It broke Tess' heart to know she couldn't give him a baby.

Tom spoke softly as he lifted her chin with his finger. "I can't believe you'd do that for me."

"I love you, Tom. I'd do anything for you," she whispered sincerely.

He rolled over and stared at the ceiling in silence. She dozed off curled up next to him and fell asleep.

In the middle of the night, he stirred pulling her into his embrace. "I love you so much, Tess. I don't want to have a baby. To be honest, if you and I could make our very own baby together, I would, but I'll be perfectly happy having grandkids someday. It means so much to me that you love me enough to offer."

She tucked her feet between his and snuggled closer. "I think you're just going to have to settle for three young adults instead."

Christmas Eve had finally arrived. The kids snowboarded all day, Lisa and Benny ran into town to get a few last minute gifts, and Tom had helped Tess wrapped presents in her room.

Tess wanted to make Tom's Christmas Eve memorable. Tom waited for her when she got out of the shower.

"I have something for you," he said with a gift in his hand.

"Can we put presents under the tree first?"

"We can if you'd like," he flirted, taking her towel. "Or we could do presents later."

"Let's do presents first." Tess slipped into her silky robe and strolled toward the door.

Tom tossed Tess' present on the bed. They headed downstairs to put gifts under the tree and were back upstairs after midnight.

Tom untied her robe, holding her close, placing her hand in his. Dancing with Tom had turned into one of her favorite things. Tom swayed her slowly around the room, and Tess couldn't contain her excitement any longer. "I have something for you, too." She went to the closet and retrieved a wrapped box.

"Can you wear this present for me tonight?" he questioned suggestively.

"No, that's hanging in the closet. This is something you'll like even more."

Full of intrigue, he grinned curiously. "How *much* more will I like it? Are we going to use this together tonight?"

She playfully swatted at him. "No, *that* is not what's in the box. You make me feel so incredible that I haven't had an urge to get anything like that for us. But judging by your face, you have definitely thought about it."

He smirked sexily. "Maybe."

Tess suspiciously eyed his box lying on the bed, wandering if there was a toy inside. Tom burst out laughing. "No. That's not what I have for you. I think you should open your gift first."

"Please, can you open mine first?" She practically wiggled in her seat with anticipation.

He conceded and proceeded to open her gift. "Are we going somewhere warm, Tess?"

"Maybe!" she squealed.

Inside the box, Tom found new swim trunks, a bikini, a bottle of Monoi oil, flip-flops and a bottle of Vodka for martinis, as well as reservations to stay at her new favorite place in Bora Bora, the private island he took her to their first night together.

"Are we going back to Bora Bora for our honeymoon?" Tom grinned.

His smile made her deliriously happy. She threw her arms around his neck, tackling him on the bed, rolling him over to sit on top of him. "Yes, we are! I checked with the woman on the phone and they didn't have any reservations under your name. I figured you hadn't made plans to go back yet. These were the only dates they had available."

"No, you're right. I haven't made any plans to go back there, yet." Tom wore the most immense cocky smile.

The grin on his face made her nervous. "Did you make other plans for us? I can change the dates, or we could go someplace else if you'd rather."

Tom couldn't quit laughing. "No, it's perfect. We leave in three weeks. Trust me. I can't wait to go back."

"I didn't book a flight, because I don't know how you do that so…"

"I'll take care of the flight."

"Merry Christmas, Tom."

He held her gift. "Sit up for a second. Close your eyes, Tess. No peeking." He kissed her fingers as he fastened something around her wrist.

She squirmed and giggled with her eyes closed. He held her face kissing her softly. "You can open them now."

Tom clasped a beautiful silver watch with a royal blue face

around her wrist. "I love it, I don't have a watch."

"I know. You always check the time on your phone. There's an inscription on the back."

No more wasted time.

Tears stung her eyes as she smiled. "I really love it, Tom! No more wasted time. It's perfect."

"It's a dive watch. I know you wouldn't care for a showy watch. I think you'll get a lot of use out of it." Tom paused for a moment. "I won't waste one more day of my life without you, Tess."

Completely enamored by his words, tears pricked her eyes. What he didn't know was that Tess also had a dive watch for him downstairs under the Christmas tree.

"Merry Christmas, Tess. Did you say you have something hanging in the closet for me?"

"Yes, I do, but I think I'll just wear this tonight." She held up her new watch. "I'll save that for tomorrow night. It's not very much, really."

"Oh, good, those are my favorite kind, the ones with not very much to them." He tickled her side with his teeth and unshaven face. "Turn over." He reached for the monoi oil. "Do you remember the first time I did this for you?"

She became aroused instantly from the memories running through her mind. Tess squeaked, "Oh, yeah. I remember." Goose bumps covered her back as oil drizzled down it.

"You were wearing your blue bikini. My favorite." His tongue traveled up the small of her back. "You had goose bumps all over your body, just like you do now. I wanted to touch you and taste you so badly that day, Tess." Tom massaged her back, working his way up her inner thighs, getting so close, trying to tease her. Her passion accelerated thinking about their spa day in Bora Bora. "Do you want me to touch you?" He murmured.

"Jesus, Tom. I'm not even sure if you need to touch me." The words came out as a whisper.

"Oh, I think I do." He slid his fingers too close and she guided her hips to find them. Overly excited, Tess peaked instantaneously, moaning loudly. "Shhhh, Tess," he whispered sweetly in her ear.

Out of the corner of her eye, Tess saw the satisfied grin on Tom's face. This just made it worse or better for her, knowing he enjoyed driving her to the edge only by touching her. Her eyes rolled back as she slowed down for just a moment, squeezing her legs around him, flipping him on his back. Staring down at him, she could see the lustfulness in his eyes as she teased him at first, taking in only his ridge.

A low groan escaped his throat. "Tess."

"Wait for me." She sat motionless atop of him, giving him a moment to regroup, needing him to last.

"I always wait for you, Tess," he said, watching her face intently.

Tess entwined her fingers in his hair and kissed him fervently. She lowered herself down fully, taking him in. Tom rolled her over, drawing her leg over his thigh. Straining to get closer, her fingers dug deep into his side, pulling him forcefully into her body.

He peeled her fingers from his side, placing her hands above her head, moving slower and more aggressively. Her heavy breathing turned into a very loud moan mixed with a lot of, *Oh, shit! Holy crap! Oh my God!*

"Shhhhhh, Tess," he murmured.

He asked her to *Shhh*, but Tess couldn't *Shhh* at all because the louder she moaned, the more stimulated he became. His movements came in strong deliberate strokes, fueling her hunger. He covered her mouth with his, quieting her cries as she peaked. Tom waited as long as he could before allowing his own release.

Tom spoke to her, but she couldn't hear him. She stared directly at him, watching his lips move, but could only hear buzzing in her ears. Tess laughed softly, holding her pointer finger up to say *just a minute.*

Tom nuzzled his face in the hair by her neck panting, "Merry Christmas."

"Holy cccrap," were the only words she could utter. "M…Merry Christmas."

"This is by far my best holiday ever." He held up the monoi oil. "This is our new Christmas Eve tradition. Every year, Tess, from now on."

"Every year," she agreed, still trying to catch her breath.

As they lay sprawled out across the bed, Tom snickered. "Don't be surprised if you catch crap about this from somebody tomorrow."

"I was not that loud. Besides, we're upstairs." She smirked, positive no one heard her.

"Yes, you were loud enough. Aren't Benny and Lisa below us, Tess?"

"Oh, great!"

"Ten bucks says you catch shit from one of them tomorrow," he chuckled.

"Even if I was too loud, I don't care." She curled up next to him. "It was definitely worth it. That may have been a first for me."

He still wore a haughty smile. "Really?"

"Fine, ten bucks says they didn't."

Christmas morning came four hours later. Kim woke up Tracy and JC with giddy squeals of delight that Santa had been there. Tess' girls knocked on their door at six thirty. Tess glanced at Tom, making sure he was covered up. "Come in."

"Merry Christmas," both girls mumbled, half-asleep, dragging themselves into the room, plopping down on the bed next to Tess.

Tess and Tom both said, "Merry Christmas."

"What, no coffee this time?" Tom asked.

"It's not finished brewing," JC groaned.

"I'm kidding, but thanks," he said.

"Come on girls, Kim's waiting. We can take naps later," Tess said as Tracy and JC stumbled out the door.

Kim had begun opening presents before they'd even made it downstairs. Tom hadn't experienced a morning like this since he was a kid, and Tess was happy simply watching him snap pictures.

Tom appeared completely baffled when he opened his gift. "We think too much alike," he said, shaking his head at the handsome dive watch with a black face.

"I'd like to put the same inscription on the back."

"I'd love that."

Tom gave her a sound system for their bedroom and her favorite perfume. She gave him a couple of things for the cabin. What he loved most, however, were his pictures Tess had framed for the bedroom.

That afternoon, Tess and Lisa hung out in the living room. "Thanks for having us, Tess. We've had a great Christmas. I wish we could stay longer," Lisa said.

"I love having you here. It's been wonderful."

"Benny's a little upset with you, though," Lisa sighed with disappointment.

"Me? What did I do?" Tess asked curiously.

"Benny was exhausted last night, plus he had one glass of wine too many." Lisa struggled not to laugh. "I had to wake him up in the middle of the night to drown out the noise coming from upstairs."

Tess flinched and her mouth dropped open. "You're lying. Tom told you to say that."

"Benny wasn't happy at first because he was so worn out, but he got over it in a hurry." Lisa teased, laughing her ass off.

"Great!" Tess scoffed, absolutely mortified.

Lisa mocked. "I'm sure it was!"

"Very funny. Don't say anything to Tom or I'll never hear the end of it."

"Oh, I won't, but Benny already gave Tommy shit first thing this morning. And you're right, you probably will never hear the end of it."

Tess tried to read Lisa's face. "You're screwing with me, aren't you?"

"Not me. blame Tommy. Good thing you didn't give that room to your kids."

"Shit." Tess slumped back on the couch, humiliated.

"Thank god I have a guesthouse for you two to stay in when you come to visit."

"All right, I got it. I'm sorry I kept you up last night."

Lisa laughed. "Hey, don't apologize. It worked out great for me, too."

When Tom was upstairs in the shower, Tess left a ten-dollar

bill on the counter for him. He ambled into the kitchen before dinner, leaned into her ear, and breathed in deeply, imitating her moan. Her body covered itself in goose bumps and she elbowing him in the ribs.

"I've had the best Christmas, Tess."

"Me, too." she whispered.

CHAPTER TWENTY-SEVEN

"Good morning, Tess."

She opened one eye, peeking at the clock. "It's dark outside. I don't want to get up yet. Christmas was yesterday."

He pulled the covers down, kissing her tummy. "Tess, I need you to get up. Come on."

"How come we have to get up so early?"

"It's snowing outside and I want to take you for a ride."

"Right now? It's not even light outside."

"Come on. Just throw your jeans and a shirt on. We need to hurry."

She rolled out of bed, brushed her teeth and hair, and threw on some clothes. Overly enthused for five o'clock in the morning, Tom kissed her sensually as she sat on the edge of the bed, putting on her shoes.

"If you're going to kiss me like that, why don't we just stay in bed?"

"Let's go, sleepy head."

Snow had fallen all night long, turning the forest into a winter wonderland. They barely made it out of the driveway without getting stuck.

"Where are we going?"

"Someplace I want to take you. If we don't leave now, we won't make it because of the snow," he said coyly with his crooked grin.

Tom passed through town, heading for the highway. She glanced around, confused and half-asleep. "I thought you were going to show me something pretty in the forest or something. Where are we going?"

He only smiled and ignored her question.

Tess laid her head back, dozing off, waking up when the car stopped. "Why are we at the airport?"

He grinned mischievously and opened her car door.

"Where are we going?" she asked again.

"Come on we need to hurry. It's a surprise." Tom chuckled, grabbing the luggage out of the back of the car.

"Did you pack for me? When did you do that? What about the kids? Did you tell them we're leaving?"

"Of course. They knew days ago. They're staying at the cabin. John's going to take the girls back to school before he heads back to Vegas. I think the girls might have a couple of their girlfriends come up from Vegas to go skiing. I hope you don't mind, but I told them it would be okay."

"My kids are getting way too good at keeping secrets from me." Her excitement started to build as they boarded the plane. "Where are you taking me?"

"You know me better than that, Tess. Let's go back to sleep first. I've been up all night packing, trying not to wake you up. You sleep through just about anything."

"Seriously, you're not going to tell me?'

"Nope." he said, snuggling up to her.

Tess only crashed for a little bit, but Tom slept for hours. She had coffee, breakfast and watched two movies. She couldn't take it anymore. He could sleep later. Tess peeked into the dark bedroom. Tom lay on the bed sound asleep, looking gorgeous, lying on his side. She lay next to him, but he didn't move. She pulled the sheet back to his waist, wanting to reach out to touch and kiss his body, but he was tired.

"What are you looking at, Tess?" His voice filtered through the darkness.

Her breath hitched. "My husband."

Tom stretched his hands behind his head.

Tess noticed a dark spot on his side above his hip and she touched it.

"Oooh, hey, that's sore." He winced, examining his side.

Tess inspected the dark spot closer. "Is that a bruise?"

He placed her four fingers over the bruise, and they matched perfectly.

"Is that from me?" she asked, covering her mouth with her hand. "I'm sorry. I didn't mean to do that!"

"I'm not complaining. You can cover me with bruises." He pulled her next to him.

"I feel horrible."

"Don't feel bad, Tess, Christmas Eve was the best Christmas I've ever had."

She kissed his bruises and her lips traveled to the muscles at the bottom of his abs. He wiggled out from under her, stepping out of bed.

"Where do you think you're going?" She tugged on his finger, pulling him back so he stood naked, directly in front of her as she sat on the edge of the bed. Obviously, he didn't want her to stop. She bit her bottom lip, gazing up at him.

"Don't do that, Tess. Not yet. Come on be nice. Please."

He might have been saying *Not yet*, but his body was saying *Hell yes*. "I'm going to be very nice." She slid her tongue across the length of him.

Tom pulled her up on her feet.

"Are you going to tell me where we're going?"

"Are we negotiating now?" He laughed.

"Maybe."

"Do you really want me to tell you?"

She let out a big sigh and sauntered into the other room. "No, you don't have to tell me."

Tom got dressed and joined her on the couch with a box in his hand.

"Isn't that the same box my watch was in on Christmas Eve?"

"It is. It's funny how much we think alike sometimes. I had something else in the box to give you. But after you gave me my present, I decided to wait and give the rest of your gift now. It's not much. Open it."

She peeked inside the box to find a dark, brown bikini bottom. "No top?" She burst out laughing. "Did you give me the same thing I gave you? Are we going to Bora Bora right now?"

He nodded. "I couldn't believe it when I opened your gift. I hope you're not disappointed."

"Disappointed? Don't be ridiculous! I knew you were up to something, I could tell by your devious smile. I asked if they had any reservations under your name and they said no."

"We're staying someplace different. I made arrangements a long time ago." He flashed a grin.

"How long ago?"

He ignored her question. "You might want to get ready. We'll be there in less than two hours."

"I'm so excited!"

Standing under the hot shower, Tess reminisced about previous trips. Her memories started with meeting Tom on her last trip, but quickly turned to unforgettable moments she and Richard shared. Bora Bora filled Tess and Richards's lives with romance, making their marriage stronger. Unexpected emotions overwhelmed her as tears streamed down her face, crying uncontrollably. Tess hadn't broken down like this since she let Richard go in the lagoon.

Richard and Tess shared a great life together, yet the connection between she and Tom was undeniably more powerful than anything she'd ever experienced. She loved Tom, but still missed Richard immensely and would never stop loving him.

Tess had set Richard free into the ocean so he could see the manta rays put on their show every day, but it felt awkward heading back there now with Tom. Even though Tom was her husband now, at that moment, she couldn't escape the feelings of unfaithfulness. *If Richard see's me in the lagoon with Tom, it'll crush him like a bug. It'll kill him to see me with another man. That's the most ridiculous thing you've ever said, Tess. Richard's already gone.*

Tess felt different with Tom. She was the same woman, just at a different stage in her life. She loved Tom passionately, and felt free to give all of her love to him. She didn't need to worry about the daily responsibilities of raising a family. Her children were adults now. She could be Tess again. A woman, not a mother.

It saddened Tess knowing Richard didn't get to experience her this way. In a way, Richard was cheated out of the best years they would've spent together as a couple, and he would've loved this stage of their life together.

At the same time, Tess was sad that Tom had to miss out on the stages of raising a family. He had never experienced any of the things she shared with Richard; babies, broken bones, wrecked cars, dates, curfew, and all of the stress and worry that comes with having kids. Tom missed out on all of the love and happiness of a family. Babies, birthdays, holidays, vacations, graduations, and all of the firsts; first words, first bike rides, first dances.

Tess' heart ached, torn between what was then, and what is now. Richard and Tom were both wonderful, and she was lucky to share her life with both men. She'd been a great wife to Richard and the best mom she knew how to be. Now, with Tom, she'd become the best woman she could be. She wasn't Mom. She was Tess. Tess Clemmins. She already figured out who she was in life as a person, Tom just made her better. A better woman, a better lover and a better friend. She felt alive and passionate and empowered by the love they shared.

Tess didn't want Tom to find her sitting on the shower floor, sobbing. She looked down at her wrist, taking off her watch, running her fingertip over the words etched into the back. "No more wasted time," she uttered between snivels. *I will not waste one minute with this man. Life is too damn short! No more tears. Pull it together, Tess!*

Tess threw on cut off shorts and a black tank top. Clearly she'd been crying, so she put on makeup and did her hair, eventually joining Tom on the couch.

"Are you all right, Tess?" He stroked her shoulder.

"Umm hmm." She tried to sound joyous.

"Are you sure?" he questioned in a concerned tone. "I came to see you when you were in the shower."

Shit. She leaned her head on his shoulder, forcing herself not to cry, peeking down at her watch again. "I'm fine."

Tom sighed. "I don't expect you to forget about your trips here with Richard. I don't mind sharing your old memories while we create new ones. You were married for a long time, and I won't make you feel guilty for missing him, Tess. You haven't given me shit one time for the life I led before we met, and let me tell you, it's a relief. You don't judge me. Ever. You only love me for who I am. I'm sure as hell not going to be upset because you loved your first husband." He wiped the tears from her cheeks. "But, we need to be able to come here."

"I know. You're right. I just had a little bit of a meltdown, but I'm fine now."

"Talk to me, Tess. I want to understand what you're feeling. I know you miss him and I'm okay with that. I'm not okay with sitting here feeling helpless, watching you suffer by yourself." He spoke tenderly while stroking her hair.

"Do we really have to talk about it? I'm fine now."

"Yeah, I think we do." He nodded somberly.

She exhaled deeply. "I feel guilty because he didn't get to experience me the way I am now...with you. And you didn't get to experience me the way I was before...with him, as a mother and a wife."

"What do you mean *before?* You're the same person now as you were then." He said it sweetly, concerned that she sounded a little crazy.

"Oh, no, I'm not the same! I feel powerful and more confident with you. I'm free to love you as myself, as a woman. There's a huge difference. I get to be Tess now, not John's mom or Tracy's mom or JC's mom. I get to be me! Your wife, and lover, and best friend."

"It's odd you describe it like that because I do get a bit envious of him knowing he got to share *that* life with you. The life I could've never given you."

"I know, Tom. But you have a part of me he would've really, really loved." She grinned through her tears.

"I'm sure," he agreed, smiling back.

"I promise I haven't been feeling guilty at all. It's just...he's here in the ocean, watching us now. And I put him here on purpose." Tess silently wondered if she might've made a mistake releasing Richards's ashes in the lagoon.

"Maybe you're looking at it backwards, Tess. Everything happens for a reason. Richard's only watching over you, not spying on you. I'm sure he'll be happy to see you."

"I feel better being able to talk to you about it."

"Me, too. You have no idea. I was worried when I heard you crying in the shower."

He held her hand walking into the bathroom. Tess fixed the mascara smeared down her face. *Tom's right. Richard is just watching over me.*

It was almost time to land and they lay across the bed. Tom embraced her, gently running his fingers though her hair. Tess stood, pulling him to his feet. She placed her hand in his so he would dance with her. Tom chuckled, swaying her around the room.

"Thanks, Tom, I feel much better now."

"You're welcome."

Mr. Rene waited at the dock with a joyous smile. "*Ia Orana*, Mrs. Blue Eyes and Mr. Tom. I'm happy to see you again." He wrapped his brawny arms around them. "I knew you would be back here together."

"*Ia Orana!*" they both replied.

"Mr. Rene, I am Mrs. Tom now," she said, squeezing Tom's waist.

"I knew you would be his *Vahine*, I told my misses. Mr. Tom I told you too, do you remember? Mr. Rene is always right about these things. I am happy for you, and I am glad you are back here to see me so soon."

Tom smirked with flush cheeks. "Yes, I remember."

Tess' eyes narrowed curiously, knowing *Vahine* stands for wife in Tahitian.

"The day we saw the manta rays, when you asked me to meet you for dinner, he informed me that I was in love with you," Tom explained in her ear.

Her mouth dropped open. "How could he possibly know that?"

"Apparently, he's always right about these things." He grinned, mimicking Mr. Rene.

This is exactly how it started for Tess and Tom: Mr. Rene singing his beautiful Tahitian songs, sharing a boat ride, staring out over the serene turquoise water. She sat between his legs with her back against his chest. Tom's hand lay across her heart. His fingertips moved up and down with the hammering in her chest. He glanced at her with concern, skimming his fingertips across her shoulders.

"I'm fine. This place is magical," she whispered.

He nuzzled her neck with his unshaven face. "Yes, it is. I couldn't wait to come back here."

Mr. Rene was still singing when they approached a small exotic *motu* Tess had never seen before. Pink and yellow hibiscus bloomed everywhere and tall palm trees swayed in the light breeze. Black lava rock jutted out into the lagoon at both ends of a lovely U-shaped beach.

Mr. Rene pulled up to the dock. A sailboat and a speedboat were already tied to the dock. "I will see you soon. My misses will be very happy for you. You are a blessed man, Mr. Tom. Look at how beautiful Mrs. Blue Eyes is. See? I told you." Mr. Rene began singing again as he pulled away from the dock.

Tom draped his arm around Tess and waved goodbye. Looking down, he said, "*This* is our honeymoon." He stared hungrily at her, as she ran her hands over his back and butt. "Oh, yeah. It feels like Sunday to me."

The path at the end of the dock led them through the palm trees to a gorgeous bungalow all but hidden by lush tropical flowers.

"Holy crap! This is absolutely breathtaking."

"Let's check it out."

Overlooking the perfect beach lay a gorgeous plunge pool on the deck in front of the magnificent bungalow. Tom slid the disappearing glass doors all the way open, exposing the amazing view of the lagoon. They could lie in bed gazing out over islands in the distance. The luxurious white bedding popped with large orange, yellow and pink pillows. This bungalow was larger than others she had stayed in, with a beautiful full-size kitchen and a living room furnished with teakwood tables and an off-white modern sofa and chaise. It was by far the most exquisite bungalow she'd seen.

At this point, Tess was done inspecting the bungalow. She focused on Tom. *He wants Sunday? I'll give him Sunday.* He headed into the bathroom to look around. She slipped her clothes off and pulled the comforter off the bed. Tom turned back to see where she was and he grinned the crooked grin she loved so much.

"Come here, Tess."

She ambled into the bathroom, staring only at him. Tom lifted her up onto the counter as her legs fastened around him. He pulled off his T-shirt as she unbuttoned his shorts and slid them to the floor. Tom tugged on her hair and tilted her head back. He kissed her neck, trailing hot, wet kisses down to her breast. His arms wrapped around her waist, attempting to take her to the bedroom.

Tess shook her head. "Wait, kiss me." Tess wanted to give herself to him again just by kissing. She was filled with desire and already on the edge, it would happen this time.

Tom stopped abruptly. His warm mouth found hers, kissing her eagerly, sucking on her bottom lip. He tugged gently with his teeth and tongue. The longer, harder and deeper he kissed her, the more it turned her on. Tess squirmed to the edge of the counter, sliding against the length of him, breathing in long sighs. Tom plunged his tongue deep between her lips, bringing sweet spasms, making her cry out beneath his lips as she melted over him.

"I want to feel you, Tom."

He carried her to bed and gave her what she craved. Tom took her from the back, the front and the side. Tess rolled him onto his back, grasping his hands over his head and pinning him to the bed.

She whispered in his ear as her hair fell around his face. "Do I feel like Sunday?"

His strong and powerful hands shifted her hips, thrusting himself deeper. "Do I feel like Sunday to you, Tess?" At that exact moment, it turned into Sunday for both of them. Tess laid her head on his chest, gasping for air.

"How did I ever get so lucky to find you?" he said earnestly.

Thirty minutes later Tess dragged Tom to the beach. They grabbed their masks, drifting in the warm turquoise lagoon. Black lava rocks swarmed with vibrant fish as well as one turtle. Several reefs beckoned in the distance, but they would have to wait until tomorrow.

Tess traipsed through the sand and rinsed off before dipping into the plunge pool. "How long are we staying?" she asked inquisitively.

Tom walked past. "I'm going to fix us a drink."

"Not so fast."

"I'll be right back." He returned minutes later with martinis and stepped into the water.

"So how long are we staying in paradise?"

"How long would you like to stay for, Tess?"

She floated in his lap. "Forever. I love it here."

"Me, too. I don't know what it is about this place, but I can't keep my hands off you." He kissed her and carried her to their room.

"Oh, you know...It's the blue sky, the turquoise water, the scent of the Tiare flowers growing everywhere, the heat and humidity, the stars in the sky at night and-"

He dumped her onto the bed. "I think it's just you lying on the bed naked." His lip pulled back into his crooked grin. "I know we just had Sunday a few hours ago, but I want to make love to you."

She stretched her arms above her head, pretending to yawn, acting as if she was too tired, but she couldn't keep a straight face. Tess slid her hands down her body. "Well get over here and make love to me then."

"I need to tell you something first."

She sat up on her knees, pulling him on top of her. "You can tell me later."

Tom took his time, touching her tenderly while he talked. They normally didn't talk much while they made love, but that afternoon they did. "I've waited so long to find you," he said, gazing into her eyes. "I hope you're ready for the rest of our lives together because it's going to be more than either one of us expected. I won't waste one minute with you. Not one. No more wasted time." His breathing accelerated and he put his lips next to her ear. "No more tears, Tess. I won't ever disappoint you or make you unhappy. I love you too much." He tried to kiss her, but her head dropped back off the side of the bed, cresting a wave of pleasure simultaneously.

When Tess opened her eyes the next morning, she could smell coffee brewing and climbed out of bed. Tom stood down by the water, skipping stones across the lagoon.

Tess joined him on the beach, grinning as she handed him a cup of coffee. The only thing either of them had on was their sunglasses.

"Morning, Tess. What's so humorous this morning?"

"I think it's funny. Here we are, naked, having coffee on our own deserted island. Where else can you do this? I love it here."

"Nowhere that I know of. Do you really like it here, Tess?"

"I hate it. It's terrible. We should find someplace else to stay." She laughed sarcastically.

"Let's check out the other side of the *motu*." Tom held her hand as they walked and talked.

Tom's eyebrows creased and he unconsciously squeezing her fingers tighter. "Tess, I need to tell you something."

His death grip on her fingers made her flinch. "I didn't think you were serious yesterday. What is it?"

"I've been keeping something from you and I'm not sure how you are going to react when I tell you."

Her brows automatically wrinkled, mimicking his. He looked entirely too serious and very uncomfortable. She didn't like where this conversation was going. "What is it?"

Tom turned his eyes away from her, staring solemnly toward the lagoon. "Do you remember when the photo of me was released? When you ran over your phone."

Heat rose to her cheeks. "Yes, I remember all too well."

"I was here in Bora Bora when that happened."

Tess attempted to process what he said, but could only envision the photo of him with that girl. "By yourself?"

Tom gave her the strangest look. "No, I wasn't by myself. But that doesn't have anything to do with it."

Tears stung her eyes as her lip quivered. "It matters to me. Why were you here? You told me that you were in Germany filming. Did you lie to me? Do not tell me you were really with her."

He looked at her as if she had lost it. "No, no, no, no, Tess. No. Tess, that's not it at all." He embraced her, but she stiffened under his touch. "Stop it, Tess." He held her face, staring into her tearful eyes. "Stop it right now. That's not what I'm trying to tell you. I most definitely have *NOT* been with another woman."

She sighed heavily, hugging him tightly. "Sorry. You just made it sound like you were going to tell me something about that picture. You have a horrible look on your face like you're afraid to tell me something."

"I am afraid to tell you something."

"Well, spit it out. Who were you with?"

"If it makes you feel better, I was with Lisa."

"Lisa? Why were you in Bora Bora with Lisa?"

He dropped her hand, pacing anxiously, digging his toes in the sand. "Okay, fine. She made me swear not to tell you so you cannot tell her you know she was here. All right."

"I wish you'd just say it. You're freaking me out, Tom. Fine, I won't tell her I know she was here. What's the big deal?"

"You make me nervous sometimes, Tess. Sorry. I don't get this way very often. Nothing comes out right."

"I make you nervous?" She huffed sarcastically.

"I know you find it hard to believe, but for some reason you make me nervous once in a while. I happen to really love that about you because I never get uncomfortable." He attempted to grin.

"I'm still waiting for you to tell me something, Tom."

"When Benny took over the film for me, Lisa flew to Germany with him to say goodbye. I was coming here to Bora Bora and she wanted to tag along. She mentioned something about your dancing at the premier. Apparently you were a twelve and she seemed somewhat pissed about it. Lisa asked me earlier where you learned to dance and I told her I thought some of it came from Bora Bora so she wanted to take a Tahitian dance lesson while I took care of some…business. Lisa's slightly competitive, and you dance better than she does. That's why she was with me at your house when John came after me. I flew straight from Bora Bora to Las Vegas when I found out about the picture in the magazine."

Tess grinned, but was losing her patience. "You're rambling. Please, just spit it out."

"I told you I had a plan, but everything got screwed up when that ridiculous picture was released. When I came to Bora Bora, Tess, I had already planned on asking you to marry me. I came here to…make a purchase for you, a wedding present for the both of us."

"Why? Are you worried I'm not going to like it? I love everything about this place."

"Good. Because *this* is your wedding present."

"I know. This is our honeymoon."

"No, Tess. This *place* is ours."

"What place?" she asked.

He grinned immensely. "This *motu*, the bungalow, the boats. They're ours. I had this built for us. It's your wedding present."

"You bought this island?" Tess' mouth hung open in complete shock. "The whole thing? Are you kidding me?"

"Nope. I'm not kidding you. We don't have to go home. This is home."

"Get out of here! How the hell do you buy an island? I don't even know what to say. I love it! You're serious, aren't you? The bungalow? Everything?"

Squeezing her tightly, he lifted her up until her toes came out of the sand and he could kiss her lips. "The whole thing. We can learn how to sail, too. We may never go back."

"You're crazy!" She chuckled, completely taken by surprise and still in shock.

"I am crazy! About you. We're going to have fun together for the rest of our lives. No more wasted time." Tom set her back down, stroking her arm from shoulder to wrist, glancing at her watch.

"Wait a minute." Tess said, mystified. "Why are you so afraid to tell me about this? You know how much I love it here, Tom. Why would I be upset? Why were you freaking me out just now to tell me this?"

The smile fell from Tom's face. He inhaled deeply, hesitantly pointing to a long stretch of dark blue water that followed the lagoon by the outer reef. It wasn't very far from their *motu.* They could kayak to it.

"Do you see the dark area in the water? It's an underwater highway for marine life." Tom paused, sighing heavily again. "It's like a cleaning station for fish. The Tahitian people say the manta rays come to this spot daily to be cleaned by the reef fish."

The world seemed to slow to a crawl. Tess nodded her head as tears stung her eyes. It all came together now. This is why he wanted an explanation when she broke down in the shower. And yesterday when they made love, he said he wouldn't make her unhappy.

"We need to be able to come here," she quietly repeated his words.

"That's right. We need to be able to come here," he nodded. "We live here."

"No more tears, Tom, I promise." She bit her lip, trying not to cry.

He grinned his crooked grin for her, trying to make her smile before kissing her softly. "Are you sure, Tess? I don't want this to make you unhappy or uncomfortable. When I bought this place, they told me about the manta rays that visit every day. That's what really sold me on this particular *motu*. I knew it was perfect, or at least I thought it would be perfect, but now I'm not sure."

She stared at Tom, thinking of Richard and the manta rays.

"The day we saw the manta rays means a lot to me, Tess. We were both so happy and excited. Without even thinking, you practically climbed into my lap and wrapped your arms and legs around me. My heart was pounding in my chest," he said very quietly. "That's never happened to me. Not like that. Not ever."

"I remember that exact moment. I was so relieved after seeing the manta rays, it felt like a weight lifted off my shoulders. It was the first night we stayed together," she whispered.

"Tess, I realize now that the manta rays have a different meaning for you, don't they? They hold a special place in your heart for Richard."

She could only nod her head as tears streamed down her cheeks, thinking of Richard and the manta ray box that held his ashes. *How could he possibly know that?* "How did you know? How do you know about the manta rays?"

"I'm not sure, just a gut feeling, but when you said you were afraid he was watching us in the lagoon together, I knew I was right. I thought this *motu* would be perfect because you can visit him here, but….did I make a mistake, Tess?"

Tess took a deep breath. "Richard and I tried to see the manta rays several different times, but they never showed up for us. On our last trip here, we were shopping at the market when he found a wooden box with a carved manta ray on the lid. He thought the box was the perfect souvenir to take home. Richard kept it on the counter next to his sink in the bathroom, that way he could look at it every day, determined to see them the next time we came back here. He never got the chance."

Both of them stood in the sand with tears streaming down their faces. "After he died, I looked at that box every single day, knowing how badly he wished to swim with the manta rays. I woke up one morning and decided to bring him here, so he could see their show every day. I needed to say good-bye to him. My kids thought I had completely lost my mind, but ten days later, I was on my way here to Bora Bora with his ashes in that manta ray box."

Tom nodded his head, listening to her story.

"I set him free so he could be here in the lagoon forever. The next day you invited me to go with you. When the manta rays actually showed up, I couldn't believe it. I know it sounds silly, but at that moment, I could've sworn the manta ray was Richard waving goodbye telling me, *Hi, baby! It's me. I made it. Thanks. I love it here.* It was okay for me to be happy again. I allowed myself to feel again. I wanted to be with you, Tom." She laid her head on his shoulder. "I love it here. It's better than perfect. Thank you so much."

Tom tilted her face up to his own. "I was hoping you could have the best of both parts of your life. Your old life and your new life. I want you to love our home here, and you can visit him, too. I don't mind sharing you. You're with me now, but I understand you miss him. I want you to be happy when you see him, not sad or stressed out. Don't you think he deserves to know you're happy?"

Tess agreed nodding her head. "How can you be so

understanding? How do you know me so well? You're so wonderful to me."

"Because I love you, Tess, more than I thought imaginable. I'm sorry you had to go through the pain and heartache of losing Richard. I'll admit, I do get a tiny bit jealous of him, well envious is probably a better word. But in my mind...I almost feel as if he took good care of you until I could find my way to you."

"We're meant to be together. Soul mates," she whispered.

"Do you feel better?"

She nodded and he held her for a long time. Finally, Tess said, "I'm hungry."

A huge grin lit up his face. "Come on. Let's go."

They headed back to their bungalow. Right after breakfast, she put on a bikini. "Are we kayaking or taking the boat tied up to the dock?"

"Where are we going?"

She pointed to the dark water. "The sooner the better. I need to do this."

"Let's kayak."

They tossed their gear in the kayak, and paddled for the dark water. Slipping into the warm blue water, Tess sensed Tom's uneasiness, unsure if he should hold her hand. His eyes smiled beneath his mask when she reached for his fingers. They drifted above the underwater trench, watching schools of the fish, turtles and even a few sharks swim beneath them.

This time Tess saw them first. Three huge shadowy black figures came from the deep, gracefully twirling, rolling, and dancing to the underwater music. Each one glided effortlessly through the water doing back rolls and somersaults, coming so close they both could've reached out and touched it. They drifted alongside the manta rays, watching in awe as they performed underwater ballet before returning to the depths of the underwater trench.

Just like the first time, she wrapped herself around him and both wore huge smiles. "You don't think I'm crazy, do you?" she asked.

"No, Tess, I don't think you're crazy. I told you he'd be happy to see you."

"Thanks." She beamed.

They paddled back to their own private paradise. Tess lay on the bed content and happy. Tom came to lie beside her.

"I'm so lucky. You're so wonderful. I can't believe you bought this *motu* for us. How long are we staying? Seriously, how long?"

"Indefinitely. Tess, the last time you were here, did you really decide at the last minute to come on your trip?" Tom questioned inquisitively.

"Yes, ten days before I got on the plane. Why?"

"I arrived here the day after you and I made my reservations eleven days before I left. That's the *exact* same day you made your reservations to come to Bora Bora," he said with a look of astonishment.

She sat straight up in bed.

"Everything *does* happen for a reason," Tom and Tess said simultaneously.

"I knew it was love at first sight." Tess smiled.

Tom grinned. "From the very first moment I laid eyes on you."

For the past twenty-one years, Beverly Preston has been a stay at home mom, although she prefers the title Domestic Engineer, raising her four amazing kids. Along the way, Beverly worked side by side with her husband Don, the love of her life, designing, building and selling custom homes. As her children begin to venture out on their own, she's left to shed a tear—for a minute—wonder what's next in life, and embrace the feeling of empowerment that surely must've been wrapped in a present she received on her fortieth birthday.

Beverly lives in Las Vegas and if she isn't at home riding her spin bike, you'll find her spinning richly emotional and sinfully sexy romance stories.

Don't miss the next novel in this sensational new series. Visit Beverly at www.beverlypreston.com

Made in the USA
Charleston, SC
15 September 2012